Claire McGowan grew up in a small village in ˌ n Ireland. After a degree in English and French from Oxford University, and time spent living in China and France, she moved to London and works in the charity sector and also teaches creative writing. A SAVAGE HUNGER is her fifth novel and the fourth in the Paula Maguire series.

Praise for *A Savage Hunger*:

'*A Savage Hunger* is a taut, compelling thriller that merges ancient beliefs with a very modern crime' Elly Griffiths

'A complex, disturbing, resonant novel that remains light on its feet and immensely entertaining' *Irish Times*

'The best of the Paula series yet' Stav Sherez

'Plenty of intrigue makes this a must read' Fanny Blake, *Woman & Home*

'The intricately woven plot builds to a level of tension that's almost unbearable' traceybooklover.wordpress.com

Praise for *The Silent Dead*:

'I read *The Silent Dead* with my heart in my mouth . . . brilliant' Erin Kelly

'In Dr Paula Maguire, she has created a wonderfully complex character' *Irish Independent*

'A breathlessly exciting and intelligent thriller with a brooding atmosphere' *Sunday Mirror*

'I was gripped by *The Silent Dead* and was fully immersed in the world created by Claire McGowan's fine storytelling' forwinternights.wordpress.com

Praise for *The Dead Gr*

'Fast-paced and engaging

'Enthralling . . . evoked ˌ

'It's a gripping ˌ hriller writer of exce ˌ

'McGowan's book is bloody and brilliant' Angela Clarke

'McGowan is a brilliant writer who knows how to keep the reader turning their pages waiting to see what happens next . . . This is a fresh, exciting and completely readable thriller' louisereviews.com

Praise for *The Lost*:

'Compelling, clever and entertaining' Jane Casey, author of *The Burning*

'McGowan's style is pacey and direct, and the twists come thick and fast' Declan Burke, *Irish Times*

'Engaging and gripping' *Northern Echo*

'Taut plotting and assured writing . . . a highly satisfying thriller' *Good Housekeeping*

Praise for *The Fall*:

'There is nothing not to like . . . a compelling and flawless thriller' S.J. Bolton

'She knows how to tell a cracking story. She will go far' *Daily Mail*

'The characters are finely drawn, and it's concern for them, rather than for whodunnit, that provides the page-turning impetus in this promising debut' *Guardian*

'Hugely impressive. The crime will keep you reading, but it's the characters you'll remember' *Irish Examiner*

'Highly original and compelling' Mark Edwards

By Claire McGowan and available from Headline

A SAVAGE HUNGER

CLAIRE McGOWAN

Headline

First published in Great Britain 2016 by
HEADLINE PUBLISHING GROUP

First published in paperback in 2016 by
HEADLINE PUBLISHING GROUP

1

Cataloguing in Publication Data is available from the British Library

ISBN 978 1 4722 2812 3

Typeset in Sabon by Avon DataSet Ltd, Bidford-on-Avon, Warwickshire

Printed and bound in Great Britain by Clays Ltd, St Ives Plc

HEADLINE PUBLISHING GROUP
An Hachette UK Company
Carmelite House
50 Victoria Embankment
London EC4Y 0DZ

www.headline.co.uk
www.hachette.co.uk

To my sister and brothers

Acknowledgements

Thank you to everyone who helped me keep going with this book, especially when I said I hated it and wanted to burn it (difficult as it only existed on my laptop at the time). Thank you to my agent Diana Beaumont, and everyone at Headline especially Vicki Mellor, Caitlin Raynor, and Jo Liddiard. Special thanks for the wonderful new-look covers.

A big thank you to everyone who reviewed my previous books, whether online or in print – it is hugely appreciated. You rock.

Thank you to all my fantastic friends, and to all readers of Paula's adventures, who tell me they want to know what happens next. I hope that at least some of your questions have been answered in this book.

Thanks to my dad for finding my long-lost copy of *Alice's Adventures in Wonderland* somewhere in the attic, and to my mum and siblings.

Thank you to Phil Murray for help with the police bits – if it's still wrong (quite likely) then it's obviously my mistake (I mean a very well-considered bit of poetic licence).

I'm indebted to the book *Ten Men Dead* by David Beresford, a fascinating and harrowing account of the 1980s Hunger Strikes, and also to *Hunger Strike* by Susie Orbach, about the psychology of eating disorders. If you get a chance, do look up about holy relics in Ireland – I promise you that bit is all true. Someone really did steal the preserved heart of a saint from a church in Dublin. Oh and it is entirely possible to buy hair shirts and other penitential equipment online (you're welcome).

I love to hear from readers, so if you have any comments, please do drop me a line on Twitter at @inkstainsclaire or via my website www.ink-stains.co.uk.

Part One

'Alice had got so much into the way of expecting nothing but out-of-the-way things to happen, that it seemed quite dull and stupid for life to go on in the common way.'

Lewis Carroll, *Alice's Adventures in Wonderland*

Prologue

Belfast, Northern Ireland, July 1981

The corpse on the bed was still breathing.

Hardly at all, in a harsh, erratic rhythm, so every few seconds you thought it had stopped. One. Two. Three. Four . . . Then it would start again and you'd drop your head in your hands and think: I can't bear this. It got so bad you were counting the seconds of silence – one, two, three, four – just hoping in a terrible part of you that it would stop for good, just stop with this bloody agony and let it all be over, for God's sake. Sixty-seven days of it. No one ever thought he'd be here after so long, still clinging on, still somehow not dead, while outside the walls the world marched, waved banners, howled insults. You wondered could he hear the racket, in this room with bars on the windows, or if his ears had gone as well as his eyes.

He'd gone blind ten days ago, his eyes turning milky, and then a sort of black colour that was terrible to see. He was stretched out on a sheepskin rug, the waterbed under him wobbling obscenely with each snatched breath.

3

His skin would crack and split if he moved, opening in red, sore mouths that quickly turned black. At the foot of the metal bed, like a bad joke, sat a plate of bread; white, with the crusts cut off. Some beef spread; three apples, dried up. Just in case, they said. In case what? He was too far gone now to eat – a bite of that apple would kill him straight off.

You felt a hand drop on your shoulder. It was Rambo. Or so they called him, anyway; a tiny wee rat of a man. Sort of a bad joke. 'Seen enough, son?'

You couldn't answer, so you just nodded. You'd not expected this. You didn't know what you'd expected, but not this. The hospital stink of shit and bleach, the skin so pale you could nearly see the blood struggling underneath, the black, gaping gums – Christ. It was all you could do to keep a lid on it, and you knew suddenly that if you tried to speak you would burst out crying like a wean.

The doctor, who hadn't said a word or looked at either of you the whole time, took the corpse's pulse again. Every hour at this point. Checking. Counting. You were waiting, he was waiting, all the crowds outside and watching around the world were waiting for the last moment, where the long, slow slide towards death finally ended, hardened into something permanent. When he finally let out his last breath. You could almost feel the hands on the triggers. The match held to the touch paper.

''Mon.' The other man gestured and you got up, numbly, and followed him out to the corridor. It was less like a hospital out there and more like what it really was – a prison. Your DMs echoed on the stone floor and you blew on your hands. When you'd touched him, he'd been cold as ice, and you just couldn't get the feeling off your skin. The man was dying. He was dying right in front of your eyes and you weren't doing a thing to stop it. Somehow, you hadn't understood that until now.

Rambo lit a roll-up, breathed in. 'It'll be soon, they said. Next three days. But it's not too late – if they get an IV in him—'

'They can *help* him?' It didn't seem credible. The man was so near death you could feel it in the room, see it moving up his body with his slow blood.

'Aye. I know he's far gone. But there's still a chance to bring him back. They sometimes ask for it, when they're near the end. When they don't know where they are.'

You'd heard that. About the families who'd had to swear not to feed their sons at the end, as they screamed in broken voices for someone to take the pain away. Swear to just stand by and let them die.

'And if he doesn't go – well, you know how it'll be. It'll all be called off. The whole hunger strike. If he stops, they'll all stop.'

'But—'

'The demands. They still don't agree.'

'But I thought we were close.'

Somewhere across the water, in leather-lined office rooms and under green shaded lights, people were deciding the fate of this man. Mrs T and her top men. Whether they should bring him back. What would happen if they let him die. Suicide, they'd been calling it, but to the people outside the walls, it was murder.

'Aye, they're close. Not close enough. Yet.' It had gone so far now – the man drawing in death with every breath, the Army outside, the world watching. The Brits couldn't be seen to back down, give in to terrorists. Your lot couldn't accept less than they'd asked for at the start. Not when six men had already starved to death.

'So . . .'

'Word has it they might give in. Brits never thought it'd go so far. And there's your man down in Ballyterrin calling for an end to it. People listen to him. If word gets out we're close to an agreement – well, you see what'll happen. They'll take all the fellas off the strike. It'll be over, and we won't get what we started this for.'

And the man in there on the bed, the corpse, they could bring him back from the brink. Lazarus, walking out of his tomb.

You didn't understand. 'So what—'

'Son. We need you. Are you ready to do your duty?'

At first you thought they were asking for this – your life, your body, the slow pain of starving to death over months. But then he spoke again, and you saw it wasn't that they were asking for at all. It was worse.

Chapter One

Ballyterrin, Northern Ireland, July 2013

'There now,' said Pat. 'Isn't that lovely?'

'Lovely,' agreed the salesgirl, whose eyebrows had been so over-plucked she always looked like she was first glimpsing the prices of her own merchandise. 'Add in some wee shoes and a veil, it'd be gorgeous, so it would.'

'Gorgeous,' Pat echoed. 'What do you think, pet?'

Paula regarded herself in the mirror. She'd lost some weight since Maggie's birth two years ago, but the lace dress was still cutting into her ribs, with its complicated architecture of hoops and boning and petticoats. Above it was her face, irritated by the overheated shop and confection of fascinators, shrugs, white satin shoes, and general frippery, none of it costing less than two hundred pounds. 'It's . . . nice,' she tried.

'It's beautiful!' the girl urged. 'Handmade lace. French.'

'Hmm. Yeah, it's nice, but . . .'

'If you're not sure we can try more. There's plenty more!'

Pat was giddy, overjoyed that her difficult son was finally

marrying his childhood sweetheart, who was also, as of two years ago, her own stepdaughter. Paula herself felt some more complicated things about the situation. She'd have liked Aidan to be there, to examine the handwritten price tags, and give out a low whistle at the cost, and raise his eyebrows at her when the girl gushed about two grand being 'nothing at all', not for the 'most special day of your life', while telling dire tales of brides who'd ordered their dresses for cheap online and sure wasn't the wedding ruined when it never turned up? Pat ate all this up, adding in 'she never' and 'God love her, what did she do then?' at the right moments.

The dress was lifted off by the woman's claw-like hands, and Paula stood in the narrow cubicle, looking at herself in her M&S pants and bra, legs unshaven, toenails unpainted. Her red hair was scraped back in a plait, already plastered to her forehead with sweat, because for once the Irish summer was actually a summer. Her body had scars too – a neat one from the Caesarean that had birthed her daughter, a puckered white one where she'd once been stabbed. Paula thought of Maggie for a moment – toddling on the beach with Aidan, if he got organised enough to take her, in a little green swimsuit, her red hair in chubby bunches, Aidan lifting her up to splash over the waves. She wished she was there with them, not stuck here in womanland.

She wriggled back into her jeans and T-shirt, rattled the curtain. 'That's me changed so. Better get back to Mags, I've been ages.'

Pat said, 'Oh, she'll be grand. Aidan dotes on her, so he does.'

'With her daddy for the day!' twittered the girl. 'Ah, isn't that nice, he's babysitting.'

Normally Paula would have retorted that it was hardly

babysitting when it was your own child, but Pat's sudden interest in a cabinet of costume jewellery was a sobering reminder that they could play dress-up weddings and happy families all they liked, but it didn't change the fact no one knew if Aidan was actually Maggie's father or not.

She allowed herself to think of the other, just for a moment – his straight back, the fair hair brushed off his face, his English accent clipping on the edge of words – and then she cut it off. There was no use thinking about Guy, because he was gone.

She drove up the road, afternoon traffic snarling the town, horns blaring in the unexpected swelter of the warm day. She'd taken off work to try on those dresses. What a waste of time, when she could have been doing something useful.

Opening her front door, she was greeted with a cloud of dust and a strange man in paint-stained overalls and a face mask. 'Sorry, love. Be out in a minute.' The builder was extracting a cigarette from his pocket. She was torn between wanting him gone so she could get into a cool shower, and the need for them to actually finish the work they'd been contracted for. The kitchen had been unusable for weeks now, since the builders had thoughtfully ripped out the cooker and sink then disappeared on other jobs, leaving most of the brown seventies cupboards still attached to the walls. Some of them had missing doors, like gaping teeth in a beaten-up face. Paula's childhood home would soon look like a different place – somewhere that wasn't haunted by memories.

Paula averted her eyes from the dust sheets and tools left in her kitchen, a place that used to be just for her, and pushed out through the old-fashioned fly curtain to the garden behind. The garden had been her mother's place, where she'd pegged out roses in the square of uninspiring soil, until the search team had dug it up in 1993. Looking for her body. Paula couldn't be out there and not remember watching white-suited techs as they pulled up each long-nurtured plant. Wondering if they'd find anything. Hoping against hope they wouldn't. This was before she'd got to the point of just wanting an answer, even if it meant knowing for sure her mother was dead.

'Hiya.'

Aidan and Maggie were on a blanket on the dry, yellowed lawn. The last rays of the day filtered down between the roofs of the terraced houses. He was wearing khaki shorts and a Springsteen T-shirt. His forearms were tanned from the summer; bits of the paper were spread about him. Bustling around, Maggie ferried sand from her little pit in the corner to another pile by the back wall. She wore a yellow sundress, clashing wildly with the red hair that was already curling over her ears. What with the hair and the milk-pale skin, she looked nothing like Aidan. Not even a bit.

'Did you put cream on her?' asked Paula.

'Nah, I thought I'd let her get skin cancer, like. Course I did.'

'Sorry.' She collapsed down beside him in her jeans and T-shirt, kicking off her sandals and digging toes into the parched grass.

'So are you all kitted out in the frock of your dreams?'

'Don't. I can't cope with much more of this. I'm having an allergic reaction to the lace, look.' She held out her arm to him and he rubbed it absently, engrossed in the paper.

'Offer it up, Maguire. It makes my ma happy, anyway.'

'I know.' As usual his touch was enough to make her curl into him. Even after two years she didn't take it for granted, having him there every day when she turned her key in the lock. 'What are you doing there, Mags?' she called out.

'Sand,' came the succinct reply.

'I can see that. You're making a bit of a mess, pet. Come here till I see you.' She scooped up the toddler onto her lap, breathing in the smell of warm skin and sun cream. Aidan had indeed slathered the child with it.

'Where were you, Mummy?' Maggie twined her hands in Paula's loosening hair, like a little monkey.

Aidan said, 'Mummy was away getting a big nice dress for her wedding to Daddy. And you're going to be flower girl, aren't you?'

'Yessss!' Maggie had no idea what being a flower girl entailed, and Paula had no desire at all for a big nice dress, or for any of it. But it seemed important to Aidan, to Pat, to Paula's father PJ, who'd been married to Pat for the past two years. So she was doing it. The church, the big nice dress, the works. She rubbed her finger, where her engagement ring chafed in the heat. White gold, diamond and emerald. Not huge, but respectable. Something she'd never thought to see on her own hand. But there it was, there she was, there they all were, a happy family of three.

'Can I've some juice, please, Daddy?' Maggie tugged on his hair. Dark – so unlike her own.

'Juice? Well, I don't see why not. On you come.'

She watched Aidan walk to the house, Maggie trotting after him in her green Crocs, holding up a hand, trusting. He was her daddy. That was all she knew. It could be true. They were making it true, with every day together and this wedding coming up. And although Paula was trying, so hard, not to search the child's face for hints of resemblance – a breadth to the forehead, a turn of the cheek or mouth – she still found she could no more put the other out of her mind entirely than she could stop herself picking up Maggie into her arms whenever she was near.

She paused in the garden with her arms curled round her knees, alone for a moment, feeling her mother around her in the pretty tiles on the wall, a plant that had survived the police digging, and wondered how that trip to the wedding shop would have been if things were different. If everything was different. But it wasn't.

Aidan stuck his head out through the fly curtain. 'Will I go for a takeaway? I'm not cooking in this mess.'

She pushed herself up. 'Yeah, OK. Do you reckon they'll ever finish?'

'God alone knows. He just told me he has to knock off early as he's getting a "wee tickle" in his throat.'

'I'm getting a bloody massive tickle in my throat from all the dust they've left everywhere. It can't be good for Maggie. Is there anything we can do?'

'I dunno. Now the recession's over they'll be off doing someone else's bathroom if we let them go. He said they'd *maybe* be finished this month.'

'In the meantime we've no hob and we have to wash the dishes in the bath.'

'We could always move in with Ma for a bit.'

That really would be it sealed, her and Aidan and Maggie and their respective parents. A family. And she wanted that, she really did. It was just the wedding throwing her into a panic, the dresses, the fuss. The finality of it. That was all.

Paula heard her phone trill on the counter, and got up

and moved to the door, going inside to the cool of the kitchen.

'Leave it,' said Aidan, with his head in the fridge.

'But—'

'If it can't wait till tomorrow they'll ring you. Now, do you want Chinese or pizza or what?'

Paula looked at her phone. It could be work. Someone missing, needing to be found and put back in their proper place. As a forensic psychologist, these were the cases that kept her up at night. She felt little hands round her leg – Maggie, toddling over. 'Mummy, will you read me a story?'

She reached down and picked the little girl up, feeling small legs and arms wrap around her. 'Of course, pet.' To Aidan she said, 'Get fish and chips. We had to bust that Chinese last week for immigration violations.'

He picked up the car keys. 'Right so, fish and chips and mushy peas it is.' The door slammed. Paula remained in the kitchen, standing by the sink in the last place she'd ever seen her own mother, her daughter in her arms, before Maggie started to wriggle down.

'Mummy, I want a story *now*.'

'OK, sweetheart, go and get one.' The phone stayed on the side, ignored.

Alice

He's watching me through the door.

Please go away, *I ask.*

He doesn't move or speak.

Please. *I'm getting upset again.* I need to go . . . please don't watch me. Please.

I know there's no point in asking. It's the rules. He has to watch everything I do. Pissing, showering, crying, bleeding – there are no doors in this place. Nowhere to hide.

That's what I want more than anything. A door. I'd give everything I have for one, even though I don't have anything, not any more. I'm crying now. Or I would be if I had any liquid in my body. There's a lot of that in here – dry crying. Squeezing more out of something that's totally empty. I'm making a sort of huh-huh *sound, like a dog after it's been out in the rain. I've got no choice. I need to go, and he won't leave.*

I cry as it starts to run out of me. I can hardly bear for anyone to see me like this, so I shut my eyes tight and imagine how it would be to totally disappear.

Chapter Two

'Morning, Maguire.'

Paula banged her pass over the entrance to the police station, looking up at the familiar face. Gerard Monaghan, now Detective Sergeant, in a newly sharp suit to match. 'Well, Sergeant. How's Avril? I never see her these days.'

'They have her on nights. Making her work for it, like.'

'Any word on whether she'll make CID?'

'Dunno. The new boss's not such a fan. He reckons we were all too matey with you-know-who.' She and Gerard passed through another door. He swiped the pass which hung around his neck, waiting for it to work. 'Fecking thing. You ever miss the old days?'

Paula sighed. 'All the time. But no point in looking back.' She was willing Gerard not to say the name that went with the face in her head, and he didn't, and they both shifted off to their desks with desultory goodbyes. The PSNI station on the hill was a very different place to work from the missing persons unit she'd started out in. There were rules, and rotas, and phones were always buzzing and people shouting out codes. But she had to be there. There was no more unit now, just her and Gerard up here, Bob retired, Fiacra back in Dundalk with the Gardaí, Avril training as a PC, and – that was all she could think about.

'There you are.' A woman was sitting at Paula's desk;

15

fair-haired, in her forties, wearing a grey trouser suit. Helen Corry had retained the designer outfits from her days as Head of Serious Crime, even though she'd been demoted back to DS.

'Here I am, yes.' Paula put her bag down.

'Fun time wedding shopping?'

'About as much fun as stapling my eyes shut.'

'I remember. Want something juicy?'

'Yes, please. If I do one more internal assessment I'm going to scream.'

'I've got a missing persons. Right up your street – a student from out at Oakdale College.'

'Female?' This was Paula's area of expertise – missing women, lost girls. Trying to find them and bring them back.

'Yep.'

'Tell me the circs?'

Corry spread out the missing persons form, complete with a grainy photo of a blonde, very slim girl. 'Alice Morgan. Twenty-two, doing research into holy relics and Irish folklore. English. Her dad's Tony Morgan.'

'Should I know him?' Paula picked up the photo.

'You would if you were in uniform. He's a life peer, high up at the Home Office. Lord Morgan, I should have said. Alice has been over here studying for a year or so.'

'Oh, right! So it's all hands on deck on this one?'

'Yep.' Corry stood up, straightening her suit. 'Don't take your jacket off, you're coming straight out with me.'

'Did Willis OK it?' Usually, Paula was not supposed to go to crime scenes.

Corry made her usual face at the mention of DCI Willis Campbell, their new boss. It was like someone chewing on a pickled egg. 'Oh yes, nothing's too good for Mr, sorry, *Lord* Morgan's daughter.'

'When was she last seen?'

'Yesterday. It just came in this morning.'

At least she hadn't missed it by ignoring her phone last night. 'Wait, what are you not telling me?' Ordinarily, a missing person's case wouldn't be dealt with so quickly. She looked at the photo of Alice. A little slip of a girl. It was back, the pulse, the spark. She could do this, at least. She could find people when they were lost.

Corry had started walking. 'She was last seen in that church with the relic. You know, Crocknashee. She'd been working there. And they found blood.'

'How much blood?'

'Enough. Come on, let's go.'

'Right. We're meeting Willis at the scene, he's already there, and then we'll search Alice's cottage.'

Paula had never heard Helen Corry talk about her demotion. Two years ago, there'd been a leak in a major case. A forensics expert had falsified evidence, and Corry had been sleeping with him at the time. People had died, and the fallout from it had knocked her off her hard-won perch. Outwardly, she was enjoying being in a more hands-on role, and only the look on her face when DCI Campbell was mentioned ever betrayed her.

When they got to the site, which was some way out of Ballyterrin, the man himself had left his Mercedes, a car that cost more than a one-bed flat, right across the gate of the church. 'Typical,' muttered Corry. 'I'll just park mine on the road. I mean, it's only a Fiat, clearly doesn't deserve the room.' She pulled up. 'How much do you know about this place?'

'A bit, I suppose. From school. They were trying to get away from that side of Catholicism when I was wee. You know, this kind of – idolatry.' For years Paula hadn't known what religion Helen Corry was. It didn't matter, of course, but somehow you did need to know, you had to be sure where to put people. Never English friends, she'd no idea what religion most of them were. When they'd started working together properly, Paula had learned that Corry was indeed a Catholic name, but that her mother was Protestant, and they'd tried to bring their children up with no religion at all, in the cauldron that was seventies and eighties Belfast. Corry had gone to that rare thing, an integrated school, and so she often displayed strange gaps in her knowledge.

'This land belongs to the Garrett family,' said Corry, opening her door. 'Mother and son, they live in the big house over there. But the church is owned by a trust which the son chairs. I just want to know if we'll be treading on any religious toes.'

'I think it's deconsecrated now, so we should be OK.'

She and Corry went up the path to the church. It was another close July day, a sigh of wind rustling dry blades of grass. The graveyard was full of ancient stones, collapsed like drunks, and the eroded faces of stone angels watched the two women as they slogged up the hill. Paula took off her jacket and carried it over her arm. 'He's here already then, Willis?'

'Of course. There'll be TV cameras. He's not going to miss that.'

'What is it you hate so much? Is it the hair?' Streaked and bouffant as it was, Willis Campbell had more hair than any man of forty-eight had a right to.

18

'That doesn't help. Or the suits.' Handmade, the paisley linings always prominently displayed as Campbell whipped his jacket off in order to patrol 'the shop floor', the suits were a source of great amusement in the station. When he was well out of earshot, of course. Corry went on, 'But no, mostly it's a Belfast thing. Every time he talks I just hear that posh Malone Road accent.'

Fair-haired, well-dressed, smooth on TV – but for the upbringing, Willis wasn't a million miles from Corry herself. Not that Paula ever would have said it.

The door of the church was open. It led into a low-ceilinged drystone space, an old chill stippling Paula's arms with gooseflesh. A dark smell of damp, and maybe something worse. She pulled her jacket back on as her eyes adjusted. Below her feet were stone slabs marked with names and dates. They were walking on graves.

DCI Campbell himself was up near the cordoned-off altar, talking to someone in a white boiler suit. 'Ladies.' He advanced on Paula and Corry, smoothing back his hair with one tanned hand, his wedding ring glinting on a well-fed finger. He was married to Greta, a well-turned-out woman who worked as a primary school headmistress as well as bringing up four clever, musical, sporty children. Paula knew all about it from the Christmas round-robins they liked to send.

Corry said, 'I've brought Dr Maguire along – she has a lot of experience in this kind of case.'

He gave Paula the kind of look he might give a man-made fibre. 'Well, I suppose I don't mind you consulting. This could be very high-profile, given who her father is.' That explained why the Head of Serious Crime was at the scene of what was on paper a medium-risk missper.

Corry was looking at a glass display case someone had installed near the entrance desk. Its door was closed, but it was empty. 'That's where it was? The relic?'

'Was is the word. It's gone, but the case is still locked and the alarm's not gone off.'

'And Alice is gone too?' asked Paula.

He gave her another pained look. 'It seems that way. She was seen by a volunteer – a Mrs Mackin, she's in the vestry – at around six last night. This morning Mrs Mackin came in to find the place lying open, no sign of Alice. So she went to get the chair of trustees, Mr Garrett, who owns the surrounding land, and they find the relic gone, and this mess on the steps.'

'Can we have a look at the blood?' Paula tried to see behind him.

He gave her another look. 'Let's see if the techs have finished.'

Behind him, steps led up to the altar of the church, which was carved all over in religious symbols, twisting sheaves of corn and crowns of leaves. Above the tabernacle, the face of Jesus had been painted onto the stone wall in odd lurid colours, his eyes looking up to Heaven. Below him, the steps were splashed in dark red blood, several small pools of it, dried and clotting. A suited tech was crawling about the space, taking pictures. Campbell waved him aside. 'Let the ladies see, please, there's a good lad.'

The man stood aside and took down his hood. 'Kemal!' said Corry. 'Couldn't tell it was you in that get-up. How are you?'

'Very well, thank you, ma'am.' Kemal, an Egyptian who had somehow fetched up in rural Ireland, always spoke in polite RP tones. He nodded to Paula, who gave him a smile, which quickly faded as she looked at the floor.

'This is all you found?' Corry asked Kemal.

'Yes, just like this, spattered as you see.'

Campbell was growing impatient. 'So what do you think, Dr Maguire? I hear you can diagnose everything just by *looking* at a crime scene.'

Behind his back, Corry was rolling her eyes. Paula didn't rise. 'I'd have to find out more about Alice. Anything that might make her disappear – boyfriend issues, mental health problems, if she'd ever tried to kill herself . . .'

'You think this could be self-inflicted?' He pointed at the blood. It had partially dried, but you could see there'd been a lot of it. Too much for a small injury.

'It's possible. But then there'd be a body, wouldn't there?'

'Should we be treating this as high-risk, is what I want to know?'

In other words, did he leave it with Corry and the miss-per team, or did he take it for Serious Crime and himself? If it was likely to be a messy one – no easy solve, no obvious answers – he wouldn't want it. Paula said her usual spiel. 'Well, for someone her age, the most likely thing would be she's gone off voluntarily. But when people do that they don't leave blood everywhere, and they don't tend to take priceless holy relics with them. Alice was working here?'

'She was doing her dissertation on the place, and she ended up with the caretaker job.' Corry was examining a rack of postcards as she spoke, the usual Irish scenes of cows, churches, crosses. On the reception desk was a collection box for Trócaire, the Irish hunger charity.

Campbell was wincing. 'We have to keep a lid on the relic angle. Otherwise we'll be overrun with every tree-loving hippy in Ireland.' He looked at Corry. 'Did you tell her the rest?'

'No. I wanted to see what she'd make of this first.'

'What rest?' Paula glanced between them.

Corry said, 'We didn't want to tell you until you'd seen it yourself, but this has happened before. In this exact spot.'

'What, a missing girl?'

Campbell clicked his fingers to Kemal, who handed him an evidence bag. Inside was a photograph, smeared in blood. For a second Paula thought it was Alice, but it was just a strong likeness – this picture was of a different blonde girl. Not recent.

'This was found on the steps,' he said. 'Does the name Yvonne O'Neill mean anything to you?'

Chapter Three

'Who's Yvonne O'Neill?' said Paula.

'You didn't come across her name down the road?'

When the unit first opened they'd been dumped with all the unsolved missing person cases in Ireland – the ones that made things messy, the ones they couldn't close. Ones with no body, where the person was simply gone forever, leaving in their wake day after day and night after night of unanswered questions. Now it was shut and the remaining files were all in a storage locker. Paula tried to think. 'Nope. No bells ringing.'

Corry sighed; she hadn't wanted to be telling this story. 'Yvonne was twenty-six – bit older than Alice. Pretty girl. Teacher. She was very religious – in fact she even started training as a nun. But she met a man, got engaged instead. Then the man was killed. Car crash.'

'That's rough.'

'It gets worse. She used to come here a lot, to pray. She only lived down the road. That farm we passed on the way in, you know. Her mother's still there. Well, one day Yvonne tells her ma she's away down to the church. She's walking – it's a nice day. An elderly neighbour was driving past, saw her on the road. She waves hello, goes up the path. No one ever sees her again.'

Paula frowned; that didn't make sense. 'Why didn't she

go round the back way? Would that not be quicker?' A path looped round the back of the church, linking the O'Neill's farm, the Garrett home, and the cottage where Alice had been living.

'Apparently she didn't like to walk past the Garretts' house. The families were having some dispute over the land. And yes, before you ask, they looked at the son back then. He was alibied.'

Paula digested this. 'So – she was also last seen at this church?'

'That's right. Same as Alice. They searched everywhere round here. They even took in cadaver dogs – they alerted in the church, but the place is full of old bones, so that didn't help. No sign of her. Yvonne had a look of Alice too – wee and blonde, like she wouldn't say boo to a goose.'

'When was this?' Why had she never heard about it? '1981.'

That explained it. The year of the hunger strikes, when every day someone else was being killed in the North. No surprise if Yvonne got forgotten. 'Ah.'

'Yeah. So, everyone was a bit distracted, shall we say. People getting shot all over the show. Everyone thought the UVF got her, or the UDR maybe. Retaliation for the hunger strikes. Yvonne nearly being a nun, you know.'

'But you don't think so?'

Corry shook her head. 'Why no body? If they wanted to make a point, they'd have left her where the RUC could find her. No, I think she just got lost in the chaos. No one cared, when there were ten men starving themselves to death.'

'So. We have a missing girl, same spot, same look, thirty-two years apart. You reckon that's significant?'

Corry sighed again. 'Maguire, there's more. Yvonne went missing on July the thirty-first, 1981.'

'Shit. Same *day*?'

'Same day. Lúnasa – the old Celtic fire feast, right?'

Paula bit her lip. 'Right.' Sacrifice. Fires on the hillsides. Blood in the soil.

Corry gave a grim ghost of a smile. 'I told you this one was juicy.'

Willis Campbell had been listening to their discussion, and was again looking like a man with severe heartburn. 'As I said, we need to stay away from the pagan angle – it could just be coincidence. But we'll do everything we can on this one. Dr Maguire, I'm redirecting you to this case full-time.' Clearly he had decided that this would be a messy one. 'Maybe if we find Alice fast we can keep the press out of it. Can you manage?'

'If you like, sir.' Thank God – something real to work on, instead of dull-as-ditchwater psychological assessments.

A knock at the church door, and a nervous uniformed officer. 'Sir . . . DCI Campbell? There's a reporter here, they said—'

'Christ, the word's out already.' Smoothing his hair again, Willis rushed off.

'Hope he's brought his Touche Éclat,' said Corry. 'Come on, we need to talk to the person who last saw Alice.'

'This is a disaster. It's a priceless relic!' The chair of the Crocknashee Church Trust, Anderson Garrett, was wringing his hands as he paced around the nave of the church.

'Don't be getting on so, Anderson,' said a grey-haired and grim-faced lady, who was sitting bolt upright in one of the pews. She was dressed in lemon-yellow slacks and carried her handbag on her knee like an offering. 'Just tell them what happened.'

'It's Mrs Mackin, is it?' Corry looked at her.

'Mrs Maureen Mackin, and I'll need to get away soon, I've to pick my grandchild up from nursery.' She peered over her glasses at Corry in her suit and heels, and Paula, somewhat less groomed with her hair falling out of its plait and slightly-too-short summer skirt (she'd grabbed it out of last year's clothes, not realising it had shrunk from too many washes). 'You're from the police, are you? Well, I told the ones in uniform everything.'

'You were the last person to see Alice, as far as you know?'

She nodded. 'She said she'd close up last night, so I went off – I'd to make my husband his dinner, he goes to his Rotary meetings on Wednesdays. Then this morning, the door's lying open.'

'So you went to get Mr Garrett?' Corry turned to the man, who was still pacing. He was about sixty, with an oddly stiff gait and a belly that must have been five feet around.

'Really, you have to find it,' he said. 'You've no idea how valuable it is, I . . . It's been stolen, I'm sure of it. Lots of relics are being stolen these days, you know, there was one in Dublin just the other month, and—'

'Mr Garrett, we're going to do our best to find Alice. And the relic.' Corry's tone could have cut glass. 'It would be very helpful if you could tell us the relic's history.'

'It's irreplaceable.' He stopped walking for a moment, a sort of tremor of panic going through him. Through the gap in his strained shirt buttons, Paula could see his pale flesh. 'It's really . . . I can't explain. There's nothing like it.'

'Yes, but why? What is it?' asked Corry.

He turned, resuming his fevered pacing. Paula wished she could ask him to sit down. 'It's the finger-bone of Saint Blannad. Verified by the Pope.'

'Assume we're not Catholic for a minute,' Corry said drily.

Maureen Mackin tutted under her breath and Garrett expanded: 'Saint Blannad was the abbess of a convent in five AD. She helped convert the local chieftains to Christianity.'

'And why's she a saint?'

At her question, Garrett glanced at Paula, distracted. 'Because of the miracles, you see, she . . .' He stopped, taking in air with a kind of gulping noise. 'The relic. It can perform miracles.'

'Such as?' asked Corry.

'It made the harvests multiply. Fed the hungry. During the Famine people prayed at the shrine, you see, and the area was spared.'

Paula was sceptical. Everyone knew South Down had largely avoided the potato blight, but this was likely due to its ring of protective mountains. 'Anything recent?'

'Many people find it a source of great healing and comfort,' Mrs Mackin said, glaring at them over her handbag. 'We get visitors from the missions all the time. Places where the wee black babies are starving, you know. They pray for food.'

'OK, but . . .' Corry was giving Paula a look, so she subsided. 'Can you tell us about Alice, Mr Garrett?'

It didn't seem to have occurred to him. 'Alice? Miss Morgan started coming here several months ago. She was interested in the relic.'

'Very interested,' added Maureen Mackin.

'Meaning?'

'She used to be in here every day God sent, staring into the wee case. We'd have to chase her out when we were locking up.'

'But you gave her a job?' asked Corry.

Garrett was working his hands together like he was kneading a piece of dough; over, under, over, under. 'We set up a caretaker post to run the place, put on events and so on—'

'Weddings,' Mrs Mackin chipped in, 'though I don't think it's right, having civil weddings in what used to be a holy Catholic church.' She was that kind of speaker, fussy, correcting. The type that made useful witnesses.

'And how was she as an employee?' asked Paula, looking at Garrett.

'Oh, she was, she was . . . diligent, yes. Though I didn't like her habit of staying late in the church. It should have been locked every day at six, I told her that.' Corry gave Paula a brief look; that might be worth checking out, if she'd been here alone at night.

'But apart from that?'

Mrs Mackin conceded, 'Aye, she wasn't so bad. Not that any of these young ones would know a hard day's work if it came up and hit them in the face.'

Corry pressed on, mild irritation seeping into her tone. 'So it would be out of character for Alice to disappear.'

Garrett was pacing again. 'I don't know. I didn't know her very well.'

'So let me get this straight,' said Corry. 'The relic is missing. The case has been locked up again with the code.'

'Yes. And only Alice knew it.'

'Apart from you?'

He made a gesture of annoyance. 'Of course, apart from me.'

So it was possible she'd been forced to open it. Corry said, 'And where were you, Mr Garrett, overnight? I gather that's your house on the road that runs behind here.'

'My mother, I care for her, you see, she had a fall so I took her in to Ballyterrin Hospital. We were there till about eleven, then I took her back and put her to bed.'

'Did you see anything at the church, or at Alice's cottage?'

'No. No, it was all quiet. All dark.' He kept staring over at the empty case. 'I can't believe it's gone. It's really priceless, you must find it!'

Corry said, 'I'm a bit more concerned about Alice right now. Especially with the previous disappearance from this church.'

Garrett looked blank for a minute. 'This is nothing to do with that.'

Maureen Mackin looked up sharply. 'Oh aye, wee Yvonne. That was a long time ago. You don't think it's connected?'

'It's a big coincidence if not. So we'll need to examine the building, of course.'

'What?' Garrett turned pale. 'We can't have you, you, swarming all over the place. It's bad enough that forensics man's been in here with his brushes, touching everything . . .'

'Ah now, Anderson,' remonstrated Mrs Mackin. 'He's respectful enough for one of those Muslim fellas.'

Corry shot Paula a quick glance. 'Mr Garrett. We will need to search the church. You must see that.'

'But the relic's gone. It's not here. Why would you search the place?' His hands were wringing again. Up, over, down, around. Of all the things that were lost, the relic seemed to be the only one he cared about.

Alice

Today's one of the days we aren't allowed up. We wake up, we go to sleep, and in between we have to just lie here, looking at the ceiling. If you make a fuss, if you turn over in bed too much, then you get the bands.

That makes them sound nicer than they are. Cuffs is what they are. Restraints. They're made of a kind of Velcro that's soft, but impossible to break. You don't want to be in them, so you lie really still, but he's always watching. Even a flicker of an eye, or breathing too deeply, or moving to scratch an itch, and he notices. Then you can cry and scream and beg and promise all you want, but it's the cuffs. The woman helps him. We think she's in love with him. She stinks of cheap perfume and sweat, and when he's here her eyes follow him round the room. I can smell her breath as she straps me in. She doesn't care if she hurts me.

Please, I say. Please. I'll be good.

I might as well have said nothing. She doesn't even look at me. Now my arms are pulled up over my head, my chewed fingers hanging over the cold metal bedhead. If I'm very bad, if I move or complain, it will be the ankle cuffs too. So I shut up. I stare at the ceiling and the brown stain where water has dripped through. It looks polluted. Ruined. It's all I'm allowed to look at for the next ten hours, until it gets dark and we just look into the blackness with dry open eyes.

Down the room, someone starts to scream. I can't see who; my shoulders have seized up. The man and the woman rush to shut her up. I've already lost all feeling in my hands. It's been ten minutes. There's eleven hours and fifty more minutes to go.

Chapter Four

'So Alice didn't live on campus?' They were walking down the hill at the back of the church, Corry's heels getting stuck in the parched grass.

'She did till about six weeks ago.'

It seemed an odd place for a twenty-two year old. Your nearest neighbours would be the skeletons in the graveyard, and the yews around the church rustled and chattered, almost like they were whispering. Alice Morgan clearly didn't scare easily.

The lintel of the cottage was so low that Paula, at five foot ten, had to stoop to go in. Gerard Monaghan was loitering at the door, stabbing at his BlackBerry. Corry eyed him. 'For the love of God, Monaghan, would you put your tie on right. Your neck's not *that* thick.'

They were technically the same rank now, which neither of them could get their heads around, but Gerard hadn't lost the habit of deferring to her. He twitched his tie. 'Nothing here. I've had a wee look in already.'

'Well, let's see anyway.'

The cottage was just a living room with an open grate, in it a small pile of ashes; a modern kitchen, cold and ugly, and a sliver of bathroom with terrible seventies fittings. It reminded Paula of a bad B & B in the west of Ireland, the kind of place her parents used to take her on their holidays.

Before everything. Alice seemed to have spent most of her time in the bed, which was dragged up to the fireplace in the living room, and heaped with books and paper. Baggy tracksuits and jumpers, even in the relative warmth of July. Paula glanced at one of the books. 'The Paleo diet?'

Corry rolled her eyes. 'My Rosie came home the other day talking about that. She's fourteen years old, for God's sake. Here, don't touch anything.'

She took some gloves from her jacket. Paula snapped them on, examining the books more carefully. They were on two main themes – Irish history, or dieting. 'Alice wasn't overweight, was she?'

'Hardly. Her description has her at five foot two and seven stone.'

'Eating disorder?'

'Most wee girls seem to have one now.' Corry moved into the kitchen as Paula's eye was caught by another book. *Hunger in Ireland: From saints and visions to the famine and the hunger strikes.* 'Wasn't there some story about Saint Blannad?' she called. She was trying to remember back to school, the drone of her RE teacher on a soporific afternoon. 'She was starved, wasn't she, and she had holy visions or something like that, and . . .' She turned over another book. *The Body as Power.* A history of the 1981 hunger strikes. Same year Yvonne had gone missing. Had Alice known about the other girl?

Corry's voice echoed as if she was looking in a cupboard. 'Come in here,' she said.

Paula moved towards the kitchen – there was barely room for the two of them. 'What?'

Then, she saw.

*

The kitchen units and doors and fridge were entirely covered with pictures. Torn out of magazines and papers. Female bodies. Torsos, legs, arms – the faces cut or ripped off. Here and there were actual photographs of another female body. One hand could be seen holding the camera phone, the other lifting up whatever she was wearing. In some, a hank of blond hair was visible, but the face was always missing. 'Is it her? Alice?'

Corry nodded. 'Selfies, is that what they call them?'

'God, she was thin. Is there any food at all here?'

With her gloved hands, Corry opened the fridge – nothing but a wizened apple and some dark nail polish. In the cupboards were some stale-looking packets of cereal and dried fruit and that was it. Even houses during the Famine probably had more to eat in them. 'Her Facebook page is like this too – she posts one of those selfies every day. Even yesterday.'

'Did we get her computer or phone? Bet we'll find loads of links to pro-ana stuff.'

'We've not found anything yet. She might have her phone with her.' If she was alive, of course. At this stage – and this was what got Paula really hooked on missing persons work – everything was still possible. Alice might be perfectly fine. There was still hope. There was still a chance.

Gerard had followed them through the kitchen doorway, and his face creased as he saw the pictures. 'What's that?'

Paula opened another cupboard. 'Thinspiration. Pro-anorexia stuff.'

'That's a thing?'

'Be glad you're male, Monaghan,' said Corry, poking through a cutlery drawer.

Gerard squinted. 'So does she do this every day, take photos? Bit up herself, is she?'

'It's an eating disorder thing,' said Paula. 'She needs validation from people online to reassure herself she's thin.'

'Load of rubbish.'

'Look at this.' Paula indicated a headless picture of Alice in a bikini, her hipbones lifting the fabric like buttresses. 'I'd say her self-esteem isn't the best. She'd be at risk of drug use, self-harm – and suicide, sadly. And I bet if we have a look we'll also find a bad boyfriend in the mix.' Paula's fingertip hovered over the picture, not touching.

Corry shook her head. 'Give me a nice gangland killing any day. Clean and simple.'

Gerard said, 'Like that one last month where the fella's kneecaps were shot out all over the kitchen floor?'

'At least that made sense. He didn't do it to himself, did he?'

Paula was still looking at Alice's ribcage. She was gaunt, like an animal starving to death. She'd have hated how she looked, most likely. Probably explained the baggy clothes. But she'd chosen to cover her fridge with pictures of her near-naked body. Maybe so she'd punish herself if she allowed one morsel of food past her mouth. 'Mortification of the flesh,' she muttered.

'Eh?' Gerard was on his phone again, perhaps hoping for an assignment to something more clear-cut.

'That was what Saint Blannad did, wasn't it? She fasted for a year in captivity, supposedly, and was rewarded with divine visions. And Alice here is obsessed with the relic by all accounts, she's spent the year studying it, she's even moved out here – and she's starving herself.'

'A girl with anorexia at a shrine for the hungry,' said Corry. 'That's strange.'

'This is beyond me, Maguire,' said Gerard irritably. 'Women and food. Just eat if you're hungry, then don't if you're too fat. Easy.'

'I hope you don't talk to your girlfriend like that,' Corry scolded him.

'She's all right. She can eat what she wants, she's a fast metabolism. She says she never diets.'

'How long is it now you're together?'

'Year and a half.'

Corry did her trademark eye-roll. 'God love you, Monaghan, you've got a lot to learn.'

'Eh?'

'Nothing. Let's talk to her friends, see if we can get the name of a boyfriend, if there is one.'

'There'll be one. There always is.' Paula peered at the photos, the dismembered body parts. The angles seemed impossible – a stomach curving in on itself, legs that didn't meet in the middle. She looked down at herself, the roll she'd never quite shifted from her middle after Maggie's birth. How thin could you get, before you'd actually disappear?

'I better tell Willis,' said Corry, shutting the kitchen door. 'This is adding up to suicide, right?'

'But the blood in the church, and the relic missing? The photo of Yvonne?'

'I know. Which is why I've asked Willis to make it high-risk. Then we can put all the resources we have on it.'

'Will he give it to Serious Crime?' said Gerard, sounding wary. He preferred the more straightforward cases, scumbags to be hauled in and banged up. Simple.

Corry shook her head. 'I want to hang onto it. He's

enough on his plate and she's only missing for now.'

Until they found a body, that was. Paula looked around the cottage. 'Is that it? Two and a bit rooms?'

'There's a wee garden outside.'

'Can I see?'

Corry shrugged and led her out of the side door to an overgrown back lawn. At the bottom was a shed. It would have been the outside loo at one point. Paula tramped down, the dying weeds crunching underfoot. There was no sound but the birds in the trees, and far away, the noise of a farm vehicle droning over the land. The door had not one but two padlocks on it. New and shiny.

'This is weird. Nothing else is in such good nick.' The door itself was old and rotten.

'I'll ask the search team to get a warrant.' Corry beckoned to Gerard. 'See if you can get in there, Monaghan, OK?'

'Can we not get a DC on it?' He lowered his BlackBerry. Now he'd made DS, Gerard was at pains to stay ahead of the pack.

'I'm sure you can sort it. Let's get back to the station and sort our paperwork, and then we better go to Oakdale. I think this lot are more concerned about the relic than they are about poor Alice.'

Paula wondered was Corry saying 'poor' because Alice was gone, or because she'd clearly been an unhappy, suffering girl. As they left the cottage she saw Corry pull the front door shut on its old-fashioned latch. 'It wasn't locked?'

'No. She left it open, Garrett says. It didn't have a lock.'

'Trusting.'

'Well, it's in the middle of nowhere. Who'd be coming round here?'

But Alice was gone all the same.

Chapter Five

On the screen were two pictures. In one, a woman was dying in a famine in Sudan. Flies crawled on her face, made ageless by starvation. In the other, another woman was almost as thin, the skin stretched over the bones of her face. Only difference: she was smiling. On a website that gave tips on how to lose weight, hide your eating habits from friends and family. How to cheat at weigh-ins. How to never eat in public. How to die, slowly and willingly.

Paula sighed and clicked out of her research, feeling the weight of the internet press on her. The Famine. The hunger strikes. Anorexia. It was all too much to process. There were already some news stories online about Alice disappearing, and the phones in the station had been ringing since their return from the church. She turned again to the picture of Alice which Corry had put on the incident room board – frail, lost. *Where are you?* Paula couldn't help but feel that the signs – the empty kitchen, the blood in the church – were all crumbs someone had left, if only she could follow them.

Gerard appeared at her desk, a ham sandwich in his hand – if he didn't eat every fifteen minutes he would slip into a coma, apparently. 'Corry wants you,' he mumbled, chewing.

Behind him was a young policewoman in uniform. Paula smiled at her. 'Well, Constable Wright. Not arresting me, I hope.'

Avril blushed. 'Ah, stop it. It's bad enough I have to wear this. I just hope I make CID quickly.' The black police uniform, slacks and a stab vest, wasn't Avril's usual pastel attire, but her face was flushed and pretty as always when Gerard Monaghan was nearby.

The two were very careful to be discreet at work. Gerard, at twenty-nine and already a DS, was her senior. Avril had been an intelligence analyst for the missing persons unit before getting a taste for policing. Paula wondered how it was working out for them. Gerard's Republican family and Avril's parents – her father a Presbyterian minister – had so far refused to meet. Avril would also not countenance living with a man she wasn't married to.

Gerard shoved the last of his sandwich in his mouth, chewing exaggeratedly to make Avril laugh. She shook her head. 'You're awful. Sorry, Paula.'

Paula thought they were doing OK. Gerard's big lug of a face was also trying hard not to laugh. 'Isn't she a sight in that get-up?' he said to Paula. 'I keep expecting her to Taser me.'

'Ah, give over.' Avril slapped him lightly on the arm. 'I better head on, Paula, but I'm dying to hear all about the wedding. What's your dress like?'

Paula grimaced. 'Um . . . I haven't got one yet.'

'Oh! But is it not . . . eh, a bit late?'

'When's it again?' said Gerard, through lumps of ham.

'The seventeenth.' Avril shook her head at him. 'Honestly. I've told you a million times.'

Paula got up. 'I know, I don't have much time. Soon. I'll do it soon. I'll see you anyway. Better find out what Corry wants.'

*

38

'Your man Garrett might be weird, but he was right – this is the third relic theft since last year. In Dublin they lost a preserved heart out of a church, and another place had the jawbone of Saint Brigid nicked, if you could credit it. People were seen hanging about the church both times – seemed like a professional job.'

Paula said, 'What do they want them for? Some kind of ritual?'

Corry laughed. 'Nothing so voodoo. They probably just want to sell the gold casings. The recession, you see.' Saint Blannad's finger appeared to be a white half-moon of bone. In the pictures it rested in a gold, velvet-lined reliquary, which had been locked in the glass case in the church. 'So that's one angle,' continued Corry. 'Burglary gone wrong. Also, as you suspected, Alice was anorexic. Listen to this: in her teens she was in a private clinic for two years, and she dropped out of her first university in England because of it. Explains why she's twenty-two and only an undergrad.'

'What are her parents like?'

'Well, you know about her da. This is the mother. Rebecca Morgan.' Corry held up a picture from a newspaper. A woman hurrying from court, with short blond hair and a grey suit. The kind who got manicures, and went to the hairdresser's once a week. 'That was taken when there was that hoo-ha, the affair allegations about our esteemed Lord Morgan – when he was made a life peer, remember? They sued the paper that broke the story. Rebecca swore blind he was at her side on the nights he was supposedly with those girls. Paper had to give them half a million.'

'How old would Alice have been then?'

'Let's see, 2005 – about fourteen. Anyway, the Morgans

have been at a conference in Dubai, so they're travelling over.'

'Anything else I need to know?'

'Well, the blood in the church – it's same type as Alice's.'

Part of her had been hoping it was animal blood, or even a Halloween prop or something, not evidence that a living girl had been done some terrible harm. 'Did they get into the shed at her cottage?'

'God, the shed. What a palaver that was. It's a listed building or something. Anyway, look what was in it.'

Corry pulled up a picture on her phone and Paula leaned in to see. 'Is that . . . food?'

'Yup. Alice's little secret.' Even on the small screen, it looked as if the shed was packed out. Boxes of biscuits, multipacks of crisps, jars of peanut butter, sugary cereals, and bags and bags of sweets. 'It looks like my kids' dream meal,' said Corry, putting the phone away.

'So what, she was bulimic?'

'Looks that way. We're trying to get her medical records but she hadn't registered with a GP since she left the college. And they aren't exactly cooperative over at Oakdale. You'll see.'

'Do we know much about the rest of her life, her friends and so on?'

'We're going to the university in a minute. I say we – that means you're coming too, so don't get comfortable.'

'Any boyfriends?' Paula had been hoping for an obvious suspect, a jealous lover, a rejected friend, someone with an 'arrest me' sign on their forehead. She had so much on with the wedding and Maggie, it was entirely the wrong time for a girl to go missing. Because Paula knew herself, and she would never be able to let it go until Alice was found.

'There's a fella she was seeing, according to the college secretary. Bit of a gossip – best kind of witness, for our purposes. I don't know if they even have boyfriends these days, it's all Tinder and hooking up and what have you. So come on, get your things.'

'Have we time for a bite to eat first?' Paula hadn't got around to buying lunch – all that research into starvation had put her right off – and she and Aidan never had anything in the house to make a packed one. She wondered if that would magically get better once they were married. If they'd be like proper grown-ups.

Corry shook her head. 'You should have brought something. Will I make you a packed lunch when I do Rosie's, is that what you want?'

'That'd be good actually.'

'Come on. You can get a sandwich on the way.'

Alice

I'm throwing up. I hate this normally, I can't stand it, choking my throat, panic in my chest – what if I can't breathe? – but it's all they've left to me. All the poison they've fed me, I can feel it coming out, leaving me clean. I'm hugging the toilet, the lovely ceramic curves of it cold under my arms. I rest my head against the seat. It smells of piss and bleach but I know I'm safe here. The floor is checked in black and white. Eight tiles each way. I count as I vomit, trying to stay in control.

Into the toilet I am puking my guts. I heave and heave, feeling the body take over, the terrifying power of it. Out. Out. Getting rid of it. Everything they've forced down me over the past weeks. I can beat them. I can puke it all out. It's all gone, in stringy ropes of bile. The smell is so disgusting it makes me want to cry. I imagine it leaching out of me, off my stomach and hips and thighs. They won't have won. I won't swallow this poison. In this place, everything is so controlled. They weigh you, they watch you bleed, they calculate every ounce of you. Well, this is my revenge.

Down the corridor I hear the alarm start to scream, and the sound of running feet. They will find me. There's nowhere to hide. But I've still escaped, for now, because I am purged and clean and new. I lie down on the floor and wait for them to come, and as they wrench the door open I put my head on the tiles and start to cry.

Chapter Six

'Do they know we're coming?'

'They should do.' Corry was looking grumpy as they stood in the reception of the college. 'There was meant to be someone here to meet us. We've an appointment with the principal.'

Oakdale College, a small private university, was still fixed up like the stately home it had been – apple-green carpets muffling the stairs, clocks ticking quietly in the corners. And the calm of the place – despite the students gathering books and preparing for lunch, passing Corry and Paula with curious looks.

'No one seems to know Alice is gone,' Paula said, as the lobby, once the hallway of the house, filled and emptied, filled and emptied, busy with chattering students, the girls dressed for the hot weather in tiny shorts and vests, the boys loud-voiced. High sounds of laughter clashing round the wooden walls of the place.

'They know. Honestly, you'd think they didn't even care one of their students is missing. Come on, I'm not waiting.'

The library at Oakdale stopped Paula in her tracks. Polished wooden shelves of old books, and above on a high mezzanine, lines and lines of them running into shadowed corners. Students worked at the desks, the buttery summer light reflecting off glasses and Macbooks. Though they were all over eighteen, the place felt more like Paula's old convent school. Jam-packed with hormones and tears, everything constantly on the brink. Everything full of meaning. Where you sat, who you had lunch with, how you wore your clothes, how you carried your bags. 'Why haven't they gone on summer break?' There seemed to be as many students around as you'd expect mid-term.

'They're allowed to stay all year round. It's like an extension of boarding school for a lot of them – often they've no homes to go to, if Mummy and Daddy are overseas or it's too much hassle to have them. So they carry on with research projects. That's what Alice was doing with the relic.'

A woman in a short-sleeved shirt and polyester trousers approached. She looked cross. 'Yes?'

Corry showed her ID and the list of names she'd got from the secretary. 'We're looking for these students. Any of them in here?'

'Dermot Healy's in Mathematics,' the librarian stage-whispered. 'But you can't speak to him here. You'll disturb the students.'

'Where then?' Corry was speaking at her normal volume.

'Well, there's my room, but—'

'Good.' She tapped the edge of her ID card on the librarian's desk. 'Would you send him in to us, please? It's urgent.'

Even the office was nice, a small room with wooden cabinets. Corry crossed to the kitchen area and flicked on the kettle. She saw Paula looking. 'It's the least they can do. One of their students is missing, for God's sake, and they're acting like we're here from Ofsted or something.'

It took a few minutes for Dermot to be summoned from the depths of the library – or perhaps he wasn't keen on helping either. By the time there was a reluctant knock on the door, both Corry and Paula had cups of tea. Corry had shamelessly nicked some Earl Grey from what looked like a private stash. 'Come in.'

The boy in the doorway – you couldn't really call him a man – had horn-rimmed glasses and the fair, rosy skin of a chorister. His brown hair, ungelled, fell in curtains round a child-like face. Paula clocked the crimson college hoody – she'd noticed others in the library. She remembered boys like him from her own university, sometimes emerging in groups from labs and libraries, blinking in the light.

Despite her impatience, Corry's voice was kind. 'Hello, Dermot. I'm DS Corry from the Ballyterrin PSNI, this is Dr Maguire. We need to ask you a few questions about Alice Morgan.'

'Did you find something?' He stepped into the room, rubbing the back of his head. Afterwards, Paula would think it was a strange thing to say.

Corry didn't seem to notice. 'No, she's still missing. I'm afraid we're a bit worried about her.'

He looked puzzled but reacted slowly, his features somehow flat, as if under glass. Paula found she was looking to see if his pupils were dilated. 'Oh. Where do you think she is?'

'Well, we don't know, Dermot. She's missing, as I said. We were hoping you might know something.'

'Where do you think she could be?' It was Paula's standard question when people went missing, one that often yielded surprising results.

'We thought she'd just gone off again,' he said. Offhand.

'Again?' Corry flashed her gaze to Paula, steely. *Let him talk.*

'Well – sometimes Alice wanted, like, headspace. You know. She said that's why she was moving out of campus. So she could work on her summer project.'

'You said *again*. Do you mean she's gone missing before?'

Dermot rubbed his head. 'Uh – she told me once she used to run away a lot. At school and that. So we thought maybe . . . she went off.'

Paula asked, 'What about Facebook? When did she last post?'

'Um . . .' He took out a phone and scrolled through it. 'She liked something Katy – that's Alice's room-mate, or she was before – put up about friendship. Katy's always posting these crap statuses, oh I've had such a bad day, blah blah, just had the worst time ever. Just to make the other girls go *are you OK, babe?* and all that. She's so pass-aggy. That was yesterday.'

'Tell me about you,' said Corry, changing tack. 'What are you studying?'

'Applied Maths.'

'And what's that?'

'It's complicated. I don't think it's worth explaining.'

'And you've known Alice a while?'

'We met in freshers' week. There's a small class here so it's easy to meet people.'

Corry said, 'I gather you dropped out of Trinity before this.'

He looked irritated. 'I didn't drop out. I get anxiety. It wasn't that bad. My parents over-reacted, made me transfer here.'

Paula asked, 'And when did you last see Alice, Dermot? I mean actually see her yourself.'

He screwed up his eyes. 'Um . . . I'm not sure. Not that long ago, I guess. A few weeks, maybe.'

'And she seemed OK?'

'Well, yeah. Same as normal really. Honestly, she's probably just gone off for a bit of space.'

Corry regarded him steadily, and Paula could almost hear her thought as if she'd said it: *he's lying*. 'So you aren't worried about her, then?'

'Well . . .' For the first time Dermot paused. 'I mean, of course I'm worried. She's my friend.' He straightened up. 'Anyway, is it not early for you to be here? I thought you normally waited like twenty-four hours to do anything about missing people.'

'We don't wait if we have reasons to be concerned.' Corry stared him down. 'Do you think we do?'

'I don't know. Like I said, she needs space sometimes.'

Corry held his gaze for a few more seconds, before nodding. 'Well, if you hear anything that might help, please get in touch.'

'We're friends. Best friends. She didn't have any other girl friends here. She got on better with the boys mostly.'

Katy Butcher was a large girl, with thick-framed glasses that matched the nondescript brown colour of her hair. Katy was sitting hunched over, cross-legged on one of the single beds in the room she'd shared with Alice, also wearing a college hoody, despite the warmth of the day. Sad, low music played; Paula thought it was maybe Snow Patrol.

Corry leaned against a dresser. 'Would you give the music a rest, Katy?' The room was small for two girls, one single bed under the window and another in the corner, stripped and unused. Katy's posters – Sylvia Plath, Virginia Woolf, Marilyn Monroe; all the dead girls – crept over half the wall, then stopped, in an invisible line of demarcation.

Katy put out a hand to turn off the iPod dock, and Paula saw it, underneath the thick black wristband the girl wore: a network of broad raised scars, crossing Katy's arm, right where the skin was thinnest and the veins showed through.

'How long have you known Alice, Katy?' asked Corry.

'Oh?' She had a habit of opening her eyes up wide under her glasses like a child. 'I guess since we got here? A year? They said we'd be roomies, which was like the best thing ever, cos we got to be best friends. She told me everything.' Katy bit her lip. 'Do you think she's OK?'

Corry said, 'What do you think, Katy?'

Katy paused. 'Alice . . . sometimes she needed, like, space. Headspace, you know. So maybe she went to . . . you know, get a break.'

Corry said nothing to that. The silence in the room felt like an extra person, especially unfamiliar since a girl like Katy had likely never known a moment without snap-chatting or WhatsApping or something. As if to underline this, her phone vibrated. Paula noticed it was an old, beat-up one, of the type only her own father insisted on still using. Katy glanced at it and stuck it into the pocket of her hoody. Paula felt Corry tense; she'd be wanting to tell the girl to put the phone away and listen. To break the silence, Katy spoke falteringly. 'You know, she moved out there on her own. So. We thought she just wanted to be alone.'

'But Katy – we found signs of a struggle in the church. And a quantity of blood, too, I'm sorry to say.'

Katy sat up straighter. 'How much?'

Corry glanced at Paula. 'Well. Some.'

'Maybe she cut herself or something?' Katy fiddled with the band on her own wrist. 'Did you find anything else? Like anything that makes you think, you know, she's been – hurt or something?'

'We don't know yet, Katy.'

She slumped back down again. 'Right. So she could have gone off.'

'All the same, we're worried. Also, the relic is gone. Saint Blannad's finger-bone.'

To Paula's surprise, the girl sighed. 'Not that again. We were all totally sick of hearing about it. After she had that lecture on relics she just went on and on about it. Wasn't it amazing and wasn't it so cool we had one right near here and—'

'You said we,' Corry interrupted. 'Who's we?'

'Oh, the gang of us. Like me and Dermot and Peter.'

Corry looked at her list of people to interview. 'Peter Franks, Alice's boyfriend?'

Katy sat up again. 'Er, they're not together.'

'We were told by the college that—'

'It's wrong. They kissed but like ages ago, only once or twice. He said she was too needy.'

'So he's not her boyfriend.'

'No,' she said, and her sullen mouth curved into a smile, despite what they'd told her about the blood in the church, despite her missing room-mate. 'He's mine. He was with me last night. He spent the night here.'

Paula looked at Corry quickly, but she hadn't blinked. She was good. 'Right. What about this other boy? Dermot Healy?'

'Oh, he's like my brother. You know, we're totally close.

You could tell him anything, that's what Alice always said.'

'But you weren't romantically involved with him, either of you?'

'God, no. It's like he's gay.'

'But he's not?'

'He says he isn't. Me and Al thought he was.' Her mouth lifted again in that glassy smile. 'I think he's just kind of in denial?'

Paula asked, 'What did you think when Alice moved out of college?'

'I was worried. It's so weird out there, and I was worried she might – you know.' She made a vague gesture. 'The anorexia, like, I mean. That it was back.'

'You knew Alice had been ill with it?' said Corry.

'Er, no *had* been. She never really stopped. You've seen her pictures, she was so skinny. And she like, hadn't had a period since she was fifteen or something.'

'Is that right?'

Katy nodded knowledgeably. 'That's what it does to you. When she was here, though, like, we've got a nurse on site, we've all got personal counsellors. They meet us once a month to see if we need pills or whatever.'

'Did you see her much after she moved?' asked Paula.

'Not so much. I'd see her in class or the buttery. Or we'd FB or G-chat, you know. But it was like . . .' She sighed. 'It was like I'd lost her. You know, we were really best friends. Before.'

'When did you last actually see Alice then? I mean in person?'

She thought about it. 'God, I don't know. I think I saw her across the library last week and waved. She didn't see me but we G-chatted after.'

'And how did she look?' asked Corry.

'Eh, same as usual? She was wearing this big, baggy jumper and had a hat on, even though it's been boiling. I didn't really – but I should have realised maybe that was a sign.'

'What?'

'When you get really bad with anorexia, you sometimes wear massive clothes, cos you think you're big. It's like body dysmorphia or something?'

Paula nodded. 'Right. That's useful to know, thank you.'

Corry said, 'So you can't tell us why she liked the relic? It seemed to almost . . . obsess her?'

'Oh yeah. It did. She told me she was interested in what it could do.'

'What do you mean, do?'

At this, Katy looked up, her face smooth as a child's. 'The powers that it had. You see, she was looking for a miracle.'

Chapter Seven

'A miracle?' said Corry.

'You know. She was sick of being how she is. All the time. Not being able to eat.'

'And she thought the relic could help her?'

'Well yeah, because it's for hungry people. She—' Katy broke off as there was a brisk knock on the door and it began to open.

'Katy?' said a woman's voice. 'Are you in there?'

Katy straightened herself on the bed, tucking her phone under herself. 'Ms Hooker . . . hi. The police . . . um. They're here.' She gestured towards Paula and Corry.

'Can I help you, ladies?' The woman in the doorway was dressed in riding clothes – jodhpurs, jacket, boots. 'I take it you're the police then?'

'DS Corry, Dr Maguire,' said Corry, indicating Paula. 'You wouldn't be the principal, by any chance?'

'Well, yes, I'm Madeleine Hooker.'

Corry narrowed her eyes. 'I thought we had an appointment earlier today. You weren't about to assist us.'

'Well, I see you've gone ahead anyway.'

'We have. Can we have a word now?'

She looked at her watch and gave a small sigh. 'Come to my office. Katy, shouldn't you be studying? I hope you won't let yourself get behind.'

*

The woman who ran Oakdale kept a riding crop on her desk, apparently with no sense of irony. Paula was trying hard not to look at it. The walls of Madeleine Hooker's office (she was called Hooker too – Gerard would have had a field day) were hung with equestrian rosettes, pictures of her jumping horses, meeting the president in a hard hat and jodhpurs. You could tell from her voice she was old money, old Ireland. 'I hope you won't upset things here. We run a very delicate ecosystem. Lots of police questions might create an atmosphere of distrust, stress.'

Corry, not one to be intimidated by a woman with a real Hermès scarf and a non-ironic riding crop, geared up. 'One of your students is missing, Ms Hooker. If they feel anything at all, the others are most likely already stressed. Now, please try to help us with our inquiries – I imagine you'd also like Alice found, and fast. The press must be all over you.'

Madeleine Hooker drew her brows together. She was much younger than Paula had expected – not even forty, maybe. 'We want Alice found because she's a member of our community. But you need to understand, Oakdale isn't like other universities.'

'How so?' Paula could almost hear Corry thinking – the other universities would be worried about their damn students going missing.

'It helps if you think of it more like a monastery, or convent. Somewhere cloistered. And we're lucky that we have a lot of private bequests, so we don't have to rely on government funding. We're fully accredited, of course. We just take a different approach. And we're fortunate that applications are always high, so we can be selective.' She swept her hand to the window, indicating the graceful building, the acres of green grounds, the lake like a pewter bowl in the afternoon sun.

'Does that have to do with your reputation for emotional support?' Corry asked.

Madeleine Hooker darted a look at her. 'I'm not sure what you mean. We offer high levels of pastoral care – being so small and cut off, it's important.'

Corry obviously wanted her to say something about money, and she was far too wily for that. 'You take care of the students here, Ms Hooker?'

'Of course. Some of them come to us a little lacking in the . . . robustness to survive a larger university. All that drinking and partying.'

'No parties here?'

Her lips vanished in a thin line. 'They are adults, Detective. But we often attract a more reflective type, students who want to learn without distractions.'

'Was Alice one of those?'

'I admit, I didn't know Alice all that well. I can't, with over three hundred of them. Of course we did know all about her background.'

'Her anorexia, you mean?'

Madeleine Hooker sat back at her desk, her face reflected in the shiny iMac that dominated it. 'Alice was being well looked after here. She was in the best place – but unfortunately, as we're dealing with adults, we can't always protect them.'

'Isn't it true that she hadn't been seen in college much for a while?'

'It's not compulsory. We prefer to let them learn in their own time.'

'It's not a cause for alarm, a girl with severe anorexia moving out of campus like she did?'

'Alice is twenty-two. You can't expect us to police her life – no joke intended.' Both Hooker and Corry looked as far from joking as it was possible to be.

'Well. Yes. I just hope you'll make sure the staff and students cooperate with our inquiries. It seems impossible to know where anyone's supposed to be at any moment.'

'It's not a school. But I'm sorry to hear if anyone hasn't been helpful. Perhaps you'd give me their names?'

Corry stared at her over the table. 'Just ask them to show us every courtesy. A cup of tea wouldn't go amiss either, now and again.'

'Tea?'

'Yes.'

'Well.' She blinked. 'I'm sure we can set you up with cafeteria cards. But – will you be here much longer?'

'Ms Hooker, Alice is still missing! I don't see why no one here feels the urgency of that.'

The woman didn't react. 'A young adult with a history of disappearing, with mental health issues, and she's not in her house for a day . . . I don't see that this is necessarily any concern of the college's, no.'

'A student goes missing and there's blood at the scene? I think that's everyone's concern, to be perfectly honest.'

She was frowning. 'I was under the impression that a small amount of blood had been found. And that Alice was prone to self-harm—'

'Nothing we've heard suggests that. We're treating Alice's disappearance as suspicious. I'd suggest you do the same.'

Madeleine Hooker sighed. 'Detective. I hate to have to

say this, but about six weeks ago, at the end of term, there was an incident on campus.'

Corry was on it like a wolf. 'What kind of incident?'

'Alice was seen in the grounds, apparently having taken something. Quite out of it, by all accounts. Stumbling around, making a show of herself.'

'Drugs?'

She nodded, a look of distaste on her made-up face. 'So maybe you'll see why I wouldn't necessarily be surprised if Alice had gone off somewhere.'

Corry batted it right back. 'No activity on her phone? No use of her bank account? If she's gone off, then where is she? And why is her blood on the church steps? A significant amount of blood, and in the same place another young woman went missing over thirty years ago?'

'I didn't know about that,' said the principal stiffly.

'Well, I'm telling you. This has happened before. Now maybe *you'll* see why I can't be as blasé as you and Alice's friends seem to be.'

To this, Madeline Hooker had no answer. She shook her head a few times, as if to clear it, then picked up the phone and said, 'Shona. Make sure our guests get everything they need. Finding Alice Morgan should be our top priority.'

Alice

It'll hurt, *Charlotte says, out of the corner of her mouth. I just roll my eyes up at her. Like I care about hurt by now. Every day is hurt, in this place.*

Charlotte has a razor blade hidden in her little-child's hand. She smuggled it in, then smashed it up and threw away the moisturising bits. We aren't interested in smooth legs here. We don't care about anything except getting out. Just there. *I feel her hand on my skin, cold as ice. She has it up my robe, holding my pants aside. I bet he would have loved it. Little does he know. As if you feel sexy when you're one step ahead of death. That's one of the best things about it.*

Then Charlotte, in her strange crazy way, slashes the blade against my upper thigh, way high up, almost in the crease between my leg and my bits. I gulp and she claps the hand holding the pants over my mouth. The material digs into the cut. Shh. Don't say anything. When they weigh you, just let it drip out.

I nod. That way, he'll think I'm bleeding. He'll think I'm a normal girl and that I'm fine, and then maybe, if I'm very lucky, just maybe I'll be closer to getting out of here one day.

Chapter Eight

'They all have alibis, the kids?' Corry and Paula were walking down the main staircase of the house. Despite herself, Paula had to admit it was nice – the kind of place you could imagine being young and earnest.

'Dermot was working in his room all night, his room-mate says – sounds like a fun lad – and Peter and Katy were supposedly together. That's been backed up by Peter's room-mate, who says he didn't come back to the room. Which by all accounts is a fairly regular occurrence. Why, are you hearing alarm bells?'

'Well, Dermot was lying about something. Did you see the way his eyes kept moving?'

Corry put less faith in behavioural science. 'They seem to think she's gone off by herself. Get some time alone.'

'Katy and Dermot both used the same word. Headspace, they said.' They were heading back out to the car. The day at Oakdale was winding down, students starting to gather up books and jumpers and sun cream and head indoors from the lawns. No indication at all that just a few miles down the road, one of their classmates was gone, leaving only a trail of blood. 'That suggests to me they've been discussing it.'

Corry unlocked the car. 'I wouldn't pay too much heed to what they say. Alice isn't the only one into drugs.'

'Yeah, I clocked Dermot's eyes. Spaced out.'

'Aye. Uppers and downers, I'd say. Anxiety my foot. Katy seemed a bit glassy too. Then there's Peter Franks – who Katy claims is her boyfriend.'

'You don't believe it?' Paula looked at Corry, her profile strong against the low evening sun as she started the car.

'Maguire, wait till you see him. His picture's on the website of this place, because he's rowing captain or some nonsense – a great big hunk of a fella. Whereas Katy, not to put the girl down, but unless she's in some soppy American romcom, she's not the one who gets the guy.'

'So what's his story? Peter?'

'Well.' Corry took her hand off the wheel and rubbed at a spot on her trousers, where she'd dripped tea earlier. 'I couldn't get much out of the secretary on that, waffling on about data protection, but Peter doesn't even have his Leaving Cert. He didn't finish school, for some reason.'

'And they still let him in here?'

Corry gave a small snort. 'The wonders of money, Maguire. Not that your woman Hooker there would admit it. She's a tough customer.'

Paula looked round at the university, the early evening light soft on the building's grey stone walls. Horses in the fields, bending their heads to the rich grass. No drought problems here. 'Seems a weird place for a lord's daughter.' There'd been a few of Alice's type at Greenwich, where Paula had studied – privileged, brought up to let their voices ring out loud and proud, no regional accent to be ashamed of. No one asking them to repeat themselves or had they grown up on a farm. Ski tans and rowing hoodies. She'd been permanently weighed down by the chip on her Northern Irish shoulder – part of the reason she'd got a first was she'd hated everyone on her course too much to socialise with them. Or maybe she was just prejudiced.

'She missed a lot of school, remember,' said Corry, as they drew down the long driveway. 'She went to Warwick but couldn't hack it, dropped out last year.'

Paula said, 'Did you go to university?' There was still so much she didn't know about Helen Corry, despite having worked with her for nearly three years now.

'Me? No, straight into the job. Didn't see the point.'

'I guess they don't think much about the point, here. Alice probably felt at home, if she spent her life in clinics and boarding schools.'

'It's a haven for the mad and rich, Maguire. For when their parents want rid of them and are happy to pay. Question is, why did Alice leave? If she chose to live in that damp wee cottage, she wanted away from something. Or someone.'

'Katy?'

'Could be. Sharing small quarters can get tough – though she was at boarding school all her life, she'd be used to it.'

'We need to speak to this so-called boyfriend. Whoever's boyfriend he is.'

'That's what we're doing.' Corry had parked on the edge of a playing field. The sun had dipped now, and a breeze with a slight chill picked up. Across the pitch, with the lake at their backs, came a troop of warriors. Four young men, all over six foot, every muscle visible in Lycra suits. On their shoulders, like some pagan sacrifice, they carried a boat. Corry opened the door and called them over, but even without being told Paula already knew which one was Peter Franks. He was the one everyone else looked to.

*

Men and their attractions was something of a difficult topic between Paula and Corry. Occasionally the older woman would offer a bit of parenting advice, like how to stop Maggie's teething pains or deal with her nursery. Corry's children were now sixteen and fourteen, and she'd long since divorced their father, who she described as 'a useless streak of piss'. But she'd never asked Paula whose child Maggie might be, or what exactly had been the relationship between Paula and her former boss, Guy. In her turn, Paula didn't ask how Corry felt about the fact she'd been sleeping with a killer, one who'd hacked into her emails and used them to derail the investigation, and also Corry's career. One who'd died for it, with a bullet in his head.

But this boy had a gravity, she didn't deny it. Once Peter had showered – he'd begged ten minutes so he could change, with a smile it was hard to say no to – he met them in the common room. Students sat at the desks or in the seats, talking quietly. Peter returned in soft jeans and a floppy-collared shirt, the same blue as the fading sky outside. The sleeves were rolled up to show his tanned arms, the hairs touched with gold.

'Ladies.' He was all charm, but Paula felt Corry bristle slightly.

'It's DS Corry and Dr Maguire.'

'Of course, sorry. Can I get you a drink?'

It was the first one they'd been offered all day. Corry nodded. 'I'll have tea. Decaf, please.' He went to the bar to get them, chatting easily with the girl working there, coming back all smiles with three drinks held in his large hands. Corry caught Paula's eye. 'We'll have to watch ourselves with this one,' she murmured. 'Fancies himself.'

He sat down, passing them the drinks in paper cups. 'Sorry that took a while.'

'So, Peter. What is it you're studying?'

'History,' he said, easing back in his chair. 'I'm interested in, you know – the past. What was it you wanted me for?'

Paula caught the steel in Corry's voice. 'We're here about Alice.'

He eased back more. Didn't bat an eyelid. 'Oh yeah. She's run off again, I hear.'

'We're treating it as suspicious, Peter.'

'Is that really necessary? I mean, she's known for doing this.'

'Have you known her to disappear from the college?'

'Well, no, but she moved out to that cottage, and that was weird. We all thought something was up.'

'We?'

He shifted, the leather of his chair creaking. 'A few of us hang out a bit. We were all older than the rest of the first years, see. She made friends with her room-mate, Katy, and a guy she met at the therapist's office.'

'Dermot, is that who you mean?'

His voice was light, skimming the conversation like a boat on a lake. 'Yeah, Dermot. He's OK, bit nerdy. I'd never normally hang round with someone like him. But Alice – she was good at bringing people together.'

Corry said, 'We heard you and Alice were involved.'

Again, he didn't bat an eyelid. 'Ah no. We might have pulled a few times, you know, freshers' week stuff, it's only natural. But we were friends mostly.'

'And Katy? She calls you her boyfriend.'

At this, Peter looked momentarily surprised. 'She does?'

'You're not?'

'Sergeant.' He rolled out a smile, a yard of white, dimples creasing his mouth. 'I'm a young guy. I don't want to settle down yet. And this place, it's full of girls. You know what I'm saying.'

'Yes, Peter, I believe I can crack your code. So you weren't with Katy last night?'

He was wrong-footed. Just for a second, then he righted himself, but Paula and Corry both noticed it. 'Oh – well, I was. But we're not – you know. A couple.'

'You might want to have a chat with Katy, then. She thinks you two are an item.'

'Of course. I'd hate to hurt her feelings. She's a nice girl, if a bit – clingy. That's why Alice went, I thought.'

'Go on,' said Corry, carefully. It was the same thing Katy claimed he'd said about Alice.

'Well, Katy was always wearing Alice's clothes and using her make-up, and like, cuddling up on her bed. Plus she'd cry a lot, tell Al all her woes. A bit, you know – hello, stalker? So I think Al just wanted some space.'

'Headspace,' said Corry.

'Right,' he nodded, as if grateful for the word. 'Headspace.'

'She couldn't have just switched rooms?'

'Katy would have been hurt. And when you hurt her, you *hurt* her. You know?'

Corry frowned. 'Explain?'

Peter held up his forearm and mimed slashing at the soft underside. 'Bit razor-happy, you know? Did you see her arm?'

'Sounds like a lot of pressure on Alice not to upset Katy, drive her to self-harm.'

'Like I said. You'd want space, wouldn't you?'

Paula leaned in, casually. 'I'm surprised you'd get involved with Katy then, knowing what you know.'

At that Peter went silent. 'I wouldn't say *involved*.'

'What would you say?'

Corry shot Paula a look – they'd hit home. 'Look,' he said, fighting to get the smile back on his face. 'I'd really hate for you to waste your time. I honestly think Al, she just needed a bit of space. She'll be fine. She'll be back in a few days.'

'So we shouldn't be worried.' Corry watched him.

'Well, I don't know obviously, but I think not. No.'

Unexpectedly, she sat back, changed tone. 'Thanks, Peter, you've been very helpful.'

He looked up in surprise as they rose. 'That's it?'

'For now.' Corry buttoned her jacket. 'You won't be going anywhere, of course, if we need you.' She gave Paula a look, the meaning clear: *enough*.

Chapter Nine

'This is the one you want?' The wee lad who ran the storage facility was about eighteen, in a green polo shirt that bit into the painful acne on his neck.

'Yeah.' Coughing on the dust, Paula stepped into the unit. 'Thanks, I'll be grand here.'

He went, his feet clanging on the cold stone floors. Down below, he was playing the local radio station, Radio Ballyterrin, with important breaking news such as a herd of cattle getting loose on the road, and a suspicious package being blown up by Bomb Disposal. Northern Ireland was that kind of mixed-up place.

Paula had been given permission to access the archives earlier that evening, by an unnaturally helpful Willis Campbell. He'd said, 'It's hard to credit it. This other case happened on the same day, thirty years back?'

'Thirty-two. I need to get the file out of storage, check a few things.'

He'd waved her on. 'Yes, yes, do what you must. Oh, Dr Maguire?'

'Yes.' She'd paused, hating herself for adding: 'Sir.'

'I hear you get good results. I also hear you think the rules don't apply to you.' She said nothing. 'I'd like to see more of the former, less of the latter, please. Then we'll get along just fine, won't we?'

'I'm sure we will.' She paused again, thinking – *Oh, Guy.* 'Sir.'

'Lovely.' Then he'd added, as if remembering something he'd seen in a management manual: 'You're doing a good job, Dr Maguire. Carry on.'

But she wasn't, she thought now, seeing the piles of archive boxes, labelled in what looked like Avril's neat handwriting. *Women 30–45.* Yvonne would be in the box marked *Women 18–29.* A safe one, where Paula wasn't likely to accidentally find her mother's file. Of course, she had a copy of it in the desk at home. She hadn't opened it in two years, but all the same it was there, while life went on around it. A nasty little secret on the underside of everything.

No, she wasn't doing a good job. Alice had already been lost a day, and that meant the window for finding a missing person was closing. And with Alice's background, suicide was the most likely thing. But why no body? Had she gone off somewhere alone to die, like an animal? And what of the strange coincidence about Yvonne? Paula found the right box, labelled *1970–90* (thank God for Avril; policing's gain was admin's loss), and pulled it out, grunting with the effort.

Paula read the file sitting on a squashy pile of boxes, by the dim light of the unit's bare bulb. Soon she forgot about the cheerless surroundings, and the chill of the concrete walls. She was back in 1981, the year of her birth, and feeling it again – the first time in so long – the rush, the need to find and bring home the lost. Yvonne O'Neill, she noted, did indeed have a look of Alice Morgan. The fiancé who'd died had been the only man in her life, according to the RUC. No boyfriends, not even many friends, just her teaching job, among the same nuns who'd once been her family, and the invalid mother she'd gone back to every night. Yvonne had helped out with Girl Guides, visited sick neighbours. A good girl, you'd say. Paula looked at the old grainy photo of Yvonne, smiling, her hair falling in pale waves. Someone else had been cropped out of it – an engagement photo, maybe. There was a funeral order of service in the file too, the front reading *David Alan Magee, 1 May 1981*. A picture on that of a young man in a denim shirt, also smiling. Paula fitted the two together, the edges making one photo, David's arm slotting in place around Yvonne's shoulder. So it wasn't long after her fiancé's death, the disappearance. Him dead. Her gone.

She ran a finger over the signature on one report in the file – *Patrick Maguire*. Her father. He'd remember this case – like her, he never let go of the ones he couldn't find. She took the file and locked up the cold little room. Full of names. The ones they would maybe never find.

Paula couldn't get used to her dad living at Pat's. She'd been going to this house all her life, since her mother had taken her as a child, whispering admonishments to keep quiet and be good. Then as a teenager, the odd time for parties or Christmas visits, keeping an eye out for Aidan, who hadn't uttered a word to her at all between the ages of thirteen and seventeen. When suddenly they'd been going out and she'd been round here all the time to sneak into his room, burrowing her hands under his school shirt, gulping in the smell of him as if he was the air she breathed.

She was remembering all this as Pat came to the door, slowly, visible through the panes of coloured glass. 'Ah pet, there you are. She's asleep. Will I wake her?'

'Ah no, I wanted a word with Dad anyway. Leave her be

a while.' Pat was looking tired, Paula thought. Dark circles under her eyes, a stiffness in her shoulders. She hoped it wasn't from running around after two-year-old Maggie all day, who was currently into everything she shouldn't be. PJ helped, but his old leg injury meant he couldn't do the running, stop Maggie from slipping out an open door or feeding her sandwich into the video player or her fingers into the electric socket (really, it was exhausting).

'He's in the lounge. I'll make you some tea – I haven't baked, but I'm sure you're not eating biscuits anyway, with the big day so soon!'

Paula was, in fact, still eating all the biscuits she could get her hands on – the lack of a functioning kitchen didn't lend itself to healthy eating – but she let it go. PJ was in front of the horse racing, his leg propped up on a pouffe, the *Irish Times* crossword open in front of him with his glasses folded on it. Somewhere between now and Paula leaving for university – her eighteen, him mid-forties – her father had aged. 'Well, pet.' He took the glasses off and rearranged some cushions for her to sit down. 'Where's Lady Muck?'

'Having her nap. I'll leave her for a while yet. Wanted a word with you.'

'Aye?' PJ always looked wary at such things. When he'd told her he was marrying Pat, three years ago, and Paula had told him in return about Maggie coming, they'd had a lot of awkward conversations that veered closer to the emotions than PJ, being an Irish man, would have liked.

'A work thing. An old case that's come up again.'

'Oh, right so.' Relief. Work was safe in a way the topics of her mother and her child were not.

'Did you work on Yvonne O'Neill's disappearance? Remember that?'

It took PJ a moment. 'Oh aye, the wee blonde girl. God, that was a bad summer. We were up to our eyes in riots and shootings. The hunger strikes, you know.' He turned his eyes on her, suddenly alert. 'What've you found? Did we miss something?'

'No, no. It's just she went missing from the same place Alice Morgan did. You know, this new case.'

PJ nodded. 'Aye, I never thought. Crocknashee church. Strange old place. But that was thirty-odd years back. You're thinking there's a connection?'

'No idea.' Paula sank back in Pat's squashy armchair. Once, in here, in 1999, when Pat had gone into the kitchen to make tea, she and Aidan had pressed themselves into the carpet, kissing with a blind fury. She blinked, trying not to let the memory show on her face. Even the ornaments and pictures were the same – the photo of Aidan's father, John, holding the boy on his knee. 1983. Three years before he'd been gunned down in his office, in front of Aidan. Pat and John's wedding picture, all seventies hair flicks and sideburns, had been tactfully taken down, replaced by one of Pat and PJ on their own wedding day two years back. Paula in a bridesmaid's dress on one side, hugely pregnant, and Aidan on the other, ignoring her. And of course there were photos of Maggie on every possible surface. Maybe the only grandchild Pat would ever have, even if she wasn't exactly . . . 'So was there anyone?' she asked her father. 'You know, someone you suspected?'

PJ was thinking. 'I was working with Hamilton then. We were still partners. You could always try him.'

Paula nodded. She hadn't seen Bob Hamilton much since he'd retired two years ago, something she'd mistakenly had a hand in precipitating. She could have gone to visit, of course, but it was always there, the vague panicked feeling that Bob, who'd also been lead investigator on her mother's case, knew more than he'd ever told her about it. And that whatever he knew, it was something that would shatter Paula and her father, bury the shoots of happiness they'd found for themselves in the rubble.

'The fella who owns the land,' said PJ, as if running through a database in his head.

'Anderson Garrett? Yes, he's odd. I think he had an alibi, though, did he not?'

'He was a strange one.' PJ tapped the paper for emphasis. 'He'd an alibi, though, right enough – he was in his work in town all day. He couldn't have got back to the church.'

'Why not?'

'See the date? Well, one of the IRA head honchos was killed that day. Shot in his house, here in Ballyterrin. Whole town was shut down from lunchtime on, riots, petrol bombs, you name it. I was in uniform, couldn't get home to see if you were even OK. You were only wee, and—' He'd come dangerously close to mentioning her mother there.

'Garrett's alibi held then?'

'Aye. We checked with the other solicitor he worked with – guy called Andrew Philips, if I remember right. He backed it up – Garrett was there all day, he said, nine to seven. It's the Garrett family's firm, see, though I don't know if Anderson ever did a stroke of work in it. Doesn't need to work now, mind. Oakdale College bought the family land not long after Yvonne went missing, paid them a fortune, so he hardly needs to.'

'This Andrew Philips – is he still about?'

PJ shook his head. 'Died in 2003, I heard. Heart attack – seemed a nervy kind of fella.'

'So there's no one who can prove it?'

'Garrett's ma backed it up as well, he'd been out all day. And Yvonne was safe at home until well after two. Garrett never made it back till near midnight, he said – roadblocks. Yvonne's ma had already reported her gone by then. So that was that.'

'That was that.' Paula made a note anyway. Andrew Philips. All these names from the past, shut away in dull brown folders for over thirty-two years. Suddenly coming to the light, like things crawling away when you lifted up a stone. She wondered if Alice had heard. Did she know another girl had gone missing, and that her boss had been the chief suspect?

Alice

When they come into the room, Charlotte turns off. I don't know how she does it. It's like flicking a switch, no light in her eyes. Charlotte is past the point of wanting to escape. It's a battle now, them against her. They sweep in, the man and the woman. He's in his white coat, brisk bad-Daddy air about him. I start to shake on the couch – I can't help it. She's all starched up, hair pulled back, steady at his elbow. Yes. No. Three bags full. It makes me sick.

Alice, *he says. To the woman, not me. She snaps my wrist, moving me to the scales. Huge things, like for cows at market. She's rough and I stub my bare toes but I don't make a sound. I know Charlotte will notice, and approve. I step up on the horrible wobbly things and he's so close. I can smell the old-man breath under his aftershave. I think he drinks. He looks me over like a dog at the vet, calling out things to her, which she writes down. I refuse to hear the numbers. I refuse to hear how fat they've made me. He feels down my arms for hair growth, and in my mouth for the gum recession that would mean I've been puking up. His hands move over my ribs and down. He stops at my legs. I close my eyes.*

Alice. You're bleeding.

I act stupid. Oh?

Yes. *I feel his gloved hands on my thigh, moving up the line of the blood that has come down. I close my eyes, bite my lip so hard it must be bleeding too.* Alice, have your periods started again?

I don't know. I never have any.

I'd be surprised if menstruation recommenced at this

bodyweight. *To the woman again. Not me. I catch Charlotte's eye and there's a glimpse of her back again. We're winning. We beat them. But of course, no, we're not. We will never win. He pulls my knickers aside and puts his finger inside me, right up inside. In me. I nearly scream.* I thought it didn't look like menstrual blood. For reference, girls, that's much darker and thicker. I doubt either of you have seen much of it.

Charlotte is suddenly alive. You stupid fucker! You've never had a period, you never will! Stop telling us what it's like!

He smiles at the woman. Would you please restrain Miss Yu? And be careful, because I think we'll find some cutting implement about her person.

They go at her like she's an animal, and the energy is back, the strength. She's cornered. The woman reaches for her wrist to put her in restraints, and I know it's the hand with the razor in it, and I almost pass out – go, go, do it, Charlotte. And she does. A flick of her hand and the woman is howling, and there's blood pattering to the floor. Big red drops of it. Hey, guess what, we all bleed the same.

He's on it, of course – the drawer, the needle, Charlotte's eyes closing – but it's enough. It's enough to see the rage in his eyes, and hear the woman sobbing, as if her face was anything nice to start with. Do stop crying, *he says. He looks at me as if he'd like to sedate me too, but I'm meek as a lamb. From somewhere in my deep self, dry as a bare riverbed, I find some tears.* She cut me, sir, she made me.

I know it's what Charlotte would want. It doesn't matter what you say. It's the words in your head that count. And mine are saying I'm going to get away from you, no matter what it takes.

Chapter Ten

Being stuck was a common feature in families of the long-missing. Instead of moving to a new place with new memories, people often refused to leave, waiting fruitlessly in case one day the lost person came walking in the door. *Hello, did you miss me?* Paula knew it well – as an RUC officer her father should have moved around every few years, for safety's sake, but they'd stayed in the last place Margaret had been seen. Yvonne O'Neill was another one of the lost. She'd gone out one summer's day to help at the church that had stood on her doorstep all her life. The height of a warm day, where it begins to collapse, exhausted, under its own heat. A haze rising up from the ground. Tarmac melting on the road. It was quicker to go the back way to the church, but that would mean passing the Garretts' house. So she went by the main road. In a yellow dress, carrying white roses from her mother's garden, wrapped in the day's newspaper. Planning to leave them at the shrine. Walking up the dusty path, the yew trees silent overhead. The flowers were found in the church, arranged in vases, but the newspaper had never turned up, and neither had Yvonne.

And now Paula and Corry were calling on her mother, stirring up memories again. Dolores O'Neill was over eighty, but still lived alone in the farmhouse. The surrounding land had been sold off over the years, and the livestock too, but still she would not go, waiting for her missing child. You could even see the church from the kitchen window, a few hundred yards down the road and up the stone path. No distance at all. But far enough to get lost in.

'This is great, Mrs O'Neill. You didn't need to go to such trouble,' said Paula.

She'd made a full farmhouse lunch for them, sliced ham, brown bread, hard-boiled eggs from her own chickens, two types of cake, a big pot of tea. She stood at the sink in her slippers and housecoat, apparently not planning on eating herself. A walking stick leaned against the door, and Paula noticed the kettle was wrapped around with insulation – she knew Mrs O'Neill had MS. 'No trouble. It's a long time since anyone came asking about our Yvonne. In them days it was all big strapping men from the police.'

Paula heaped her plate with ham and cheese, then narrowed her eyes at slim Helen Corry, who sighed and took some sliced egg.

Mrs O'Neill was fiddling with the tea towel. 'I don't know what you'd find after all these years. Could there be some DNA or any of that?' She spent a lot of time watching *CSI*, she'd told them.

'Possibly. But the search was thorough back then, from what we can see.' Corry ate some ham. 'The reason we called to see you is actually the Alice Morgan case.'

'Aye. She come to the door a while back, asking for some water. The cottage pump was playing up, she said. I had a shock. You've seen Yvonne, her pictures?' She indicated a school photo on the wall, of a slight, fair girl who could have been a younger Alice. 'Short wee thing, with this great big jumper on her, even though the sun's splitting the stones.'

Corry nodded. 'There is a resemblance. You're saying she came to see you?'

'We talked the odd time. She'd come in to say hello if she was walking past the place. I'd give her a good tea like this.'

Corry paused with a slice of buttered bread in her hand. 'I'm sorry – you're saying Alice ate when she was here?'

'Oh aye, every pick. She's a good appetite for such a wee girl. Must have one of them fast metabolisms.'

Paula looked at Corry. Strange. 'And what did you talk about?' she asked.

'This and that. She asked me about Yvonne and I told her – you know, it's a long time since someone wanted to hear, and I like to talk about her. All my ones and our Mary, that's Yvonne's sister, they're sick of it, I think. No news in over thirty years. They've just given up. But wee Alice, she'd ask me a lot of things. Did Yvonne ever go in for fasting – of course, I said, we all fasted back then, on holy days of obligation. So lax now. You know what Lough Derg is?'

Paula nodded, and Corry looked blank. 'I'll explain later,' Paula said to her. 'Yvonne went there?'

'Aye. Trying to make up for what she did, giving up her vocation. I told her God wouldn't blame her for leaving the convent – married love is sacred too. But she said when David died – you know he was killed in a car crash, God rest him – that was her being punished.'

Paula knew the police had speculated about suicide back then – but then where was her body? In some boggy ditch or crevasse?

Mrs O'Neill said, 'Alice asked about the hunger strikes as well. And did I think it was connected, to Yvonne? Because of all those riots in town that day. I said not at all. If the Provos or the UVF shot her to make a point, they'd have left her body, wouldn't they?' She said it matter-of-factly, and it was close to Paula's own thoughts on why the IRA probably hadn't taken her mother, despite everything. They generally wanted people to know what they'd done. But you never could be sure. Terrorists were not a reliable source, after all.

'What did you think, Mrs O'Neill?' Corry cut a slice of cheese.

She sipped from a china cup of tea. 'I always remember it. She went out after lunch, and I said bye. She wanted to lay some flowers in church for the strikers – you know, they were dying. It was an awful time. Then next thing I looked up and saw it was near four, and her not back. And I thought – that's strange. And you start to worry, just a wee bit. You tell yourself it'll be grand, she'll walk in the door any minute. Then she still doesn't come. I went down to the church, she wasn't there. I even went over to the Garretts', though I was far from welcome there. Wanted me to sell a bit of our land, see. On and on at me they were. Course they got it in the end, once Yvonne went. Anyway, the son's car was outside, but nobody answered. So I came back.' She took a sip. 'At first I hoped she'd run off – maybe she'd go and be a nun somewhere else, where nobody knew her. I'd see her in Spain . . . Seville, maybe. We went there once, when she was wee, for Holy Week. All the white hoods and the chanting. She'd have liked that, she loved all the incense and singing in church. It was why she went down there, to Saint Blannad. She loved that place – said the land was sacred. She didn't like the idea of selling up to the university, wouldn't let me do it.' Sip. 'But now I think someone took her and killed her.' Another sip. 'I just hope it was fast.'

Corry was speaking gently. 'And Alice – Mrs O'Neill, did

it occur to you they might be connected, the two cases?'

'No.' She looked confused. 'Alice ran off, did she not? That's what her friend told me.'

Corry stopped. Set down the piece of bread in her hand, slow and measured. 'What friend?'

'The young fella. The boy who called in yesterday. Wanted to know if she'd told me she was going. I said no, but he said she did it all the time, she'd come back.'

Paula and Corry exchanged a look. And then Corry explained about the blood in the church, and watched as the woman's face changed, and she shakily set down her cup.

'Mother of God. Jesus, Mary, and Saint Joseph. That poor wean.'

Corry was on her feet. 'Sit down there, Mrs O'Neill.' She pulled a chair for her. 'I'm sorry we've given you a shock.'

It wasn't right, Paula thought, pouring out more tea and stirring in sugar. The woman should have her daughter there. Things should be in their proper place. None of this was right.

'Blood,' Yvonne's mother said, when she could speak. 'Do you think someone hurt her, wee Alice? In the same place . . . Mother of God.'

'We don't know,' said Corry. 'It's true Alice does have a history of running away, but because of the blood, we're treating it suspiciously. And the relic's gone too, of course.'

'And you think my Yvonne . . . it's the same person? Who would it be? There's nobody round here; we know every man, woman and child on the land.'

'We don't know. But we're looking into it. We just wanted to keep you updated.'

'Aye,' she said, distracted. 'Aye, aye, look into it, please.'

'Mrs O'Neill?' Corry clicked open her phone. 'If you're

feeling all right in a minute, would you look at this picture for me and tell me if it's the boy who came?'

She hunted for her glasses, found them on her head, then peered at it. 'Oh – I don't think so, no.'

'No?'

'I think he had darker hair.'

Corry gave Paula a look, then scrolled through. 'How about this one?'

More peering. She gripped the phone, holding it away from her. 'Oh – I think that's him, yes. He had glasses. Well-spoken.'

Paula leaned over to see the picture. Dermot Healy.

Corry put the phone away 'And – I'm sorry, this is the last question, I promise. Could you tell us if you think you're missing a photo of Yvonne? One where she's at her graduation?'

'Well, I don't know . . . Wait there a minute.' She left the room shakily, leaning on her stick, and they heard her open the door of the living room. For a moment there was silence. Then she came back. In her old hands she was holding a picture frame. Empty. 'I don't understand it. The picture's always been in there, but I don't be in that room much these days.'

'Mrs O'Neill . . . I think we've found the picture.' And Corry explained, as delicately as she could, about finding the picture in the pool of blood. By the end of it, Yvonne's mother was weeping. 'I'm so sorry,' said Corry. 'Believe me, we're going to do everything we can to find out what happened. I know they tried in 1981, but this new information—'

'I always knew she was dead,' said her mother hoarsely. 'They said maybe she'd run off, gone with some fella . . . but she never would have. I always had this feeling, in my bones, that she was nearby. If only I could just get her, put her to rest.'

'Like I said, we'll do everything we can to—'

'Please.' She tried to steady herself. 'Please. I know it's been more than thirty years. But please, I just want to know where she is, before I die. I just want to put her to rest.'

'I promise we'll try everything,' said Corry. And Paula knew that she meant it.

'But it doesn't make sense.' They were walking to the car, Corry stepping over mud in her good heeled sandals. 'These kids are barely twenty. I'm surprised they would even know about Yvonne's case.'

Paula was struggling with it too. 'So why did Dermot come to see Mrs O'Neill? He must have gone after we spoke to him.'

'Well, maybe Alice told her something important and he wanted to know what it was. Or maybe he wanted us to think there's a connection to Yvonne – get him off the hook, since he wasn't even born in 1981.' Corry sighed. 'God knows. But I'd certainly like to know what he was doing out here yesterday. Let's get back to the station.'

Chapter Eleven

'Was Alice Taken By Pagan Cult?' Corry read aloud. She leafed through the paper. 'I'm not seeing the part where it says, "No, don't be daft, of course she wasn't."' She lowered it and glared at Paula. 'Top-notch investigative reporting there from your fella.'

Paula made a noise of annoyance, trying to indicate that while Aidan might indeed be 'her fella', she had no control over what he chose to print in the *Ballyterrin Gazette*.

The wider media had picked up on Alice's disappearance – *Affair Lord's Daughter Vanishes* and so on – but it was the loss of the relic that seemed to rouse the town. Aidan's paper led with *Bring Her Back to Us* – and the 'her' in the headline meant Saint Blannad, not Alice. It turned out it was a quote from a distraught pensioner, who credited the relic with helping him win the pools.

'Saint Blannad,' Corry muttered, tossing the paper aside. 'Feeds the hungry, magics up pool wins for those behind on their fag consumption. Oh bollocks, look who's coming.'

A brief flurry of desk-straightening went through the office; Willis Campbell was on patrol. He stopped by Paula and Corry's desks. 'Ladies. Any updates?'

'We don't have any strong leads,' said Corry in the measured voice she used for him. 'We know that one of

Alice's college friends was in the vicinity of the church yesterday.'

'That's all you've got?'

'Everyone seems to think she went of her own accord,' said Paula, earning herself another dark look.

'I don't follow you.'

'Just that. No one even seems to be worried about her. It's like they almost . . . expected her to be missing.' She looked to Corry, who nodded. That was the thing which wasn't there. Shock. Surprise. That 'it can't be happening to us' slap in the face people felt whenever crime entered their lives.

'We're going to question the friends again,' said Corry. 'See if we can get some sense out of them.'

He sniffed. 'Well, you may hope you come up with something soon. Alice's parents have just arrived. I want you to go and update them.'

'What took them all the way out here?' Paula asked, as they wound up the seemingly endless driveway to the hotel. She could hear the thunder of the river that ran past the place. Alice Morgan's parents had insisted on staying outside of Ballyterrin, in a golf resort and spa that had opened pre-recession and been struggling on ever since.

Corry swung the wheel of the car. 'Nowhere in Ballyterrin good enough. And I think they wanted to be away from the press. They've not got the best track record with newspapers.'

'You'd think they'd want to be nearer. For the search.'

'Yes, well, I don't get the feeling they're very concerned either.'

As they entered the hotel a deep calm settled over Paula.

Despite the heat, a fire crackled in the lobby, which was scattered with soft grey sofas, the kind you could just sink into, like a cloud. The girl behind the desk wore so much make-up you felt it might fall off her in a perfect oval if you tapped her head. She spoke with a thick local accent. 'Good morning, ladies, how may I help yous?'

Corry took out her ID. 'Rebecca and Anthony Morgan, please.'

The girl's face changed – though it was hard to tell with the make-up. The way people looked when they sensed something not right. A human instinct, to get away from the bad thing, protect what was yours, hope it wouldn't come looking for you as well. 'Oh yes. We've put yis in a nice wee room, so we have.'

It was a shame about the hotel, Paula thought, as they entered the small meeting room. She liked to meet families in their homes, if possible – get a feel for them and their worlds, where they felt relaxed. In this room they were almost in an office, complete with notepads, uncomfortable chairs and little bowls of sweets on the boardroom table. A man in a polo shirt and slacks was pacing by the window, which looked out on the river. The woman at the table, tapping into her phone, was Alice a few years on. Same fair hair and tiny frame, the skin on her face pulled tight from tropical suns and surgery. The father was also ruddy, fit-looking. No more than fifty, she guessed. The wife could have passed for forty.

'Lady Morgan, Lord Morgan.' Corry was good at this. Victim liaison stuff, working the press angles, always thinking how things looked. 'Thank you for coming over. This is Dr Maguire, our forensic psychologist.'

Interviews held by Paula, an outside expert, could be

shaky in court, so she usually did the background stuff, filling in gaps, trying to create a picture of what had happened. Feeling a piece of the puzzle that didn't fit was a technique that often worked, and here was one – Alice's mother was angry. Totally pissed off. And that was odd for this stage, when hope was still alive. At this point parents would usually be worried, falling over themselves to help, trying to do everything right in the hope their child would be returned. 'I can't believe we've been dragged to this place,' said Rebecca Morgan, looking round her as if the four-star resort was a backstreet slum. 'Tony had a very important meeting today in Brussels.'

Corry rearranged her shoulders slightly. 'Well, you must be very worried, so let me fill you in. Alice was last seen in the church where she worked, two days ago.'

'Who by?' interrupted Tony Morgan. 'I assume you're following all this up.'

The joys of a case where the girl's father was a Home Office minister. 'Of course, sir. I should explain, we're lucky to have a lot of experience with missing persons in our team. Dr Maguire here was part of a dedicated cross-border unit in the town.'

His eyes settled on her. The same as Alice's, pale and somehow bloodless. 'The unit that was disbanded.'

'For funding reasons,' said Corry smoothly. 'Dr Maguire is very experienced, especially with cases involving young women.'

His face changed, and she was suddenly hit with his charm, like a blast from a radiator. 'We're lucky to have you on the case. Please, anything you need to know, just ask. Alice – well, she's been a little troubled, over the years.'

'She's most likely run off again,' said the mother, laying her phone on the glass table with a click.

Paula spoke. 'Can you tell us a bit more about that?'

She sighed and began ticking points off on her fingers. Her nails were two inches long. 'Nineteen ninety-eight. We were in New York at a trade summit. Call from Alice's nanny – she's not in the house. We're at the airport, flights home booked, and she's found hiding in the stables. Quite pleased with herself, only cross that we weren't actually on the plane when they found her. Two thousand and four – call from Alice's school. I forget where we were. Darling? Where did we go that year, the Seychelles? Divine beaches. We were all the way back that time. Then in 2006, we get a call to say she's been starving herself and they've had to put her in hospital.'

'She was very ill,' said her father, not looking round from the window. 'They said she would die if she didn't eat. So it was hard, but we couldn't be here to watch her all the time and she couldn't be trusted by herself. We did what we had to do.'

Paula looked at Corry. 'You mean—'

'We had her sectioned,' said Rebecca Morgan. 'We got her into rehab, basically. Till she started eating. I mean, you don't expect to have to feed your children when they're fifteen years of age.'

'And how long was she in there?' Paula knew the answer, but she wanted to hear it from Alice's mother. See if she flinched.

She didn't. 'Two years. Listen, it worked. She did her A-levels, got into university. Then of course she flunks out again. Insisted on coming here, though, God knows why. She'd an Irish nanny once, spoiled her rotten, maybe that was it. It's been years since she pulled this kind of stunt. I thought she'd stopped.'

Corry frowned again. 'Lady Morgan – I assumed you'd been briefed by your liaison officer – we are treating this as suspicious. I'm sorry to say it, but we did find signs of violence at the church. A valuable item has also gone missing. And there was blood, even.'

If she'd expected a reaction to that, there was none. 'Oh, she can bleed, if she has to,' said Alice's mother impatiently. 'She was always getting hurt as part of her little charades.'

'That's enough, Rebecca,' said Tony Morgan quietly. A look went between them, quick and sharp as a knife. 'Look, Detective, obviously we're worried about Alice—'

They certainly didn't seem it. Paula put her elbows on the glass table, willing herself to keep quiet.

'—even though she has a history of this kind of behaviour. We can't afford the publicity, with my profile.' Meaning presumably that the old affair allegations would resurface. Paula said nothing. He went on, 'Now, a contact of mine at the Met used to work with you here, I think. I'd like to ask him to consult on this case, if that's acceptable to your team. We want Alice found with the minimum of fuss.'

Oh no. Paula suddenly knew what he was going to say. *Not him not him . . .*

'DI Guy Brooking,' said Lord Morgan. 'Do you know him?'

It had been summer two years ago. Not the still, dead centre of it, like now, but the start. June, after a spring of bodies in the dirt and blow after blow hitting the unit.

Gerard in hospital with a gunshot wound. Avril's engagement broken off. And Paula, trying to look after a newborn Maggie, to take in that she was split in two now. If someone hurt her, Maggie would be hurt too. Paula of all people knew how it was to lose your mother. And Maggie had no father to hold her together in the aftermath. Something had to change.

And then there was Aidan. And Guy. Guy and Aidan. When she was in hospital, recovering from an emergency Caesarean, Guy had given her some awkward words, stilted and confusing, about sorting things out. Maggie, he knew, was maybe his child. Paula had never told him otherwise, yes or no. But sometimes actions said more than words.

The last day was when she'd told him. A bad day, one they didn't think would actually arrive, even when the notice came that the unit was wrapping up, even when Paula was hired by the PSNI to work there instead, even when Corry's disciplinary hearing demoted her, when Fiacra left and Bob retired and Avril got in to do her police training and Gerard made DS. It was just her and Guy, in the almost empty office space, on that last day.

'Looks like crap,' she'd said. The carpet patterned in squares of grey where the furniture had been, a tangle of wires near the wall, scraps of paper and Christmas tinsel and one lone hair grip. Avril's, Paula guessed; she herself was never organised enough to pin her hair up.

'Yeah.' This was the first time they'd been alone since the decision, and the month they'd been given to shut down the unit.

'So – where will you go?' She'd heard rumours. Drugs. Gangs. Guy had a lot of credit in the Met, and this unit had been something of a backwater for him, taken only as respite when his work in London led to his son's death. *I thought I'd never have to see a dead child again*, he'd said. About that, he had been wrong.

'London. Gangs again – working with girls this time. Helping them get out, trying to improve the reporting rates for rape.'

'Sounds good. Your sort of thing.'

'I hope so. And you?'

She stared at her scuffed shoes. 'Corry offered me a job up there before she . . . A bit of a step back. More consulting work.'

'Might be good, now, with childcare.' Both their words were so neutral. He said, 'I'd hoped we'd get a chance to talk before this. It's gone so fast – and I didn't like to come to the house to see you.'

In case Aidan was there. Who was, at the very least, Maggie's step-uncle. Whereas Guy was – nothing.

He had turned to her, his hair a halo of light in the window. Paula knew this was her chance – the moment when things tilted that way or the other, one future or a different one. She turned away slightly. She'd never be able to say it if she looked him in the eye. 'Aidan proposed to me,' she said, still looking at her feet.

'What?'

'I know. It's crazy.'

'You didn't—'

'No, God no. That would be mad. It's years since we – but, you see, me and him . . .' Why was she so guilty, for God's sake? Guy was the one with the wife. 'Well. There's a lot of history.'

'I see,' he said.

'It just seemed, you know, after everything, that we should give it a try.'

'You think he'll look after you? Both of you?' He didn't say Maggie's name, and she was glad, because she couldn't have stood it.

'He'll try.'

'That's enough?' Guy knew all about Aidan's drinking, his unreliability.

'It's all anyone can do.'

The silence stretched between them, and she heard all his unasked questions, and she did not answer them, because she didn't know how. Maybe she never would now. Aidan had decided for all of them. He'd be Maggie's father, even if no test had ever said he was. Paula waited, helpless, for Guy to challenge her, fight for his own stake in Maggie, and in her too. He didn't. The silence just went on, until eventually she couldn't stand it, the empty office and the dust on the floor and the two of them with nothing more to say to each other. She went out, shutting the door on the unit and the past year. She hadn't spoken to him since.

Alice

Later, the revenge comes. We are yanked from beds, lights slapping on. It's sometime in the middle of the night. Each of us is pulled up, and a man goes round with a big set of hair clippers. He smells like fags and sweat, so thick it makes me gag. It takes a while to get round, and the girls are all screaming – so for about an hour it's a room of screeching and buzzing, girls being held down, and hair falling on the floor, dark and fair and red, dyed and natural, curly and straight. Charlotte is still out so they do her unconscious. Her head is bleeding. Afterwards we're a room of sobbing girls, bald and patchy, with huge eyes. We look like we're in a concentration camp. We look nothing like ourselves, just ghosts, with no hair, no clothes, no flesh on our bones. Disappearing.

He stands in the door. No more cheating at weigh-ins, girls. We're closing the loopholes.

Chapter Twelve

Aidan was in the living room when she got back, late. As he was the paper's editor – and it more or less ran on shoestring and paperclips – he worked from home a lot, looking after Maggie.

'Well,' she said, putting down her bag.

Aidan was engrossed in a DVD of *Breaking Bad* and barely looked up. 'Well, Maguire.'

'Is she down?'

'Not without a fight. I had to hang a blanket over the curtains before she'd believe me that it's night-time. But it's not *dark*, Daddy, she says.'

Paula smiled, feeling the twinge of unease she always got when the word was used. It had been a risk, letting Maggie call Aidan Daddy. She didn't know who'd started it – Pat, maybe. And it seemed too churlish to correct a toddler about the man who put her to bed most days, and so they'd left it, and now it was two years on, and Aidan was Maggie's father. Except that now Guy might be coming back.

She pushed the thought away and sat on the arm of the sofa, pressing up close to Aidan. He wore khaki shorts and a T-shirt, black hair flopping over his forehead, just like any dad in the town. His hand left the remote and crept round her waist, eyes not moving from the screen. It rested, strong and warm, on her hip, and she sank into the certainty of it.

Ink on his knuckles, a smear of newsprint. This was her place. This would be her husband, soon.

He said, 'So, I was thinking this weekend we should visit the hotel. Get a sense of final numbers, confirm the menu and that.'

'Um . . . might be tricky. I've got this big case on, the Morgan girl.'

'You always have a big case, Maguire.'

'I know. But this one . . . it's strange.'

'What's happening with it?' he asked casually.

'Ah, here we go, pumping for the story?' She elbowed him.

'Can I not ask my fiancée about her day?'

'Urgh. I hate that word.'

'It's what you are, Maguire. At least for a few more weeks.'

Paula felt a nasty little lurch. God, the wedding was so soon, and he was right, there was still loads to do. 'I know. No, there's no sign of Alice Morgan. Though I see according to you she's been kidnapped by tree-worshipping Satanists.'

He shrugged. 'Weird stuff sells papers. And we could be doing with the money, pay for this wedding.'

'I'm more concerned about Oakdale. It's a strange old place up at that college. What do you know about it?'

He pressed Mute on the DVD. 'Did a piece on it a while back. There's some dodgy American cash behind it, but otherwise it's just a sort of rehab with qualifications for washed-up rich kids. Hardly surprising one of them would go missing.'

'If I gave you a few names, do you reckon you could do what you do best?'

'And what's that?' He squinted at her.

'Dig the dirt, of course.'

'Maguire, I'm insulted. Who is it?'

'Some of Alice Morgan's uni friends. They're just not quite ringing true.'

'Rich kids with a dodgy past? That's my kind of thing.' His hand stroked her ribcage through her shirt. 'But here, I resent the implication that's the only thing I'm good at. What about other things?'

Paula pretended to consider it. 'Hm – can't think of any right now.'

'Do I need to jog your memory?'

Paula leaned over and paused the DVD. On screen, a bullet left a gun and never arrived. Frozen in mid-air, before the damage was done. That was a missing person, a bullet in flight, never hitting the target. After a while, you started to long for the impact. To finally feel the wound that had been done to you, at last, so many years ago. She stood up. 'Come on, then. Jog it.'

Aidan stood up too, and caught her face in his hands, and kissed her hard. Her hands went to his hair, so thick and dark. He tasted of mint, and of himself, and . . . She pulled away. He tasted like he usually did – that was the problem.

'What?' he frowned.

'You've been smoking again.'

'I have not!'

'Aidan. I can taste it on you.'

'I go in a lot of smoky places – that's where the stories are, you know.'

'Don't lie to me. It's just insulting.'

'I'm no liar, Maguire. I might be many things but I've never lied to you.'

But he had kept things from her. She put her hands on her hips. 'Aidan.'

He spoke cajolingly, hands around her waist. 'Look. OK, the odd time, I still have a smoke. It helps put people at their ease is all. Some of these ould fellas, they don't trust a man who won't take a smoke or a drink. And I'm not on the latter, as you well know.'

Did she know? She glared at him. 'Are you still buying your own?'

'No. I just cadge the odd one.'

'I don't want Maggie anywhere near it. I don't even want her smelling it on you, OK?'

'Catch yourself on, Maguire. I've grown up a wee bit now I'm a dad.'

There was a tiny pause between them, which went on for a second more than was bearable, and Paula wondered if it would always be there, that pocket of making-do, of not-mentioning.

There was a squawk from upstairs, right on cue. 'Daaaaady!'

'The woman herself,' Aidan said. 'I'll go.' He dropped a careless kiss on Paula's hand as he went out, the kind of gesture between people with love to spare, to throw away. She saw his jacket over the chair, carelessly tossed as usual, no thought to tidying up after himself. She didn't know what made her do it. She crossed the room, telling herself she'd hang it up, but then she was slipping her hand into the pocket, feeling the cold silver of the Zippo lighter which had been his father's, and breathing the spicy smell of his rolling tobacco, the onion-skin rustle of his Rizlas.

There was a creak on the stairs. She took her hand out, and left the jacket where it was.

*

Later, when they were in bed, and Aidan had fallen asleep on his back, Paula pulled his T-shirt on over her head and wandered round the house, alone, as she'd done in that year of her dad moving out, before Aidan. While she was waiting for Maggie to arrive. The night was hot, and the town restless with sirens – ambulance, police? Lives fracturing into pieces, somewhere out there. Paula eased open the door to Maggie's room – the one she'd slept in herself as a child – and watched the little girl asleep in the bed with its Peppa Pig duvet, hands clutched into fists. Paula's old desk was still in the room, now covered in stickers and cuddly toys, and in the bottom drawer of it, the sum of all the misery Paula hoped Maggie would never know.

In the glow of the street light, Paula eased open the drawer and looked in. A dull manila file with her mother's name on it. A stack of documents and interviews, read almost into flitters by Paula as she'd combed it for a bit of information, something, anything that might give answers. She'd found none. But it was still there. And she would not, could not, throw it away.

Guy. Guy maybe coming back. And just before the wedding. It was all wrong. Maybe he wouldn't. Maybe he too wanted to keep the door locked on the past, stay in London with his wife and his new job. Maybe it would be all right.

Maggie turned over in bed, making a small noise in her dreams, trusting and limp. Paula shut the drawer, as quietly as she could, and watched her daughter sleep.

Chapter Thirteen

'This is stupid. I was worried about her. She's my friend, of course I'd try to find her.'

Corry gave Dermot Healy a long look. 'You weren't too worried about her the other day.'

He scrubbed angrily at his hair. The light from the classroom window showed up the smears on his glasses and dark rings under his eyes. 'When you first came, I didn't know about the . . . you know.' His voice cracked.

'The blood?' Corry supplied.

'Yes. But when I found out, I got worried, OK? I knew she sometimes talked to the old woman at the farmhouse, so I called in.'

'Did you know that the woman's daughter also went missing from the church, in 1981?'

He paused for a second. 'Alice told me. She thought it was interesting.'

'Interesting. Not scary?'

'Well, no. It was ages ago. She thought the church was . . . kind of a special place.'

Corry gave Paula a look and tried again. 'So you're saying you went over to Mrs O'Neill's house to see if she knew anything about Alice. Did you go to Alice's cottage?'

A slight pause. 'Um, no.'

'Have you ever been there, Dermot?'

'No. I don't think so.'

'You don't think so? You aren't sure if you've ever been there or not?'

'Not that I can remember, no.' He was sounding more sure now.

'And how did you get down there the other day? It's a couple of miles, isn't it?'

'Bike.' He was barely opening his mouth to speak, arms wedged in the pocket of his hoody, which must have been in need of a good wash. Paula could hear, outside somewhere, a brief scream of laughter, which for a moment sounded like the other kind. The heat of the room lay heavy on her, frying through the glass windows. Madeleine Hooker had actually set Paula and Corry up with a base in the college this time. The room they were in was wood-panelled, with modern AV equipment skilfully inserted. Like everything else in Oakdale, it was beautiful.

Corry was saying, 'So what you're telling me is, if I take your fingerprints, Dermot, and compare them to ones we got in Alice's cottage, there'll be no match.'

He thought about it. 'It depends if it's something else there that I touched, doesn't it? Doesn't necessarily prove I was there.' He was smart. That made things harder. Paula could almost feel the effort he was putting into staying alert – and why was he doing that, if he knew nothing about Alice? What was he trying to hide?

Corry's tone changed. 'Tell me about Peter and Katy.'

He blinked. 'What about them?'

'Would either of them have a reason to fall out with Alice?'

Dermot slumped in his chair. From the corridor came laughing, confident student voices. The sound of people who'd never had anything go wrong for them. 'I don't know,' he said. 'I know Katy and Al didn't get on that well as room-mates, so maybe, something . . . And Peter, well, he is what he is.'

'And what's that?'

Dermot shrugged. 'He rows. He plays rugby. He drinks beer.'

'Does he do anything else?'

'Girls,' he said flatly.

'Alice?'

Dermot pressed his lips together. 'I don't know. How would I know?'

Corry looked at her watch. 'Well, maybe he'll tell us himself. Come in!'

As she called, the door opened tentatively. Through it, with several feet of space between them, came a wary-looking Katy and Peter, who immediately said, 'Do I have to be here for this? I've got practice.'

Corry motioned for them to sit down. Dermot was staring at his lap. 'Yes, Peter, we need to speak to all three of you.'

Katy sat down beside Dermot, so they were facing Corry and Paula across the table like an interview panel. Paula preferred to watch from the sidelines usually – it gave her a better view of the things people were trying to hide. Peter remained standing. 'But why? We already told you what we know.'

'Well, you'll need to tell us again.' Corry glared at him. 'Sit down.'

He did. Katy immediately took his hand and placed them both, entwined, on the table. 'Of course we want to help,' she said. 'We're worried about Alice. We think she might have hurt herself.'

Dermot looked up sharply and down again. Corry said, 'Hurt herself how?'

'Well, she tried to kill herself before. When she was in rehab. Did you know that?'

Corry looked at Paula. 'Did she tell you that, Katy?' Alice's parents hadn't mentioned it.

'Yes. She took pills. She told me – we were really close, like I said.'

'But not so much after she moved out?'

Katy opened her mouth and shut it. She glanced sideways at Dermot. He blinked and looked up, cleared his throat. 'Look,' he said. 'If something's happened to Alice – and I think it's too early to say that it has – she'll have done it herself. That's the angle you need to take.'

'What makes you say that, Dermot?' Corry asked carefully. 'Did she have a reason to hurt herself?'

He shrugged again. 'Like Katy said, she's done it before. And she's been a bit weird the last few months.'

'Weird how?'

'She moved out to the cottage,' said Katy, still clutching at Peter's hand. 'And before that she sort of . . . cut herself off from us. Didn't she?'

Peter licked his lips. 'Um, yeah, I guess so. We didn't see much of her and I noticed in the buttery she wasn't—' He made an incoherent eating gesture. 'You know, she was having trouble again.'

'Her anorexia was kicking in again?' said Paula.

The three exchanged looks. 'Yes,' said Katy confidently. 'I was worried about her.'

'Have you any idea why she cut herself off?'

Another short silence. 'No,' said Dermot. 'We had no idea.'

Paula muttered something about the blind – a shaft of

sun was hitting the wood of the table, filling the room with buttery light. She got up and went to the window, hovering there to watch the three as Corry questioned them. She noticed that Katy's other hand, the one not clutching Peter's, was on the side of Dermot's chair. Almost as if she was poking him. Peter's other hand was clenched tight by his side.

Corry was saying, 'So where's she gone then, if she went off by herself? We've found no trace of her.'

Dermot jerked his head irritably. 'Down the rabbit hole. I don't know. That's kind of the point, that no one would know.'

Corry again. 'So, to be clear, you all think that Alice isn't missing at all.'

He made an odd gesture. Somewhere between a laugh and a shrug of despair. 'We didn't say *that*. I guess it depends if you think being lost is the same as no one knowing where you are.'

'These kids,' sighed Corry. Across the playing fields from the car, tall figures stood against the sun. Paula wondered if one of them was Peter Franks. Thinking about his hands, how strong they were. How small Alice was in her selfies.

She asked, 'What did you think to that thing Dermot said about Peter? And girls?'

'I don't know. I don't understand any of them. Why aren't they upset? They were supposedly the best of friends, those four. And now she's missing and there's hardly a flicker of emotion between them. The only one that's shown any feeling about it is Dermot, and he looks—'

'Exhausted,' finished Paula. 'At the end of his rope.'

'Right.'

'Down the rabbit hole, Dermot said,' Paula remembered. 'That's from *Alice in Wonderland*, right?'

'I only know the Disney film. Our Rosie used to love it. You reckon he said it on purpose? He knows something else?'

'I don't know. It could just be a coincidence.' Paula thought of the illustrations in her old copy of the book, the frail, fair child, staring at the cake, longing to eat it but disgusted at the same time. What it must have been like inside Alice's head, every day. She wondered how to bring up her next point. 'Uh – you said Peter Franks had no criminal record?'

'None. His old school were very cagey about why they kicked him out, said he went of his own accord, but it must be something.'

'Well – I might have some . . . information about him. Allegations only, of course.'

Corry narrowed her eyes. 'Am I right in thinking you got it off a certain journalist you know?'

'Maybe. Maybe indeed.' Aidan was, as she'd said, very good at digging the dirt. His journalist friend Maeve worked in Dublin and knew all about the school Peter Franks had gone to, St Murtagh's. A boarding school on the outskirts of Dublin, for boys whose parents had more money than time. 'Anyway, Peter was apparently expelled just before his Leaving Cert.'

'And did your super-secret source say why?'

'There was an incident. A party in the school grounds – some girls from the local town were smuggled in.'

'And?'

'And one of them said she was raped, by Peter Franks and two other boys, taking turns.'

Corry's mouth twisted. 'Let me guess, no conviction?'

'It was all hushed up. No need to ruin the boy's futures, one mistake, etcetera, etcetera. But my, eh, source did hear there were drugs involved, Rohypnol or something similar.'

'Jesus.'

'I know.'

Corry looked back at the college, lit by the afternoon sun as they turned onto the main road. 'So we've got him with a rape allegation; Dermot . . . well, God only knows what's up with him; Katy self-harming – I saw her wrists; Alice with her anorexia, and her history of vanishing acts. She tried to kill herself, Katy says. We need to look into that. What a messed-up wee foursome they were. Question is – what happened to make them into three? And why do the others not care?'

'Do you reckon Willis would let us take a trip to Dublin?' asked Paula casually.

Equally casually, Corry said, 'Well, he did say we should throw everything we had at this. He's got the Morgans breathing down his neck, and the press can't get enough of it.'

It was the weekend, when she'd promised Aidan she'd help him with the final wedding admin. But Alice Morgan was still missing, and it was hard to care about flowers and dresses until she was found. 'Exactly. We should follow every lead.'

Chapter Fourteen

'I'm surprised she wanted to speak to us,' said Corry.

'Maeve can be very persuasive. She says rape victims get silenced, and it's like another crime being done to them.'

They were driving through one of Dublin's poorer streets, houses like weary faces, boarded-up windows and gardens full of rubbish. 'Make sure you lock the car,' Paula advised. Corry drove a sensible Fiat, and for a moment Paula thought of *him* – cars his one weakness in an otherwise straight-down-the-line personality. His BMW had been sold when he'd moved back to London. She wondered who was driving it now.

On the radio the news played. '*And police in Ballyterrin are searching for the missing daughter of Home Office Minister Lord Morgan. Alice Morgan was last seen—*' Paula reached over and turned it off. Corry glanced up, but said nothing. They both knew they needed to find something, and soon.

The door of the small semi was opened by a young woman in a tracksuit and Uggs. She had straightened hair and polished nails, chipped off at the tips.

'Colette?'

'Yeah.' Her eyes wary.

'I'm Paula, Maeve's friend? This is DS Corry. Are you OK for us to ask you a few questions?'

Colette raised a finger to her mouth and nibbled the top, as if thinking it over. Then she moved back and they followed her in. A TV blared in the living room. Colette shut the door on the rest of the house, which was filled with voices and running feet. She perched on the edge of the sofa. Paula indicated the TV, which showed a morning talk show. 'I'm sorry. Would you mind?'

Colette used the remote to mute it, though the picture continued to distract Paula. 'Maeve said a girl went missing.'

'Yes. A student at Oakdale College. And she'd been going out with one of the boys you—'

'Which one?'

'Peter Franks.'

Colette leaned forward and took a cigarette from a packet on the table, flicking a light over it. Paula breathed through her nose.

Corry said, 'There's no evidence he's involved, but we do know he has a history of violence.'

'Not proved.' She pulled a stray piece of tobacco from her lip.

'No, but are you able to tell us what happened?'

'The Guards said nothing happened.'

'I know. But Maeve believed you, didn't she?'

Colette's face, her eyebrows plucked into expressions of permanent disapproval, didn't shift. She was eighteen, Paula knew, but looked older, defeated somehow, her eyes already dull. 'Well, like I said in my report. I knew a group of lads from the school. We'd meet down the shopping centre and muck about. They asked would I come round to the gates one evening and they'd sneak me in.'

'And you wanted to?'

'I wanted to see inside. We never got to, you know. And

they were nice fellas. Smart. Cute, like. Talked like your ones off telly. They'd chat to you instead of just . . . grunting. So me and my mate Carly went. I got some whiskey out of my da's cupboard. And then. Well, we drank. But I got really drunk really fast. Like that wasn't normal, I'd been drinking since I was twelve, I can hold my booze. Carly said she was going but one of them had his arm round me and I liked him. I thought maybe he'd get off with me. I don't know after that, I was really off my face. I don't remember, except their faces, like coming at me out of a fog, and I couldn't move, and the smell – sweaty boys and aftershave. Then I woke up. Must have been hours later. They'd gone and I was lying on the ground, all by myself. I was boking my ring up. My jeans and pants were off – I found them a wee bit away. I was all – I was sticky, and I'd been bleeding.'

A moment of silence. 'What did you do?' asked Corry.

'I ran off home before I got caught. I had to squeeze through the fence, like, and it hurt – everything was sort of burning. I got into the house and had a bath. My ma shouted at me for wasting the hot water. Then I went to school.'

'When did you go to the Guards?'

'Mammy caught me scrubbing myself in the bath about a week later, and I told her the whole thing. I couldn't stop bleeding, you see, and she knew it wasn't the right time for that.'

Corry's voice, which could strike fear into the hearts of the most hardened policemen, was very gentle. 'I'm so sorry that happened to you, Colette. Can you tell me about the Guards?'

'There was no evidence – too late. And I'd been drinking with the boys. And – it wasn't exactly my first time. Someone from the college came and talked to Ma and Da, said they could even prosecute me for being in there if I didn't drop it. Trespassing. Ma said I had to be more careful. Da called me a wee slut.' She shrugged. 'So. Nothing happened.'

'Your report would be on file?'

'I guess so. Don't think they really believed me. I kept crying, and they only had men officers.' She glanced coolly at Paula, taking a drag on her cigarette.

Paula said, 'Thank you for talking to us. I know it must be hard. Do you remember anything else, anything at all?'

She exhaled slowly. 'Laughing. I remember hearing it, even though I was out of it. Someone just laughing on and on, while I was lying there.'

'Thank you,' said Corry, writing it down.

The door opened and a young girl in a tracksuit burst in, carrying a squalling tow-haired toddler. 'Ma says you've to take him.'

Colette pulled the child onto her lap, nursing him, soothing him with small noises. He wasn't much older than Maggie, three maybe, with a helmet of fair hair. 'Mammmmy, who's these people?' he said, sucking his thumb.

'Just visitors. Shush now, be a good boy.' She glanced up at them. 'I called him Tiernan. It was – I wanted to go to England. But we couldn't afford the boat or that. So. I just had to. You know how it is.'

Paula's head swam. 'Colette – do you mean . . .'

'Maeve didn't tell you? I was pregnant after it. We found out after the Guards dropped the case. I had to stop school and all, but he's – well, he's mine now. And it's not his fault, poor wean.' She continued to nurse the little boy to her, the child of her rapist, one of her rapists, and Paula found herself thinking back to the gleam of the fair hair on Peter Franks' head.

Alice

Out. I'm not sure if it even exists any more, or if it's just something I imagined. Some days in here, it's like the only world that exists is him, and me, and the other girls. The smells of blood and vomit and the white lights flickering overhead. The cuffs. The strip-searches. Being watched, all the time and every second of every day and night.

But I have to still believe in it, the idea of Out. In my head I start running through all the things I'll do when I get there. Ride a horse again, feel it breathe and strain beneath me, put my feet out of the stirrups and lie along its warm back, hugging it. Go to the beach really early in the morning, digging my feet into the cold wet sand. Go to the cinema by myself and see three films in a row, right through. Ride a Ferris wheel, and scream when we reach the top, hanging there as if by magic, as if we'll never come back down. Go to university – me, in a campus full of trees, in glasses and a scarf, laughing in a big group of boys and girls. The smell of autumn in the air – wet leaves and rain. I haven't breathed fresh air in so long. It's all I want in here. Magazines aren't allowed and of course anything you can eat is pointless. If someone was coming – which they aren't – I would ask them to bring a jar of outside air, so I could breathe it all down in one gulp. It isn't too much to ask, is it?

Charlotte asked me: What would you do to get out?

Anything, I said. Anything.

Her eyes were glittering. Pinky swear? She held up her cold finger, like a white witch, and we swore. And for a while, we played the game. The Ana game. And we were pure.

But of course she won. Because she's dead. But soon, very soon now, we're going to be even.

Chapter Fifteen

'Will we be able to use any of that?' They were walking back to the car, which was unmolested, though being watched from a distance by a crowd of young men in sportswear who looked like the most sport they ever did was running away from the police.

Corry unlocked it. 'If we can prove Peter did something similar to Alice . . . She could have been traumatised, run away, or even done something to herself.'

'Maybe he did more this time. Made sure she couldn't tell anyone.'

'Maybe. But we can't bring him in without any evidence. Still, we can use the previous allegation, if something comes up. In the meantime we'll have to watch them – all three of them.' She shook her head grimly, looking back at Colette's house. 'I can't believe they tried to prosecute *her*.'

'Let's not forget that Ireland is a country that put a teenager under house arrest in the nineties, so she couldn't have an abortion after she was raped.'

'I know. I know.' Corry sighed. 'It's just hard . . . Doing this job, you have to know you're on the right side. Otherwise you may as well give up and work in a coffee shop or something. Because if we don't have that, we have nothing. And when it's the state doing stuff like that – it makes it harder.'

Paula thought about it. They were the only people who

seemed worried about Alice. Not even her own parents. Not even her closest friends. 'If I went missing . . . I think I'd at least want to know someone was looking for me.'

'Me too. Come on, belt up.' Corry started the engine.

'Where are we going now?' Paula put her seat belt on.

'I thought we might as well pay another visit while we're down here.'

The girl was pretty in a pinched, overly made-up way, with long, straightened brown hair and a baggy cardigan over a vest top and jeans. She paused with her key in one hand in front of the tatty student house, plastic bag in the other. Hangover food, crisps and fizzy drinks and chocolate. Like a child would buy, if given money for the first time. 'What?' she said impatiently, as they approached. 'You're not the Jehovah's lot, are you? We've told you we're not interested.'

Paula heard Corry make a small noise in her throat. 'It's Alison, is it? Alison Carter.'

'Yes – oh shit, are you the Guards? I'm going to pay it, I promise, it's just I'm really busy with uni just now—'

'Not the Guards,' said Corry. 'Can we come in, please?'

She was suddenly pale and polite, ushering them into the dirty, ash-stained living room and evicting the long-haired type who was skulking in there with a stern, 'Fintan, will you go upstairs', that made Paula sure there were drugs somewhere on the premises. Slumming it, at least for a while, all of them, before getting jobs in PR or a bank, probably.

'Is something wrong?' Alison perched on the armchair Fintan had reluctantly vacated. 'Did something bad happen?'

'Not exactly,' said Corry, looking with distaste at the stained sofa cushions. 'We're from the PSNI and we're investigating the disappearance of a girl up north. You may have seen it on the news. But I'd like a word with you about Katy Butcher.'

At this, Alison's manner switched again. She groaned and sat back, so a space of flat midriff appeared between her skinny jeans and vest top. 'Christ, you're not here about Katy? That stupid bitch. She gave you my name?'

'No, she didn't mention you at all. Your school did. I just need to find out a bit about her background, her character. Before she went to university.'

'Oh my God, did she know that girl who's missing? I bet something weird happened. I bet she did something.'

'Why do you say that?' asked Paula, who was also trying not to touch any of the sofa cushions. She was sure there was a bodily fluid of some kind ground into them.

'Because, hello, Katy is a total spaz. I haven't spoken to her in like seven years.'

'Why is that?'

Alison hooked her slim arms around her legs. 'The thing about Katy is, right, she likes girls, but she's in total denial about it.'

'You're saying Katy is gay?' So why then would she claim Peter Franks was her boyfriend?

'Duh. I said it to her when we were like fourteen, hello, you're probably a lesbian and I'm not – I mean it's not the gay thing, it would be cool, I'm just not into it – but she burst out crying and told the teacher I was bullying her. Then this one time, she was having a sleepover at mine and she tried to – urgh, I don't even like talking about it.'

'She made a move?' Corry suggested.

'Yeah, she like tried to . . . touch me. In bed. So I said I wasn't like that, and she'd better sleep on the floor or something. She started to cry and said she'd go home, she'd walk – it wasn't far, see, we were practically neighbours. Then like an hour later, middle of the fucking night, I hear my mum screaming. Katy's in our bathroom, and she's well, she used my razor, and she – cut herself. You know.'

'She tried to commit suicide?' asked Corry.

Alison made a noise. 'If you call hacking at your wrists with a pink Gillette Venus suicide – like hello, do it properly . . . And there's blood everywhere, like *everywhere*, it's like a horror film, and she's all puking and groaning, lying on the floor, and she left this . . . note . . . about how she liked me.' Alison put her head in her hands. 'Oh God. It was so embarrassing. I had to explain to my folks, and her folks, and it got all round school we were, like, lesbians. Urgh. She ruined school for me. I never spoke to her again.'

'I see. Is there anything else you can tell us?'

'I bet she was in love with that girl,' said Alison shrewdly. 'Was she? I bet she's got something to do with it. She's so weird. Honestly, I bet Katy knows something about it. Bet you a million pounds. Am I right?'

'You've been very helpful,' said Corry, getting up by way of answer. 'What was it you hadn't paid, by the way, a parking fine?'

'Um . . . speeding ticket.' Alison blushed. 'I'm going to, I swear, I just—'

'See that you do. Oh, and, Alison . . .' – as a toilet flushed upstairs – 'it wouldn't be within my remit to search this place for drugs, but I could easily send someone round to do so. Make sure you clean it up. And if you have any information about Katy Butcher that we might need to hear, let me know immediately.'

Chapter Sixteen

'So I think a purple cravat would go lovely with the wedding theme, what about that?' Hearing voices as she opened the door, Paula stopped in the hallway of her house to listen.

'What's a cravat?' Aidan sounded scared.

'Ach, you know, a sort of tie.'

'Can I not just wear an actual tie?'

There was a noise of derision. 'If you want it to just be like some *normal day* . . .'

Paula went in to rescue him. 'Hiya.'

Dr Saoirse McLoughlin, Paula's bridesmaid, oldest friend, and godmother to Maggie, was sitting at the table, her godchild on her knee. 'Well, there's the bride!'

'A bride with no dress,' said Aidan.

'Er, you're not supposed to know about the dress. Hi, pet.' Paula ruffled Maggie's hair.

'Mummy, Aunty See-sha's here!'

'Yes, I can see that.'

Aidan said, 'Well then, I'll take Miss Maggie up for a wee-wee, and you two can talk about it in secret. I know you love all that.'

She glared at him as he went, scooping Maggie into his arms, shooting her a small wink.

'He's right, you know,' Saoirse started to say, then blinked as Paula suddenly asked: 'What do you know about anorexia?'

'Er, not a massive amount. I did a rotation once in psych, but it wouldn't present to Casualty much.' Saoirse was an A&E registrar, focusing on what she called the 'blood and guts' of medicine.

'Well, would you know, or could you find out, if someone was starving, say, and they suddenly started eating again – what would that do to them?'

'You mean would they put on a lot of weight fast?'

'I was thinking more of bulimia, if they developed that too.'

'Well, bulimia can easily be fatal. Puts a massive strain on the heart, which is usually damaged already with anorexia.'

'So someone could die?'

'Yeah, they could. If you're starving, even eating normally can kill you. It's called re-feeding syndrome. People had it after the war. Why?'

Paula shook her head. 'Sorry, bit caught up with this case.'

'I can see. You haven't even mentioned the wedding. Anyone would think it wasn't in, hello – two weeks' time!'

Paula shrugged off the brief burst of panic. 'Oh, you know me – I'm not good at that girly stuff. Is your own dress ready?'

'Oh yes, it's all taken in.' Paula remembered that when they first chose it – ages ago, because that one was for Saoirse and therefore not as terrifying as her own – they'd picked one with an empire line, because of the chance Saoirse might be pregnant by the time it was worn. And two rounds of IVF later, she wasn't.

Her friend was looking at her. 'Pat says you still haven't picked one.'

'You've been talking to Pat?'

'I saw her the other day in the hospital.'

This reminded Paula of two things – one, that Saoirse and Pat were basically organising this wedding for her, and two, that she hadn't been anywhere in sight on her friend's own big day. She'd been twenty-five, doing her best to stay away from the town that held so many painful memories, but still. Still still still. God, she could be a right bitch at times. 'Thank you,' she said. 'I'd not have been able to do this without you.'

'You'd not have wanted to do it.'

'No, but – it'll be nice.'

'It'll be lovely,' said Saoirse. 'You'll see. I could have become a wedding planner after mine. Dave said he'd break down and cry if he ever heard the words "your special day" again.'

Paula nodded. 'And Pat's been to about a thousand weddings. She knows everyone in town, and I mean *everyone*.'

'Is she OK then?'

'I think so, why?'

'I'm sure it's nothing. Just wondered why she was in the hospital. She seemed a wee bit off, not her usual self.'

'I don't know. Maybe she was up visiting someone. She does that a lot.'

'OK. I better go anyway, I have a shift tonight. Here, read this.' Saoirse got up, foisting a bridal magazine on Paula. The woman on the cover had teeth whiter than her veil and looked as if every thought in her head had been replaced by confetti. The cover read: *Your special day – new trends in table wear. 101 things to do with your hair. The great cake debate – three-tier or cupcakes?*

'Do I have to?'

'Yes,' said Saoirse firmly. 'You have to order your dress.

You won't get anything decent now anyway, you need at least ten weeks. I ordered mine a year in advance.'

Yes, thought Paula, because you know what you want and that you won't change your mind, and you and Dave have basically been together from the second you met and you've never had a moment's doubt about him. 'You're too good to me, you know,' she said awkwardly. They were not the hugging kind of friends. 'I don't know why you put up with me.'

'Remember that time your dad hurt his leg?'

'When were we seventeen? Yeah, why?'

'Remember you came to stay for a while after, when he was in hospital? Well, Mammy took me aside, and she said, you mind that wee girl, Saoirse. She's had a hard time of it, and you've your mammy and daddy and your brothers and sisters and everything. I said you'd be welcome to our Niamh, but she was right. She's still right, always is.'

Paula didn't know what to say to that, memories crowding her, that summer of violence and heat, her mind made up to leave town for good, even if it meant losing Aidan and her best friend in the world. 'Are you saying I'm some kind of charity case? Thanks, Glocko. If Mammy McLoughlin said put your head in the oven would you do it?'

'Anyone would,' said Saoirse. 'Have you met my mammy? She'd have put the fear of God on Osama Bin Laden, so she would.'

'Don't think he had a lot of fear of God, not as such.'

'True. Right, I'm away, these sunburn cases won't lecture themselves. Eejits. Bit of sun and they're out frying themselves in chip oil.' She gave Paula a rough pat on the shoulder. 'Come on, Maguire, time to bride it up. Offer it up to Jesus.'

Which was another of Mammy McLoughlin's sayings.

*

Ringing. Her phone was ringing. It was Monday morning, and Paula squeezed her eyes open, groping on the bedside table for her phone. Aidan was in the shower already, singing an off-key version of 'Born to Run'. Next door there was some ominous creaking from Maggie's room. She snatched up the phone. Corry. 'Hello?'

'You up? I've already had Willis on me this morning wanting an update.'

She rubbed her eyes: 7.45 a.m. Willis must be under serious pressure. 'Well, we're doing all we can.'

'He doesn't think so. Anyway, I've another angle.'

'What's that?' said Paula warily, recognising the voice Corry used when she needed you to do something you definitely wouldn't enjoy.

'I've a few contacts in the East Sussex police. Apparently Katy was right – Alice tried to kill herself while she was at the clinic there. So if she was suffering with anorexia again now, maybe she did hurt herself after all.'

'Uh-huh . . .' She was waiting for the favour.

'What do you say, fancy a quick jaunt to your old neck of the woods? See what you can find out?'

'Aw, come on. I can't leave Maggie.'

'Go and come back in a day. Seriously. I want you to go, talk to them as a colleague. See if they think she might have tried it again.'

Part Two

'This piece of rudeness was more than Alice could bear: she got up in great disgust, and walked off; the Dormouse fell asleep instantly, and neither of the others took the least notice of her going, though she looked back once or twice, half hoping they would call after her . . .'

Lewis Carroll, *Alice's Adventures in Wonderland*

Ballyterrin, Northern Ireland,
July 1981

The streets were full of dead men. It was all you could see now. The bones under the skin. What they'd look like if the flesh fell from their bodies, if their eyes were sunk and milky, if their breath stopped in their chests, something begun and not ended. Did you always die breathing out? you wondered. Maybe you'd find out, before too long.

Ballyterrin. A crappy wee town on the border, all housing estates and fields and a stinking canal, but it was home. All the same you were jumpy as a snake driving through it. A hot day, tarmac melting on the roads. The streets pressed full of traffic, peelers on every corner in their green uniforms and hats, guns cocked. Rifle green, they called the colour. The colour of injustice. You'd been brought up to hate the RUC. If someone robbed your car or your house you'd ask the Provos to sort it out. Not the peelers, never the peelers in a million years, it would be betraying your kin and country. So how come now, as you drove carefully through the town in your crappy borrowed Jetta, all you wanted was to pull over to one of the cops and tell them everything? *Please, arrest me. Don't make me do this.*

As luck would have it, today was your day to escape the random checkpoints. Every time you crossed the border or drove round Belfast, yes, it was out of the car and have it searched, spread your legs sir with the gun trained on you, just a routine search sir it's our prerogative. So many other times. Even when you'd your wee niece in the car with you, six years old, crying as the soldiers with the big guns had a good rummage through your boot. They didn't care. Children were no defence, old people, you name it. To the Brit Army you were just scum, all of you. So how come this day, and you a twenty-year-old man driving alone, with a shifty look and a gun under the passenger seat, they wave you on through, not a bother on you? Sod's law.

This town was ready to explode. You could see it in people's eyes as they walked the hot streets, even women with prams, even wee kids. People gathered on corners, waiting for news, looking at the Army and peelers out of the corners of their eyes, sun glinting black off guns. They'd had enough. Six men had starved to death already. If – when – the next one went, there'd be all bloody hell to pay. And you, wee skitter of a fella, only a foot soldier in this war, driving someone else's car, their God-awful Country and Western tape on the cassette player, you were the one who was going to make sure it happened, inexorable as the grim reaper. You were the one standing beside this petrol-soaked shitstorm bonfire of a country, and you were about to strike the match.

Chapter Seventeen

London,
August 2013

Below the Aer Lingus jet, London sprawled out, its outskirts beige, ugly and careless. But all the same Paula heaved a nostalgic sigh at the sight of it. This had been her place – somewhere to go when she'd left behind the hardened certainties of Ballyterrin, where everyone knew her and what had happened to her family. Where it wasn't possible to change. In London, she was no one. Irish Paula, at uni. No close friends, just people she'd see now and again for a drink, send Facebook messages. Colleagues that she'd share work with. She'd learned the hard way that when people got close, they could be taken away. She felt a tinge of something at the thought of Aidan – he was back home with Maggie, sorting out the growing tangle of wedding admin. Wedmin, Saoirse had called it, and Paula had nearly boked. That was all really happening, in two weeks. Old Paula could never come back again – there were rivers that could not be crossed a second time.

As the signs came on for descent, she closed her eyes and

thought about what she'd do when she got there. There was no need to actually go into London on this trip. The clinic where Alice had lived for two years was in East Sussex, not too far from Gatwick. But she felt all the same the city's gravity. And somewhere down below, among all the millions of people, was Guy Brooking. Guy, and also his wife, and his daughter, and so she hadn't, and wouldn't, try to find him.

Bustling out at Gatwick with her wheelie case, trailing jackets and WH Smith bags, she almost missed the sign with her name on it. It was misspelled, *Paula McGuire*, and she looked up, then did a double-take. 'What are you doing here?'

'I couldn't resist the mistake. I knew it'd catch your eye.' Dr Kevin Neary, one of her old university tutors. Kevin was one of the most eminent criminal psychologists in the country, and as a doctoral student Paula had naturally gravitated to him. He was also from Ballymena, his Ulster accent modulated by years in England and a London wife and kids. He had a neat grey beard and pens in his shirt pocket, a tie pin.

She eyed him. 'Putting me to shame as usual, Kevin. I was going to freshen up before I got there.'

'Ah, you're grand. It's not a formal place we're going to.'

'You're taking me?' She'd asked him to help her set up the meeting, but not expected he'd have time to come as well.

He ushered her towards the car park. 'Let's say calls were made. The girl's father is some bigwig, yes? I don't think the clinic wanted too much scrutiny on it.'

'Oh right. So you're here to keep tabs on me, is that the lie of the land?'

He laughed, stopping by the ticket machines. 'That's what they think. I've met you, of course, so I know better men than me have tried and failed. Now, how do you work this yoke?'

'I bet you don't say yoke to the English.'

'No, and it's a shame. A very useful word.'

After much perplexed stabbing of buttons – Kevin was a brilliant man, but one who referred to 'email numbers' and couldn't work his own phone – they were leaving the airport and merging onto the M25. Gatwick was barely in London, Paula thought, as they soon cut off into country lanes, trees arching together so densely that Kevin had to put the car lights on. She needn't have worried. She wasn't going to run into anyone out here. She knew it was ridiculous, but she was jumpy every time she saw a fair-haired man out the window, or someone in a suit. Just for a half-second between breaths, but enough to spin her off her axis.

He looked at her from the corner of his eye. 'And I hear congratulations are in order? Doubly so.'

'Well – I had a baby, yes. Maggie's her name.'

'I'll insist on pictures when we stop. Sandra says you've to email her one, I don't have a notion how that works. And – do I hear wedding bells? Our wee Paula Maguire?'

She squinted out the window. 'You know how it is back home – people still talk if you're not married. And with the kid – anyway, the wedding's in two weeks.' Less than that now. Christ.

'Lovely.' It was a narrative that made sense – she'd had a child with her boyfriend, her childhood sweetheart, and now they'd get married and probably have more. Except, of course, it might not be true.

'So what's the place like?' She changed the subject.

'It's like the Priory. Private rehab for kids with issues. So we've got the self-harmers, the drug users, and of course the eating disorders. They have a quite radical approach that you can't get on the NHS – supposedly they can dry out a drug addict in a month.'

'And anorexia?'

'Well.' He turned the car at a set of red-brick gateposts, almost invisible in the trees. 'Let's just say they hardly ever die. Not all clinics can say the same. So it works. In a way.'

'In a way?'

Kevin's face, placid and kind, gave nothing away. It was what made him so good at his job. 'You'll see. Come on.'

The place was like a country hotel, the kind stressed-out London couples would go to for minibreaks to try to revive their wilting relationships. They walked across crunching gravel and Paula noticed the bars on the lower windows. This was not a hotel – the people inside weren't allowed to leave.

Kevin spoke into the videophone entrance for a while, negotiating entry, and Paula looked around. It was silent, eerily so. Only the rustle of leaves and the odd cry of a bird. She wondered how Alice had felt, cut off here.

Adding to the feel of a top hotel, they were met by 'Guest Liaison Manager' Maria Holt. Paula gathered her job was to look after the paying customers, i.e. the parents who put their children in here. She drifted off during the woman's long spiel about the centre, as they were led down a wood-panelled corridor, Maria tapping in high heels. She had on subtle make-up, but a lot of it, and a blouse and pencil skirt. 'Our success rates are consistently high, because we're able to take a more aggressive approach to fighting addiction and mental disorders. Conventional therapies focus on controlling the problem, not the causes.'

They passed doors, a TV lounge with several teenagers in it, vacant, eyes glued to the screen. They wore loose grey clothes, like prison inmates. 'There are no closed doors at the Yews,' Maria said, seeing Paula look. 'It's our most fundamental policy.'

The centre director was ready for them in his office, which overlooked the thick trees at the back of the building. More yews, like the ones in Crocknashee churchyard. 'Kevin! Good to see you.' A firm handshake and a clasp of the shoulder for him. Paula was scrutinised by sharp blue eyes. 'Hello, I'm David Allardyce. Dr Maguire, is it?'

She tried not to wince as he pummelled her hand. 'Hello, yes.'

Allardyce was a short man, coming up to her eyes, and had sandy greying hair and a rugby player's nose. Beneath the Paul Smith shirt and trousers was a strong body. 'I've heard a lot about you. Kevin here used to sing your praises.'

'My best grad student,' said Kevin.

'I doubt that.' Paula brushed off the compliment.

'Well,' said Kevin. 'I've had ones who are more patient with funding applications, maybe.'

'What can I help you with?' said Allardyce. 'I heard you were on the criminal end of things – not thinking of going therapeutic?'

'Not really,' said Paula, thinking she couldn't imagine anything worse. 'It's about a former patient of yours – an Alice Morgan. She was studying in Ireland and she's gone missing.'

His expression didn't change. 'Oh yes. I think I remember. But we don't call them patients here, they're guests.'

'OK. Obviously, with Alice's history, our first thought wasn't forced disappearance. So I wanted to pick your brains really, see if you can help me put together a profile.'

'Sure, sure. Sit down.' He indicated the chairs opposite his desk, which Paula thought were by some famous Swedish designer. 'Let me get the file.'

She sat down, looking out at the cool oasis of trees outside the window. The place was peaceful, almost soporific.

'Now.' Allardyce had found a manila file in his oak cabinet. 'Alice. She was with us for two years – a long stretch. Usually we pride ourselves on having a cure within three months.'

'Can you ever really cure anorexia?'

'Good question.' He beamed a smile at her. 'We consider them cured if they gain two stone or more and are eating normally again. Obviously, a relapse is always a risk. Was Alice's eating still disordered?'

'We think so. Here's the last picture that was taken of her – the day she went missing.' Paula took out her phone to show him Alice's last selfie.

He pursed his lips. 'Hm, yes. Not quite life-threatening, but still very underweight.'

She put the phone away. 'Can I ask, Dr Allardyce, would you have expected Alice to have periods? Her room-mate at university said she didn't.'

'At that bodyweight, I'd doubt it, I have to say.'

'We also found evidence in her home of bingeing.'

'Bulimia?' He frowned. 'But that wasn't her way at all. She had a real horror of vomiting – with her it was all about purity. She had something of an obsession with medieval saints, the ones who allegedly didn't eat for years, left perfect corpses. You'd be Catholic, I assume, Dr Maguire?'

She glanced at Kevin, who shrugged slightly. It was an unusual question to hear in England. 'I was raised Catholic, yes.'

'Then you'll know about the incorruptibles. The saints with preserved bodies – they didn't rot after death, supposedly. Alice wanted to be like this.'

'You mean like. . . holy relics?'

'Yes, something like that. Things that don't decompose, that stay unchanged.'

'But don't bulimia and anorexia often co-present?' asked Paula. It wasn't really her area.

'Yes, of course. But Alice – I'd be surprised. Very surprised.'

'OK. Thank you. I need to ask—' She hesitated, glancing at Kevin, who looked peacefully out of the window. This was all down to her. 'We've heard Alice attempted suicide while she was here.'

He fixed her with a stare, and for a moment the polite veneer was gone. 'Who told you that?'

She faced him. Right on your side, Corry had said. 'We have a source in the police.'

Allardyce placed his hands on his desk. 'Well, yes, she did. A real pity. We take every precaution here – you'll see there are codes on all the drug stores, and we watch them all the time – but accidents happen. Unfortunately Alice was able to stockpile some meds from another girl, who should have been taking them. The other girl died. Heart failure, at nineteen. Such a waste.'

'And Alice's parents don't know this? They didn't mention it.'

He uncapped his pen. 'Dr Maguire . . . do you have children?'

'What's that got to do with it?' she bridled.

'Just a question.'

'I have a little girl.'

'Well, maybe you can imagine then. Imagine the pain for a parent, of watching this child you brought into the world, and all they want to do is starve themselves to death. To disappear. You'd do anything, wouldn't you, to make them eat? So Alice's parents already blamed themselves. We didn't want to worry them more. That's all.'

Alice

2013

Nothing good ever lasts. I know that. I've known it since I was seven years old and being put into boarding school by parents who blamed me for their marriage falling apart. And who had chosen to save the marriage, and lose me. But still – for a while, the four of us, here, it was good. I knew there were things under the surface. I knew Peter wanted to fuck me, and was getting more and more pissed off I hadn't let him. I knew Dermot maybe wanted to as well, or maybe just thought he should, and that he wanted Peter to like him maybe more than anything else. I knew that Katy wanted Peter, because he was popular, and that she wanted something from me, something darker. To have me, or more likely, to be me. But despite all that, it was so special to start with. I remember the first night most of all.

It was just before Christmas, so the boathouse was freezing, even when we dragged the little space heater down there. I'd told Katy to meet me there, and hinted it would be an amazing party. I'd told Dermot, who I knew from waiting to meet the stupid therapist, I'd be there too. I made it sound like I'd be on my own. I knew he would think that was the kind of thing he should do. I knew that if I pushed him, he'd probably do anything I asked. Whether he wanted to or not.

Peter was trickier. I knew he'd come, but he might be angry when he saw it wasn't just me. He was already pissed off. The night before, when we'd kissed on his bed, he had pulled away and started looking for something, a condom, I guess. I said did he mind if we didn't. Why, he said. Do you not like it?

I couldn't explain that I didn't even know. So I said I had my period. A little joke to myself, that one. And when Katy and Dermot and I were at the boathouse, and I'd introduced them, and Katy was forcing him to bond with her – sensing a fellow runt in the litter – Peter appeared over the hill. He was carrying a bottle of vodka and I smelled him before I saw him. Smoke, and booze, and aftershave, and something else. The smell of the alpha male. He stopped. He'd given me the key earlier, I guess thinking I'd be sexing myself up for him down there. Um . . . what's this?

I went up to him, stroked his arm. The way I learned from Rebecca. All men are the same, really. It's cool, isn't it? They're good people, *I said under my breath.* And Dermot – he can get stuff. You know?

Dermot's ability to 'get stuff' made him OK to Peter. He even shook his hand. I saw him look at Katy and dismiss her, but maybe even enjoy her being there, the ego boost.

There were other times too. Katy lying on my bed, laughing at Pitch Perfect. *Dermot passing me notes in the library, little jokes. Peter smiling at me across the bar, everyone turning to see who he was looking at. It was good. It's hard to believe it now, when things are so royally fucked up, but for a while, it was really good. It was the only time since Charlotte died that I actually felt I had friends.*

I should have known. If you let people in, it only makes it easier for them to hurt you. I guess that's why I'm writing it down, to try to understand what went so wrong. I haven't done that since I was in the clinic. Things aren't as bad as then. I have to remember that. I have to try and eat, and not go mad again, because whatever happens I can't go back there. I'd rather die. And when I say that, unlike Katy, I actually mean it.

Chapter Eighteen

Paula asked to see the rest of the building, and after the briefest of hesitations, Allardyce lifted his desk phone and muttered some words into it. Maria was waiting for them outside, all smiles and heels. Could she offer them a drink or other refreshment? Perhaps they'd like to see the canteen with its nutrition programme?

Kevin said equably that he'd love a coffee, so they clattered down the stairs to a large barn–like room tacked onto the back of the house. It had views of the trees, and was done up like a hotel buffet, with cutlery trays, condiments in baskets. Except for the nurses on each till point.

'The guests have to get used to eating in public,' said Allardyce. 'It's one of the biggest issues for anorexics. The alimentary act, chewing and swallowing, it disgusts them, so they often eat in secret. We have a terrible mice problem here from food in the rooms. So they have to show the nurses they made good choices – no diet foods, just nutritious items. We do more than fatten them up – we try to change their behaviour.'

Most of the people in the room were female, and in their teens. The odd boy or older man was dotted around, looking shell-shocked. The girls chattered, but with a certain nervous energy. A flock of birds, pecking at their food.

'What happens if they still refuse to eat?' asked Paula.

'Would you hospitalise them?'

'If we have to. We have the facilities on site. Under-eighteens can legally be given nutrition, on a drip or orally.'

'You mean you force-feed them?'

'If you want to call it that. It's saving them from a slow suicide, we think. Have you seen someone die of starvation, Dr Maguire?' He was speaking neither loudly or quietly. 'Everything shuts down. The eyes film over. The hearing goes. Their skin starts to crack open, even on the softest sheets. Their organs fail, one by one – the body eats itself to try to stay alive. Aside from breathing, eating is our most basic process. Unfortunately we live in a society which doesn't understand that. People think you can stuff yourself with fat and sugar and are surprised to be obese – or at the opposite end, they think you can put in nothing at all for days and the engine will not grind to a halt.' His eyes fell on one girl, who wore three layers of sweatshirts and a woolly hat, despite the warmth of the sun coming in the large windows. She was painstakingly putting milk into her coffee, drop by drop, her lips moving as she counted. Allardyce went on, 'When you're starving, the body starts to shut down non-essential systems. For girls, their periods usually stop. They may come back, if feeding is resumed. Or they may not. And the brain – no point in being able to think when you're dying. So bear that in mind, when you're trying to understand Alice. People with anorexia are mentally ill – you can't trust them to make the right decisions. Their brains are dying, and it's sending them mad.'

Paula swallowed, her mouth suddenly full of saliva. 'Dr Allardyce . . . do they sometimes fight you, when you're trying to feed them?'

His expression didn't shift. 'Hardly surprising if they do.

It's not always easy, saving someone from killing themselves. You need to think of them as drug addicts, or mental health patients. Sometimes we have to take extreme actions to help them.'

Paula stood up; she couldn't listen to much more of this. 'Is there a ladies I could use?'

He glanced at her for a second. 'Maria will show you. Maria!'

'Oh no, it's fine, honestly, I'll find it.' She fled, trying to outpace Maria in her high heels.

Once she was out of sight of the canteen, Paula went into the ladies and shut a cubicle door behind her. No lock. She held her foot against it, trying to process what she'd seen. She felt dog-tired. She'd had an early start to the airport, and Maggie had clung to her, crying, unable to understand that Mummy would be back the same night.

She took out her phone in the cubicle and thumbed through it. A message from Aidan saying Maggie was fine and he'd leave Paula some dinner, as long as she was happy to eat fish fingers because 'the bloody builders still haven't fixed the hob'. This was what having a partner meant – no need to come home alone, to an empty bed and fridge. Someone to pick up the slack. Someone waiting for you, watching for you. Maybe she'd get used to it after all.

She was about to go out when she heard a door bang and the gulp of sobs. There was the noise of a phone ringing. 'Mum?' A girl's voice, hurried, cracked with tears. 'Mum, I have to be quick, I'm not meant to have this ... Mum, please, please come and get me. Please, I hate it, you don't know what they do to us ... please let me come home.' She began to cry. Paula wondered if she should go out – but would it make it worse, knowing you'd been overheard?

Before she could do anything the door banged again and heavy feet came in. A man's voice. Paula braced herself against her cubicle door. They let men into the ladies here?

'Stephanie?' said the voice. 'I know you're in here. You know you aren't allowed unsupervised bathroom visits.'

Stephanie shouted back. 'For Christ's sake, leave me alone! I just want some privacy!'

'We know you've got the phone, Steph. You'll have to give us that. We'll be searching your room. Just come out or we'll put you in the cuffs.'

'No! I'm not going anywhere near you, I hate you!'

Another bang. The sound of the girl crying, then almost screaming. 'Let me go! Let me go!'

Stunned and frozen, Paula peered out the crack in the door. A huge man in a nurse's uniform, tattoos on his burly arms, was dragging a bird-like little girl, her arms behind her in a restraint hold. She wore a flimsy hospital gown that gaped at the back, and she wasn't much bigger than a child of eight. The phone she'd been holding fell from her hand and cracked open on the tiled floor. The man kicked it as he went past, crushing the screen. They went out into the corridor and were gone.

Paula stayed there for a few seconds. They put the girls in restraints? They manhandled them?

When she went downstairs again, Allardyce and Kevin were waiting for her in the lobby. The director's blue eyes seemed to search her. 'Maria lost you there.'

'Oh, I just didn't want to keep her,' Paula said, hoping she sounded casual.

'I hope you got what you came for.' He smiled at her, and she tried to smile back, and failed.

Chapter Nineteen

'So that's the Yews,' said Kevin, reversing out the gate.

'How well do you know Dr Allardyce?'

'Dave? Not that well. We did our training together, back in the year of dot, that's all.'

'Is there any controversy about his approach there?'

'Oh, of course. There's always controversy in this area of work. It'd be strange if there wasn't.'

Paula thought of the girl she'd heard sobbing. *Please, please, let me come home.* Something about it just didn't seem right, and she was glad when they reached the airport and home was almost in sight.

'OK now. You've got your boarding pass?' Kevin leaned out the car door.

'Yes, yes, I have everything. Thanks for the lift.'

'And you'll keep in touch this time? Bring the wee girl over to visit, maybe?'

'Yeah,' lied Paula. 'We'll definitely have to do that. You better go, look, the traffic warden's coming. Bye!'

A vague sense of dissatisfaction tugged at her as she carted her case through security, depositing phone and toiletries in the container, slipping off her shoes. It must be because she was in London. She needed to turn her back on the place again, and return to where her life was now. Kiss Aidan, and see Maggie if she made good time, smell the top of the kid's curly head and feel chubby arms round her neck.

She took out her boarding pass and passport and joined the straggling queue to get on. Then her heart did the same leap it had been doing all day. Ridiculous. Of course the flight was full of men in suits. One with fair hair wasn't unusual at all. She looked again, waiting for the dip, the slowing pulse that followed when her heart realised it wasn't him. It didn't come. She stared, puzzled, at the tall man feeling in his jacket, taking out his passport. It actually was him. It was Guy Brooking, on the Aer Lingus flight to Belfast.

For a moment she wondered if she could dodge him – get on the plane behind him, keep her head down. But that was daft. He'd only be going to Northern Ireland for one reason, and that was to consult on their case. So she waited for his gaze to swing round, and saw his visible double-take. She put on an awkward smile. He was coming towards her, moving back in the queue.

'Paula? God, hello. How are you?'

'Fine!' She thought he was thinking about kissing her cheek, so she stepped back, gesturing wildly. 'How are you? I mean, I'm over to do some digging on our current case. Alice Morgan.'

'Right, right. I've been called in to consult.'

'Yes, they said you might . . .'

'Right. Shall we . . .'

Side by side they shuffled onto the plane. She was silently hoping there might be only single seats left, but the plane was quiet. She'd have to sit beside him. He hefted her bag into the locker for her – he was always so damn polite – and let her sit at the window. 'So! It's good to see you. Been a while.'

'Yeah. How's everything?'

'Oh, OK. I'm enjoying being back on gangs, I guess. I feel I can make a difference. But I suppose I still think about missper – it sort of gets to you, doesn't it?'

She knew just what he meant. For her, murder was sad and frightening and could make her furious, but it was an answered question. What really made the pulse beat in her blood was finding the ones who were only lost – the ones you could still help, maybe, and bring home. Like Alice Morgan. 'And – the family?' She could hardly get the words out.

'All right. Katie's going to Bath University in a few months. I can hardly believe it. How's Maggie?' He asked the question lightly. As if the last time he'd seen her he hadn't still thought he might be Maggie's father. She'd never told him he wasn't. But she'd never told him she still wasn't sure, either.

'Oh, she's great. Getting big, talking.' She would have shown him a picture if he'd asked, but he didn't, and the moment slid away.

'Does she have the red hair then?' Another light question.

'Yes, God love her, she'll be as red as me, I think.' In the following silence, Paula tried not to think about what she knew of genetics, of recessive traits, and red hair and fair hair and dark.

Guy shifted in his seat and said with a different tone: 'Tell me about this case, then.'

She sagged with relief. The lost – this was solid ground to her and Guy. They'd always worked well together, their emotional tangles aside. She told him what she knew – missing girl, blood, no body, suspiciously non-upset friends, disappearance of another girl years before, the unproven rape allegation against Peter. Guy's frown deepened as she spoke. 'And the relic is gone too?'

'Yep. I think the church trust are more upset about that than about Alice.'

He pointed to the forensics on his briefing sheets. 'And the blood. This protein here – I've seen this before. It's found in uterine lining. I worked this one case where a woman's blood was on a man's jeans, and he tried to say she'd had a nose bleed. She said he'd raped her while she was menstruating. They tested it and found this protein, and he confessed.'

She shook her head. 'But that doesn't make sense. Alice hadn't had periods for years, she was severely anorexic.'

'Hmm. Well, OK. What about this shed you mentioned?'

'The food? Also strange. I've just been told Alice was anorexic, strictly not bulimic. She had a horror of vomiting, even.'

'But this is classic binge food.' Guy tapped the paper again. 'I wonder.' He spoke slowly, over the whoosh of the airplane as it cut through the clouds. 'I wonder if she'd started eating again. Gained weight, got her periods back.'

After a minute's thought, Paula shook her head again. 'No one said she looked any different. And there were her selfies – Alice posted a picture of herself on Facebook every day. It's a thinspo thing – she'd pose in her bra or a crop top so that people could say how thin she was. She kept putting those up every day, even on the day she went. She was skinny, dangerously so.' How she missed this, bouncing ideas off him, knowing he wanted the answers as much as she did. With Aidan she was always aware that he wanted something else, to find the story, to tell the truth no matter who it hurt.

He made a face. 'Facebook. I hate the thing. Those kids put their life up there, and they don't see how it can be used against them.' Paula knew a lot of the work he did was focused on getting girls out of gangs, saving them from a lifetime of exploitation masquerading as love.

The intercom clicked on, and the pilot announced their descent. Guy leaned forward to put the papers in his bag under the seat, and his hand brushed hers. She saw him notice her engagement ring, and held her breath. He paused for a second, then pulled back. 'Sorry.'

He didn't know she was engaged. Why would he? He was gone, out of her life. Or at least he had been. She stared ahead, her own hands gripping the chair arms, and they spent the rest of the flight in silence. But as they hit tarmac, and he undid his belt, she felt a deep sense that things were back to how they should be – she was hunting for a lost girl, and Guy was at her side, helping her look.

WhatsApp conversation

Katy: *Ola whatsapp buddies* ☺

Dermot: *Hi*

Peter: *Is this a good idea? Can they not tap into it and stuff* ☹

Dermot: *No it's secure. I checked. We need a way to keep our stories straight*

Katy: *I'm kind of freakin out with the police in and stuff. Do u think they'll find out what happened*

Dermot: *If they do we'll all go to jail. That's why we need to get this straight.*

Peter: ☹☹

Katy: *What will we do? Maybe if we tell them about it*

Peter: *No way we need to throw them off the sent. Don't know why you said I was with you that nite Katy . . . can they not check stuff like that*

Dermot: *It's scent duh. But yeah Katy don't just say stuff like that. Stick to what we agreed OK?*

Peter: ☹

Katy: *Um well I just was trying to help*

Dermot: *We can't tell them anything. Guys this is serious – I need to finish my degree this time or I'm screwed. This is my last chance.*

Katy: *Im just really freakin out*

Peter: *Chill dude. They don't know nothing*

Dermot: *It'll be OK if we keep our stories right*

Katy: *I was thinkin we should do something like start a campaign to find her? That's what people do you know like a Find Alice thing on Twitter?*

Dermot: *It's too risky. We have to just keep our heads down. The police know something is up and they will be watching us. I think just don't do anything for now. They have no proof.*

Peter: *Shit man* ☹

Dermot: *Just don't lose it. Either of you.*

Chapter Twenty

Aidan was in bed when she got in. Going up the stairs, tired and sweaty, she saw him through the door, turning over in bed. She eased open Maggie's door, creeping over to the child. Maggie was sucking her thumb, her other hand clamped tight on the one-eyed elephant that had been a gift from Pat (the other eye had been lost in a terrifying yet ultimately non-dangerous swallowing incident). When Paula had lived in London, when she'd been that person, Maggie had not existed. Home now was this small border town, superstitious, backwards. This drab terraced house with the same God-awful lime bathroom and Formica cupboards. This little girl, knocked out in sleep so deep she didn't stir when Paula brushed the curls from her face. Looking at the curve of the child's forehead, holding her breath. She wished the builders had finished already, so this place could be sold. There seemed to be a moment approaching where she could move on with her life, marry Aidan, put the past behind her. But if it didn't happen soon, she was afraid she was going to miss it.

She cleaned her teeth and washed her greasy face, then undressed in the dark beside Aidan, fitting her legs around him. She'd grown used to having his body there, after a lifetime of sleeping alone. She breathed in, but there was no reek of tobacco, just his skin, the smell of him. He stirred, reaching for her arm and pulling it round him, dropping a kiss on her wrist. 'Well. How are things in the big smoke?'

'Oh, you know. I didn't really go to the big smoky part.'

'Find out much?'

'Mm. Maybe.'

He yawned. ''Kay. Get some sleep. I'll get up with Mags, you can lie on.'

He was good to her. He'd be a good husband, for the most part, even if he did sneak a fag now and again. She could tell from Aidan's breathing he'd gone to sleep, so she lay in the dark and thought about how and when she'd tell him Guy Brooking was back.

The next morning was like going back in time two years. When Paula entered the station, there was a crowd of people around the meeting table, and she knew just who they'd be talking to. Sure enough, Guy was in the middle, chatting to Gerard and a uniformed Avril. More surprising was the sight of Bob Hamilton, in slacks and a short-sleeved shirt, though he'd been retired two years.

'All the old band back together, eh?' Corry had come up behind her.

'Not all,' said Paula, as lightly as she could. She felt sure everyone would be watching, see how she greeted him. They'd tried to be discreet about the situation but Ballyterrin wasn't the kind of place you could keep secrets, especially not in a team of six. She turned her engagement ring on her finger, hard and cool. She hadn't told Aidan, in the bustle of getting Maggie out that morning. She should have. She'd tell him tonight.

'Boss is back,' said Gerard, giving her a thumbs-up.

'Yes, I know. Are we reviewing the case?'

'I've pulled some slides together.' Guy indicated the laptop on the table. Of course he had. Guy was a great one for PowerPoints. Corry nudged Paula; Willis Campbell was coming across the office towards them, buttoning the jacket of his suit – he and Guy were about to have a menswear-off.

Campbell's irritated gaze took them all in, alighting first on Paula. 'Dr Maguire. Any reason you were wasting time on a trip to London, when there's so much to do here?'

Paula tried to speak calmly. 'Well, sir, we wanted to learn more about Alice's teenage years – she made a suicide attempt when she was fifteen. I was trying to put together a profile, see if she might have done it again.'

'That could have been done by mainland officers – especially with DI Brooking on his way over to us.'

'We weren't actually made aware of that,' said Corry neutrally. 'Which was a shame. I mean, it would have been useful to know.'

'Well, I'm here now,' said Guy easily, standing up and extending a hand to Willis. 'DCI Campbell, is it? Nice to meet you.'

Willis shook it, eyeing Guy. 'Good of you to come.'

'Not at all, always lovely to be back in Ballyterrin.'

Willis, a Belfastman to the core, looked as if he seriously doubted this. 'Well, you're up to speed on the case?'

'DI Brooking has kindly agreed to undertake a seven-day review,' said Corry, again in a neutral tone. 'Constable Wright. We don't need you for this, thanks.'

Avril went. 'Bye, DCI Brooking, glad to see you back.'

'And you. The uniform suits you!'

Damn him and damn his easy charm. Paula thought of Aidan, and the mound of his dirty socks that was amassing behind the bedroom door. She didn't see why she should pick them up, and Aidan apparently had selective blindness for that part of the floor. And loss of smell. The stand-off was now reaching day five and she knew she'd crack soon.

She turned to Bob as Willis Campbell told Guy a few facts about the case he most likely already knew. 'How are you? Linda and Ian well?'

'Oh aye.' He looked out of place in the station, seeming a little bemused by the lights and noise of ringing phones. 'How's the wee one?'

'Oh, she's a dote.' She should take Maggie to visit, she realised. Try to make up for the mistakes of the past, even if they weren't all hers, even if she didn't know what some of them were.

'Well, shall we get started?' Guy looked round at them.

Willis seemed wrong-footed by Guy's particular blast of efficient charm. 'All right then. I'll leave you to it. I hope you can come up with some ideas for us, DI Brooking; so far we have basically nothing. Alice's father is not particularly happy with our efforts, and no doubt you've seen it's all over the news.' He went to his office, eyes darting left and right over the unnaturally quiet and neat incident room.

Guy said, 'Bob has kindly agreed to run us through the Yvonne O'Neill case.' Calling him Bob now, not Sergeant Hamilton. Guy, however, was just as much in control as ever, his suit jacket over the back of a chair, hands braced on it. Paula tried not to look, and did anyway. He still wore his wedding ring. Of course he did, he was still married. Stupid. Only difference was she had a ring on her finger too now. An anchor to cling to. 'Bob, would you?' Guy handed over to him.

Paula and Corry took their seats, picking up Guy's

trademark stapled documents. Bob cleared his throat un-comfortably, as a picture of Yvonne appeared on the screen. 'It was a long time ago, but we'd only one real suspect. Anderson Garrett.'

'The neighbour.' Guy was already on top of the case. 'But he had an alibi?'

'Has one for both cases,' said Corry. 'At work in town the day Yvonne went, and with his mother when Alice vanished. The hospital confirmed it. Anyway, that volunteer was with him when they got into the church and found the blood.'

'Still, it's too much of a link to ignore,' Guy said. 'We should re-check all the details of his alibi. DS Monaghan – well done on the promotion, by the way – you could get a DC to do that.'

'Will do. And thank you, sir.' Gerard gave a best-in-class smile and Paula did a mini eye-roll. Guy and his charm again.

'There was no one else in Yvonne's case?' he asked.

'No.' Bob shook his head. 'We thought maybe some itinerant fella. Could have pulled her into a car. Same person as the Wicklow disappearances, maybe, if you know about those . . . but it was so far out of the way.'

'You discounted a sectarian motive?'

'We considered it, aye. Given what else was going on. But there wasn't a body.'

Guy examined the file. 'Yvonne was last seen going up the path to the church.'

'Right,' said Corry. 'She'd definitely been in the church, because the flowers were there.'

'And Alice – last seen in there, blood on the steps, picture of Yvonne left – did we find out where that came from?'

We. Who was this we? Paula and Corry exchanged a quick look. 'It was taken from Yvonne's mother's house,' supplied Corry.

'By whom?'

'We don't know. Maybe Dermot Healy. He's been there too.'

Guy frowned down at the papers. 'The date being the same . . . that's strange.'

'Thirty-two years later. Lúnasa – that's an old Celtic fire feast. A time of sacrifice.'

'Are the press onto that angle?'

'No. They're mostly interested in the relic and Alice's father.'

Guy said, 'That's probably good. Case like this, you get a lot of crackpots. Is there anything there, something about the relic? Cults, Satanists . . . burglary even?'

'I'd say burglary,' said Corry. 'But where's Alice's body? And why's Yvonne's picture there?'

'Right. So our main possibilities.' Guy sketched on a whiteboard. 'Robbery gone wrong; abduction by person or persons unknown, possibly the same who took Yvonne in 1981; or—'

'She ran away,' said Corry. 'Which is what everyone, even her parents, is telling us. No one is a bit worried about that girl.'

'And what do you think, DS Corry, did she run away?'

'Why the blood? Why the photo? Why nothing on her bank account or phone?' Corry shook her head. 'And where's the bloody relic?'

'I was also interested in her social media usage,' said Guy, glancing at his watch and then the door. 'I hope you don't mind, but I asked the tech team to check her posts again, and try to trace her phone signal.'

'Tech team? Do you mean Trevor the teenager?' asked Corry.

'Well, yes. He's a bit older than that, isn't he?'

'He looks about fifteen,' she said. 'Well, did he spot anything? We didn't find her phone. No sign of it.'

'Here he is now.'

In the door, holding a laptop aloft, lanyard swinging, came Trevor. He was a cheerful youth of twenty-four, given to zany T-shirts and technobabble about the latest computer games. Paula always wanted to sit him down with a milky drink and tell him to have a rest. 'Well, well, how're yous?' He dispensed hellos to the team.

'Find something?' asked Guy.

'Well, wait till you hear. Your woman – Alice is her name?'

'Yes.'

'Her phone's just been switched on. Picked up a signal.'

'Where is it?' demanded Corry. 'Don't explain it, just tell me.' Paula was on her feet, thinking – if they could find her, if she was safe after all . . .

'Donegal,' said Trevor. 'Over the border. You guys should get down there now.'

WhatsApp conversation

Dermot: OMG. *Guys go online right now*
Katy: *What?*
Katy: *Shit*
Katy: *The phone. SHIT*
Peter: *Someone's messin about maybe. Stole it.*
Katy: *Did one of you?*

Peter: *Uh no fuck's sake what are you saying*

Dermot: *Don't be stupid. Think what's the most likely thing.*

Peter: *Guys this is freaking me out. Maybe the police will find stuff on it. Why's it been turned on now?*

Dermot: *Stop it. You're not helping. Just calm the fuck down and wait to see what happens. They don't even have the phone they just tracked a signal from it*

Katy: *SHIT I can't believe this*

Dermot: *Look calm down it doesn't mean anything*

Peter: *Err how can you say that it might be her*

Katy: *This is so weird. I mean maybe we should just tell them what happened. She could be trying to send a message.*

Dermot: *Don't be a retard. If she's dead she can't send a message can she.*

Peter: **Fuck sake Dermot they could be reading this**

Dermot: *They're not. They don't even know how, they're stuck in the dark ages.*

Katy: *Err what do you mean D?*

Dermot: *You told the police she'd hurt herself. Make your mind up.*

Katy: *Oh well I don't know do I. I just think maybe we should tell them the truth*

Dermot: *We're not telling them anything. But both of you have to calm down. I can't do this by myself*

Chapter Twenty-One

'Look who it is!'

A familiar face greeted Paula as she got to the shore of Lough Derg, a dark oval of water on the border with Donegal. An invisible line on a map, but a different country all the same. Older now, a little less hair, a little more poise, Fiacra Quinn wasn't the angel-faced boy he'd been, but all the same she was so pleased to see him she gave him a big hug before remembering where she was. 'It's good to see you. It's been ages.'

When the MPRU disbanded, Fiacra, nursing unrequited love for Avril and guilt at his role in Gerard being shot, had gone back to work in the Southern police force. Cross-border cooperation was back to being intermittent and suspicious, the progress made by the unit all swept away.

Corry was watching them. 'If we can hold back on the emotional reunions for now; this isn't *Surprise Surprise*.'

'What's that?' said Fiacra, who was only twenty-seven.

'Never mind. God, I feel old sometimes.'

Paula kept sneaking glances at her, surprised to see Helen Corry wearing combats with zips along the side. She looked like a blonde Lara Croft.

'I know, I know,' she said, seeing the look. 'Reject from a nineties girl band. But we need to get into ditches, ponds, go digging. It'll be mucky.'

Digging – because while they said they were looking for Alice alive, they were also prepared to find her body, maybe lying in some grubbed-up shallow grave like the carcass of an animal. Her phone being switched on, that gave some hope – but for now, not quite enough.

Corry was questioning Fiacra. 'So the phone signal came from near here. Have you had any sightings?'

Fiacra's easy-going manner had also changed over time. He was more efficient, less affable. 'I went over to the island to ask that lot, though they weren't keen to let me in. One of the pilgrims thought they might have seen a girl on the lake shore, two days ago. They didn't report it before because they've no news over there, see, and phones are banned. They didn't know anyone was missing.'

Paula was nodding. Corry looked baffled. 'And for the non-Catholics?'

Fiacra explained, pointing over to the huddle of buildings on the lake's small island. 'Lough Derg. It's like a retreat. You stay on the island, and you fast and pray, and there's no contact with the outside world.' He indicated some small skiffs, lapping in the waves on the shore. 'Look, you have to go over on a boat. And guess what, on the day the girl was spotted, one of them had come loose. It was out floating in the middle of the lake.'

Paula looked at the pitch-black lake. Imagined being down there in that, the choking weeds, the silent waters closing over your head. Lough Derg – the name came from the Irish for lake of the red eye. Red like the blood in the church. Same place Yvonne had gone, atoning for her imagined sins.

'Fasting,' repeated Corry.

'That's right. The idea is they don't eat while they're

there, and they walk round in bare feet and stuff. You can have black tea but that's it.'

'Weird.'

But Paula knew what she was thinking. It might seem like paradise to Alice, already starving herself and living in a damp cottage. 'Will they talk to us?' she asked Fiacra.

'They've not been so far. It's all religious types. Practically had to recite my catechism to get in. I showed them Alice's photo and they said she'd not been over. But if that was her on the shore—'

He didn't need to say it. They all knew. Corry took a few steps, the rough sand of the beach crunching under her boots. 'How did she get all the way here, if she came of her own accord? She didn't have a car, did she?'

'Not that we know of,' said Paula. 'She might have stolen one, I suppose.'

'I'll get them to check for any stolen vehicles.' Corry keyed in some notes on her BlackBerry. 'I want a word with those people over there. An island retreat – it'd be the perfect place if you wanted to disappear. Especially if no one's been watching the news, you could hide in plain sight.'

'Should we—' Fiacra gestured awkwardly to the lake, as still as an eye full of unshed tears. Paula thought of the expense of a dive team, trawling in zero visibility, how long it would take. Especially if there was still a chance of finding her alive.

'I can't on a random sighting,' said Corry. 'Too expensive.'

'This isn't exactly random now, is it?' said Fiacra. When he'd first joined the MPRU, he'd been too scared to look Helen Corry in the face. But she'd gone down and he'd gone up, and here they were meeting in the middle. 'And look – there's this.'

He was on his hunkers now, lifting aside some bracken with gloved hands. There in the mud of the shore, tracks were still visible, where the plants had sheltered them from the overnight rain. Tyre prints. Corry bent and looked. 'All right. Let's get these looked at. Have you a gait analyst over here, in case there's footprints?'

Paula remembered the joke circulating the incident room after Corry's demotion, that she'd been brought down by Gaitgate – after her lover Dr Lorcan Finney, a forensics expert, had faked the results of footwear analysis. Three people had died as a result. It wasn't much of a joke.

She looked over to the island, glinting in the afternoon sun. The lake was impenetrable. Like Alice's life. Was she in there? Had she stolen a boat, floated out there to the deep iris of the lake, then let herself go? Would you take a long breath before you did that, or try to let it all go, sink as easily and quickly as a stone? Or maybe someone had thrown her in. Maybe she'd fought and screamed for life.

'Let's do a fingertip search,' Corry was saying, standing up. 'All this area. Did you say you have volunteers? We'll need all hands on deck. If Alice was here, she might still be – or maybe she wasn't by herself.'

Fiacra said, 'They're already here. Should someone go to the island again, though? They might prefer to talk to your lot.'

'I was going to send Dr Maguire.'

Paula didn't mind. Getting a poke around the island would be right up her street – and she was good at hearing the things people wouldn't say. 'How will I get over?' Her eye was caught by a tall, straight figure coming across the shore to them. Guy Brooking, in a blue polo shirt and jeans.

He spotted Fiacra and shook his hand enthusiastically.

'So, it's Detective Sergeant Garda now, is it? Well done, that's excellent.'

'All thanks to your teaching, sir.'

'I'm sure that's not true. You wanted me, DS Corry?' The new title sounded odd in his mouth, but he didn't let it show. It seemed wrong that Corry and Fiacra were now the same rank.

'Yes, I wondered if you were free to visit the island with Dr Maguire here. There's been a possible sighting of Alice from one of the guests.'

Paula glared at Corry, who met her gaze with a bland smile.

'Of course.' Guy seemed unperturbed by the request. 'Shall we, Paula?'

'Our Fiacra's all grown up, isn't he?'

'Oh don't,' she said, leaning against the side of the boat, a slight breeze lifting her hair and cooling her damp skin. 'I feel about a hundred already.'

'Not at all, you haven't aged a day.'

She wished he would stop being so nice to everyone. The small boat was skimming them over the lake, and Paula was trying to remember what she'd learned at school about pilgrimages to Lough Derg. Fasting for three days, walking around the island in bare feet, praying. What would Guy make of it, fresh from grappling with inner-London gang warfare?

'It's nice to be back,' he said again, breathing in the fresh air of the lake. The shifting clouds overhead changed it from black to blue and back to brown again. 'I forgot how peaceful it was.'

'Don't be fooled by a bit of sun. You know what good weather causes.'

'Sunburn? I've seen plenty of that so far. Do people here not know about SPF?'

'No, we find it hard to believe the sun could ever be hot enough to burn us. Anyway, I was talking about our annual riot season. Stick around long enough and you'll see.' She spoke lightly, but she wasn't sure if she wanted him to go back right away or not. She couldn't deny it was good to be working with him again.

Guy stretched. He was wearing sunglasses, so she couldn't see his eyes, which was a small blessing. 'Let's see what this lot have to say.'

Chapter Twenty-Two

'I can't take you onto the main island. People come here for rest and reflection, it would disturb them too much to have questions.'

'Of course.' Paula was glad, despite the difficulties, that she'd come with Guy rather than Corry, who could be abrasive and impatient with religious people. The manager, a man called Callum Manus, spoke in soft tones. They were in the visitors' centre, which was open to the public. Beyond that was the rest of the island, tranquil and green. Squinting out the window, Paula could see people walking far off, small dots in the afternoon sun.

'So is there anything you can tell us?' Guy was asking. 'You haven't seen Ms Morgan?'

Callum Manus had looked at Alice's picture for several moments, with a creased brow. He had a pale, bloodless face. 'I don't recognise her, no. But sometimes people come here for a reason. They may not want anyone to know where they are.'

'We understand that, but Alice's parents are very worried about her.' It was what you always said, but in this case Paula wasn't sure it was true. 'If we could be sure no harm had come to her—'

'I don't recognise her, as I said.' He passed the picture back. 'As I told the Garda who was over, a boat was found floating in the lake two days back. And one of our American guests thought he'd seen someone on the shore around that time. Wearing a red jumper, he thought. It was too far away to see anything else.'

Red like an Oakdale hoody, maybe. Guy said, 'Is he still here, the witness?'

'No. Gone back to the States.'

'Can we have his details?'

Manus hesitated. 'I'll contact him and ask. We have to respect people's privacy here, you see. We don't always know why they come to us.'

Guy glanced at Paula. She asked, 'Mr Manus, I know this is a place for people to retreat to . . . and I feel it would have been very appealing to Alice. You fast here?'

'Guests fast for three days. Most find it a very spiritual experience. There are no phones here, no news, no distractions. It cuts through everything.' He spoke simply, and she believed him.

'So – I'm sorry to ask again, but are you absolutely sure she didn't come here? Do you check people's ID when they book in?'

'No, why would we?' He looked puzzled. 'I don't recognise the picture. But we give people their privacy. I wouldn't have looked too closely at everyone. But she's very . . . striking. I think I'd remember.'

With her frail bones showing through the skin, Alice would have stood out all right. Paula nodded. 'Thank you.'

'I'll be praying for her. That she's found.'

'By us, you mean?'

He looked at her. 'By you, or by herself. There are other ways to be lost than just not knowing where you are.'

It was similar to something Dermot had said. Paula couldn't argue with that, so she and Guy took their leave.

'All these people came to help with the search?'

Corry spoke in low tones. 'People want to find her – and the relic too, it unsettles them that it's gone.' The village hall, co-opted into headquarters to search the area round the lake, echoed with voices, feet tripping off the parquet floor. It smelled of village plays, and music competitions, and meetings of the parish council. If they closed their eyes it could have been a pleasant gathering. Paula looked round at the variety of people – some in Oakdale hoodies and jeans, as well as older people from the area, farmers, off-duty police. Kemal the CSI was there, looking pale and attentive. Presumably in case they did find something. Alice's father was circulating, shaking people by the hand, thanking them. Paula saw he and several others wore a T-shirt with Alice's face on it – her cheekbones standing out sharp as knives. There was, however, no sign of Alice's supposed best friends – Peter, Katy, or Dermot.

She saw Guy across the room, his blue T-shirt bringing out the shifting colours of his eyes. He'd been perfectly reasonable with her all day. Pleasant, like a colleague. Maybe that was how he saw her now.

She tried to focus. Fiacra was on stage, giving the briefing. 'Ladies and gentlemen,' he said. Not too loud, not too quiet. 'We'd like to thank you so much for being here today. Alice's family are also very grateful for your support.' Tony Morgan, who stood behind him, nodded his head in acknowledgement. 'As you know, there was possibly a sighting of Alice here a few days ago.' He spoke reassuringly as a ripple of low-level interest went through the room.

'There's every chance that if it was her, we'll find other signs in the area. So we're looking for anything and everything that suggests Alice was here – damaged bushes, signs of a struggle, anything. When she disappeared, she was wearing blue jeans, brand name Prada, and an Oakdale College hoody.' Helpfully, Alice had posted a selfie in those clothes on the day she'd last been seen. In it she looked serious, presenting herself in profile to the camera phone in her hand, lifting up the jumper to show her flat stomach.

'That's all,' said Fiacra. 'Please follow your assigned group leader and fan out – but remember to stay close and shout out as soon as you see anything. Please, most important of all – if you do see something, don't touch it. It'll be your first instinct, but if you do it'll banjax all the evidence and cause a terrible headache.' Here he smiled, and some people smiled back, grateful for a release of tension. 'Thank you.'

There was movement, feet on the floor, chairs scraped back. Paula watched the team members move out ahead of the volunteers, the CSIs in their suits and masks. Alice's father remained on stage, talking to Fiacra. Outside the hall, people were heading into the woods around the lake, walking slowly, pacing the ground, looking for any clue as to where Alice might be found. Paula felt a breeze rise to her from the dark water, and shivered slightly in her vest top.

Kemal went by, walking slowly, and she smiled at him in passing. She was just thinking, *He looks pale*, when she saw his face go blank, and he stumbled suddenly against the wall and crashed to the floor. Around him, volunteers dashed to his aid.

'God! Are you all right?' She was moving forward, pushing through the gathered band of people.

His eyes fluttered as he sat up. 'I'm so sorry, Dr Maguire. I must have fainted. I'm fasting, you see. And the days are so long here—'

It took her a moment to figure it out. 'Oh! It's Ramadan?'

'Yes, that's right.'

She didn't know what to say – oh, that must be bad – or what one of the station canteen women had rather brilliantly replied on hearing he was fasting – 'Oh God love you, pet. Will I make you a wee ham sandwich?' But it made her think. Fasting all day, no food passing your lips till the sun set. People still did it, all over the world. It was happening on their doorstep right now, at Lough Derg. It wasn't only people like Alice who tried to control everything that went into their bodies. Alice had just taken it that bit further.

Paula realised a girl was kneeling beside them, having lurched to help when Kemal fell down. She wore an Oakdale hoody, like they all seemed to. 'Thank you, I think he's OK now.'

'It passes,' the girl told Kemal, ignoring Paula. 'If you're really faint you could try chewing on something, like a bit of leather or plastic. It helps.'

He was getting up, straightening his boiler suit, seeming embarrassed. 'Thank you, miss. Apologies, I'll be fine now.'

'Did you know Alice?' Paula asked, standing aside to let Kemal up.

The girl, who had glasses and short, ragged, dark hair, didn't answer for a minute. 'I wouldn't say I knew her, no.'

'Well, it's kind of you to help.'

She just nodded, putting up a hand to pull at her hair, and Paula saw her nails were bitten to the quick, smudged around with some dark tidemark. Were all the Oakdale kids messed up?

'Could we stop here for a minute?'

Corry glanced at her. They were almost back in the centre of Ballyterrin, drawing slowly through the town in the end-of-day traffic. The evening sun touched the windows with fire. 'At the shops?'

'Yeah. I just need to . . . sort something.'

'I see. Well, I'll pull up, but if the traffic lot come you can explain to them yourself that we're attending a wedding-dress emergency.'

Paula made a face at her. 'It is an emergency. Apparently I should have ordered it a year ago or something.'

'Well, you better go quick then.'

In the shop, the girl looked up as the door jangled, a pleasant smile pasted on her made-up face, fading as she recognised her difficult customer. 'Oh, hello there—'

'Hi. Right. Have you any dress that's less than five hundred quid? If so I'll take it.'

'Do you not want to try on—?'

'No. It'll do, if it's white and froofy. Oh, and has straps, I can't do strapless. If I try on one more dress I swear I'll spontaneously combust.'

The girl made an 'it'll cost you' face, the exact same one the builders always did when Paula asked if they'd any idea how long her current sink-less and cooker-less state might go on for. 'I don't know now . . .'

'I'll take anything. Look, I'll have one of these – I fit into them before, didn't I?'

'Well, yes, they're sample size, but I need to measure you—'

'I'm a twelve.'

'And what will you be at the wedding?'

Paula narrowed her eyes. 'The same, I'd say. It's next week.'

'Oh, you're not—?'

'No, I am not on a diet. Do I need to be?'

'Oh no, no, sure you must have snapped right back after the wean, aren't you lucky!'

Paula stared at the woman, who had gone quite flushed and was fiddling with the cash register. 'OK then. Just get it ready for me. Thanks.'

'Do I need to lose weight?' She slammed the door of the house behind her.

Aidan blinked slowly. 'Is that a trick psychological question? Because I don't have a PhD, you know, I'm just a humble hack.'

'No. It's just everyone keeps saying oh of course you'll be dieting for the wedding or oh Paula won't want a biscuit she's her dress to fit into.'

'You got a dress then, I take it? Well, that's good. Did you not get one that fits?'

'I think you're meant to order it in a too-small size, then shrink into it. So do I need to lose weight?'

Aidan lowered the paper and squinted at her.

'Oh my God! You looked!'

'How else am I meant to know?'

'You just know! Like, it's in your head, if Paula needs to lose weight or not.'

He put the paper up again. 'Maguire, you look great to me, always did. But if you want to, I guess a few pounds wouldn't hurt.'

'Wouldn't hurt!'

'I said if you want to! Ah Jesus.' He went back to the news. 'The situation in Syria is easier to navigate than this.'

'*Wouldn't hurt,*' she muttered, going out. 'I'll wouldn't hurt you.'

Aidan called, 'Come back, Senator George Mitchell, your peace-keeping skills are needed in the Maguire–O'Hara household.'

She shouted back, 'The peace process would never have held if Gerry Adams'd told Ian Paisley it "wouldn't hurt" if he lost a few pounds.'

In response, the sound of the TV came on. Paula stomped upstairs. Conveniently, not having to tell him who she'd been working with that day. She'd tell him tomorrow. Maybe.

Alice

I've been thinking and thinking. What did I do wrong? What did I do to make it happen? Was it my fault for doing the stupid drugs in the first place?

It was my first time with that stuff. I'd told him and told him, please look after me, please make sure I'm OK. Of course I will, he said. You can trust me. I thought it was nice, how we were friends, how he hadn't minded too much when I kissed him those few times, even let him take off my top, and then wouldn't go any further. He's cute, of course, but I just couldn't. I can't be like that.

He slipped me this little Rizla package in the middle of dinner in the buttery. Are you sure? Go on. And we smiled at each other and swallowed them down. He'd said it would be half an hour for it to kick in, plenty of time to wander down to the boathouse, meet the others – at least that's what I thought.

Right away, almost, within the time it took to put our plates on our trays and walk to the corridor, I felt my pulse racing, like a bat was trapped in my throat. I thought I was just freaking out, looking for signs that weren't there. I had time to say to him, I feel weird, and then it really hit. Everything was blurry, the colours streaked along the world like water on glass. I was suddenly intensely aware of how everything felt – my card in my hand, so shiny and cold, the wool of my jumper, so scratchy. I marvelled at it, both amazed and afraid at the same time.

I walked with him out of the dining hall – people catching on my face – are you – is she – and him making me move, saying it's fine, it's fine, Jesus, don't be weird, OK? Then we were at the boathouse, and Katy and Dermot were there, and Dermot put a blanket round me, and took me inside where Katy had all cushions and candles, and I could have lain down right there, I was so relieved to be in somewhere safe. She's just freaking out a bit, *said Peter, and I felt his hand bat at me, clumsily. I sat down. Katy hugged me, and I smelled her familiar smell of sweat and cheap perfume with an undernote of blood, but right then it made me so happy.* Oh Alice! It's going to be OK. What's wrong with her? I had some and I feel fine.

You snorted it, *said Dermot, pushing up his glasses.* Jesus, how much did you give her?

I dunno, like half.

Fuck's sake. She's five foot two and it's her first time. You basically just roofied her.

And I thought I heard him say then – which is kind of your style. *But Peter didn't hear, or decided not to, and then in a bit it all kicked in, and even Dermot was smiling, and we all sat on a rug holding onto each other, the four of us, and the only way I can think to describe it is that: afraid and amazed, all at the same time.*

That's the last thing I can remember before I woke up. And everything was different.

Chapter Twenty-Three

She was late in the next morning, having been distracted by early morning calls to the builders (cast-iron promises on their mothers' graves that the work would be finished by the following week), the wedding hotel (what vegetarian options did they want and would they like to pay an extra £5 a head for chair covers; no, they would not), Saoirse (what did Paula want her to do with her hair), and Pat (what time did she want the wedding car to come at). Since this was the first time Paula had even heard they were having wedding cars, she arrived grouchy and out of breath, to find Corry and Guy already hard at work. He had his sleeves rolled up, tie swinging free, and she had her hair in a bun, as they examined something on the conference table. Paula was already sweating, hairs escaping from her ponytail. 'Sorry,' she said breathlessly. 'Family emergency.'

'Hope it's all sorted out.' Corry knew rightly it was wedding-related.

Paula ignored her gimlet stare. 'What's going on?'

'Well, this is our lucky day. The search in the woods – we found a phone. Same type as Alice's. One of the volunteer kids turned it up in the bushes.'

'That's good.' She looked between them; there was something else. 'What?'

Guy said, 'They also found an abandoned car. It's

registered to Anderson Garrett. But he's now claiming it was stolen on the day Alice went missing.'

Paula's heart began to race. If Garrett had taken Alice there . . . 'Does that mean you'll drag the lake?'

Corry looked at her watch. 'If I can get Willis to OK it; he's up to high doh about all this. I'm waiting on his say-so.'

On cue, the man himself approached, barking out criticisms as he swept through the office. 'If we could have fewer dirty dishes on the desks, Constable, thank you, it's not a cafe . . . Oh, Dr Maguire, you're actually here. I'm still waiting for some of these famous insights. Have you anything, anything at all I can tell Lord bloody Morgan about where his daughter is? They need to get back to London, he's an important man.'

Paula shook her head in frustration; she had nothing. She hoped it wasn't the wedding and Maggie, occupying too much of her mind, but this case had left her stumped. 'I'm sorry, sir. The phone, the connection with Yvonne O'Neill . . . I don't know what to recommend.'

'In the meantime we're dragging a lake at great expense. I can't get the Gardaí to even share the costs, since Alice lived in the North.' He eyed her. 'And you have leave booked from next week, I gather.'

'Well, um, yes. I'm getting married.' She hadn't invited Willis. It might have been politically expedient, but Paula wasn't much good at currying favour.

He glared as if he would have liked to order her to cancel it all, then sighed. 'I suppose it won't make much of a difference. We don't seem to be getting anywhere anyway.'

Guy said, 'We have a number of leads now – the car for one—'

'Well, we should be dealing with those, then, not hanging

about here. I hope I can trust you to handle this, DI Brooking?'

'I'd hope so, yes.' Guy didn't rise to it.

'Well, at least *someone* seems to know what they're doing.' He went, causing another ripple of tidying-up and back-straightening and window-minimising throughout the office.

Corry rolled her eyes and stood up. 'Let's go and talk to Garrett.'

'So we're looking at him again?' Paula said. 'Despite his alibi?'

'Is the Pope Catholic? Well, you would know. We're going to see him. Just a little chat for now; Willis doesn't want him arrested. Not yet, anyway.'

'I hope it won't take long. You'll upset my mother. Could we not go to the station?'

That was odd – usually witnesses had a morbid fear of being hauled in, not seeing a distinction between arrest and interview, but Garrett seemed more concerned about the police arriving at his house. He lived in the large grey farmhouse visible from Alice's cottage, but up close it was cold and unwelcoming. Paula and Corry were in the kitchen, which was dirty, two damp dogs lying on a very old sofa. 'You live here with your mother?' Corry wrinkled her nose in distaste.

'She's upstairs. She's ill – I don't want you to disturb her. Like I said, the station would be better.'

'We like to see witnesses in their homes where possible,' said Corry briskly. 'It may take a while. It may not.'

'Last time the interviews were in the station.' Last time. He meant when Yvonne went missing.

Corry said, 'That's because you were a suspect last time. At the moment you're a witness.' For now, anyway.

He was back to the hand-wringing. Today he wore a large brown jumper, made out of some kind of coarse wool. 'Look, I've already told you my car was stolen. Maybe Alice took it, even, she knew where I parked it.'

'And why didn't you report that at the time?'

'I . . . I didn't want to bother you. You had so much on your plate.'

'You didn't think we'd maybe be interested to know?'

He looked wretched. 'I just didn't want . . . you know, last time. The interviews. Poking round the church, the house, everywhere. All the questions. And it's my fault, really, I usually leave the keys in . . . you know, living out here, you wouldn't think anyone would—' He looked up at them. 'I just couldn't face the questions. My mother couldn't stand it.'

'We need to speak to you all the same. Shall we go into the sitting room?' Corry moved towards the door of the other room.

He remained where he was, rubbing at his hands in the same nervous gesture Paula had noticed at the church. Looking closer, they were red and sore – eczema, perhaps. 'Would you come and sit down, Mr Garrett?' she said, indicating the door.

'I just—' He looked around him. 'I'd feel more comfortable if we spoke out here.'

'Why?' Corry sounded cross. 'The kitchen is quite full.' She meant untidy. Every surface was covered in clutter, plastic shopping bags, bits of scrunched paper, plates with rotting food, dog hair. The smell was sour. By contrast, a relatively tidy sitting room could be seen through the open door.

A voice sounded, which made Paula jump. It seemed to come out of the walls. 'Take the guests into the good front room, Anderson. Where are your manners?'

'I . . .' He twitched at the sound. 'I just—'

'And offer them tea, for goodness' sake.'

'Hello?' Corry peered up the staircase into the gloom. The voice seemed to have come from there. 'I'm Detective Sergeant Corry.'

'Yes, hello. I'm Mrs Garrett. Anderson's mother. I'm afraid I can't get down, I'm wheelchair-bound.' They heard the squeak of a wheel. A shape could almost be seen at the top of the stairs, hunched over.

Corry had her hand on the bannister. 'We're happy to come up, Mrs—'

'No.' Her voice was quiet but firm. 'I'm sorry but I'm not presentable. Do speak to Anderson in the front room. Can I ask if this is about poor Miss Morgan? I didn't know her myself, but of course we're all very concerned.'

'Yes, but we're also here about Yvonne O'Neill.'

Silence. 'Goodness, I haven't heard that name in years.'

'You knew Yvonne, I believe. Family friend?'

'I wouldn't go quite that far. We're neighbours with the family, obviously; in fact our land encircles theirs. They owned part of the access road, which was rather inconvenient. I'd see her and her mother in the lane sometimes, but that was before I had my accident.'

'Yvonne didn't visit you? We heard she was quite good about visiting sick people.'

'I didn't want to be prayed over with popish mantras, I'm afraid. And I'm not sick, Detective. My back is broken. It's not the same.'

'No. Of course.' Corry turned to Paula, widening her

eyes as she spoke. She called up, 'Well, we may need to speak to you again, Mrs Garrett, so perhaps you'd prepare yourself for that?'

'What help might I be?'

'You gave a statement in 1981. Providing information about movements near the church that day.'

'Hardly. I knew my son's activities, that's all. I don't get out much, as you can perhaps tell.'

Garrett's hand-rubbing had gone into overdrive. 'All right,' he broke in. 'If you insist, we'll go in the sitting room. Come on.' He called, 'Mother, I'll be up soon to check on you.'

They went in, breathing in the musty, unused air. Above them, Paula heard the trundle of the wheelchair. She looked around the room – velvet sofa, heavy brass poker set, framed pictures of grim relatives. Despite what his mother had said, Garrett didn't offer tea. He stayed in the doorway, rubbing at his hands. 'Can we make this quick?'

Corry said, 'We have a lot to get through. Is there anything, anything at all you haven't told us about Alice Morgan?'

'Sometimes she stayed in there late. In the church. Forgot to lock it. I told her something like this might happen.'

'Her disappearance?'

'No, no.' He flicked his hands, as if to dismiss that. 'The relic. She was so precious – I knew someone would come for her.'

'She? Alice?'

'No!' He threw his hands up in an almost violent movement. 'The relic!'

'To be clear, you think the relic has been stolen?'

'Yes, yes! I said this. If you look in the right places, it'll still be there. They're stupid, these people. They'll just want the gold. They don't know she's precious. So please, look harder for her? You've been looking round the church, disturbing things, but there's no point in that. She's not there.'

'That's for us to decide.' Corry regarded him stonily. 'Tell us about Yvonne.'

'I – well, I told you this. She was – I knew her a bit, she lived next door. But we weren't friends. I mean we were too . . .'

'What?' asked Paula.

'Different. We were from very different backgrounds.' When he said it, his accent, posh Ballyterrin, became more pronounced. It made him sound like his mother.

'Mr Garrett, are your family Protestant?' asked Corry. Paula had already assumed that they were, because of the name. It was a trap you could fall into in Northern Ireland. Assuming.

'Well, of course. Church of Ireland. And Yvonne was . . . you know, she wanted to be a nun. We were . . . very different.' He wrinkled his nose.

'On the day of the disappearance, where were you?'

He jerked his head, irritated. 'I – you know all this. I told you years ago, again and again. So many interviews. It was very difficult.'

'Tell us again.' Corry was implacable.

'I'd gone to work in town. They checked. Back then.'

'Did you have any clients booked in that day?'

'No. I was working in my office.'

'And no one else saw you there, or driving in or out of town, who could verify this.'

'I don't know. The police were satisfied with what I told them. And my mother said I was out. She's always here, of course. She's paralysed.'

'And on the night of Alice's disappearance? She was last seen at six o'clock, still in the church, when the volunteer left.'

He recited it, as he had before. 'My mother had a fall so I took her into Ballyterrin Hospital. We were there till about eleven. Then I just put her straight to bed. And the next day the volunteer, Maureen, she called up to say the door was open, so I went down with her and – well.'

'You saw the scene as we did, the blood, the picture?'

'Yes – and she was gone.'

'Alice?'

'Well, yes, Alice. And the relic.' He looked down at his hands.

'Then what happened?'

'I – well, I screamed. I saw the blood. It was very upsetting. The volunteer – Mrs Mackin – she was calmer. She said we should go to Alice's cottage to look for her. So we went down – you know it doesn't have a lock. Alice wasn't there, so we came back and waited for the police at the church.'

'You were together the whole time.'

'Yes.' He looked at the celling. 'I should check on my mother.'

'Could you tell us what happened to Mrs Garrett?' Corry's tone had softened slightly.

Garrett unfolded his fingers like a fan and stared at them. 'She came off Millie.'

'Millie?'

'A thoroughbred. Very good stock.'

'A horse? She had a riding accident?'

'It wasn't an accident.' He chewed his lip. 'Millie threw her. Right off, then trampled her. Mother – she really loved Millie. It was a terrible shock, you see. They said she'd never be able to walk again, and she'd need someone to help her always. That's why I stay here with her. She needs me.'

'That's a lot to ask of you, Anderson. How old were you when it happened?'

'Twenty-seven.' He was looking past them; Paula couldn't see what at.

'Did Yvonne disappear the same year?'

'Yes, a few months after.'

'And Yvonne's fiancé was killed too, I believe.'

'Yes. In a car crash. It was a bad year. Very bad. But we got through, and at least she was safe.'

'Your mother?' Corry wasn't following.

Garrett shook his head in annoyance. 'The *relic*. And now she's . . .' His face twisted. Paula found herself hoping he wouldn't cry. 'She's gone,' he said. 'Please find her. Please.'

The same words no one had used yet for the missing girl. 'We're doing our best,' said Corry. 'What else can you tell us? Did you ever see Yvonne with someone?'

His eyes flicked past them. Paula turned, wondering what he was looking at.

'I didn't see anything. I told you all this back then. I don't know what happened. And I didn't see . . . the other one. I wish you'd look harder. She's missing, you see. We need to find her and bring her home.'

He was talking about Saint Blannad again, not about Alice. Again the odd blinking stare. Paula followed his gaze. The mantelpiece, with pictures of the family and a little glass jar on it. Nothing significant.

Chapter Twenty-Four

'It's Alice's phone. We're sure. And her prints are in the car.'

Paula felt a surge of relief at Corry's news. Finally, a trace of Alice. Proof she hadn't just vanished. They'd still couldn't arrest Garrett, but at least this was something. 'What about the dive team, did they find anything?'

Guy, who was at his borrowed desk – and even Willis Campbell couldn't have found a thing out of place on it – shook his head. 'Nothing – it's murky down there, so it takes a while, but they don't think there's anything. Except for someone's massive cache of automatic weapons, that is, but that's hardly surprising in this part of the world.'

'Suppose chucking them in a lake is sort of the same as putting them beyond use,' Corry said drily. Paula smiled.

Guy looked a little wrong-footed, as he usually did when they went all Northern Ireland on him. 'So she's not in the lake, at least. There's DNA in the car, but it's looking like only Garrett and Alice's so far. His would be in it anyway. They'll keep looking.'

Corry had a look on her face Paula hadn't seen for a while – triumphant, excited. That meant they were getting somewhere. She said, 'We got a print off the phone. A nice clear one, right on the top of it, where it's all shiny. The print belongs to Dermot Healy. Get this, Maguire – he was already in the system.'

She couldn't believe it. 'How come?'

'Our wee Dermot has a drugs caution. He was kicked out of Trinity for selling speed in lectures, turns out. He was lucky not to go down for it. Dermot's dad is a high court judge, so it was all hushed up.'

'And the phone, what's on that?'

'It's sort of . . . well, I'll let Trevor tell you. Come with me.'

The man himself was in his office, music leaking out of huge earphones.

'Put that off, would you,' said Corry, tapping the back of his chair. 'I don't want to hear Jay-Zed or whatever his name is in my workplace.'

'Sorry, ma'am. Well, Dr Maguire, how you doing?'

'I'm grand, Trevor, yourself?'

'I'm sick. Just got the new CoD.' She gathered this was good but hadn't the inclination to ask; they'd be here all day. 'Have you been able to get into Alice's phone?'

'Anyone could, it wasn't even locked.'

'So we could just look?'

'Yep. Easy-peasy. You don't even need me.'

'Ah now, who would keep us up to date with all the latest game hacks?' said Corry. 'My Connor was almost civil to me for a whole hour after what you said about Grand Theft Auto. Tell Dr Maguire what you found?'

'Somebody's given her iPhone a good wee rinse, that's what. Put it back to factory settings.'

'Meaning? Remember you're talking to ancient dinosaurs here.'

'Hey,' said Paula. 'I'm only young, right, Trevor?'

'Defo. You'd pass for, like, thirty,' he said gallantly. At

thirty-two, Paula did not find this flattering. She was sure Maggie, God love her, had aged her about ten years. Trevor said, 'Well, what it *basically* means is, someone tried to delete everything she had on there. All her passwords and search history and apps, the lot. I say tried because we can most likely get it back, if I run it through some hard-ass – eh, sorry – some powerful recovery software.'

Corry patted the back of his chair. 'You're a wee star, Trevor, even if I don't understand the half of what you say.'

'Hashtag winning!' said Trevor.

'What?'

'It's a Twitter thing that you—'

'No, no, don't tell me, still don't care enough. Come on, Dr Maguire.'

In the corridor, Corry was almost dancing with excitement. 'That's it. We've got him. I want to bring in Dermot Healy, right now.'

'But she knew about it! She asked me to delete it!' said Dermot. On his forehead gleamed a fine sheen of sweat.

Corry watched him steadily over the interview room table. Paula was on the video monitor. Dermot looked very young behind the table, in his too-loose, Mummy-bought-them jeans and big red hoody. He'd been read the rights sheet, offered a lawyer. They were doing it all right this time. 'You're saying Alice asked you to wipe her phone.'

'Yes! She said she wanted to sell it or something, and she was worried about, like, identity fraud. So I helped her with it.'

'When was this?'

'I don't know. A month or so back, six weeks maybe.

After . . .' Dermot stopped himself, looking nervously at his lawyer.

'After?' Corry leapt on the hesitation.

'Um, I meant, before she moved out there for good. That's all.'

'Did you go to Alice's cottage and take her phone, while you were at Mrs O'Neill's that day?'

'No! And I'll bet you didn't find any prints of mine there, did you? Just on the phone.'

It was true, the only prints in the cottage had been Alice's, and one of Maureen Mackin's from the door. 'Dermot.' Corry took on a more soothing tone, like she might have used with her own teenage son. 'We know about your previous drugs caution, and we know that Alice was seen under the influence of . . . something about two months ago. We aren't overly concerned about students dabbling in drugs. But I need to ask – did you give Alice anything that time?'

Dermot looked at his lawyer, then briefly nodded.

'Right. We're getting somewhere. What did you give her?'

'MDMA. She wanted to try it, so I – I got it.'

'It was her first time with drugs?'

He laughed, a short bark. 'Course it wasn't. Jesus, she went to boarding school. Those places are like Studio 54, of course it wasn't her first time.' Dermot put his hands on his head. 'It's the truth. I'm telling the truth. I got it for her because she asked me to.'

'It was consensual?'

'Of course it was! People know I can get things, sometimes, so I did. That's all.'

'You took it with her?'

'We all did. The four of us.'

'And? What happened?'

'Well, it was . . . you know.' His face twisted with something – loss, maybe. 'The four of us . . . I can't explain. We were friends. Really friends.'

'Such good friends that Alice moved out of college not long after? Did something happen, Dermot? Was that it? When you were all high?'

He looked up at them. 'Look. You don't have a clue what Alice was really like. She was smart, like really smart. But she pretended not to be, so people sometimes wrote her off. Like Katy. Katy doesn't have any idea how smart Alice is.'

'But you do?'

'No. I didn't either. None of us did.' He was picking at his hands, Paula saw. The cuticles were raw, almost bleeding. 'Did you know Alice has an IQ of 170? Did you know she first ran away when she was still in primary school? Did you know it was *her* who told the press about her dad's affairs back then?'

'Seems like you know a lot about her,' said Corry casually. 'Do you also know where she is?'

He slumped. 'No. I don't. She – I don't know how she managed it. She hates the outdoors and she's always on her phone. At first I thought she'd just gone off, and she'd come back once she'd made her point, but I didn't think she'd – and now you found her phone I think maybe she's done something and . . .' He tailed off. 'I don't know. I don't know what to say.'

'Dermot? What do you mean, make her point?'

He shook his head. 'I don't know. I don't know what I mean.'

'Is there something you need to tell us?'

He straightened up. 'No. Look, this print, it's not enough for you to charge me, is it?' He looked from his lawyer to Corry, who reluctantly shook her head. 'Right then. I can't prove this, not yet, but all I can say is you didn't know Alice. Neither did I, really. But you'll see, soon enough. You'll see that I didn't hurt her. Not the way you think, anyway.'

'And when will that be?'

He almost smiled. 'When she wants us to, of course. When we're all through the looking glass.'

'So what you're telling me is, we have no end of suspects, all wrapped up for us nice and neat, and we can't pin it on a one of them?' Willis Campbell folded the arms of his Armani suit.

Corry glanced at Paula, who shrugged slightly. She said, 'Sir, everything we have so far is circumstantial. We don't have enough to charge.'

'That's just great. And I'm due on the evening news in—' he looked at his expensive watch '—half an hour, and I'll have to tell them we still have nothing.'

'We don't have nothing,' said Paula, earning herself a black look. 'The students are behaving strangely. They don't seem concerned about Alice, and they're jumpy in a way that rings alarm bells.'

'And what leads does this give us? Are any of your insights actually useful, Dr Maguire?'

Come on, Maguire, think. 'I . . .' She shook her head. 'I'm sorry, sir. I need to work on it more.'

Willis turned to the door, swinging round for one last shot. 'I hope you realise that Alice's father talks to our bosses. And if he's not impressed, they're not impressed. Just think about that.' And he was gone, in a cloud of Aqua di Gio.

Corry threw her arms out. 'I don't know what he wants from us. Everything we've looked at is a dead end. Unless Alice turns up, one way or the other . . .' Paula winced at that. 'I don't see what else we can do.'

'I think they must know something,' said Paula. 'Katy – she didn't seem exactly worried about her supposed best friend, did she? She didn't help with the search, and there were loads of Oakdale kids there who don't even know Alice. And Peter—'

'Peter is about as thick as his own eyelashes,' said Corry. 'I doubt he'd be able to cover up a crime. No, if anyone's planned all this, it'll be this one. But we're going to have to let him go.'

'Is there another way we can get to them?' said Paula. 'Make them talk?'

'I have an idea,' said Corry, looking at her watch. 'Give me an hour, will you?'

WhatsApp conversation

Katy: *He's actin really weird do u not think*
Peter: *Dunno weird how?*
Katy: *Like he said we should join the search for her. Hello why would we do that?*
Peter: *Dunno maybe so people could see us there*
Katy: *No way was I going to do that.*
Peter: *Yeah I had rowing* ☹
Katy: *So I think maybe we should talk to someone about him what do u think? Before they get onto us more?*

Peter: *I don't know I think we should stick to what he said. Keep our heads down. Stick together.*
Katy: *Umm OK but just remember what happened. Remember who gave her the stuff in the first place. who do you think they'll come for 1st?*

Chapter Twenty-Five

'Don't Taser me, don't Taser!' Gerard mock-cowered under his desk as Avril approached, in uniform.

'I will in a minute if you don't give over. Paula, what's this about?'

'I've no idea. DS Corry wanted to speak to us both.' She'd almost said DCI, forgetting that things had changed.

Avril heaved a sigh, lifting her heavy body armour. 'I hope it's away from these riots. You wouldn't believe the abuse people hurl at you. Both sides.' The uniformed police had been out all night, a spark of dissent having caught in the dry tinder of a long, hot summer. Stones had been thrown at police, and several people taken to hospital. There was talk of getting the water cannons out, as they did most summers. It being a seasonal thing, nobody was paying much heed.

There was something that stirred in the blood in Northern Ireland when summer hit – a brief heat that could take you by surprise, and equally be followed by days of stinging rain. It made people restless, reminding them they were sharing a small, wet island with another tribe. It was no surprise then that midsummer – Lúnasa – was when Yvonne had gone missing, and the hunger strikes had reached their peak. Every summer a restless wind began to blow and people seemed to decide en masse – it was time for a riot. Add in it being marching season too, when Orangemen liked to parade on the sites of places they'd beaten the Irish hundreds of years before, and the Catholics got annoyed, and the town was in uneasy ferment. From experience, it was only a matter of time before the stones turned into bullets, and the bullets into petrol bombs. And then it was usually another short matter of time before someone got killed.

'There's no such thing as sides in the police now, remember,' said Gerard, himself Catholic. And that was an achievement, Paula thought. The PSNI was not seen, as the RUC had been, as the tool of the Protestant majority. Rather it disgruntled everyone equally, as should probably be the case.

'Well, whatever. It's a pain.'

'Still, it's good for overtime,' said Gerard casually. 'You know, in case you had anything to save up for. Like a wee flat deposit.'

Avril glared at him. Paula looked politely away. She and Aidan were lucky, in that respect. They had next to no religion between them, and though Pat would have preferred them not to cohabit, the ring on Paula's finger was at least a gesture towards respectability. She spun it absently. Thinking of the burgeoning to-do list for the wedding, which she kept scrawled in the back of her diary. *Flowers. Allergies and vegetarians. Maggie headband??* Oh God, what was the point of any of it? She looked at Avril and Gerard, the little smiles and in-jokes they tried and failed to hide. They were mad about each other. She and Aidan had never got that back, the first flush of it – not since she was seventeen and he was eighteen and they'd broken up so acrimoniously. They'd both seen too much for things to be simple between them.

The door of Willis Campbell's office – once Corry's – opened, and Corry herself put her head out. 'Constable Wright, Dr Maguire, come in. Not you, Monaghan.' She gave Gerard a hard stare. 'Have you no work of your own to do?'

'Yeah, yeah.' He sloped off back to his own desk, watching as Avril went in. She sat down opposite, patting her fair hair into place. Willis made a show of shaking her hand – he never did that for Paula. She followed, slightly grouchy at being kept in the dark, her own hair flying out from its elastic band.

'Thank you for coming, Constable Wright. I gather you used to be part of the defunct MPRU too?'

Defunct. A clunk of a word, meaning dead, meaning useless. Avril said, 'Yes, sir. I was the analyst. Then I wanted to join the police properly.'

'Excellent, excellent. We need more young women,' he said earnestly. 'And let me just ask – have you had surveillance training?'

She nodded. 'I'm hoping to join CID, sir.'

'Good. That's good. Now, I must explain to you that what I'm going to ask needs to remain inside this room. You're entirely free to say no, but if you do, you must not speak about it with anyone. Same for you, Dr Maguire.'

Paula raised her eyebrows – she'd no idea what this was about.

'You understand, Constable Wright?'

'Yes, sir.'

'And forgive me, you're how old?'

'Er – I'm twenty-seven, sir.'

'Good. You could pass for younger.' Willis was suddenly embarrassed, blustering. 'Er, that is . . .' Paula hid a smile.

Corry did a barely perceptible eye-roll and broke in. 'Avril. What we're trying to say is you're not a novice to this kind of work, and you're not far off Alice's age. So we'd like to ask how you'd feel about some undercover work.'

'You mean—'

Willis recovered. 'We'd like you to pose as a student, Constable Wright. Enrol at the college as a new admission – Katy Butcher's new room-mate, to be exact.'

'Did the college OK that?' Paula was thinking of the hostile principal.

'We didn't give them much choice,' said Corry, with a glint in her eye.

Willis was looking cross again. 'Yes, well, they've agreed now I've spoken to them. All it took was a bit of diplomacy. We think someone at Oakdale has information. We want you to find out what happened to Alice. If she can be located, or if we should be making this a murder investigation.'

'No way,' said Gerard.

'Eh, it's not really up to you, is it?' said Paula.

They were gathered in the Old Shepherd, a pub which had no other virtues than being the nearest to the station and not aligned to any particular political tradition. The kind of place where the landlord kept a baseball bat under the bar and most of the drinkers were police. Paula found it strange enough to see Avril there – when she'd first joined the force, she'd never even been inside a pub. Her family were clean-living, non-drinking. But there she sat, nursing a white wine spritzer, her hair tied back and an anxious expression on her face. She hadn't said anything yet.

'It's too dangerous,' Gerard said. 'A girl's already dead,

probably – blonde girl, twenty-two, short – hello, that's not a million miles off Avril, is it?'

'I am here, you know,' she said crossly, pushing her drink away.

'Well, what do you think?' Paula asked her.

'I can't believe they asked me. I mean, it's a big deal, isn't it?'

'It is. Won't do your chances at CID any harm.'

Gerard was still glowering. 'Stop encouraging her, Maguire.' Avril put her hand on his arm and he deflated. 'I'm just worried,' he said.

'I know. But – they asked me for a reason.'

He rubbed a hand over the back of her neck. It was a neat trick, Paula thought, soothing him like that. When she and Aidan rowed – frequently – she inevitably said something that made things a hundred times worse. She wondered what he was doing now. Maggie was still at Pat's, so Aidan would be out on his beat, whatever that involved. Chatting to drunks in pubs, getting information.

'You think I should do it, Paula?' Avril's blue eyes were wide.

'God, don't be asking me. I'm not one for making sensible decisions . . .'

'You can say that again,' muttered Gerard.

Paula ignored him. '. . . But it will be an amazing opportunity, and I agree we need someone in there. We're being misled right, left and centre.' She wished Guy were there. He would know what to do, what the risks might be. And he cared about Avril – he'd worked with her for a year – unlike Willis Campbell, who only cared about his own designer-clad back. But she'd hardly seen him that day, both of them keeping busy, almost avoiding each other.

At least it meant she could get away with still not telling Aidan.

'Do you think I can pass for twenty?' With her hair back, skin scrubbed fresh, Avril looked about fifteen.

Paula smiled. 'No doubt about it.'

Chapter Twenty-Six

'So Avril's going to have a microphone on her normal phone. She won't switch it on all the time, it eats up the battery, but if something's happening she'll be able to record it without looking suspicious. Those kids are never off their phones anyway.'

'She'll be on her own?' Gerard said, too loud.

Corry glared at him. 'Constable Wright is training to be a police officer, Sergeant. It's highly likely she will find herself in dangerous situations at times. Teach her some self-defence if you're worried.'

Gerard subsided, muttering that he might just do that.

'Her brief is to befriend Katy and the others and try to find out what's been going on. Those three kids are hiding something, I'm sure of it.'

Paula had got a shock at Avril's undercover look when she'd turned up that morning, ready to be dropped off at Oakdale as a supposed new student. When they'd worked together, the younger woman had always been turned out in full make-up, hair pulled back, neat skirts and blouses and jumpers. Whereas Paula inevitably rolled up in trousers and some kind of cardy. Now Avril wore jeans and a hoody, dark-rimmed glasses. Pretty. Paula wondered if Peter Franks would notice that. After all, he seemed to like blondes.

'So,' said Corry. 'We'll monitor the operation from a

terminal here in the station. She'll turn the mic on if something important happens.' She smiled reassuringly at Avril. 'And if she's concerned about anything, anything at all, she can clock in, and we'll come and get her if she needs us to. OK?'

'OK,' said Avril, nervous. And Paula didn't blame her. It felt like they were sending her friend into the lion's den. But Avril was good with people. She knew the names of all the kids of everyone in the station, admin staff included, whereas Paula, who tended to get very caught up in cases, even forgot the names of the staff sometimes. How did you even find out the names of kids? Did you go around asking everyone and writing them down in a book? Avril would make a great Family Liaison Officer – but this was something else, something dangerous. It made Paula nervous, and Gerard Monaghan wasn't the only person who'd be hovering by the monitoring station, waiting for it to crackle to life.

It wasn't long before the first communication came through. Avril perhaps jumping too soon, turning on her mic. The first member of the trio to put their head above the parapet was Peter. Avril was in the entrance hall of the college, with instructions to look deliberately at sea, when he approached. The voice came through the terminal into the station. 'Hello. You look totally lost.'

Avril's laugh. In the incident room, Gerard tensed. 'Oh yeah. I'm new, starting next term. Just not sure where I'm meant to be.'

'Let me see.' Rustle of paper. 'You're in room thirty-five. Hmm. Good luck.'

'What is it?'

'Oh, nothing, I just know it. There's only one free, I guess. You'll be sharing with a girl I know.'

'Is she nice?'

'Well . . . let's just say, I'll protect you, if you need it.'

'Twat,' muttered Gerard. Corry shushed him.

'Thanks,' Avril was saying. 'It's freaky, just turning up like this. I've had glandular fever so I'm a bit behind. I'll be a year later than everyone.'

'Oh, that's nothing here.' The paper rustled again. 'Why don't you come down to the buttery at dinner and look for me? I'll tell you who people are. I'd carry your case but I'm late for rowing.'

'Oh, that's OK. Thanks for your help.'

How polite he was, in the midst of all those awkward overgrown teenagers. 'I'm Peter. And you?'

'Avril.' It was easier to have the same first name when undercover – hard to remember to turn around, in a split second, when called by a different one.

'Lovely name. Bye.'

God he was smooth. Avril's breath sounded panicky as she turned the microphone off. She'd been told not to speak into it unless she was sure she was alone.

'What do you think?' said Corry, to Paula.

'Not bad. She's nervous, but it'll probably seem like a new girl thing.'

'She'll be eaten alive,' said Gerard crossly. 'That sleazeball – I know what he did to that girl at his boarding school. Avril's only wee. What if he hurts her?'

'DS Monaghan. You're off this case,' said Corry. She was the same rank as him, but it was her case.

'What?'

'I'm not having you sitting about listening in for your

girlfriend like you're on Stalker FM. I have confidence in Constable Wright.'

'It's not her I'm worried about, it's him.'

'We'll put her in a burqa then, will we?'

'I never—'

'It's the same argument. Now remember Constable Wright is there to draw things out. Find out what happened. So go and do something useful.'

'What?' he said sulkily.

'Dig up the Yvonne O'Neill files again. We're going to have to go through it more carefully, check every bit of evidence. There must be a link between the cases. I want to know if we missed something.'

As he went, stroppily, Paula shuddered. 'I hope Avril can handle this.'

'She's brave. She can manage.' But Corry didn't sound convinced, and for the rest of the day they both continued to watch the terminal for any signs of life.

'So how come this bed's empty?' Avril's voice drifted out. Corry signalled to Paula from across the room.

'Oh, it's my old room-mate.' Katy's voice. 'You know on the news – the girl who's missing.'

'Oh my God! She was here?'

'Yeah, but like, she'd moved out before. She was living out of town in this weird cottage.'

'Ew, why? Was she mental?' Avril sounded totally convincing as a twenty-year-old.

'Kind of. She . . . well, Alice has some issues.'

'God,' Avril was saying. 'Why did she do that? I mean, she must have told you everything; did something happen to make her go?'

There was a pause. 'Why do you ask?'

'Well, God, it's a bit spooky, isn't it? I mean, someone could have *killed* her. It could be someone from here. My parents didn't want me to come because of it.'

There was a noise as if Katy was moving around. 'You came really early. Term doesn't start for like a month.'

They'd invented a backstory where Avril had failed her first year because of glandular fever. 'Yeah, I know. They wanted me to get caught up. I was sick all of last year.' Avril tried again. 'So did you not get on with her, Alice?'

There was a pause before Katy answered, quietly. 'We were best friends. I mean, I thought we were. Then she just took off. I hardly saw her any more.'

'You must be really worried about her. I mean, what if something happened to her?'

'It didn't.' Katy said this in a flat monotone.

Avril sounded confused. 'But how do you . . .'

'Look, I knew Alice really well. Like I said, we were best friends. And this is what she does. Things get too much for her and she runs.'

'But – I heard the police found blood.' Avril needed to be careful here. A twenty-year-old arts student shouldn't know too much about the case.

'I know, but . . . there'll be a reason for all that. She'll turn up. She had her reasons to go.'

'What do you mean?'

The thump of Avril's heartbeat. *Keep calm*, Paula urged her silently. *Don't push it. She wants to tell you.* She saw in the corner of her eye that Corry was listening intently.

Katy didn't say anything for a while. 'Do you mind if we don't talk about it? Sharing with Alice – it wasn't easy sometimes.'

Avril said quickly, 'God, I'm sorry, asking all these questions when you must be worried sick. I was just, you know – bit nervous being the new girl.'

When Katy spoke again her voice had changed. 'God, it's nice to share a room with someone *normal*. Don't worry about being new. Everyone here's had it at some point. Trust me.'

'Aw, thanks, you're sweet. So . . . I met this guy earlier. Peter someone?'

'Peter Franks.' Katy's voice narrowed.

'You know him?'

'Tall, fair hair?'

'Yeah. He's sort of cute. What's his story?'

Katy was probably trying to sound light, but it didn't come out that way. 'Oh, I'd stay away if I were you. He's a hot mess.'

'Really? You've never . . . gone there, then?'

Katy gave a dry laugh, which aimed for sophisticated and fell into cynical. 'God, no. Not my type.'

'I guess the posh boys are usually a bit up themselves, right enough.'

'More than that. Peter kind of thinks that if he sees it, it's his, you know?'

'What do you mean?'

'I mean, he's bad news. Don't take a drink off him, like.'

'God, really?'

'Really.'

Paula wondered if Gerard was in earshot – thankfully he seemed to be out actually doing some work for a change.

Avril said, 'I'll stay well clear then. Any other cute boys here? I saw this one guy in the library. Glasses, sort of nerdy chic . . .'

'Dermot?' Katy seemed to be warming into the role of wise friend. 'Hon, you're barking up the wrong tree there.'

'You mean—'

'Yeah. I mean he's so in denial about it, but you can tell. Think he has a thing about Peter as well. He's good if you ever need anything, though.'

'Like what?'

Katy said, 'You know. Stuff. Meds the doctors won't give you. Or for fun. Dermot's your man. He can always get stuff.'

'Wow. Are there any non-fucked up guys here?'

Katy laughed, and this time it was the first genuine sound of warmth Paula had heard from her. 'Nope. Welcome to Weirdsville. Nothing but druggies and fuck-ups here.'

'And us,' said Avril chummily.

Katy laughed again. 'Yep. We'll just have to stick together.'

Corry looked at Paula as the feed turned itself off. 'She's good. I think she might actually get through to the girl.'

'Katy's changed her story . . . she didn't spend the night with Peter after all?'

'Right. And if not, that means neither of them has an alibi for Alice's disappearance.'

Alice

I have a memory that I just can't shake, from the clinic. I wake up and his fingers are inside me. I'm wearing a hospital gown, the kind that opens at the back and leaves your bum cold. I'm lying on the examination couch, my legs all splayed out like a doll's. And his fingers are in me. Oh, there's a glove, and a nurse to chaperone, and it's some officially sanctioned test, but all the same I know what's happening to me. I just can't call it the word you're taught to call it when someone's inside you and you don't want them to be.

Now I have another memory to add to that. I wake up, and I'm lying on the grass outside the boathouse. It's dark and I feel sick. My mouth is full of puke and my legs are all splayed out again. My knickers are tied round my ankles, biting into me, the elastic stretched.

He has his fingers inside me. Stabbing, poking. This time it's Peter. It's my friend. My boyfriend, almost, until he found out I can't do sex. I can't move or speak but I'm awake for a lot of it. Then he takes his fingers out and he pushes my knees apart, so they press against the stones, and it hurts, and he's panting and cursing under his breath, and then he's in me. But in a different way.

Sometimes this memory is different. Sometimes I look up and it's Dermot – the security lights reflecting off his glasses, one side slipping off as he jerks inside me. His feet are grinding in the stones. I still can't move. Dermot, my sweet friend, my GBF except he doesn't think he's gay. And I hear Peter laughing. Just laughing and laughing on in my head. Mate, I never knew you had it in you . . .

I don't know which of these memories are real – or maybe

they're all real or maybe not at all. Maybe the one from back then isn't real either. They always said I made things up. Maybe I do. But I know that when I woke up properly the next day – in bed, but in my clothes, like someone put me there – I could still feel deep inside me, that someone had been there. I was bleeding into my pyjamas, and I don't bleed. Ever.

Sometimes, when I get this memory, Katy is there too.

Chapter Twenty-Seven

On her second day at the college, Avril attempted what was, for her, the most unnerving aspect of the operation. She approached Dermot in the canteen, her phone on in her bag, picking up the high cadences of young voices, laughter, clashing plates and cutlery. In the office, Paula and Guy were listening.

'Hiya.' Avril sounded nervous, but that fitted with what she was going to do.

A pause, then Dermot's voice. 'Hi.'

'I'm Avril. I'm new.'

No answer. There was the scrape of metal on a plate.

Avril said, 'It's Dermot, right? I'm Katy's new room-mate.'

'They put someone in there already?' A brief burst of anger.

'Oh, yeah, why – you mean cos of Alice? The girl who's missing?'

A pause again. 'Never mind.'

Avril cleared her throat, lowered her voice. 'Listen, sorry if this is a bit weird to ask, but I get a lot of anxiety, and sometimes I take stuff for it. You know, calm me down if I have a test or that.' No reply. 'Starting here, it's a bit – hello, head fuck, you know? So someone told me . . . Um, sorry. I don't mean to be weird. Someone told me you might be able to get me stuff?'

Dermot didn't answer for a while. 'If you want meds, there are doctors on site.'

'Yeah, I know, but . . . they took me off it. There's this one kind that really works, but you can only get it on prescription, and they said I needed to come off, I'd taken it for too long.'

'Then you should come off.' There was a rustle, as if Dermot was standing up.

Avril sounded unnerved. 'Oh. You can't get stuff then?'

'Look, I don't even know who you are. Did Katy say to talk to me?'

'Well . . .'

'Tell her I know what she's doing. Peter told me. And that I can tell people plenty of things about her too if she wants to play that game.'

There was a noise of feet stomping away, and on the mic, Avril let out a small sigh.

'He's not biting,' said Guy. 'What do you make of that?'

'I don't know,' said Paula. And she really didn't. She had no hunches, no clues, no idea. 'If they're not getting along, we need to watch Peter and Katy. They'll probably do something stupid soon, if Dermot's not helping them out.'

'So what do we do?' Guy was waiting on her, swift, alert. Ready to do what she suggested. For a moment she let herself remember what it was like to be a we, him and her, a team. So in tune they barely had to speak sometimes. Before he'd gone, and she'd agreed to marry Aidan, and she'd had Maggie, and it was all so late, far far too late to even think about.

'I can't think,' she said. 'This case . . . I can't get my head around it somehow. It's come at a really bad time. And working here – well, you can see it's nothing like being at the unit.'

Guy looked around them. The office was quiet, no one in earshot. 'Paula,' he said quietly. 'I wanted to ask you something.'

She stared at her computer, willing her face to remain composed. 'Yes?'

'This might sound strange. But – I've noticed you're not working all that well with DCI Campbell.'

She bristled. 'It's him who—'

Guy held up a hand, spoke soothingly. 'I know. I know. I can see Helen Corry's not a fan either. So I wanted to ask if you'd ever thought about moving on from Ballyterrin. Weren't you only here on secondment anyway?'

She had been, but that was nearly three years ago. 'Things are a bit different now.'

'I know. But I just thought I'd say this: I have an opening in my London team. For a researcher. You know we do anti-gang work. Looking at the best ways to reach out to teenage girls, running stats and so on. I think we could help these kids. The government's getting very worried about radical-isation. So there's funding around, and who knows, maybe the chance to actually do something good.'

'And you thought I could do it?'

'Yes, you have a research background, don't you? I know you don't like working with Campbell and I can't blame you, the man's a prick.'

She blinked. That was most unlike Guy, to criticise someone at work. Or swear, for that matter. 'Um . . .'

'I'll get them to make you a good offer. It could be your chance to come back. I mean – if you want to.' He looked at her with his clear grey eyes. Kind. Tired. Always just out of reach.

'But – I've Maggie.'

'You can have Maggie in London. I know there's not built-in childcare like there is here, but you'd be on more money, and I think – I got the impression you wouldn't mind a bit of distance now anyway.'

Paula tried to think of some words. 'But . . . Guy, I'm getting married.' It was hard, somehow, to say it out loud to him.

He was suddenly embarrassed. 'Oh! I know! I meant you would all come. I certainly didn't mean that you . . . Look, Paula, Tess and I are . . . things are going OK with us. We're trying to work things out. Perhaps I should have said that sooner. So I didn't mean . . . you know.'

Paula was staring at the keyboard, scarlet with embarrassment. 'Right. Right. I just meant I'd have to talk to him, think about it . . .'

'Of course, of course. I'm just putting it out there. Just an idea. Get you out of Ballyterrin, if that's what you want?'

Was that what she wanted? Would Aidan ever go, leave Pat and the paper his father had built up? Could she take Maggie away? 'Eh . . .'

'Think about it. Just think about it. Did you want me?' Guy turned, almost gratefully, to the desk sergeant who'd just come over. Paula couldn't remember her name. Susan, something like that? Avril would know.

'I was looking for Dr Maguire. Your mother-in-law's here, is all.'

Guy looked at her sideways. She gave a weak smile. 'Not yet anyway.' It was hard, trying to sum up who Pat was to her. 'Excuse me a second.' Guy nodded and Paula went out to reception, where Pat was indeed sitting. She looked pale and tired and Paula again felt a needle of guilt. Pat was doing too much for her. But worse – skipping around the reception, with its grim posters of domestic violence and rape, was Maggie. Dressed in a pink top that clashed with her hair, she saw her mother and called out, 'Mummy! Granny brung me!'

'Brought me,' murmured Paula, without thinking. 'Hi, pet.' She went through the barriers and Maggie clung to her.

'Mummy, Granny says I can see your work?'

'Sorry,' said Pat to Paula. 'It's just a friend of mine's been taken into hospital so I need to run down – I didn't like to bring the wee one with me.'

Paula disentangled Maggie from her feet. 'OK. Well, I can go home now, I suppose. I just got held up.'

Paula saw Pat looking behind her. 'Is that not your old boss?' Oh no. Oh no no no.

Guy was indeed standing behind her in reception. His eyes were riveted on the child. 'You left these papers, Paula, and . . .'

Too late, Paula recalled that Pat and Guy's last and only meeting had been on the day Paula went into labour. She made her voice sound steady. 'You remember DI Brooking, Pat? He's over consulting with us.'

'Hello!' Pat shook hands. 'And you're keeping well? You'd a wee girl yourself, hadn't you?'

Oh shut up, Pat! Couldn't she see this was no time for chit-chat?

'That's right, she's off to university soon.'

'She never is! Doesn't time fly!'

Paula busied herself with Maggie, doing up the clasps of her dungarees. But her daughter was a friendly, open child, and was staring at Guy. So naturally Guy dropped down to her. 'Hello! What's your name?' Suddenly shy, Maggie shot a side-eye at Paula. 'It's Maggie, is that right?' said Guy.

She laughed, suddenly deciding to trust him, and reached out to pat his face. Paula let the moment crystallise – they were finally side by side, her daughter and the man who was maybe—

'She's beautiful,' said Guy, straightening up. 'Looks just like her mum. Excuse me, Mrs O'Hara, I have to get back to work. See you tomorrow, Paula.'

He went without looking at her, and Paula felt Maggie heavy in her arms, hot breath and racing little heart. She wouldn't do it. She would not look for a likeness. It was far too late for all that now.

Chapter Twenty-Eight

'What's up? I slaved away over a hot microwave making that for you.' Aidan indicated the scrambled eggs Paula had left on her breakfast plate. He liked to cook, but it was always stodge, chips, burgers, toast – he had a large appetite, and like most Irish men, not much truck with salad.

'Oh, it's just this case. All this stuff about girls starving themselves, you know. It's got to me.' And also Guy being back and having offered her a job, of course. Not that she was planning to tell Aidan any of that.

He shovelled eggs in his mouth, glancing at the clock. 'I'm going to be late for this interview, bollocks. Have you time to ring the builders?'

'Do I have to?'

'Come on, Maguire. We're away from next week and still no hob.'

She sighed. Being on honeymoon would also mean no more Alice Morgan case. If they didn't crack it by the end of the week, she'd likely be off it for good. 'All right.'

'It's either that or ring the hotel about final numbers, and I bet you don't want to do that either.' Paula mimed bashing her head off the table. 'Thought so. I'll take wedding, you take builders.'

'Fine, fine. You drive a hard bargain, O'Hara.'

He came up behind her, stooped to kiss her cheek.

'Less than a week. Can you believe it?'

'No,' she said, and she really couldn't. She reached for him, drew his face down to hers. 'We'll be OK, won't we?'

'With the wedding? Aye, no doubt it'll hang together. Saoirse and my ma will make sure of it.'

That wasn't really what she'd meant, but she let it go. Maggie was happily messing with her own breakfast, Weetabix all over her face and hands. Paula reached over and wiped her chubby cheeks. 'All done, Mags?'

'All done!' came the cheerful echo.

Paula lifted Maggie onto her knee, where she played with Paula's engagement ring, holding it to catch the light. Out of nowhere she was poleaxed by a memory of her own mother. They were a horded treasure, finite. But of course she hadn't been paying attention, hadn't known they would run out at thirteen. In this one Paula was sitting at the table, home from primary school, and Margaret was cooking at the stove, and the kitchen was warm and she heard her dad's car in the road and relaxed, knowing he was home safe for another day. No bombs or guns or bad men had got him; not that day at least. Back then, she'd never imagined it would be her mother she'd lose instead.

Paula squeezed Maggie tighter, breathing in the shampoo smell of her red curls. Watched Aidan dump dishes in the sink, the easy movements of his hands so familiar to her now. You never knew. You never knew when would be the last memory you had of someone. She wondered when Alice Morgan's parents had last seen their daughter, and if they remembered it now, if they'd told her they loved her, or if they'd fought, or been indifferent or hurried. And if that would be the last time they ever spoke to her. As the days went on, that chance grew and grew.

Aidan was still footering at the currently broken sink, the same sink Paula's mother used to stand at. She hadn't told him Guy was there. Worse, that he'd seen Maggie. But was that so bad? He'd be gone again soon, and she'd ordered her wedding dress, hadn't she? That meant something. That meant a lot. The wedding was on Saturday, and then it would be too late for these doubts and worries. She would be safe.

Just then her phone started ringing on the side. She could see Aidan moving towards it – and something, she didn't know what, made her spring up, almost dislodging Maggie. 'I'll get it. Might be confidential.'

Aidan just nodded OK, going back to the clean-up. He wasn't the suspicious type. And there was nothing to be suspicious of, was there? Even if her heart was hammering and she took the phone into the hallway to answer. 'Hello?'

'We've a problem.' Guy's voice in her ear, making her heart pound harder. She moved back slightly, into the doorway of the living room. 'Dermot Healy's just been reported missing. His room-mate says he didn't come back to college last night, and Dermot's also apparently taken the guy's car.'

'You need to find my son right way.'

The reaction of Dermot Healy's parents – a professional couple in their early fifties – was very different to that of the Morgans on hearing their child was gone. They had set off from their home in Bangor as soon as he was reported missing, and been in the station ever since, haranguing Corry.

'We're doing our best, ma'am,' said Corry equably. 'It's Ms Ryan, is that right, not Healy?'

'Dr Ryan.'

'I'm sorry. Well, as I think your FLO told you, Dermot has only been missing for twelve hours. He told his room-mate he was going away for the night, but he didn't return in the morning. Now. We've checked with all the petrol stations, and we believe CCTV shows him filling up near Derry yesterday afternoon. He took his room-mate's car.'

'Londonderry?' Dermot's father – a high court judge, with steely silver hair to match his demeanour – glowered at the word. 'What would take him to a place like that?'

'We think he might have been travelling to Donegal. There was a sighting of Alice Morgan there. It's possible Dermot wanted to help with the ongoing search, or to find her himself.'

'Why would he do that?' The mother had a Radley hand-bag and newly set hair. 'He has his studies to think about.'

'Well, the girl who's missing, Alice, she and Dermot were very close friends. He didn't mention her?'

They looked at each other and Dr Ryan shook her head stiffly. 'We didn't know he was caught up in that. I spoke to him at the weekend and he never said. I even asked was it affecting his work, the investigation. I gather the police presence has been *very* intrusive.'

'How did he sound?' asked Paula. She wondered how they would react if they knew their boy had given Alice drugs. Wiped her phone. Maybe stolen the picture of Yvonne O'Neill out of Yvonne's mother's house.

'Normal. I mean, the thing about Dermot is—'

His father interrupted. 'He's a very anxious boy. Always has been. Too clever for his own good. Over-thinks every-thing. We sent him to Oakdale because we thought they could manage this kind of thing. Obviously not. I'll be speaking to the principal.'

'Isn't it true Dermot also has a drugs caution, sir?' Corry spoke blandly.

Mr Healy glared at her. 'He started using drugs to manage his anxiety. It went too far. All that's in the past now.'

'I'm afraid we have good evidence that Dermot was selling drugs on campus. And he most likely gave some to Alice.'

There was a silence. Dr Ryan put her hand to her mouth. 'Are you not going to look for him?'

'Of course we are. There's a link to Alice's case, for one thing. But I think the most likely thing is that he's gone to find her, and hasn't suffered any harm himself. But we will need to bear in mind he could be in a very agitated state.'

What Corry was trying to say, as tactfully as possible, was that they had to treat Dermot as if he was on his way to find Alice, and if she was alive, to kill her.

'Right. So the question as I see it is, does this disappearance have anything to do with Constable Wright's presence at Oakdale? And if so, do we remove her?' Willis looked round the table at Corry, Paula, Gerard, and Guy. Behind him a muted TV played a news alert about Dermot, showing the same CCTV clip of him buying petrol, wearing the same red hoody and dark jeans. The kind of boy you wouldn't look at twice.

'I don't think she's in any immediate danger,' Corry said, looking to Paula. 'Dr Maguire? What kind of situation are we dealing with here?'

Paula opened her mouth and closed it again, shook her head. 'It's very hard to say. The reactions of all three friends suggest they were never worried about Alice – which could be because they knew what happened to her. And I've been sure all along they were concealing something, I just don't know what. But I don't know why Dermot would have gone, in that case.'

Willis looked between them, barely concealing his impatience. 'So we think this Dermot Healy is responsible for Alice's disappearance, is that it?'

Guy said, 'We think he's gone to find her. That suggests he isn't directly responsible, but he may know where she is. So it could be she's in Donegal, but she went there herself.'

Paula wasn't so sure. 'Why has her phone not been on before, then, if she went there herself? She's the kind of girl who'd be glued to it. And then there's the blood. And the Yvonne link.'

'In the meantime I have two sets of parents breathing down my neck, not to mention the Oakdale principal.' Campbell looked at Paula. 'Dr Maguire. As you assess it, do you think Constable Wright is in immediate danger?' Paula had spent the morning weighing it all up, trying to imagine it was an anonymous member of staff, not someone she'd worked alongside for years, seen crying and covered in Gerard's blood when he'd been shot that time, watched the break up with her fiancé, kiss Gerard in the corridor, figure out the fact Fiacra was in love with her too.

She spoke carefully. 'It depends if Dermot has worked out she's undercover. He's a smart kid.'

'Is there anything to make us think he has?'

Paula could feel Gerard watching her, willing her to say they should take Avril out. She turned away. 'I don't believe so. She should be careful, of course. Especially of Peter Franks. But I think we need her there more than ever now – to watch what Peter and Katy do, with Dermot gone.'

'And I gather Constable Wright is coming to your wedding anyway?'

'Well, yes.' They had decided there was little risk of anyone from Oakdale seeing Avril there, or noticing a weekend's absence.

'All right,' said Campbell. 'She stays in. But I want a plan in place. What exactly is Constable Wright trying to find out for us, and when do we decide to pull her out?'

Paula looked at Gerard. He was too professional these days to get up and storm off, but she saw the look he gave her over the table, and knew she was in for a bollocking as soon as Willis was out of earshot.

WhatsApp conversation

Katy: *OMG D where are u?*
Peter: *Hello??? Mate whats going on?*
Peter: *Police said ur missing whats that about*
Katy: *Hello . . . please D, I'm scared. Where are u???*
Katy: *Have you gone to look for her*
Katy: *D TELL ME WHERE YOU ARE*

Dermot has left the conversation.

Chapter Twenty-Nine

'Nice one, Maguire. It'll be on your head when Avril gets hurt by that dick Franks.'

Paula looked round; no one important could hear what Gerard was hissing at her. She pulled her seat round to face him. 'Look, this is what she wants, yeah? She wants to be in the police.'

'She doesn't know what it means. Look at you and me, Maguire. I've been shot. You've had a knife stuck in you. And we've sent Avril in to that bunch of weirdos, who've more than likely done their own friend in?'

'We don't know that.'

'Well, someone probably has. It's not safe!'

'I know! It's never safe, though, is it? We just have to make the decision, is it worth it to us to try. And it's Avril's decision to make this time.'

'Dr Maguire is right.' Guy was coming over. Though she was glad of the support, Paula's heart sank. Gerard was well aware that things between Guy and Paula were not strictly professional, and she didn't want to be seen as a favourite. 'Gerard,' Guy was saying soothingly. 'I know you're worried. But we'll be monitoring her the whole time. She's been well trained. And this could be our last chance to find out what's happened to Alice. Help protect other girls from danger. All right?'

'All right,' said Gerard moodily. 'But I want to monitor the mic station.'

'Sure, why don't you go and tell them I okayed it?'

Paula watched him go. 'It's not that I don't—'

Guy cut her off. 'I know. You think this is the best course of action, and as you said, nothing we do is ever really safe. Nothing anyone does is. Could I have a word with you?' A dart of distrust went through her. No one used that tone of voice, careful and polite, when they had good news to impart.

'All right.'

'Not here. In room four. I'll get some tea.'

She sighed and stood up. The room, just along the corridor, was empty. She sat on the sofa waiting for him, enjoying just for a second the upholstered quiet of the small room, blinds drawn. Unbelievable to think she'd be getting married in just a few days' time. How had it crept up on her? It had been easy when someone else was organising it, when it was still months away, just to push it out of her mind and get on with things, not stopping to think about what that meant. Being married to Aidan. Being his wife.

'Here we are.' Guy was in the doorway with two paper cups. Something complicated flashed through her – the familiarity of his face, his voice, the length of his body.

'Have they found something? Dermot?'

'No, it's . . . something else has happened. Not about the case. I wanted to speak to you.'

That meant something about her mother, most likely. She swallowed hard.

'They asked me to tell you,' said Guy. 'We just got word of it.'

Paula tried not to frown. She hated anyone using their

'giving bad news to relatives' voice on her – she'd spent too much time developing a version of her own. 'Just tell me, whatever it is. Don't do all that softening me up bollocks. Is it something about my mum?' She tried to say it casually, but her heart had started to race all the same. How annoying. After almost twenty years with no news, her mother declared dead and her father remarried, she'd told herself she had given up, along with PJ and the police and her mother's family and everyone else. But still the quickening of the pulse. It was a hardy little bugger, hope.

'Not exactly,' he said gently. She glared at him. 'It's about Sean Conlon,' he went on, more briskly. 'He's going to be released from prison.'

Her heart stilled. 'When?'

'Tomorrow.'

Nothing to feel sick about. Just a man, a man who'd served his time, getting out. She'd been expecting it, hadn't she? He'd served fourteen years, more than many terrorists. They didn't even know for sure if he'd been involved in her mother's disappearance. He had hinted at more knowledge, dropped riddles, but that was all. She found she was imagining his low voice, the watchful hunter's eyes of the man, and rubbed at her arms, suddenly goose-fleshed. 'Will he be back in town?'

'Yes. He's on full parole, and he has children here, of course.'

Innocent kids, going to local primary schools. Maybe even the same one Maggie would be at in a few years. Paula took a deep breath. 'I suppose there's no avoiding it.'

'He served his time. It was a long sentence, as you know, compared to others. And there's nothing concrete to link him to any other crime.'

'Aidan,' she said suddenly. 'Will Aidan be told?'

'I think they'll only tell the families of known victims.' Sean Conlon had also been a suspect in Aidan's father's murder – perhaps one of the masked men who'd shot John O'Hara dead in his newspaper offices. But again there was no proof. Aidan had been there too, hiding under a desk, and had watched his father die, but he'd been too young, too traumatised to tell the police anything. He hadn't spoken for a whole month after the attack. Paula had been six, suddenly afflicted with nightmares, waking up screaming for her mother. They hadn't known much worse was ahead, that Margaret too would be lost when Paula was thirteen.

'I'll have to tell him,' she said. 'I can, can't I? I mean, I have to. He's my—' She didn't know the end of that sentence. Aidan would be her husband after the weekend. It seemed so unlikely, especially with Guy perched on the low table, leaning on his knees, looking at her with his kind grey eyes.

'Of course you should tell him. But Paula—'

'What?'

'Are you sure he won't . . . well. He can be . . . impulsive, can't he?'

'What's that supposed to mean?' Guy bowed his head. She knew what he meant.

Aidan's drinking. His fearless, reckless reporting. His firm belief that terrorists should never be forgiven, even if that was the price of peace. She said, 'I don't know what you're talking about.'

'I'm just worried about you.' He took her hand and stunned, she let him. 'You seem so well these days. You're doing great. I don't want this to . . . throw you off.'

Paula took a deep breath and held it, trying not to lose her temper. Her hand lay in his warm one, as if she didn't know how to remove it. 'I'm getting married.'

'I know that.' She hadn't invited him. He'd been away, and it was unthinkable anyway.

'What I mean is, I don't have time to be thrown off. It's too late. Do you understand? It's too late.'

Guy said nothing. *Don't look at him don't look at him.* She looked up. His gaze floored her. 'I . . . I have to tell him.' That was all she knew.

Guy sat back, his tone changing, the moment passing. 'Of course. It's not a secret. He may know already – good at finding things out, isn't he?' She bristled, but he'd meant it as a compliment. A small offering, perhaps, and she took it. She dropped his hand, stood up.

He said, 'Paula . . . I'm sorry if this is maybe out of line. But would this not be a good time to get away from Ballyterrin? Take the job?'

She scrunched up her face until she was sure she wouldn't say something rude back. How could he ask her that now? 'Maybe. I better go now. Thank you for telling me.' She turned in the doorway. 'Conlon. He'll never talk now, will he? I mean, if he ever did know what happened to her, if they hid her body somewhere. No incentive.'

'No,' Guy admitted. 'I imagine he'll want to keep his head down.'

And so her mother's case, like so many others, would be swept under the carpet of reconciliation and peace and it's-not-really-worth-the-bother, if it meant people not dying in the street again. Paula nodded again. 'All right.'

'Is it?'

'It'll have to be. It's no more than other people have to

stand. And some of them know for sure he killed their families.'

'Some of them don't, though. Stand it.' He was referring to a case from two years ago. The one which had brought Corry down. The relatives of bomb victims, who'd abducted and killed the terrorists they thought responsible.

'Well, I sent them to jail. So you can hardly think I'd do anything to Conlon.'

'It wasn't you I was thinking of.'

The silence stretched, and Paula looked at Guy, his unswerving moral compass, his belief in the law, his bafflement with Northern Ireland's 'leave it be' approach to prosecutions. And thought of Aidan, his temper, his smoking, his small betrayals. And she made her choice again, as she did every day. 'I better go and tell my fiancé.'

Guy stood up. His eyes were unreadable. 'If I don't see you before the weekend, I hope it all goes well,' he said. 'You deserve every happiness.'

She could hardly bear it, his best wishes for her marriage. 'I have to go.'

She didn't stop or look back till she was in her car, where she sat for a moment, breathing, hands on the wheel. She'd known this was coming some time, Conlon's release, but all the same there was a small cold pocket in her stomach. The grit of soil under her nails, scrabbling in dirt, bones white in the moonlight. Only a dream, of course – she had no idea where her mother was, dead or alive. And now any possible answer seemed to get buried deeper with each year that passed. Maggie growing up, knowing no granny but Pat. It would be confusing later on, to explain why Granny and Gramps were the parents of Mummy and Daddy, but they'd find a way.

She started the car, pulled out into the heavy traffic. Headed to home and another difficult conversation with the man she'd chosen. Not her fault, any of it. But she couldn't shake the sense that somehow, she had failed.

Chapter Thirty

'Hello?' No noise of Maggie running around or watching *Peppa Pig*. She must still be at Pat's. The house was quiet, all the worktops neat and clean; well, neat as they could be with half the doors still missing. Dammit, she'd forgotten to ring the builders. She was letting too many things slide.

She saw the flutter of the fly curtain and poked her head out the door. He was sitting on the back step in his jeans and T-shirt, nursing the one Beck's he allowed himself per day. She hated to admit it, but she counted what was in the box. One, one was OK. One was not a habit. One was not a problem. 'Hiya.'

He didn't answer. He was staring at the back wall, turned orange by the last of the sun. Paula sat down beside him. It was where she used to eat her lunch during school holidays in summer, her mother passing out a little plate of ham sandwiches with the crusts cut off, a beaker of warm Kia Ora. 'Did you – Aidan, did you hear?'

He nodded slowly. 'Yeah. I need to tell Ma.' His voice sounded hoarse. 'Couldn't face going down for Mags yet. Sorry.'

'It's OK. Do you think she'll—?'

'Well, yeah, Ma'll take it hard, but he can't be inside forever.'

'Right, right. I mean, he's been in since 1999, that's a

long time . . .' She tailed off. Sean Conlon, for all his suspected crimes, was actually serving time for a bomb which had killed two police officers. Samuel Walker. Oran Collins. She knew their names by heart. Oran was only nineteen. Walker had a three-year-old child. It seemed wrong to say fourteen years was a lot of time to serve for that.

'You refused him parole once, didn't you?' Aidan took a swig of his beer.

'I – well, I recommended he shouldn't get it. It's not really up to me.' Two years ago, Paula had gone to see him, the man who'd hinted he knew something about her mother. 'He was just messing with me, really. He has no remorse. He'll never tell the truth now.' She said it in a flat monotone.

'Aye.' Aidan set down his bottle with a chink and put his arm round her. 'Come here.'

Shoulders dropping in relief, Paula leaned into him. The warmth of him. Hers to touch, and hold, and come home to. 'I'm sorry. It's crap. All of it's crap.'

He played with a strand of her hair. 'Well now, Maguire, as you say, fourteen years was a long time to be in. Plenty of murderers get less, or none at all. And if they'd got him for my da or . . . anything else before the Good Friday Agreement, he'd be out by now anyway, same as all that other scum.'

It was all true, and reasonable, and toed the line of what you were supposed to say in Northern Ireland now – in the spirit of putting down weapons after a thirty-year war and trying to live on together in the same small country. So why did she not believe him? 'You can tell me if you're not – I mean if you—' She was trying not to look at the bottle but he picked it up all the same, removing his arm from her to pick at the label.

'One beer. Same as always. I'll not let that man affect one step I take from now on.' He shifted, looking her in the eyes. 'Maguire. You know I was a mess about my da for years. Could hardly bear to think of it.'

She nodded. It was true, yet he worked every day in the same office where it had happened.

'Then I got ashamed of myself. Wallowing in it. Christ, my ma would cut off her arm if she ever thought she was being selfish by having something she wanted – but even she'd moved on. Even she had some kind of life. And then you were back, messing everything up—'

She said, 'Sorry. Didn't mean to.' He laughed a moment, soft, and her heart pulsed in gratitude. She grabbed his hand. 'You're right. Christ, they destroyed our parents, these men – him or whoever did it, someone just as bad – but they don't need to ruin the rest of our lives.'

Aidan was looking off again. His hand enfolded hers, warm and calloused. 'Thank God for you and the wee one, Maguire. Thank God.'

They sat for a moment. 'What if we see him around town? I mean, you're always in those scummy pubs.'

'If it happens, it happens. What about you, though – he knows you said no to his parole?'

'Yes, but I can't start avoiding every lowlife that might have a grudge against me; I'd never leave the house.'

'Just be careful. None of your mad running off to places or parking in dark streets.'

'Oh, you're the boss of me now, are you?' His hand crept under her top, finding the place where her skin had torn, the knife splitting her. 'OK,' she relented. 'I've been better, haven't I?' They both had. Aidan working hard, drinking less, being a perfect father. Her less obsessed with work, getting the house sorted, not putting herself in danger, staying one step removed from most cases. Pat and PJ down the road, Maggie growing up. The two little families, blown to pieces by bloodshed and war, were doing fine. Paula had even, as much as she could, managed to mute the desperate need to find out her mother's fate. 'We're fine,' she said, out loud, hearing the uncertainty in her voice.

'We've been through worse,' said Aidan. He too sounded faint, unsure.

Paula took a deep breath. 'Um – it was Guy Brooking told me about Conlon.' Aidan said nothing. 'He – he's back helping on this case.' She looked at him sideways. He hadn't reacted, went back to picking at his bottle. 'You already knew?' He squinted at the sun. Of course he'd known – he made it his job to know everything in town. 'I'm sorry,' Paula said. 'I didn't want to tell you – well, I thought he'd be away again soon, and with the wedding coming up . . . Do you understand?'

Aidan spoke. 'Maguire. I don't care about Brooking being here or in London or wherever he is. I've no beef with the man. But I care if you don't tell me things. We're both a wee bit too good at that, aren't we?'

'Yeah.'

'So he's here. Still with the suits and the Beemer and all?'

'Well . . . I think it's a Merc this time.'

'Course it is.' Aidan continued to stare out across the garden. 'You'll always have a choice, Maguire. We both will. Getting wed doesn't change that, not really. As long you keep choosing me, I don't mind if you work with him, or any God's amount of fellas in sharp suits. So . . . will you? Choose me?'

She laid her head on his shoulder, feeling the warmth of him through his threadbare T-shirt. The smell of the washing powder they used. This was home. This was it. 'You know I will. Do you need me to say it? Out loud? Cos I was planning to save the vows for the weekend.'

In response he got up, draining his bottle, holding the other hand for her. 'Come on, Maguire. I'm making you your dinner.'

She peered into the wreck of their kitchen. 'Er, I assume something that doesn't require a cooker?'

'When I say make, you need to understand I mean "ring down to the pizza place".'

'Jamie Oliver, eat your heart out.'

He turned and kissed her suddenly full on the mouth, hard and fierce so she could hardly stand to look at him. 'I mean it, what I said. Thank God you came back when you did.'

'Oh, you're glad I messed things up, are you?'

'Aye, I am, but don't expect me to say it again until one of us is dying. I am an Irish man, for all I can change a nappy. I've my reputation to think of.'

Alice

I go to the Madwoman. She always bangs on about wanting to make Oakdale a safe place, a place of tolerance and equality. If anything happens, go to her. I'm quite pleased with myself in the corner of my brain that isn't going 'it happened, it actually fucking happened' on some stupid loop. What seems to be the trouble, Alice? *She keeps all this riding crap on her desk, like she's secretly a dominatrix. I bet she is.* I gather you were quite out of it the other night. Care to explain?

Well. Something happened that night. *Look at me! Being the reasonable girl who 'tells someone'. I imagine me crying prettily, and her with her arm around me, offering tissues, like my actual mother never would in a million years. I imagine that after I tell her, I'll feel clean again. Maybe I'll even be able to eat. Ever since it happened, I look at food and imagine it going into me and settling on my hips, my stomach, my face, and all I can think is how disgusting I am, how disgusting all of it is. I know I am getting bad again, and I know where that ends – the clinic. I will do anything to stop that. Even this.*

Happened? *She's impatient. Her eyes keep hopping to the computer, a nice big Apple one.* You'll have to be more specific than that, Alice.

I've thought a lot about how I will phrase it. I won't come out and say the word. That would sound melodramatic, and anyway I'm not ready to say it, not even inside my head. So I try: A few nights ago, I was attacked.

She frowns. You mean mugged or something? I'm not following you.

I – there were two boys. Friends of mine, who go here.

And I think they gave me something and I woke up and they were . . . attacking me. *She's supposed to bring on the tissues and sympathy now, and the* oh Alice you're so brave. *Where's my fucking tea and sympathy? She just looks at me over the desk, narrowing her eyes.* Are you saying you had sex with two boys from this college? While using drugs?

No. Yes. No, I mean I didn't consent. *That's it, the legal definition.*

But you went somewhere with them, alone?

Well, yes, like I said, they're my friends. Were my friends, I mean, so . . .

And you were using drugs? Drinking?

I pause, confused. I – that isn't the point, is it? I mean, it doesn't matter what I was doing.

Alice. *She leans in, doing this faux-caring tone.* The thing you have to realise is, it's a very difficult process. It's very hard to prove, and they'll drag you through the courts, and if you were drinking, and I imagine you were wearing something quite revealing too, weren't you, it won't go well for you. So, I would urge you to think very carefully.

I am speechless. I can't believe she's spouting all these bollocks clichés at me. I – but are you not going to . . .

I'm just trying to help you, Alice.

No you aren't, I think. You're just trying to protect your precious college, which you filled full of rapists and coke-heads and rich mentalists, hand over a big fat cheque and no questions asked. That's all Oakdale is, really. An asylum with good-looking inmates and posh furniture. And I can hardly fucking complain. I'm one of them, after all.

I don't say anything for a while, feeling it open out below me, a new level of rock bottom where my college principal, women's champion, tells me not to report my rape – there I said it my rape my gang rape – *because I'd been drinking and maybe my top was tight or something.*

I could say – but I was a virgin. I woke up with blood all over me. I woke up with bruises on my wrists and my ankles and – other places. But I don't say anything. And the Madwoman nods and says: If you like we can up your counselling sessions. Help you feel better, and maybe discuss your substance misuse, if you're worried things like this are happening.

Things like this. Like my rape. By two of my best friends (by three friends Alice but no I can't think about that not yet).

On my way out I see Dermot in the corridor. I'm crying a bit. What were you doing? *he says, licking his lips in that gross way of his.*

Just leave me alone. *My voice is full of tears.* For fuck's sake, leave me alone.

Did you go to the Mad— did you . . .

Just fuck off! *I push him. But when I touch his horrible hoody and feel his bony chest underneath, the heart fluttering like a little trapped bird, I want to be sick.*

Alice, *he says, and he sounds so sick too.* Please – we need to talk, all four of us.

Fuck you, *I say, trying not to puke.* There is no four of us. I hate you all. I never want to see any of you again.

It was a mistake, *he says, and I think he is going to cry too.* It was just a mistake. It got out of hand. The drugs . . .

It was. It was a huge mistake, by him, by Peter, by fucking Katy. By the Madwoman. By Garrett. By Charlotte, stupid cow, giving me the pills that didn't work, then dying and leaving me here on my own. By Rebecca and Tony. By Una, who left me. By Nurse Twatface and Doctor Dickhead and everyone, everyone I've ever known. But the thing about mistakes is, sooner or later they have to be paid for.

Chapter Thirty-One

'Right. Here's what we need to do – I want to search Dermot Healy's room at the college. I want his picture out to every unit in the North-West. He can't have vanished. And I want someone to monitor Constable Wright's feed at all times, OK?' Corry was in full action mode, handing out instructions the next day. Paula, Gerard, and Guy took notes, along with a group of uniformed officers whose names Paula also didn't know. She would have to try harder. 'Everyone on board with this?' said Corry. 'Monaghan – I don't want any interference from you. I know you're worried, but you need to hold steady.' It was hard to believe she was no longer a DCI – and Willis Campbell had also noticed.

'What's going on, DS Corry?' he said, materialising with his customary frown.

Corry swung around. Her hair was in a high ponytail, which usually indicated she meant business. 'I'm directing the search for Dermot Healy.'

'Don't you think you should come through me? Your dealings with Oakdale so far haven't exactly been cordial.'

'They'd be more cordial if they would actually help—'

He held up his hand. Corry looked at it, mouth open. Campbell said, 'We can cover Oakdale later. I need you for something else first.'

'With respect, the search should be our top priority—'

He cut her off again. 'Dealing with the fallout is our top priority. Which is bad, and getting worse. Now I need you to explain what's been going on. Alice's father is here. He's seen the news.'

'Please,' he said. 'Is my daughter dead?' Tony Morgan looked like he hadn't slept in days. His shirt was rumpled, so were his eyes. He'd come over on the first flight that morning. 'You've made arrests at the college. And that boy is missing too – one of Alice's friends?'

'No arrests have been made so far,' said Corry blankly.

'Please. Do you think someone hurt her? I need to know.'

Corry showed him little sympathy. 'We don't know, Mr – sorry, Lord Morgan.'

'God.' He raked his hands over his face. 'Don't call me that, OK, it's—'

'As far as we know, Alice is alive. It's important to remember that.'

'But this boy. He's gone after her, you think?'

'We believe Dermot might have gone to find Alice, yes. He was seen near the Donegal area. But we can't be sure.'

'Please find her.' The man reached over the table and grasped Corry's hands. His face, so familiar from television and papers, contorted in grief. 'I – we weren't good parents to Alice. Rebecca didn't really want her and I always put my career first. I keep thinking about the day we left her at boarding school. She held onto my leg and cried. Like a dog being left at kennels. I – I shook her off. She was only seven.'

'Lord Morgan—' Corry tried to extract her hands.

'They say that when girls have issues with men it's because of their father, isn't that right?'

'There's no evidence that—'

'Alice had a lot of nannies. There was only one of them she really liked – Una. Irish girl. From this neck of the woods. She was very sweet, innocent really. One day Alice came home from school – she'd have been seven, maybe. Seven or six or something like that. And Una and I were . . . and she saw. Oh God.' He dropped Corry's hands, slumped on the table. 'It's my fault. It's all my fault. She's never been right since.'

'Lord Morgan,' said Corry crisply. 'I hope very much that Alice is still alive. If she is, she'll need the support of you and your wife to get past her ordeal.'

'Oh, Rebecca wouldn't support a cat. She's never loved Alice. Or me, really. That's why I – the other women . . .'

Corry almost rolled her eyes. 'This isn't appropriate, sir. I'm sorry you're distressed. We're doing everything we can to find Alice, please believe that.'

'Is there anything I can do? Do you need more money? Resources?'

Corry said, 'You could do a TV appeal. If Alice can hear it, it might help her to know she's missed. There's a chance she ran away. We think her anorexia had returned – perhaps she wanted to avoid being sectioned again.'

He bowed his head. 'I know. I know. She hated it at that clinic. But we thought we were saving her life. She almost died, you know. We couldn't watch her just starve herself to death. Her life was in danger.'

'It may be in danger again,' said Corry severely. 'I think it would help, an appeal from you and her mother. If Alice is able to see it, that is.'

Tony Morgan cleared his throat. 'Alice. This is Daddy here.' The word sounded false in his mouth, rolling like a marble.

The cameras had assembled with haste for a morning press conference. He sat at the table, alongside Corry and his wife. Tony went on, speaking without notes. 'Mummy and I miss you very much. We just want to know you're safe. If you can hear this, please come home.' He looked down at his hands, as if choked by emotion. Beside him, Rebecca Morgan sat frozen, behind her helmet of fair hair. Her expression was the same as in that image of her leaving court. Implacable. 'And if you're holding our daughter . . . if you took her, we'd like to beg you, as parents, please let her go unhurt. Alice is a wonderful girl – bright and loving, popular with everyone . . .'

Paula watched from the back row of the press conference, as journalists clicked and snapped. No Aidan today; he was busy sorting out last-minute wedding details. While she continued to hide from it. This was how it went, she thought, listening to Alice's father. When you were missing, or you got killed, and the smallest details of your life were dragged under forensic lights, everyone had to say the best of you. That you were lovely, loved, loving. No one could say you'd been awkward, unhappy, sometimes cold and manipulative, sometimes hurt and abused. She wondered – if Alice even could hear this, wherever she was – if she would recognise herself at all.

On stage, Lord Tony Morgan had produced some tears. The press snapped away. In the glare of the lights, he took his wife's hand. 'Please – Alice's mother and I are frantic. Please give her back to us.'

There was the scrape of a chair. Rebecca Morgan, dropping his hand violently, had risen to her feet. In her lilac suit, she quivered with something. Grief, or perhaps rage. Thin as a rail, the skin of her face stretched like a drum. She addressed the TV cameras. 'Alice,' she said. 'We've had enough of this now. Stop it. You've made your point. Now come back. Come back and stop punishing us.'

Chapter Thirty-Two

'Is this really necessary?'

Today, Madeleine Hooker was wearing a thin cashmere jumper, dove grey, the kind of thing that would cost you hundreds of euros in Brown Thomas in Dublin. Underneath, more jodhpurs. She was standing in her office at Oakdale with her arms folded – not happy. But Corry was a match for her.

'Ms Hooker, two of your students are missing. We need to get in and search Dermot's things.'

'It's very disruptive – his room-mate has term starting soon and—'

Paula could almost hear the sound of Corry's last nerve snapping. 'I should think your students are a damn sight more worried about their missing classmates than their work. If not, they should be. And frankly so should you. I've been very disappointed with your attitude here, ma'am. Now, I can tell you don't give a damn about Alice, and you don't care if all your students are in crisis, so long as your reputation's intact and the money keeps coming in, but let me tell you that reputation won't last long once all this gets out.'

Delicate muscles moved in the principal's face. 'All what exactly?'

'We'll know soon. There's a reason Alice and Dermot

aren't here. And I plan to find out what happened here back in June, why Alice moved out to that cottage, why she's missing. Now let us into that room before I arrest you for obstruction.'

She opened her lipsticked mouth as if she might say something. Then she seemed to deflate. 'Please . . .' she said. 'Do what you need to. Find them.'

'Is there something you want to tell us, Ms Hooker?'

She looked at Corry and Paula. Outside in the corridor, uniformed officers were waiting. Gerard had been dying to come, but the risk of running into Avril was too high, so he'd been left to cool his heels at the station. 'If I tell you something that's only anecdotal, no proof, will there be repercussions for the college?'

'You mean you've concealed something from us?'

'Not concealed. There was no proof – just allegations. But there is something, yes.'

Corry motioned to her desk. 'Sit. Tell us now.'

'I . . . you remember I mentioned Alice had been seen under the influence of drugs. Well, I had her in here to discuss it. We have a reputation, as you say, and when the students behave badly, it reflects on us.' She was trying to sound assertive, but Corry was almost growling beside Paula.

'Just tell us what happened, for God's sake. We don't have time for excuses.'

Madeleine Hooker squeezed her hands together, her expensive rings pressing white into the skin. 'Alice made a disclosure to me. She said she thought she'd been raped.'

'Who by?'

'She didn't tell me a name.'

'And you didn't ask?'

'There was no proof. She'd been taking drugs that night,

and – I knew she wasn't exactly a nun, if you see what I'm saying.'

'So you did nothing?'

'I – I encouraged her to be more careful, and see her counsellor more if she felt unwell.'

'You did nothing.'

'I . . .' The woman bowed her head. 'Perhaps I was wrong. Shortly after that, Alice moved out of campus.'

Paula wondered if she'd see steam come out of Corry's ears in a minute. Instead, the other woman stood up. 'Let us into Dermot's room. Now.'

Paula didn't take part in the search of Dermot's room; they had to do everything exactly by the book. Feeling suffocated by the air of Oakdale, hot and close, full of whispers and suspicions, she went outside to the lawn, where the lake glinted in the August sun. Her phone had sprouted an array of message icons while she was inside – wedding guests, caterers, suppliers. It was overwhelming. She put it back in her pocket.

'Miss?' A breathless voice. One she'd heard recently, but only over a radio.

'Yes. Hello, Katy.'

Katy had been sweating in the heat, and her upper lip was furred with it. Despite the sunshine, she had on her usual jeans and crimson hoody. It was creepy, how they all wore it. Almost like a uniform. 'You're with the police, right? Do you know what they're doing here again? Is it true Dermot's gone missing? Dermot Healy?'

'I can't tell you that, Katy. You just have to let them work.'

'Do you know where he's gone? What's happened to him? No one's telling me anything!'

'We don't know yet, but I'm sure he's—'

'Has he said anything about why? Did he, like, leave a note or something?'

Paula looked at the girl. For once, her air of disaffection had slipped and she looked genuinely afraid. 'What do you mean, Katy?' She had to be careful. Nothing the girl said to her now would be admissible.

'I just – I don't know what's going on.'

'Katy?' Another girl was approaching. Slim, also in jeans and a vest top, flip-flops. Avril. Paula let her eyes train over her friend, trying to give no flicker of recognition. Avril also pretended not to know Paula. 'I'm going now. You know, I'm away for the weekend. Will you be OK?' She was going away for Paula's wedding. Paula squinted at the gravel she was standing on.

'Yeah,' said Katy distractedly. 'It's just – where would he go? I don't understand it.' There it was, the concern she hadn't shown for Alice.

'I'm sure they're looking for him,' said Avril soothingly. Even her voice sounded different undercover – higher, less sure of herself. 'Anyway, I need to go say bye to Peter. I know he's worried about Dermot too. See you Monday, hon?'

Katy's eyes narrowed, just a fraction. 'Peter? He talked to you about Dermot?'

Avril flushed slightly. It might have been having Paula there, or it might even have been slightly real. 'Well, yeah. I think he's scared.'

'Why didn't he talk to me? I'm his friend. He hardly knows you.'

Avril's eyes flicked to Paula's, just for a second. 'I don't know, hon. Maybe he didn't want to worry you, since you and Dermot are so close, like. Anyway, I have to run.'

Katy hesitated. Her manner had grown colder. 'All right. Bye.'

'You can text me anytime, OK?' Avril gave her a hug, which was barely reciprocated, and managing not to look at Paula, dashed off down the path to the lake, where a small wooden boathouse could just be seen in the distance. Standing on the path, outlined in shimmering haze, was a tall boy, straight as a tree. At that distance he looked like a god – beautiful, even. It was hard to imagine the things he'd done to Colette, and maybe to Alice too. It was almost too easy, if you didn't stop yourself, to look for answers. *Oh she led him on, oh she was drunk, oh he wouldn't. He wouldn't.* Would he? Paula hoped Avril remembered that he had. She even ran like a student – young, light, happy.

Paula realised Katy was watching too. She said, 'I'm sorry, Katy, I really can't tell you anything more. We're looking for Dermot, and for Alice. We're doing everything we can.'

Katy met her eyes for a moment. They looked hollow behind her glasses. Despite the heat of the summer her skin was pale, as if she'd never been outside. 'You're not doing anything,' she muttered. 'You haven't a clue.'

'I'm sorry?'

'Never mind.' She hurried off, shoulders hunched.

'Was that Avril?' Corry appeared beside Paula, shading her eyes.

'Yeah. I don't think Katy picked up on it, though. Did you get something?'

In answer, Corry held up an evidence bag. Paula peered into it. 'His phone?'

'Found it in his desk drawer.'

'Why would he leave his phone behind?'

'He knows we can track them, that's why. Not stupid, Mr Healy.'

'That means he doesn't want to be followed, so maybe he's done something to Alice. We should—'

'What's this we?' said Corry. 'It's Friday, Maguire. End of the road for you, I'm afraid.'

She'd forgotten. Tonight, of all things, was her hen do (under extreme sufferance). And tomorrow . . . 'Bollocks,' she said softly.

'Yep. Two weeks' leave for you. And if we don't have this sorted by then, I may as well hand in my notice and get a job selling wedding dresses.'

WhatsApp conversation

Katy: *Hello*

Katy: *Hello?*

Katy: *Are u ignoring me?*

Katy: *Look we need to talk. D is gone off now it's just u and me. Do you know why he went? Did he tell you where?*

Katy: *Hello?*

Katy: *Ur making a big mistake if you think you can just blow me off like that. Warning u.*

Peter has left the conversation.

Chapter Thirty-Three

'Cheers!'

Paula looked with distaste at the cheap white wine, the summit of the pub's meagre 'cellar' – i.e. one fridge half-stocked with alcopops. For a Friday night the place was quiet, a few old men in flat caps and some couples enjoying the two-for-one deal on steak, chips and a Portobello mushroom. The steaks were so large they were hanging over the side of the plates.

Her hen do – something she had thought, and secretly hoped, would never happen – was here. And that meant her wedding was suddenly tomorrow and she was meant to be off for two weeks. The honeymoon in Spain was booked. Maggie was staying with PJ and Pat. Paula had supposedly handed over her case notes that afternoon – though Alice and Dermot were still not found, and that meant she was turning it over and over in her mind, like a stone worn smooth with handling. No answers. Nothing put back in its place. It didn't feel right to stop.

'So,' said Corry, setting down her own glass with a small grimace. 'I don't think we can make any jokes about your last night of freedom and so on, seeing as you've already a wee one at home.'

'Please don't.' She'd stipulated it: no willy straws, no sex jokes, no innuendo, no pink. Avril had still turned up with a sparkly pink tiara. Paula had worn it for ten minutes then accidentally on purpose left it in the ladies. The pink L-plates she had refused entirely. She wondered if Avril was feeling sad about her own aborted wedding – she loved all this, the fake-naughty screams, the glitter, the teary laughter. Hers had never taken place, the engagement to all intents and purposes falling apart the minute she'd met Gerard Monaghan. As it was she seemed subdued – out of her cover for the night and with the wedding the next day, it could be hard to manage the shifts in tone. Corry and Paula were deliberately not asking her anything about it. Paula herself just wanted to go home and drink gin in front of *Newsnight*. She forced a smile. 'It's hard to believe sometimes – I never thought I'd get married.'

'I knew you and Aidan would end up together,' said Saoirse, who was waiting to start IVF again, and drinking J2O. 'They were the cutest couple at school,' she confided to the table. 'Like Angel and Buffy or something. Dawson and Joey. All intense and lovey-dovey. So much angst and drama!'

'He never climbed in my window. My dad would have arrested him on the spot.'

'My da's still like that.' Avril fished around in her wine spritzer with a straw. 'Mind you, Gerard's lot are as bad. I was round the other week and his mammy got out the holy pictures and started testing me on the saints.'

Everyone laughed, though Avril's strained expression did not ease. Sectarianism was now a gentle joke, and no one would really stand in the way if Gerard and Avril got married. It was all easy, too easy. Paula felt a prickle of anxiety between her shoulders.

This feeling was exacerbated when the door opened and two striking women came in, one with short dark hair and a trouser suit, the other fair-haired, in a print dress. She lit the place up, though she was leaning on a stick. Paula jumped up. 'It's Maeve and Sinead.' She had a brief moment of wondering how her uber-Catholic cousin Cassie would take to this, Aidan's best friend and her new wife, then reached out to them.

'I was expecting more pink,' said Maeve, scrutinising her. 'Do you not need an L-plate or two?'

'Don't you dare.'

As Maeve leaned to hug Paula, the left side of her face was exposed, still red with scar tissue. Two years before she'd been badly burned, her lovely face damaged. But her hair was salon-shiny and her blue eyes sharp as ever. 'We'd have been here sooner but the missus refuses to use Satnav.'

'And *my* missus can't drive to save her life. Hi, Paula.' Sinead, a razor-sharp lawyer, hugged Paula. Ever since Aidan and Paula's *rapprochement*, the four had become good friends. Paula was slightly ashamed she'd ever suspected Maeve of designs on Aidan; some behavioural expert she was.

The party shook down, with greater and lesser degrees of success. Saoirse and Maeve were soon nose to nose talking about IVF. Sinead and Corry were having a good bitch about Southern court judges. Paula's cousin Cassie, who'd got married the previous year, was telling Avril a very long and complicated story about some issues they'd had with their hotel: '. . . and I told them and told them, there's English people coming, we need a vegetarian choice, and they said it was extra . . .'

After a while, Paula saw Avril get up, swaying, and head to the ladies. Saoirse, the non-drinker, cocked a head at her. Paula nodded – she'd go.

It was cool and quiet in the ladies, a respite from the

pounding Shania Twain in the bar, which apparently was stuck in a nineties time warp. 'Avril?'

A voice came out of a stall. 'Yeah.'

'You all right?'

'Yes, I just . . .' She sighed. 'I'm really tired. The wine's going to my head.'

'Well, nothing wrong in taking it easy. The wedding's tomorrow, we don't want to be too hungover.'

'No. OK.'

The door opened and Avril came out. Up close, Paula saw there were dark circles under her make-up. She was wearing a short floral dress and lots of foundation, her fair hair straightened, as if trying to distance herself from her student get-up. She washed her hands under the tap.

'Is it getting to you?' asked Paula. The psychology of being undercover was harder than people imagined. The strain, day and night, of pretending to be someone else. Holding yourself rigid even in your sleep. Not to mention the fact that if someone had hurt Alice, they might still be around.

'I can handle it.'

'I'm sure you can.'

'But – it's just so hard, Paula.' Avril leaned her head against the hand dryer. 'It's so hard. Even if I'm nice to Katy I just feel like I'm lying – she's really upset, you know, even if she doesn't show it sometimes – and I keep thinking of Alice, if someone did something to her . . . I'm sleeping in her bed, even. It's weird. And now Dermot going too—'

'It'll be over soon,' said Paula soothingly. 'You don't have to go back after the wedding if you don't want to. Especially now we know about this rape allegation.'

'No, I do. Someone knows something, I'm sure of it. I just don't know who. Or what. I think Peter likes me, so he might tell me something – and Katy, she's starting to trust me, so maybe I'll be able to find out what—' Avril shook herself. 'Listen to me. It's your big night! I shouldn't be talking shop. Let me get you another drink.'

'Oh, no, I don't—'

She was gone. Paula turned to look at her own reflection. In the mirror she too looked pale and tired. A discarded feather from a pink boa hung in her hair, clashing horribly with the red. Tomorrow she'd be primped and preened to within an inch of her life. And one person, the one who should be lacing her into corsets and driving her as mad as Auntie Phil had driven Cassie, would not be there. Her mother was still gone, and all these milestones – Maggie's birth, the wedding, renovating the house – just felt like throwing more dirt on her grave. Kicking over her traces, until it would be one day as if she'd never existed.

There was a bang and Maeve hobbled in on her shiny pink crutch. Paula moved to hold the cubicle door for her.

'Ta.' Maeve went in and closed the door, calling out as she peed. 'Where's the quare fella tonight?'

'Oh, he's out with Saoirse's husband and a few guys from the paper.'

'And the wee one?'

'She's at her granny's.' Paula had wondered about inviting Pat tonight, but baulked – you could invite your stepmother to your hen do, of course, but not your soon-to-be mother-in-law. 'You're sure you don't want to stay at mine?'

'No thanks, I'm not too good with stairs. We're booked into a nice hotel. Well, nice-ish, I mean, it is still Ballyterrin.'

So that meant Paula would spend the night alone – Saoirse couldn't sleep over as she needed Dave to inject her with hormones in the middle of the night, and Aidan was supposed to be staying with them too. She could have slept at PJ and Pat's, but she felt it would be fitting, to have one last night truly alone. Just her and the ghost of her mother.

Maeve came out and leaned her stick against the sink as she washed her hands. 'He seems great, I must say. I've never seen him so well.'

'Oh. Good. This Conlon news threw him a bit.'

'He'll be OK. He's a daddy now, it's changed things for him.' Maeve caught her eye in the mirror. 'I heard your man was back. Brooking.'

Of course, as a journalist, Maeve always knew things. 'Um. Yeah – they brought him over for this Alice Morgan case. I didn't know.'

Maeve hesitated. She wanted to say something, clearly, acknowledge the elephant in the room, and Paula suddenly couldn't let her. 'We're doing our best,' she said in a rush. 'Aidan and me. I didn't want any of this, the wedding and that, but we're OK. He loves Maggie. He's a great dad.'

'Ah, I know he is. Sure he never stops going on about her.' Maeve nudged her affectionately. 'Anyway, I knew it as soon as I saw you, Maguire. I said to myself, that's the woman who's fit for Aidan O'Hara.'

'You did?'

'Oh aye. Only person I know who's even nosier and more stubborn than he is.'

'You're a fine one to talk, Ms Investigative Journalist of the Year.' Maeve had won this award the year before, despite her injuries.

Maeve pulled another feather from Paula's hair. 'Thank God for Google, eh? My days of running down alleys are over, I think. Now come on, Bridezilla. You've got a big day tomorrow.'

Chapter Thirty-Four

'You take this one.' Saoirse, sober and bossy, was putting people in cabs, checking her phone. Avril was already slumped in one, eyes closed. Paula hoped she wouldn't be sick.

'How are things on the "lads about town" stag do?' Paula nodded to Saoirse's phone.

'Dave says he's home already. Got a dodgy pint or something. Couldn't handle his booze, more like.' Saoirse's husband was a huge, rugby-playing bear of a man, and Paula imagined he'd actually come home early in order to see his adored wife.

'Any sign of the groom?' she said lightly, thinking how odd that sounded.

'Not sure. Still out, I guess.'

'Well, just make sure he gets there tomorrow.' She had visions of Aidan passed out in a ditch. 'I don't want to be standing up there like a gom in a big white dress and no groom.'

Saoirse's phone bleeped again. 'Dave says he behaved himself. Only on the beers.'

'Good.' She hugged her friend, loosened up by booze. 'Thanks for this. See you tomorrow for getting Tangoed?'

'You will indeed. Hair and make-up at nine.'

Paula shuddered. 'Promise you won't let them make me

too orange? I mean, seriously, with this hair I can't pull it off.'

'I'll do my best. Off you go.'

In the cab she leaned her head against the cool window, checking her phone. There was a chaotic text from Pat, who had just discovered emojis, or the 'wee picture yokes' as she called them, about how she'd be up at six to steam her hat and how Maggie had gone off to sleep clutching her headband for tomorrow. Tomorrow Paula would marry Aidan. Her fingers hesitated over the screen, thumbing his number. He'd behave. It was his stag do, she wasn't going to bother him.

She paid the driver and let herself in. In the hall she saw a light was on upstairs. A memory grabbed her – the day two years back when she'd come home to find an intruder there, fleeing, but not before stabbing Paula and leaving PJ for dead. He'd been lying on the kitchen floor in a pool of blood. She flicked on the lights – nothing, of course. Silly. 'Hello?'

From upstairs, Aidan's voice, muffled. 'Maguire. You're back early.'

'Yeah, early start and that – are you not meant to be at Dave's?'

'Ach. I didn't want to disturb him. Can't handle his drink, for all the size of him.' She stood at the bottom of the stairs. The bathroom door was ajar, but as she watched, Aidan moved to shut it, and she heard the lock go. Aidan rarely even closed the door when he was in the bathroom – she was always moaning at him as he peed in full view, whistling a tune.

'What are you doing?' She could hear running water.

'Shaving. Get a head-start for tomorrow.'

'Did you not leave your gear at Saoirse and Dave's?' He didn't answer. Frustrated, she went into the kitchen. Maybe he'd overdone it on the booze and come home hoping he'd be passed out before she got back. His jacket was over a chair. She looked at it, but didn't touch. That was a road she did not want to go down. One of Maggie's toys was on the side, an irritating Barbie-like doll, all legs and boobs and fake blond hair. A present from Paula's Auntie Phil. Paula saw it had been dressed up in a confection of lace and net – a bride. Maggie had scribbled on its face with red crayon, perhaps in a cry for greater diversity. Paula set it down carefully, decided she couldn't be bothered making herself a cup of tea. The kitchen looked surprisingly clean – she'd meant to give it a wipe before people landed in the next day, but she hadn't managed it. It was unlike Aidan to notice dirt, yet she saw a streak of cleaner drying on the floor. Had he mopped? She didn't think he had ever mopped before; in fact it was a source of some discord.

On impulse, an impulse she hated, Paula opened the high cupboard where they kept a bottle of whiskey. She wasn't even sure why they had it, except it would seem wrong in an Irish home not to have one round the place. She squinted at the level of the amber liquid. It hadn't gone down. At least she didn't think so.

She went up. Rapped on the bathroom door. Silence. 'What?'

'I'm going to bed now, I have to be up early. Can you let me get in?'

'Just a minute.'

Why was he shaving at one a.m., for God' sake? She listened to him splash around, irked. The door opened.

There he was, stripped to the waist, his jeans dark with water. 'You took your time.'

'I thought you'd be out still.' He looked at her, and she couldn't tell if anything was wrong. 'Relax, will you. Is this going to set the tone for our married life?'

'If you hog the bathroom it might.' She looked behind him. 'Can I go in now?'

'It's all yours.' He stretched, the muscles in his chest shifting. She couldn't imagine a time when she wouldn't want to touch him, run her hands over his skin just for the sheer pleasure of it. 'Like what you see?' He did a mock body-building pose.

'Just checking out what I'll be stuck with.'

'Stuck with, she says! Listen, I'll go in Mags's room, then I'll head out early before you're up. Preserve that sense of mystery, or whatever the bollocks reason was that I had to stay at Dave's.'

'I think so we can hoodwink God into thinking there's been no extra-marital badness.'

'Let's hope the priest doesn't notice Herself, then.' He leaned in and kissed her on the cheek, chastely. 'Sleep well, Maguire. Cos tomorrow's gonna be a long one.' He went into Maggie's room and shut the door. Paula found herself looking around for his T-shirt. Usually Aidan would leave it in his wake, but there was no sign of it in the bathroom or on the landing. She went in, and saw the smear of drying red on the underside of the basin.

She regarded it for a while, but she'd come across enough blood in her time to know it when she saw it. He'd cut himself shaving, maybe. In a hurry, with her hassling him. She tore off some toilet paper and wiped it, flushed; all gone. In the mirror her face looked pale and worried. Paula took a deep breath. She could not do this. Could not suspect her husband all the time, of terrible crimes, of lies, just because she spent her life unpicking other people's. Just because her mother had kept secrets, and was gone, it didn't mean everyone had. And just because her mother had left a man, and a daughter, left them alone in this very house – by choice or not, there was no way to tell – it didn't mean Paula would. It didn't mean she and Aidan couldn't manage this. Of course it didn't. And so she was going to do it, and give it her very best shot, because that was all anyone had to offer.

Paula was very good at opening Maggie's door without making a sound. She peered in at Aidan, already curled up and asleep on the bed. His hand was thrown back, and in the street light Paula could see the cuts and scrapes on his knuckles.

Paula was woken in the morning by Maggie, her red hair in bendy rollers, but still in her Peppa Pig pyjamas, bursting through the door and jumping on the bed. 'Oof! What are you doing here?'

'Granny brung me.'

'*Brought* me.' Maggie ignored her, burrowing under the covers. She was developing a real Ballyterrin accent, which had come as something of a shock to Paula. If she'd thought of it at all, she'd imagined her future children would grow up in England, with polite little Southern accents.

'Where's Daddy?' Maggie had found no one else in the bed, just her mother in an old vest top and pyjama bottoms. Where *was* Daddy? A good question. Paula had lain awake for hours, hearing every car up and down the main road, listening for sounds next door, but she must have fallen asleep by the time he left.

'He's at Auntie Saoirse's house, getting ready.'

Maggie was worrying at Paula's plait. She liked to lay it alongside her own, to see the matching colour, pretend she had long hair. 'Auntie Saoirse's *here*, Mummy.'

'Is she?' Paula could indeed hear voices downstairs, Pat and Saoirse, and the make-up girl, and she was still not even showered. 'Mummy better get up then.'

'Yes, get *up*, Mummy.'

'OK, OK. You go on down then. Be careful on those stairs.' In the bathroom, she confronted her own pale face, the shadows under her eyes almost green with exhaustion. Hungover and tired, and worried sick about the groom – exactly as a bride should be. She sighed. Aidan was right, it was going to be a long day.

Afterwards, it had all somehow blurred into one. Several hours went by of people sticking clips in her hair and running hairdryers and curling her eyelashes and jabbing at her cheeks with sponges. The make-up girl had foundation three inches thick herself, and Paula kept saying, 'Please, not too much, I honestly don't wear a lot.' Saoirse was there, her hair already done but wearing her glasses and a checked shirt over jeans. Flowers were being put in water by PJ. White roses in bud. Paula thought of Yvonne, carrying her blooms up the road, and she wished they'd chosen any other flower for the bouquets. Pat was buzzing about steaming her hat, and putting on mascara, and fretting over when the cars were arriving. Maggie had an unaccountable tantrum over her beaded headband and Paula had to scoop her onto her knee, smudging her make-up and causing exclamations all around. Finally Saoirse was helping her put the dress over her head, the world momentarily muffled in all that silk and lace.

'Ah, look. You're beautiful.' Saoirse stepped back.

'You better not cry, Glocko,' said Paula sternly. 'There are things worth crying about, and me stuffed into a dress made in a Chinese sweatshop isn't one of them.'

'OK.' Saoirse dabbed her eyes. Paula regarded herself in the mirror of her parents' old room. The dress, for all it was cheap, sparkled with beads and lace. She'd insisted on a halter neck, not having the chest for strapless. The dress clung to her down to her knees, then the heavy silk pooled round her feet. Her hair was up, strikingly red against her pale skin and dress. 'Hmm. Could be worse, I suppose.'

Saoirse was gathering the folds of her own lilac dress. 'I'll tell them you're ready.'

'Just – yeah. I just need a minute.'

Alone, for the last time in a long while, she drew in her breath. The room was quiet, the clothes hanging in the wardrobe, the blinds casting shadows. It had been her and Aidan's for two years now, but Paula could still feel her mother there. Feel the secrets she must have been hiding that day in October almost twenty years ago. Imagine how things would be if her mother hadn't gone, if everything was still in its proper place. Maybe she'd still be marrying Aidan, never having left Ballyterrin. Or maybe she'd have gone with her parents' blessing, married some English fella, or no one at all.

It didn't matter, in the end. This was the life she'd ended up with. There was no other. She took a deep breath. It was time.

In the car, squashed in beside her suddenly silent father in his grey morning suit, Paula convinced herself Aidan wouldn't be there. That's what last night was about. He'd

probably done a runner and she'd get some message saying
he was already on a ferry to England . . . she fumbled in her
clutch bag for her phone, which was blank of messages.

'All right?' asked PJ.

'Yes, just . . . um. Bit nervous.'

PJ said nothing for a moment. 'Don't be worrying. He's
been down there this ages.'

'Who?'

'You know who. I got your man Dave to text me, just in
case. He's there all right. Don't you worry.'

Her hand snaked over the folds of silk, found her dad's.
She wasn't going to say anything maudlin about wishing her
mother could see her, and neither was he. They were just
going to get on with things and try to be happy. Because
when it came down to it, that was all you ever could do.

Now they were at the church. Everyone inside. The photographer snapping away. Saoirse with Maggie by the hand,
ready to go in first. PJ asking was she ready, taking her arm
to guide her up the steps. She was trying to breathe. Then
they were in the porch, and she could see rows and rows of
heads through the glass of the doors.

Was that him, up at the front? Dark hair, a suit. She
couldn't see his face properly. The light in the church was
dusty, opaque. Her legs under the stupid, itchy dress were
heavy and she held her breath. There was the team, Avril in
a little hat, hair and lips glossy. Gerard beside her, red and
scrubbed in a suit. Fiacra, some look of sadness on his face,
making him very old and very young all at once. Dave all
spruced up too – a reminder that she'd missed his and
Saoirse's wedding, how unforgivable. Pat in her 'mother of
the bride and groom too, it's awkward, let's not mention it'

outfit of old gold. She was pleased to see Bob had come with Linda, his wife. Someone must be minding Ian, their disabled son. Her father had gone in too, stumping to his seat with one last squeeze of her arm. She'd asked not to be given away, thinking it old-fashioned, sexist even, but as she stood in the porch she wished there was someone to propel her forward, show her the way. She heard Maggie's voice rise above the hubbub – *Mummy* – and the sound went up, light as a balloon. They didn't know she'd arrived yet, and so she got to watch her own wedding for a moment, in the church where they'd held her mother's memorial, the smell of damp hymnals and rubber hassocks, the heavy weight of gilt – and guilt, for that matter. Oh God. She was frozen. She didn't think she could actually take a step forward on her own. Where was Aidan? Why couldn't she see him properly? God help him, if he was late for this . . .

'Paula.'

Him. What was he . . . ? At first she thought he'd come to give her away, walk her down the aisle – and she was almost grateful for a second. Later, she would not forgive herself for that small moment, that slip, of being pleased to see him.

'What are you doing here?' Had she invited him? No, of course she hadn't.

'I'm sorry.' He stepped into the church porch in his navy suit, his eyes finding hers. 'I'm so sorry to do this today, believe me, I . . .'

Paula was suffocated under the veil. She threw it back. 'Do what?' Outside there was a white car. Blue markings. She understood it was a police car, same as she saw every day, but her brain couldn't work out what it was doing here, parked outside the church. On her wedding day. Then she saw the uniformed officers, and realised she'd let her bouquet fall to the ground, the white roses landing with a damp flump.

Guy was coming towards her, talking rapidly, quietly. As if time was running out. 'It's Sean Conlon – he's been murdered.'

Again, her first thought was odd – some kind of regret. What if he'd known something? They'd never be sure now.

He was still moving, speaking fast and low. The officers were at the door. 'It's Aidan. He was the last person to see Conlon. They had a fight. Last night. Everyone in the pub saw. Now Conlon's dead. I'm sorry to come here but I thought it might be easier if it was me – they wouldn't wait – I'm sorry.'

Aidan was coming down the aisle. That was the wrong way round. She was meant to go to him. She had a moment to see his face – pale under the dark hair – his grey wedding suit – the single white rose in his buttonhole.

Then, too late, she finally understood.

Alice

When I was little – shortly before they packed me off to boarding school and moved to Africa – Tony and Rebecca took me to a circus. I was almost sick with excitement. I remember the popcorn, the smell of elephant poo, the way the steel poles of the tent dug down into the mud. The red and blue dome overhead, the man in the top hat and whip.

The thing I remember most is the magician. He had a sparkly red cape and a moustache, and a lady in a spangly swimsuit I thought must be his wife. He did tricks, pulled rabbits from his hat – and then he chopped his wife into pieces. It worked like this. She went into the giant box with stars painted on the side. Then the magician began pushing swords through it. When the first one went in, I screamed. Rebecca tutted and told me to be quiet. But Tony smiled at me, and a minute later I felt him take my sticky little hand in his big one, and I knew everything was OK.

Then of course the box fell apart and the lady wasn't there; she'd vanished and appeared at the top of the tent, on the platform for the trapeze artists, shining like a star. I clapped so hard my hands hurt. It was like a miracle. Later on, when it became clear I'd been taken to the circus to soften the blow of being sent away, I wondered what it would be like to actually be the magician's wife. Never knowing when he might make you disappear, or when he might cut you to pieces.

Part Three

'If there's no meaning in it,' said the King, 'that saves a world of trouble, you know, as we needn't try to find any.'

Lewis Carroll, *Alice's Adventures in Wonderland*

Ballyterrin, Northern Ireland, July 1981

There were freedom fighters, in other countries, who strapped their bombs to their own bodies. Pulled a switch, went sky-high along with everyone else, straight to the afterlife in a blaze of glory. Died for the cause, and willingly.

That was not the Republican way. If you got blown up with your own bomb it was because you'd made a hames of it. No, your way was to plant it, walk off, then pull the switch. Ring in a warning, if you were feeling nice about it. Stand back and watch it go up. Today, there had been no bomb. And yet the feeling as you drove away from Ballyterrin was the same. A sort of excitement, that made you tap your fingers on the wheel and fidget your feet on the pedals. Waiting for it to go up. It was lunchtime now. They'd find him soon, and then . . .

He'd known you when you came to the door. Smile on his face. *A chara.* Friend. *Come on in.*

Your hands convulsed at the memory. It had to be done, friend or no friend. It was your duty and you weren't about to shirk it, not when those lads in the jail had given body and blood to the struggle. The least you could give was a bit of your soul.

It was over quickly. The surprised look on his face, the light in the eyes going out, the slump down the hallway, a dark red stain sliding behind him. Nice wallpaper, with bobbly bits. Ruined now. Behind him, under the coatrack, a pair of child's welly boots. Yellow. Duck's faces on the front.

But you weren't going to think about that. You were driving fast, the radio playing. 'Ghost Town'. That was nearly funny. You were passing the old church now, almost away from Ballyterrin. For a moment you imagined pulling up, going in, out of the heat in that cold stone, and gulping in the air, and saying your penance. But no. Better to get away. In the gate of the church a girl was standing, her eyes shaded against the sun. Yellow dress, yellow hair. Something in her hands – white roses? As you passed, the air from the car moulded her dress around the shape of her, and you noticed, and that was good. You'd feel OK again soon. You'd smile at pretty girls on summer days. You'd bring them roses. Everything would be grand. Soon.

The radio. 'In Belfast, another hunger striker lies on the brink of death . . .' He would die now. Because of what you'd done. You did what you had to, for the struggle.

But the smile on his face. Welcoming you in. *Sean*, he'd said. *A chara. Come on in.* You weren't sure if you would ever forget that.

Chapter Thirty-Five

'But miss, you can't—'

Shaking, Paula rounded on the desk sergeant. 'It's *Doctor*. What's your name? I've been working here nearly three years, for Christ's sake. I'm entitled to go into the station if I want.' She'd even brought her work pass to the church, among the cards in her wallet. God knows why.

'But, you're . . .' He waved a hand at her dress with its stiff cream layers, the flowers falling down from her head.

'That's because it's my wedding day, you eejit. Only you lot arrested the bloody groom.' She'd watched Aidan being loaded into the police car – moving like a sleepwalker, not looking at her – and she'd collared some late-arriving guest, made them drive her up the road. She wasn't even sure who, one of Aidan's colleagues at the paper, maybe? A youngish fella. Rude to turn up late, anyway.

The desk sergeant was gesturing helplessly. 'But you can't . . .'

'All right, let her in.' Helen Corry appeared, clattering through reception in sky-high heels. Paula had a moment to think how well she looked, in an oyster-grey silk suit, a little hat on her fair hair. She must have come straight from the church. 'You couldn't have gone home to change?' she asked Paula, not unkindly.

'No! Aidan's been arrested!'

'I know, I know.' She had buzzed them in, was directing Paula down a corridor. The station was as full as it always was on a Saturday, and she felt the curious looks from officers she knew and ones she didn't. Flicking over her skin like little scratches. Corry opened a door and switched on a light. 'In you go.'

'An interview room? For God's sake.'

'The nice one, at least. Come on, you can't be running round here like Runaway Bride.'

Paula relented, sinking with shaking hands into the sofa. It was the place they took victims, or families, people in deep shock – that was her now, the family. Of the suspect.

Corry stayed standing. 'I rang around. I asked why in the name of God would they do this at your wedding – apparently there's good evidence against him.'

She was running it through in her head – Aidan at the house. The blood. 'Sean Conlon.' Her voice was muffled, like it was coming from far away. 'He's dead.'

'Well, yes. He was drinking in Flanagan's pub last night. The punters said Aidan came in about eleven, saw Conlon, started on him. Conlon went out back, Aidan followed. Neither came back in so the barman just thought they'd gone off home.'

Paula knew the owner of Flanagan's well. He'd stayed open all through the Troubles by turning so many blind eyes it was a wonder he could see at all. 'And what then?'

Slight pause. 'Well, they found Conlon's body this morning, in the car park. He'd been beaten to death – Paula, someone smashed his head off the tarmac.'

She made a small noise in her throat. The bruises on Aidan's hands. Paula suddenly thought she might be sick.

She closed her eyes. 'It – it was my wedding day,' was all she could think to say.

'I know. It's a crap thing they did. Willis said they thought he'd be a flight risk – you probably even had a honeymoon booked . . .'

Oh God. Another layer of things to cancel. The flights, the hotel in Granada, the meal for seventy-five guests – all that money . . .

Paula realised her breath was coming thick and raspy. 'What do I do? I don't know what to do.'

'He could get bail maybe – he needs a good lawyer. Do you know anyone?'

Lawyers. She had to think. The only ones she knew had defended some of the worst terrorists in Ireland. But they'd often won, of course. 'Colin McCready,' she said. 'Call him. Tell him it's Paula. Tell him it's Margaret's girl.'

'Isn't he—'

'Yeah. So he'll do it.' Her mother's old boss. Paula was fairly sure he'd been in love with Margaret – even though she'd been suspected of stealing information about the Republican prisoners they defended, giving it to Special Branch. More than enough, in the eyes of the IRA, to execute someone.

She lurched to her feet. 'Where's Maggie?' Dear God, she'd run out of the church without even thinking about her child. She'd be so confused, frightened . . .

'She's with your stepmum. I don't think anyone knows what to do – but I persuaded Pat to go home with the wean. Your dad's outside.'

'I need to see her . . . she'll be upset, she was so excited—' She reached for the door.

'You don't want to see Aidan? I can get you a quick chat, he's in the cells—'

She shook her head. 'No. Maggie needs me.' And all she could think about was Aidan's hands, his missing T-shirt, the way he'd kissed her so gently on the cheek. Judas kiss. She turned to Corry. 'Will you call the lawyer? I don't think I can . . . I couldn't talk to him today. I need to go. I need Maggie.'

'Of course I will.' Paula could hardly stand the look of sympathy on Corry's face, normally so stern and professional.

Her voice wobbled. 'Thanks.'

Outside, the office was a blur. Ringing phones, sympathetic faces. She had to get away from it.

'Paula—' He was in the doorway. His face so kind she could hardly bear it. Before she even knew it she was walking away from him. No. She wouldn't do this. She wouldn't go to Aidan, to where he was locked in one of the cells – in this very building! – but she wouldn't go to Guy either, not after he'd come to the church on her wedding day, bringing with him nothing but doom. She shook her head and walked past him, out of the police station that held both men, her wedding dress hanging around her, useless. In the car park, her dad was leaning against his Volvo. In his new grey wedding suit, his face grim, his bad leg held out stiff. She went to him, rustling silk with every step. 'Oh Dad,' she said, the tears finally coming as she sobbed into his shoulder.

'Just visiting today, Dr Maguire?'

She forced a smile. 'Yes. A personal visit this time.'

The prison officer, what Paula's father would call a 'wee hard man', who had a white moustache and shoulder epaulettes, signed her into the visitors' room without further comment. Paula had been in prisons many times. She was an old hand at the clang of metal doors, the bleach and cabbage smell of the places, the suffocating heat. The blank file of women heading to the visitors' room, occasionally casting glances at each other's shoes or hair. But she'd never been here before as one of them.

Aidan looked different behind the table. Smaller somehow – he'd been in here two nights already, while Paula tried to sort out the mess he'd left. He was fidgeting about in a way that meant he wanted to smoke. Paula thought of the cigarettes she'd found in his pocket, and for a moment loss got her by the throat – he'd lied to her about that. Maybe he'd lied to her about everything. She started to walk towards him, willing her feet to move.

He was the first to speak. 'Are you OK?'

'Me? I'm fine.'

'But the wedding – Jesus, what a mess.'

'Dad handled it. People got fed, I think, and then they went home.'

'Your big day.'

'For God's sake. I never wanted all that, and you know it.'

'But you were there, in your dress – I hardly saw you, Maguire, they were hauling me off. But you looked—'

'*Stop* it. I never wanted a big white wedding. I wanted you. And now you're . . . Christ, look at you.'

He looked down at his knuckles – one hand was shining raw. 'Yeah. He's got some buddies in here.'

'But you didn't do it. Just tell them you didn't do it.' Aidan said nothing, and she watched the moment sail away. 'Will you at least tell me what happened, for God's sake?' She lowered her voice. 'You had blood on you. That night you came in.'

She waited for him to explain it all away. He didn't. 'Aye. If they ask you, tell them whatever you know. Don't lie for me. I won't have you losing your job, it's too important.'

'Don't be stupid. I can't—'

'Listen to me, Maguire. You've work to do, finding that missing girl and all the other ones too. You have to be above suspicion. Tell them it all and I'll sink or swim on my own.' His face tightened for a minute. 'Is Mags . . . did she see them take me?'

'No, she was – she was up front with Saoirse. She wants to know where you are, of course.' Paula didn't say that Maggie had cried herself to sleep the last two nights, inconsolable, wanting Daddy to put her to bed. There'd even been a search of the house. Quick, and discreet as possible, thanks to Corry, but all the same hands running over her things, opening up all the secret places of the life she and Aidan had been building. Until two days ago. 'But, Aidan, listen—'

'She likes the *Hungry Caterpillar* story at bedtime. And *Goodnight Moon*. And I make up a story and do the voices – and she likes the jammies with the ducks, but not the ones with teddies. She thinks they have a funny look in their eyes.'

'OK.' She knew all this, but it seemed to soothe him. 'But you'll be back soon. You'll get bail, surely, and then a trial—' Bail wasn't guaranteed in murder cases, but surely they'd see he hadn't done it. See he wasn't capable of such a thing.

'I'm not sure I'll get bail.'

'What?' Paula felt a lurch in her stomach. 'Aidan. You need to tell me what's going on! Did you see him? Conlon?' She was remembering the man, his soft voice, his watchful eyes. Imagined Aidan lunging at him, Aidan who was all bluster and fire. Getting Conlon by the throat and pushing him down, and banging his head again and again on the rain-slick surface of Flanagan's car park. Beside the bins with their stink of stale booze. Smashing the man's head until he stopped moving.

No. She couldn't imagine it. But Aidan was nodding.

'You went to Flanagan's?'

'Aye. I just wanted . . . well, I thought I could have one for the road. One last time.'

'And he was there.'

'Aye. He said—' Aidan swallowed. 'He knew who I was. The paperman's boy. I said he'd a lot of nerve coming to the pub, after all the people he'd killed. He said he'd served his time and if I'd a problem drinking with murderers he suggested I found myself another establishment. I said he never served his time for everyone he killed. He tried to push past me, go outside for a fag. I smelled it on him. You know my da, he used to smoke in the office. You were allowed to, back then. It's why I always – well, I should quit, I know, but the smell always reminds – I just like it.'

Paula found she was conjuring John O'Hara, his spicy tobacco smell, the mints he always had in his pocket. She'd only been six when he was killed, but she knew exactly what had happened. Like all children in Northern Ireland, she was very well aware she was living somewhere that was not safe, where bad men could walk in and shoot your uncle John, who was so kind and always said *there's wee Paula* when he saw you and gave you a Polo to suck down to a sliver.

'When Da died, he'd been smoking. I watched it burning away in the ashtray when they left, and he was—'

Paula knew the rest of this story. John, dying, not knowing if the gunmen who'd shot him had seen Aidan, had motioned to the child not to move from where he was playing under a desk. So he hadn't, even after the men did their work and left his daddy to bleed to death on the floor. She bit the side of her mouth in frustration. This was old sorrow. This should have been gone and buried, not still giving more. 'I asked you to tell me what happened.'

'Aye, I – well. I followed him out. I said, Conlon, you lying prick, tell me what you know about my da. And he just says, he's dead. I know he's fucking dead, I say. What I don't know is who killed him, but I'm thinking you do. You said you served your time – well me and my ma are still doing ours.' Aidan swallowed again. 'So he stubbed out his fag on the wall. Says, son, you want to be careful who you ask those questions. Or you'll get in the same kind of trouble as your da. My da was a great man, I say – I'd had a few, Maguire, I admit – and he says – your da was a Brit-licking traitor, son. This war is over now, and your da was a casualty. He knew what he was doing. I suggest you let it go. So I pull him back – he's . . . he was a big lad, you know, must have kept in shape inside – and I shut the door in his face. And he goes . . . he goes . . . *you're the same weak wee shite as you were back then.*'

Paula let out all her breath. No one knew Aidan had seen his father die – the police were afraid the men who'd shot his father might not baulk at killing a child witness. 'So you mean . . . he admitted it? He said he was there that night?'

Aidan put his face in his hands. 'Aye. Maybe. What does it matter? Even if he didn't pull the trigger he knew. They all knew. They assassinated my da in cold blood and nobody gave a damn.'

'So what did you do?' Her voice sounded dull, like a clanging bell.

'I saw red – I hit . . . I hit, God. I hit him. He went down . . . I kicked him. Then I ran. I ran off, came home. I washed off the blood – you saw. It was all over my T-shirt.'

'Did you put it in the bin?' It was surreal. A chat about laundry.

'Aye, it's in the big bin outside. They'll have found it by now.'

'Aidan—' She prepared to ask the question that could change everything. Because despite what he'd said, she couldn't see him beating a man until he was dead. 'When you stopped – was Conlon still alive? Was he breathing?'

Aidan looked at his raw hands. 'I – I thought so. I thought he was making a noise. And I sort of – time went funny. I was on the whiskey, and it's been a while – and I just can't be sure, you know. God help me, Maguire, I just don't know.'

Paula sat staring at the table. Coffee rings marked its plastic surface. Dirty, and ruined, just like everything else. 'How could you do this?' she said quietly.

'I didn't mean—'

'I asked you. I asked would you be OK. And you told me we'd be fine. You promised me. And I put on a fucking white dress for you and I went to the church and . . . all for you!'

Aidan looked stung. 'Maguire, come on. I wanted to marry you. I wanted us to be a family. Is that so wrong? I know you never wanted the wedding, you've been dragging your heels since day one, but—'

'No, I didn't want it. But I did it for you. I did it, and I stayed in this bloody town for you, though I should have gone years back, and this is how you repay me. And Maggie. How could you do this to her?'

He jerked as if she'd slapped him. 'I'd do anything for her. Anything.'

'Anything except keep your bloody temper for one night. One night you go out, and you're back on the booze, back in your seedy old pubs, fists out – Christ, Aidan, I thought you were past all that.'

'It's been two years! Have I ever given you a moment's worry? Have I not made your dinner, and minded your house, and looked after your child, and—'

'My child!' She was aware that people were starting to look over, and tried to lower her voice to a savage whisper. 'Since when is she *my* child?'

As soon as she'd said it, Paula wished she could take the words back. Push them into the dark again. Go back to how things had been, the comfort of silence, the gentleness of lies.

When he spoke, Aidan's voice was soft. 'Maguire. That's the thing, see.'

'Look, I shouldn't have—' She wanted to keep talking, fill the space with words, make a dam against the thing he was about to say, rushing towards them like a wall of water, so big she could already feel the shape of it.

'I'm not,' he said. 'I should have – God help me, I don't think we can get past this now but I have to tell you – I'm not.'

She should have said, *not what?* But she didn't. Because she knew.

Aidan said, 'I'm not her dad. It's – well, it's not me, so you can work it out. I thought it wouldn't matter – I thought he didn't love you like I did, back off to London with his wife. I thought if I could get you back, I'd be worthy of it, I'd take you both as mine. And I did. I did, didn't I? She wouldn't have felt the difference? She knows I love her?'

Paula found her voice, choked up in her throat, and spoke carefully. 'What the hell are you saying? We don't know who her father is. You can't tell by looking. I know we learned in school you can't have a blue-eyed child if one parent has brown eyes but it's not true, it's more complex than that—'

'Maguire. There was a test.'

And the world stopped.

'You did a test on Maggie?' Her voice flattened out, cold as marble. She felt rage seep into her blood. 'You need my permission for that.'

He was looking down at the table. Aidan had many faults, but he was a terrible liar.

'Not you. I know you wouldn't do that.' No, like her, he would have been too scared to know the result. Her dad wouldn't have either, he preferred to leave things be and hope for the best. So that meant . . . 'Your mother did a test? Pat did it?'

'She was minding Maggie ages ago, after she was born – she got a wee test out of Boots and I suppose she just – did it. It's just a cheek swab, you know, Mags didn't feel a thing—'

Paula snarled. '*For fuck's sake.*'

'OK, I know, that's not the point. Please don't be angry with her, Maguire. She's eaten up with guilt. She did it because – she thought it was keeping us apart, that she married your da – her selfishness, stopping Maggie from having a family. I don't think she ever believed you would, you know, sleep with someone else. She thought it had to be me and she wanted to prove it, make us get together. It's just not in her world view that you would – do that. But then – well. The results came back.'

Despite his words, Paula had so far been sitting inside a bubble of denial. Aidan was upset, talking nonsense. Pat wouldn't do that. Aidan couldn't love Maggie like that if he wasn't – but suddenly the world was tilting.

'Say something,' said Aidan, pleading. 'Look. Brooking – he loved you, in his way. He's just English. And I've taken his wean away these past two years. God forgive me, it was wrong. But I thought it was the right thing. I honestly did. I've done my best by you both, I swear I have. Last night, it was just – I fucked up, Maguire.'

Paula gradually became aware of her surroundings, the rise and fall of voices, children shouting, the bleach smell of the place. The enormity of what he was telling her sank in. For a long time, minutes or maybe even hours, days, neither of them spoke. Then she stirred. Her hands felt numb. 'Just tell me one thing.'

Aidan could barely move his head. She'd never seen him like this, so sunk under misery. It made her heart race in her chest with fear, made her want to run right out from those concrete walls and snatch up Maggie and never come back. 'What?'

'When was this?' Her voice came out strangely. 'How long have you known?' Suddenly, everything depended on his answer.

Aidan said, 'When I asked you to marry me. The first time.'

When he'd come to her in the hospital, after she'd been attacked. Maggie just weeks old. And he'd said let's not do a test, I'll be her dad, no matter what. 'You're saying you *knew* . . . you mean . . .' Aidan was not Maggie's father. It was as certain as writing on a page. Guy Brooking was. She'd been raising Guy's child. And Aidan had known about it for two years.

'I'll tell them what happened between me and that man

Conlon, Maguire. They can judge as they see fit. But I reckon I'll be in here a while. Maggie will be—' His voice hitched and she bit her lip, hard, to keep the tears from her eyes. 'She'll maybe be a big girl by then. So don't fall out with Ma, Maguire. You'll need her. Don't blame her. I just needed to tell you, so that you knew. So you can choose. And I hope that the past two years – I've loved you, Maguire, God help me I have, and the wee one too – I just have to hope that counts for something.'

Her world had shrunk to the rickety coffee-stained table between them. And with a sudden rush Paula understood this was real, this was happening. Aidan was in prison. He might not get out. And that the carefully constructed shell of the past two years – happy years, happiness that seemed to cut her to ribbons now – was shattered and fallen to pieces around them.

Alice

I don't understand why you're going. *Katy's voice is quiet in the dark, but it doesn't matter. We both know neither of us can sleep.*

I could say, of course you know. I know you know. I could say, I know you were there. But I can't speak.

Al . . . I don't know what's happened. Why are you leaving me? For that horrible cottage?

My voice is very small and hard. I have to.

But do you . . . do you not like me any more?

I almost laugh. She can ask me this, after everything? When I'm dying? When I haven't eaten a bite since it happened?

I realise Katy is crying. Al . . . you're my best friend. *She's out of bed. I hear her heavy footsteps on the square of carpet between our beds.* Al – please don't be mad with me. I can't – I can't take it.

She's kneeling beside me. I can feel her breath – warm, damp. And suddenly I am back there. That night. Everything. I love you, *she says.* You know I love you.

I'm out of bed before I know it, shaking. Get away.

Katy cries harder, sitting on the floor. I don't understand. What did I do?

I could say, Oh, hey Katy, you know how you were actually there when it happened? You didn't happen to see if it was Peter or Dermot or maybe both? (Or you, you're there sometimes when I . . .)

I say, Katy. *Louder.* Katy.

I know she can hear me but it takes her a while to say, What.

Why don't you help me?
She doesn't answer.
I try, I know you know what happened.
Nothing.
Katy, I could tell them, you know. I could tell them what you did to me and . . .
Nothing again, and I think she's just going to ignore me. Then I hear her voice, hard and low across the room. I don't know why you think they'd believe you. Everyone knows you're fucked up. So fine – if you want to go, just go. Leave me. Disappear, if that's all you know how to do.

Chapter Thirty-Six

'Listen, pet, I know what happened, Aidan told me—'

'No, Dad. It's not OK – I didn't want this! Aidan and I, we discussed it, it was no one else's business . . .'

'I know.' PJ put his hand on her arm. He was not a demonstrative man, and it stopped Paula in her tracks. She'd burst into their house, nothing in her head but anger at what Pat had done, what Aidan had done. 'I know all that. She had no business. She knows it too. She was just in a bad way. Thinking it was her fault you and himself couldn't get your heads together.'

'No one told me! Did you know too?'

He shook his head. 'I didn't, pet, I swear it, I just found out—'

'Lying to me! For *two goddamn years*! About my own child!' Vaguely, she wondered if Maggie was in earshot. She was too angry to care.

'I know. Listen, would you. Pat did a wrong thing, and it's been eating her up ever since. But you need to know something else before you go tearing into her. She was down at the hospital the other day—'

'I know, Saoirse told me, but—'

'*Paula.*' She subsided. Her father – did he have tears in his eyes? She'd never seen him cry, not even when her mother went. He'd kept it from her, tried to pretend everything would be fine, in the grand tradition of Ireland.

'Dad.' Her heart fell like a stone. 'What—'

'She's not well.' PJ's voice was suddenly thick with tears. 'She – she went for some ould tests, and they said . . . well – she's not well. She didn't want to tell you till after the wedding.'

'Is it – what is it?' Paula could hardly force the words out. 'Cancer?' He nodded dully. 'What kind?' PJ opened his mouth, nothing came out. Made a shapeless, desperate gesture with his hands. 'Breast?' she tried. He nodded again. 'Well, that's – it's often OK, isn't it . . . I mean did they say . . .'

'Aye, aye, they're going to try – things.' He gave a big juddering sigh. 'Look at the cut of me. Grown man bawling like a wean. There's things they can do, or so they say. But she needs us to help her get well.'

'Where is she?'

He indicated the living room. 'But don't . . .'

'I won't. Let me see her.'

Pat was lying on the sofa, an unprecedented sight. She had her eyes closed and a blanket draped round her. She stirred as Paula went in, groping for her glasses. 'Oh, pet . . .'

'Don't get up.' Paula went over to her, sank to her knees. 'Oh Pat.' Suddenly she was choking back tears too, her nose aching and eyes blurred. 'God, what a mess. It's all such a bloody mess.'

'I'm sorry, pet,' Pat croaked. 'I did a terrible thing. It wasn't my place. And I love her, you know I love her like she was . . . and you like you're . . .'

'Shh.' Paula grasped Pat's hand, which was shaking, cold despite the blanket and warm day. 'We'll get you well. None of that matters now. Leave it. We had to find out sometime.'

'I never treated her any different,' Pat was saying. 'She's my wee dote . . . And my Aidan, locked up in that place, because of what that man did . . . When's it going to be over? When will we have a bit of happiness?'

Paula didn't know the answer to that. It hadn't seemed so much to ask for; a wedding, a happy family. But that wasn't going to be the way of it now. 'It's OK. It'll be OK.'

She looked up at her father, who was stooped against the door lintel, as if he was sick too. She knew two things – one, that although this changed everything, she would never reproach Pat for what had happened. It was done, it was crossed, it was too late. But two, that every moral and reason in her being told her she had to let Guy Brooking know he was Maggie's father.

'Paula.' Colin McCready rose from behind his desk. 'I'm very sorry . . .'

'Yeah. Thanks.' Paula sat down, dropping her bag on the floor. She didn't want to hear how sad it was. She wanted to do something about it, and quick. She hadn't slept a wink all night – her wedding dress staring at her like a ghost from inside the wardrobe, Maggie limp beside her, having cried herself to sleep. She'd sent everyone away – she couldn't bear the looks, the pity. Now she was here to do something. If that was even possible. There had to be something she could do. She just had to focus on that, and keep going, and maybe it would be all right, and she wouldn't have to think about the fact her wedding hadn't gone ahead and Aidan was in prison. 'So you've had the details, I think. It seems . . . well, I wouldn't say they had a watertight case.' They. She was used to being on the side of the police. Of right, as Corry said. But now . . . she didn't know.

'No. Unfortunately your . . . er, Mr O'Hara did admit to assaulting Mr Conlon that night. That will make it difficult. Any of the blows he dealt could, of course, have killed Mr Conlon. Mr O'Hara was seen drinking by several people, and his dispute with Mr Conlon is well known—'

'Yes, yes,' said Paula impatiently. 'It's not good. I know it's not good. I just want to know what's likely to happen.' So that she could make some decisions.

He hesitated. 'If we're lucky they won't be able to prove he intended Conlon's death . . . manslaughter, even. But they might say Mr O'Hara went to the pub with pre-meditation. He hadn't been in there for a long time, the owner said.'

Typical of the landlord, dropping Aidan, who had been one of his most loyal customers, in it at the first sign of trouble. 'Aidan's been off the drink. It was his stag do.'

'I know. That may . . . go against him. You also had a trip booked for a few days later, I believe. That doesn't look good.'

'It was our honeymoon.' She stared hard at her hands. The wedding manicure was still in place, not even chipped. But everything else was broken, wrecked beyond repair.

'I know. I'm very sorry. There's other evidence too – they've matched Mr O'Hara's shoes to some footprints on the deceased.'

She didn't understand. '*On* him?'

'It looks like he's been stamped on.' Aidan, planting a trainer on Conlon's chest – the distinctive star of the Converse he always wore – standing on the man, kicking him till he stopped moving.

She wasn't going to be sick. Not here. She would hold it together. 'Right. And how many years would it be for manslaughter?'

'With good behaviour . . . maybe eight.'

Eight. Maggie would be ten then, at least. Paula tried hard to breathe.

He hovered, his kind face red and anxious. 'I'm very sorry, Paula. I wish I'd better news.'

She stood up. She couldn't bear pity, not from him, or anyone. 'Not your fault. Will you take the case please, Colin? I want you to do it. I know you'll see him right . . . or as right as anyone can.'

'I'll do my best, Paula. Of course I will. But—'

'I know it's not good. Just whatever can be done.' Compassion on his florid, fat face. Colin McCready, a lifelong bachelor, did not look after himself all that well.

Suddenly she knew she had to get out of there, the sad little office with its out-of-date calendar and wilting pot plants, the very same desk in the reception that her mother had sat at, in another life. 'Thank you, Colin.'

Outside, the town felt febrile. Ready to pounce, ready to topple. The murder of a prominent Republican like Sean Conlon, coming in the restless heart of the summer, would not pass peacefully. The streets were full of men, young and old, hanging about. Waiting for something, even if they didn't know what. Hoods pulled over their faces. Stones in their pockets, and maybe worse.

'There'll be more trouble tonight,' PJ had remarked that morning in a 'talking about normal things' voice. Because for everyone else, this was normal. Life was going on. They'd riot and burn things, and everyone would enjoy themselves, except the police, who'd get spat at and dodge stones and wonder if anyone in the crowd happened to have a gun.

No one cared about Paula's problems. It mattered to no

one that her wedding had been cancelled and her fiancé was in prison. It was high summer in Ballyterrin, and that meant riots would be held, and maybe someone would die, and Alice Morgan would still be missing. Nothing had changed, but all the same everything was different.

Alice

It was a while before I heard about Yvonne. I was already working here when Maureen brought it up. Bloody old gossip. I don't know how you can stay alone in here, Alice.

Oh really? *Thinking – shut up, you nosy old bag. Trying to sound light and perky.*

Oh aye. Well, you know about the girl who vanished here? *And of course I didn't and of course she told me every gory detail, ending on:* and they never found her, not even a hair off her head.

Are you saying I'll vanish too, Maureen? *I said.*

You never know, *she said, with that usual vague dread that Irish people seem to like. Then off she pops for an evening at home with her awful husband, leaving me out here all alone in my damp cottage with no lock. Thanks, Maureen! But I maybe I should thank her after all. Maybe that gave me the idea.*

I looked Yvonne up, later that night, all alone in my horrible spidery cottage. Anything to take my mind off things. And there was her photo – and it was like looking at myself. As if I'd died and this was my memorial. And I'd never even heard of her.

How awful, to be gone and not be famous. To be missing and the world just keep going on, as if you just slipped out of someone's pocket and down the back of a sofa. The people who hurt you just carrying on with their lives, as if you didn't matter. Not being punished. Not being stopped.

It won't be like that for me. I'm going to make sure of it.

Chapter Thirty-Seven

Paula paused with her pass at the door of the station. She couldn't bear it. She just wanted to get on with work, forget that she'd been up all night again with a sobbing Maggie who wanted to know why Daddy had to go away. Paula had hardly been able to leave her that morning, with a quivering-eyed Pat and silent, miserable PJ. And she hadn't even thought about the news that Aidan had given her, what she was going to do about that. No sign of Guy, thank God, but she'd encounter him sometime. And then what?

She was walking to her desk through the main office, head ducked down, when someone planted themselves in her way. She looked up, but she'd already recognised the handmade shoes. 'Sir.'

'Dr Maguire,' said Willis Campbell. 'I'm surprised to see you here.'

'Why?' She met his gaze, thinking she really didn't care any more what Willis Campbell thought of her. There were more important things.

'You have leave booked, for one thing.'

'It's been cancelled.' She knew it was him who'd authorised Aidan's arrest, right in the middle of her wedding. It was him who'd ruined everything. But he couldn't send her home because of it – could he?

She could feel the waves of annoyance roll off him, along

with his Aqua di Gio. 'Are you sure you really want to be here? With everything?'

She looked past him, trying to keep her temper. He was just doing his job. She'd do the same. 'I think work is the best place for me, sir. Especially with Dermot Healy missing as well.'

'I hate to say this, Dr Maguire, but you've not exactly added much to the investigation up to now. And with your family . . . situation, I'm not sure you should be working here.'

Paula looked him in the eye. She was two inches taller than him. 'Are you saying you're suspending me? Because last time I checked I hadn't done anything wrong.'

'No, but—'

'I don't know what you expected me to add, either. This is a complex case, and no one has any more insight than I do. I'm not a miracle worker.' She had left out the sir, and God, it felt good. Not to care. Not to worry about what might go wrong, because everything already had.

He seemed to think about it for a moment, almost waiting to see if she'd mention his role in what happened. 'If you're absolutely sure your work won't be affected.'

Paula gave him a tight smile. 'All I can do is my best. *Sir.*'

He stood back, but she knew he was watching her as she walked off.

Corry was at her desk, and thankfully she didn't offer any platitudes. 'Well. I wasn't sure we'd see you today.'

'I just need to . . . is there anything?' The room seemed busier than usual.

'Still no sign of Dermot or Alice, no. We're searching everywhere.'

'Did you get anything off his phone?'

'Loads. Dermot, Peter, and Katy have been exchanging messages all the way through this.'

'They're in it together?'

'They're in something. You were right, they've been lying to us the whole time.'

'Can we bring Katy in?' said Paula. 'We need to try and catch her out. And now Dermot's gone, we might have a chance.'

'Why am I here? Did something happen to Dermot? Did—'

'Katy, Katy. Please calm yourself.'

Katy was in the interview room at the station. A change of scene. Not her own bedroom, where she felt safe. This room was stark, unforgiving, the dazzle of harsh lights in your eyes. Katy wore her usual misshapen clothes, the black band prominent on her pale arm. Corry said, 'Your parents are on their way. We've recommended they engage a lawyer for you. In the meantime we've supplied one. You've understood the rights that were explained to you?'

She narrowed her eyes. 'I didn't need a lawyer before.'

'No. This is a bit different. Katy – I have to tell you that we've seen the messages.'

Katy looked blank. Almost bovine. 'What messages?'

'On WhatsApp. From you to Dermot and Peter. You see, Dermot left his phone behind when he went.'

Still the blank look. 'I don't know what you mean.'

'Come on. I'm telling you, we have them.'

'Er, I don't even use WhatsApp. I had it once, like, ages ago, but I couldn't figure it out.'

'Katy. I must ask you to tell us the truth. We've seen your messages. Talking about what happened. Saying you needed to tell the police about it?'

'What?' She looked at her lawyer, puzzled. 'I honestly don't know what they're on about. I don't have it. It was on my old phone, I think, maybe, but I don't use it.'

Corry stopped. 'Your *old* phone?'

'Well, yeah, I had a smartphone, but I lost it a while back. I just have an old crap one now, a Nokia.'

'But Katy, we've seen messages that come from your number. It's registered to you.'

She just stared at them, slack-jawed. 'My *old* number. It must have been, my phone can't even . . . Honest, I don't know where that one is. I lost it. So I just got a pay as you go one, till my contract runs out and I can get a new phone. It was Alice's idea.'

'What?'

'I didn't want to tell my mum I lost it – she'd have killed me, the phone cost a fortune. So I just got a new SIM. It was a real hassle to tell everyone, such a pain.'

'Alice told you not to cancel your old number?'

'That's right. She said the phone might turn up and then my mum wouldn't need to find out.'

'Katy, when was this?'

She screwed up her eyes, remembering. 'Um, I guess it was like, a month ago? Two months?'

'Before Alice went missing.'

'Yes, right after—' Katy stopped, bit her lip. For a moment Paula, watching, felt a surge of annoyance. How could she be so stupid, so slow, and yet still run rings around them? What were they missing?

Corry leaned in. 'Katy. In these messages, which purport to be from you, there's a lot of references to "what happened". Something that involved you, and Alice, and the boys. They seemed to know what it was. There are references to drugs. Now I need you to tell me, do you know what that was?'

Katy looked all around the room. At the video recorder, at the blank walls. At Corry. At her lawyer, who was just as puzzled as anyone. She seemed to be weighing up her odds. Then she let out a small noise, like a child about to have a tantrum, and burst into tears.

'Katy would like to make a statement,' said her lawyer, a while later.

Katy was red-eyed, shredding a tissue onto the table. 'I want to tell you what happened,' she said. 'I should have before, but – I was afraid. I thought maybe they would hurt me.'

'Who would, Katy?' asked Corry. She sounded tired. In the interview room, the recorder was running.

'Peter. And Dermot too. It was them, you see.' Katy spoke formally, as if she'd rehearsed it in advance. 'They raped Alice. They gave her drugs – MDMA, I think. I didn't want to take any, but I think they put it in my drink because everything went all funny that night.'

'When was this?'

'About, I don't know, two months, maybe. At the end of term. We used to go to the boathouse, the four of us. Just to hang out, talk. Peter has a key, you see, he's the rowing captain. But that night . . . I don't know. He was weird. He kept trying to kiss Alice, touch her. Even though she was really out of it. I don't know what happened. I must have passed out. Everything was sort of blurry. Then I woke up at one point and—' She shuddered. 'Alice's clothes were half-off. She had her top on but her jeans were . . . round her ankles. And he was on her. He was . . . raping her.'

'Peter?' Corry spoke gently.

Katy shook her head. 'No. Dermot.'

'Dermot raped Alice?'

'Yeah. Peter had already . . . done it.' She shuddered again. 'I didn't remember properly for ages. When they realised what they'd done they carried us back to our room. I could hardly walk. Then the next day Alice woke up and she didn't know what had happened . . . but she was bleeding. I said she should go to the nurse, or the police, but she said they wouldn't believe her. I think she told the principal, though.'

'Why didn't you tell us this before?'

'I – I wasn't sure what I remembered. And Alice wouldn't have wanted me to tell you. She was ashamed.'

'Do you think that's why she ran away?'

'Yes,' said Katy promptly. 'I thought she would come back again, see. Once she'd got her head straight.'

'You should have told us sooner, Katy.'

'I know.' She lowered her head. 'I was just trying to help my friend.'

'Peter?'

'No! Alice, I mean. I was trying to help Alice.'

'But you said Peter spent the night with you before Alice disappeared.'

'I know, I . . . I was just trying to help. Honestly, I thought she just wanted some time away.'

'And did he? Spend the night with you?'

Katy seemed to weigh this up for a long time. What would best serve her need. To be important. To matter. Then she said, 'No. No, he wasn't. I just said that.'

'You lied.'

Her lawyer muttered something. Katy shied in annoyance.

'Yes, but I – I thought I was helping Al, you see. I thought she wanted—'

'Headspace,' said Corry, with irony. 'Tell me this, Katy. When did you actually see Alice last? I mean see her with your own two eyes?'

Katy thought about it. 'I don't know. I was sure I'd seen her a lot . . . but when I think about it, I guess it was mostly online. I saw her in the library about a month ago. I suppose that was the last time.'

'And how did she look? What was she doing?'

'She was looking at some books. She had on like a big jumper, and a hat, I think, even though it was hot, I remember thinking that was weird . . . I called out to her and she looked round, but she just went out. She said afterwards that she didn't see me.'

'You saw her face?'

'Yeah, it was her. But she looked funny, I guess.'

'Funny how?'

'I don't know. Puffy. Like she wasn't well or something.'

'All right. We're going to need your phone, Katy. Your current phone, that is.'

'There's nothing. Just texts. I don't . . . I didn't send them, I swear. The WhatsApps and that. I don't know how. I swear.'

'One more thing. Where do you think Dermot is?'

'I think—' Her lip trembled. 'Now that I think about it, maybe he went to get her. To make her shut up about it. About what happened.'

'To hurt her, you mean?'

'Yes.' Katy blinked. 'Please find them. Please don't let him hurt her.'

*

'She's lying,' said Corry. 'Not about the rape. I think that took place, but I think she knew more about it than she's saying. I want to keep her in custody, if we can. We can charge her with obstruction if nothing else.'

Paula was thinking it through. 'She was trying to protect Peter at first, saying he was her boyfriend, but now he's not interested – he's going after Avril – and she's ready to drop him in it. She's smarter than we thought.'

'Not that smart – she may have taken away his alibi, but that's her own gone as well. I think she may be right about one thing, though. We need to find Dermot Healy, and fast, before he hurts someone.'

'And who's got her old phone? Someone was sending those messages.'

'I don't know,' said Corry, frustrated. 'I don't understand how it works. We'd need to ask Trevor the teenager again.'

Paula said, ideas forming in her mind – *puffy*, Katy had said, *great big jumper*, Mrs O'Neill said, the food buried near the cottage. 'Um—'

'What is it?' Corry saw her expression. 'Are you having one of these famous insights? Should I get Willis?'

'Well, you know, I might just be . . . We need to speak to someone who actually *saw* Alice before she went. Not Garrett. The volunteer. The one who found the church open that morning. What's her name again? Maureen? Do we have a number?'

'In the file,' said Corry. 'But . . .'

Too impatient to explain, Paula rifled through the file and punched in a number. It being Ireland, people still answered their landlines. 'Ballyterrin 64578,' came the crisp tones.

'Hello, Mrs Mackin? This is Dr Maguire from the PSNI.

I'm sorry to bother you, I just had to ask a quick question about Alice Morgan, if you don't mind.'

'Well, I suppose so, but what—'

'What did she look like?'

'*Look* like?' The woman sounded impatient. 'But surely you've her picture, I saw it in the paper.'

'Yes, I know it sounds daft, but what did she look like when you saw her last? What dress size was she, for example?' Paula was aware of Corry staring at her. 'I know it might seem like a silly question, but please.'

'Well, she . . . I suppose she'd be a size twelve, something like that?'

Corry was making 'what are you doing?' gestures. Paula ignored her. 'You're sure about that? A twelve?' In her selfies, Alice would barely have been a size eight.

'Aye, I take my granddaughter shopping and she'd be about the same, though she'll be a fourteen soon if she doesn't stop with the chips after school.'

'Was Alice the same size when she first started working there?'

Maureen Mackin said, 'No, she put on a powerful amount of weight in a wee while. They say they do, students. All the chips and pints of beer, like navvies they are. In my day we just stuck to a small sherry.'

'Thank you,' said Paula. 'I'm afraid I need to run on now, but that's very helpful.' She hung up, but not fast enough to miss the tut of disapproval at her lack of phone manners.

Corry was looking at her. Half-exasperated, half-pleased. 'Well?'

Paula said, 'She'd started eating again. She looks different from what we thought. We've been sending out the wrong description.'

Alice

What's the matter? *Katy's face was twisted up, her hands balled inside her hoody. I could tell she'd been crying from the sheen of snot on her lip.*

I can't find it anywhere! It's gone, it's gone! Someone must have nicked it!

What's gone?

My – my phone! Oh God, I can't believe it. My whole life is on there.

On top of her other great qualities, Katy loses stuff. Canteen card, so I have to buy her lunch – I'll pay you back, honest! *And then she never does, of course. Her towel, her hairdryer, money. She's a walking disaster area. Now she was full on sobbing.* Mum and Dad will kill me! I've only had it a few months!

Calm down, you can easily replace it. Do you have an old phone somewhere?

She wiped a hand over her face. Uh, maybe, like a crappy Nokia.

So go back to using that.

But – how?

For God's sake. I was the one who'd been in institutions all my life, but I swear to God Katy would never survive for a minute on her own. Go back to pay as you go. Don't tell your mum and dad you've lost it. Your contract is up soon, right?

Otherwise I'd have to lend her mine, and I didn't trust her with it. The drama of Katy's phone went on for days. Everyone we saw in the canteen or quad – God, did you hear? I've lost my phone, nightmare. *And her FB posts: so* sorry for radio silence. Lost my phone sadface. Contact me on here, thx! *As if anyone would even notice. Stupid cow.*

Then when at last she'd gone back to her old number and stopped moaning, after everything, I was changing my sheets, getting ready to move out of college – Katy didn't do hers at all, all term, I watched – and I heard a thud as I pulled the bed out from the wall. It was down there – the stupid pink cover gave it away. I remembered now she'd been using it on my bed, snuggled up – too close as usual, watching Pitch Perfect, *and she'd fallen asleep. I'd had to sleep on her bed. Urgh. My hands closed over it. The battery was run down, but I plugged it in to my charger – we had the same make – and it came to life. There were message icons. WhatsApp and Facebook still coming through. I clicked on WhatsApp – I remembered that Katy had set it up at the start of term, because everyone else had, but she didn't use it because she couldn't really work it. Normally she texted, now she'd gone back to her old Nokia.*

I heard a noise – she was coming back from the shower, singing Taylor Swift. Charlotte would have puked at the sight of her, all red skin and rolls of fat.

I slipped the phone into the pocket of my hoody. I had her.

Chapter Thirty-Eight

'Right. I've just spoken to the photo techs and they say they think Alice's last selfie was actually taken in March. The light doesn't look right for this time of year. Same goes for the last month or so – all her photos are old ones.' Guy was showing them the pictures on the big screen, not that a casual observer would be able to see what he was talking about. People believed what they were shown online, and a picture of a girl posted in July was how that girl had looked in July. Even if it wasn't. 'I've asked them to trace Katy's old phone too, but it's been switched off. The last signal it gave was in Donegal.'

'So Alice could have it?' asked Corry.

'Maybe. Or Dermot, of course.'

Paula had not spoken to Guy since the wedding – God, it still hurt to even think of it, a gnawing animal in her stomach – and did her best not to meet his eye. Corry said, 'So for all we know, no one's even seen Alice for months. Do we trust this Maureen Mackin?' She looked at Paula.

'I don't think she'd lie. Pillar of the community like her? And it's backed up by what other people said.'

'All right. I think she's legit too. So Alice has put on weight. Quite a bit of weight.'

'Is that even possible?' asked Paula. 'How much weight could someone gain in six weeks?'

Corry said, 'I checked with an eating disorder specialist

at the Royal – you can put on about three stone in a month, if you really go at it. And Alice was tiny before, it would make a lot of difference to how she looks.'

'So we need a photofit,' said Guy. 'What she'd look like now, as a size twelve.'

Willis Campbell had been listening in, looking cross. 'Do I assume from this discussion that we now believe Alice to be alive? Because it seems to me this investigation has suffered from a *serious* lack of focus.'

'We still don't know,' said Paula. 'If we knew, we'd tell you.' He looked askance at her tone, and she could see Guy trying to catch her eye. She ignored him.

'I think there's a strong chance she's alive,' said Guy, smoothing the moment over. 'Or she was before Dermot Healy set off, anyway.'

Corry ran her hands over her face. 'Real question is, should we take Avril out of Oakdale? After what we've just been told about Peter?'

Willis folded his arms. 'We have Ms Butcher in the interview room, yes?'

'For now. We'll have to let her go soon or charge her with something.'

'And we need something concrete. We've had two of them in so far – I'm not hauling in the other boy just so we can let him go as well. We need something that sticks. A confession, ideally. Constable Wright has established contact with the Franks boy?'

They all looked at Paula. 'Um . . . she thinks that he likes her, yes.'

'She might be in danger,' said Corry. 'We're not sure if Dermot had worked out she was undercover. It's possible they all know.'

Willis spoke carefully. 'If we let Constable Wright carry on, what are the chances she could get some actual proof – make Franks show his hand?'

Paula digested what he was saying. Bait. He wanted to use Avril as bait. 'He might, yes, but . . .'

He was looking at her with distaste. 'Dr Maguire. You've said several times you thought Dermot Healy was the brains of the outfit. So there's a high chance Franks will do something stupid now, yes?'

'I don't know, but maybe, I—'

'Right. So here's what we do – we send Katy Butcher back in. Drop some hints that if she helps us out, she might escape charges herself.'

Corry blinked. 'Her lawyer wouldn't let that get by.'

'Well, tell her without the lawyer, then. Honestly, DS Corry – ' he seemed to pronounce her demoted title with relish – 'anyone would think you'd never run a major investigation. If Katy helps get us Franks, we'll maybe overlook the fact she lied to us. Or we can at least let her think that.'

Corry tried again. 'Sir, I don't know if we can trust Katy to that extent.'

'We don't have to tell her about Constable Wright. Just hint that if she can help us get Franks in some way, we'll go easy on her.'

'But sir . . .'

'Listen to me. This speculation, this running about, it's all very well, but someone around here has to actually make a decision,' he snapped. 'DS Corry, talk to the girl. Get her assistance. And brief Constable Wright that we need to draw Franks out. Maybe he'll do that stupid thing sooner than we think.'

As long as that something didn't get Avril hurt. Paula wanted to protest, convince him to pull Avril out, but she had no other ideas. Corry met her eyes, grim-faced, as she got up to follow Willis.

Guy lingered. 'Paula. Are you all right?'

She busied herself gathering her papers. 'I'm worried about Avril. She's my friend.'

'I didn't mean about that.'

She looked away. Of course she wasn't all right. 'I'm dealing with it.'

'I'm so sorry for the way I – I honestly thought it would be better coming from me than Willis. There was nothing else I could do. I promise you. I wasn't trying to . . . you know.'

She said nothing.

'Was I wrong? Did I make it worse?' He looked wretched.

She honestly didn't know; could anything have made that moment better? Watching Aidan be packed into the car, and taken away, and her left in the porch with all their guests and her stupid wedding dress?

'I don't know,' she said. 'No. It doesn't matter anyway. I just want to get on with my job. Can I do that, please?'

'OK. But just please know that – if I could have stopped it, I would have.'

'Yeah,' said Paula tonelessly. She wasn't ready to forgive him just yet. Even if she knew that, really, it wasn't his fault. Because she couldn't forgive herself for that moment in the church porch, when he'd appeared in his suit, and she'd just for a second been happy to see him.

It took Paula almost an hour to drive to work the next day. A night of more riots had left the town broken, roads closed with burnt-out cars, stones and rubbish littering the streets.

She'd lain awake in the double bed, which now seemed huge and empty, and seen the glow of fires over the town. Wondering if Aidan could see it too, in his prison cell. She hadn't been back to visit him. She couldn't face it, not until she'd decided what to do about Maggie. How she would tell Guy. Whether she could ever forgive Aidan. Or herself.

In the morning Maggie came charging in, jumping on the bed and rooting about in the covers. 'Where's Daddy? Where's Daddy, Mummy?'

'He's not here, pet. We talked about this.'

But Maggie was too young to understand. She looked everywhere. Under the bed, in the wardrobe, in the bathroom. 'Where's Daddy? Where's Daddy?' The tears starting. The sound of a two-year-old crying inconsolably was more than Paula could bear.

'Come on, pet. We'll see Daddy soon. He's just gone away for a wee bit.' She scooped Maggie into her arms, her pyjamas quickly getting wet with tears. She felt like crying herself. *He isn't your daddy. I'm sorry, Mags. We lied to you. He isn't your daddy at all.*

Downstairs, she was greeted by the half-built kitchen, the cupboards hanging loose, everything in limbo like a bad metaphor for her life. This had to stop. They had to finish the work, so she could actually make some decisions and move on, to whatever life was now left to her.

'You're saying this happens a lot?'

'Well, yeah. Do you not know the joke?' Gerard was explaining the riots to a bemused Guy Brooking when Paula finally made it in. 'What does the calendar go like in Northern Ireland? January, February, March, March, March . . . we just like a bit of a riot every now and again. Trash the place up a bit, throw stuff at the peelers. Conlon's death is just an excuse. Could be anything.'

'Like in London the year before last,' said Guy.

'Not like that,' said Paula irritably, dumping her bag at her desk. 'Remember when everyone said let's get the water cannons on the London rioters, and all the more liberal ones said no it's too brutal? Well, the reason there aren't any in London is that there are three in Belfast. For our annual riot *season*.'

'You have to win everything here, don't you?' He spoke lightly, almost teasingly, though his face was anxious.

Ah, bollocks. It was hardly Guy's fault Aidan had lost the head and ruined everything. And could she blame him, when she still hadn't found the strength to talk to him about Maggie? She just had to get through this case, then everything could be sorted out. She tried to match his light tone. 'Come on, if rioting was an Olympic sport we'd have medalled in every Games.' Saw his look of relief.

'Every summer, is it? There were riots the year Yvonne went missing too, weren't there?'

'Yeah. Shut the whole town down, my dad said.' How history repeated. In 1981, a missing girl, a dead terrorist. Same now. And no answers to any of it, all of it a mystery tangled in on itself.

Paula stopped suddenly. Yes, there had been riots the year Yvonne O'Neill was lost. It was why the police had taken so long to get out to Crocknashee – the roads had been blocked. No one getting in or out from lunchtime till nearly midnight.

'Paula?' Guy was watching her. 'Is something wrong?'

'Um. Maybe. I don't know.' She pulled a piece of paper towards her and quickly made some sketches. Her lips pursed as she moved it, then counted on her fingers, muttering to herself. 'No one in or out – not till late – but he was back in the afternoon. Yvonne's mother saw his car! She said so!'

'Who?' Guy was looking baffled. He glanced at her scribbles. 'Is that a map?'

Paula tapped the big blob she'd drawn. 'Ballyterrin.' Then the small house shape. 'The church. That's where Yvonne was last seen. And Garrett's alibi was he was at work. But Yvonne's mother said his car was there during the day. Why would his car be there? There was no way he could have been there at four o'clock. Unless he never went into town at all.'

She saw Guy was nodding, getting it. 'What should we—'

'Wait. I just need to check something first.' Paula scooped up her bag. 'I'll be back as soon as I can.'

She knew she wasn't supposed to. She knew she was meant to sit in the office, looking at files, observing, writing reports. But this, this she could do – find things out. Talk to people. Hear what they were actually saying, in the spaces between their words. And at the moment, she could not do anything else, not comfort her child, not save Aidan, not make Pat better. So she was going to do this instead – Willis Campbell be damned.

'Can I help you?' The woman had a small child by the hand, a little older than Maggie, eating a rice cake and wearing a blue T-shirt. A boy, maybe. They were almost in the door of the terraced house; the woman was fumbling with the keys.

Paula smiled, tried to look non-threatening. 'I'm looking for the family of Andrew Philips.'

'I'm his daughter. Suzanne.' Straightforward, but not warm.

'Suzanne, I'm Dr Maguire from the PSNI – we're

investigating an old case which your father gave evidence in. The Yvonne O'Neill disappearance.'

Suzanne put the key in the lock, without taking her eyes off Paula. 'I think I remember hearing about that, yes.'

'We interviewed Anderson Garrett at the time – your father gave him an alibi.'

'That's right. Dad worked for them for years and years. Then he set up on his own.' Paula was surprised at the shabbiness of the terraced house, if her father had owned his own law firm. 'What do you need from me?' asked Suzanne.

'Well, I think that Garrett couldn't have been in work that day after all. There were riots, the place shut down – he'd not have been able to get home in time. But we have a witness says his car was there that day.'

'So you're checking if I know anything?'

'Your father was the only one who could alibi Garrett, Suzanne – I need to check it out.' She couldn't explain that it felt like a loose end. One tug and the whole fabric might unravel.

'Dr Maguire. My dad's been dead a long time. I don't know about that year – I wasn't born – but I know the Garretts had some hold over him. Even after he'd his own firm, Anderson or the old lady could call – Anderson wasn't much of a lawyer, by all accounts – and Dad would always go running. Mum used to tell him, that family says jump, Andrew, and you say how high?'

'You don't have any idea why?'

'No. Like I say, I wasn't born then.' The little boy pulled at her arm, grizzling. 'OK, OK, we'll go in now.' She turned to Paula, ponytail flipping. 'I'm sorry I don't know more. I hope you find something. Terrible, to be lost all this time.'

'Thank you.'

At the door, Suzanne turned back. The boy was inside, taking off his shoes with great song and dance. 'Dr Maguire? I don't want to speak ill of my father – but if it helps, well, we lost the law firm when I was twelve. And the house.'

Paula stopped. Under her hand the wood of the gate was rough, sun-warmed. 'Do you know why?'

'Well, yes. The bookie's shop. Dad was a gambling addict. So.' She shrugged. 'I don't know if that's something to do with it. Maybe he owed the Garretts money.'

Paula thanked her, and she went into the house, and Paula went to her car. If Andrew Philips had lied, if the Garretts had forced him to because of debts, that could be it. The dangling thread they needed. And if Garrett had killed Yvonne, maybe he'd killed Alice too. She found herself thinking, what strangers our parents are. The people who bring us up, make our breakfast, give birth to us. They have whole lives we know nothing about. Her own mother's life was as dark and impenetrable as the waters of Lough Derg, just like this case. But there was one person who might be able to shed some light on both.

Alice

It takes time to disappear. First, you have to plan. You have to get money out, a little every day, and put it away so you don't spend it. Or if you have access to, say, a church collection box, you can get money there. Saint Blannad doesn't mind – she protects the hungry. Seeing as I've been hungry since I was seven years old, she must really like me. Then you buy everything you need – clothes for sleeping out rough, a little tent maybe – but you get them a long time before. Because people remember, and they have CCTV – so wait until it's been wiped. Move out of town so people get used to not seeing you every day. Pretend via Facebook you're still skinny. Post up some old pics. G-chat your former room-mate to say you just saw her in the buttery – she's there every day, stuffing her fat face, so she'll believe you. Ask your nerdy friend – ex-friend – to wipe your phone for you. Get rid of all that search data about how to disappear. Make him think you've forgiven him. Laugh to yourself, because you never will.

Next, you have to change your appearance. There are easy ways to do this – black hair dye you bought a long time ago, with cash. Scissors to cut it all off, glasses. But to really look different, you have to be different.

You have to start eating is the main thing. I mean really stuff yourself. Put as much as you can in your mouth – it doesn't matter if you see people who don't know you well. They won't comment on it to the police, because for all they know you always look like this. They won't say, OMG, Alice got fat. The only person who seemed to notice was the Creep. I saw him look a few times, but of course he didn't say anything. And he'd do his best not to talk to the police. Because when you're trying to hide something, you do what you can to avoid them. And fuck me, did the Creep have something to hide.

How can I do this? Me, who struggles to eat at the best of times? Well, it's simple really – I got the miracle I asked for. Saint Blannad. I prayed to her, and then I could eat. She showed me I had to do it. So that I could die, and live again.

Next, you need transport. You can't get a bus or a train because they'll have CCTV. I recommend, if you can, finding someone with a nice car they leave the keys in, because who would steal it all the way out here? Then you steal it. Trust me. They won't tell the police. They won't want the attention. You need to save the petrol, but you can buy some once you're far enough away. Use cash. Everyone here still uses cash anyway, they like the feel of it in their fat country hands or something. Put a hat over your face. You'll look different by then – they'll be looking for a small blonde girl, and you'll be neither blonde, nor small.

Next, you book yourself into an island retreat where they take cash and don't ask too many questions, so long as you look holy enough. Stay there till the heat dies down. It's perfect, because they don't even watch the news.

I'm not saying I achieved the perfect disappearance. I mean, of course I didn't. I wouldn't be writing this if I had. Duh. I made some mistakes. All the same, it was easier than it should have been. My so-called friends hadn't seen me in a month or more, and my so-called parents longer. All they knew was I looked like my daily selfie. Blonde. Size six to eight. Funny how we believe what we see, even if we know the reality must have long moved on.

Turning my phone on, that was a big mistake. I'd been

using Katy's – stroke of genius, that, pretending to be her. Copying her dumbass dyslexic style. Again, it was too easy. We believe what we see. But I couldn't resist turning on my own phone, just for a second. To see the messages. To see if anyone wanted me home, loved me, missed me. I thought a minute would be OK. I was stupid, and I had to ditch the phone because of it. But – thanks to that fingerprint of Dermot's, it all turned out well. Saint Blannad was looking after me.

If it hadn't been for that, I might have gone back by now. Pretended I'd gone mad or something. Just long enough to force them to tell the truth. Force them to admit they hurt me. But Saint Blannad had other plans for me, and so I stayed missing. Not going further away was a risk. Staying on the island was a risk. Going to my own search was a risk – I even talked to that red-haired woman they have working for the police. She looked right in my face and she didn't know me. Because I've disappeared. In the realest sense of the word. And I ask myself sometimes – if I really want to be dead, why am I still around, haunting the place? Because I want to achieve the impossible. I want to be at my own funeral. I want to see my own search party. I want to see people cry for me. I mean, who could resist that?

I think, if you're honest with yourself, you would do the same.

Chapter Thirty-Nine

Paula was accustomed now to the look Bob Hamilton got when she showed up at his door. Wary, tired, and a tinge of something like sadness. Nonetheless he showed her into his dust-free, airless living room, and she sat down on the overstuffed cream sofa. Linda was out with Ian at a physio appointment, he explained. Bob's only son – same age as Paula – was severely disabled.

'I bet you're glad to not be out policing these riots,' she said.

'Aye, it's terrible. You'd think they'd catch on by now, with the peace process fifteen years ago.'

'I think they enjoy it, to be honest. Bit of a hooley.'

He sat down opposite her in a matching armchair. On the mantelpiece, a clock ticked in the still air. 'Did you want to ask me something about the O'Neill case?'

'Sort of.' She explained her epiphany of earlier, and her visit to Suzanne Philips.

Bob, never one to react quickly to anything, thought it over for a while. 'We missed that, then. I don't know if the mother mentioned seeing the car, she was so upset at the time. There's no way to prove it, though, if the man's dead. You'd have to break Garrett.'

'Or his mother.'

'Well, yes. If I remember rightly, she doesn't give much ground.'

'You mentioned the families were having some kind of boundary dispute?'

'It's a long time ago now. But if I mind it, the O'Neills owned part of the access road, and the Garretts wanted to buy it so they could sell the lot to Oakdale College. But Yvonne's family wouldn't let it go.'

'That's a possible motive.'

'Aye, maybe. But short of a confession or a body turning up, it'll be hard to prove now.'

'I know. But we have to try all the same.'

Bob looked up slowly. 'I want to tell you something else, while you're here. It's not my place, but . . . that Conlon fella. I heard about what happened – and I'm sorry for you.'

She flinched. Immediately it poured into her, the shock and horror, like ice in her veins. Aidan killing a man. Aidan in prison. It could still catch her out, when she'd managed to think of other things for a while.

Bob went on. 'Do you know much about the hunger strikes?'

'Yes – well, I was only born the year before. But people talk about it a lot.'

'The year Yvonne went missing, there was a murder in town. During the hunger strikes. Local IRA commander, high-up. Had a direct line to the families of the strikers – and he was pushing for a deal. Rumour had it the British government were close to settling. There were six men dead by then. This fella thought they should take the deal, end the strikes.'

'I heard about that. The riots it caused, I mean. But why wouldn't they want to settle?'

'Think about what happened after. One of the strikers elected to Parliament – it was a big, big thing. Huge. After that, thon Sinn Fein lot, they got taken seriously, like a real political party. But if it had all ended sooner, before ten men were dead . . .'

'You're saying they deliberately extended it? To get more capital from it?'

Bob looked uncomfortable. 'People have been saying that for years. There's rumours there was a deal on the table, but they told the strikers there wasn't. So they'd carry on, starving themselves to death. This fella that was killed, supposedly he'd found out the truth, was threatening to go to the press. His brother was on the list to strike next. They timed it, you know, so there'd be a wave of deaths, one after the other. Oh, it was very well thought out.'

'So what's that got to do with anything?' She was impatient. Why this now?

'Conlon. There was talk he'd done the murder. I had all this out of a Provo we lifted in the eighties. He'd have said anything to get his sentence cut. But we couldn't tie Conlon to it, no more than we could tie him to your friend's da's murder.'

He meant John O'Hara. Just one of many crimes Conlon had likely carried out over the years. Was a man like that better off dead? She pushed the thought away. 'You couldn't prove it?'

'We hadn't DNA in those days. It's one of the cases the Prosecutor said we'd have to let go. Too far in the past. But Conlon was fingered for it, aye. Said he had an alibi. One of his women lied for him, like as not. He'd usually a few on the go.'

'Why are you telling me this, Bob?'

'We were told he was a marked man. Conlon. Knew too much, you see. The kind of fella who wouldn't last long once the prison gates shut behind him. And . . .'

As soon as he'd set foot out of jail, he'd been killed. Finally, she understood what Bob was driving at. She shook her head, struggling. 'But Aidan hit him – he admitted it.'

'Aye, but there's hitting, and there's killing. And who'd know how to kill a man like Conlon – your friend there, or some hardened Provo that's been waiting thirty years to get revenge? I just thought, you know – maybe it might be worth a look.'

Paula let out a long breath. 'OK. Thank you. I'll – I need to think about it.' She got up. She saw his face slacken, no doubt with relief that she hadn't brought up her mother again. Then she realised she was going to anyway. 'Bob – I know you suppressed the statement. The one that said my mother was – seeing someone. A man. I just want to ask – did you do it to spare us? Me and Dad? Just tell me if I'm wrong.'

Bob said nothing. The clock ticked a few more times.

Paula nodded. 'Thanks. Thank you for doing that. I don't know if it – but I know you meant well. Do you know anything else at all? Did someone take her? Did she go with that man?'

Silence.

'Please, Bob. I'm – I can't do this any more. I gave up, before. But if you do know something, please tell me now, so I can – I have some decisions to make. For me, and Maggie, and what we do next.'

She turned to find Bob's eyes on her. Tired. Kind. 'Paula.' He never called her that. 'I know it's hard, that you don't know, and you with a wean now yourself. I know you think I didn't look hard enough. But I looked everywhere. I searched high and low for your mammy. The statement – I didn't show your da because I owed the man, and he didn't need to know his wife had some fella coming to the house. But if I thought she'd run off with him, I'd have said. I wouldn't have left you all this time, not knowing.'

'So you don't . . .'

'No. There was nothing to find. I promise you. Nobody could have looked as hard as I did.' He took her hand – Bob, a man who would hardly look her in the eyes when she'd first started at the unit. She felt tears gather, bit her lip hard. 'I promise you, pet. You can stop now. There was nothing to find. Nothing.'

Paula felt her shoulders sag, and a terrible punch of sadness went through her. It was over. They would never know. And with the sadness came something else – something not a million miles from relief.

Back in the car, she took out her phone and rang Corry. 'It's me. Any word from Avril?'

'There's going to be a start of term party tonight. They'll all be there, Peter and Katy too. Avril said she'd be in touch every hour up to then, so we can be on standby.'

'Right. Well, you know you said I should stop interviewing people? I *maybe* did it again.'

Corry sighed. 'Did you at least get a result?'

'I think so. You might want to meet me at the Garretts' house.'

Alice

The blood, I admit, I hadn't thought of before. That was the hard part, I guess. But it came to me as I sat in the church thinking about what was under the floor, the bit that looks like a gravestone but if you look very carefully, lifts up. I thought about what he'd done to her. What they'd done to me. And about all the people who'd led me to be here, fat, my hair rat-brown and chopped, about to leave my own life. It was then I felt something on my thigh, running down it. Just like the day Charlotte cut me. I saw my jeans darken in a spot, and I touched it. When I took my hand away it was red.

The blood was a shock to me. That's weird, right? I'm twenty-two and I've only had like two periods in my life. The first time I was thirteen. It was at home, in the Easter holidays. I woke up in a pool of blood. Sticky, with black bits, tarry at first, brown when it dried. I was stuck to the sheets with it. And the smell – it stank. I thought I was dying. Yeah, I know, how stupid can you be, but I'd been at boarding school and they didn't go in much for sex ed. I knew about periods, I wasn't dumb, but I didn't realise that was the reason for all this shit that was coming out of me. So I'm in there, crying, blood all over my feet and legs and the toilet and the bath mat, and I hear Rebecca come up the stairs. Alice? What is that racket . . . ? She stops. Jesus Christ. You dirty little bitch.

The second time was at the clinic. He fed me up so much I started to bleed again, like a pig for market. So I had an idea it might happen this time. What could be better – a splash of blood on the ground. A way to make them look, not just for me, but for Yvonne. A trail to lead them home.

This time I was ready. I didn't use a tampon. I can't bear the idea of putting something inside me ever again, and I hate to lose a drop of this. When I felt it – the wetness, the slow course of it out of me, I didn't cry or make a fuss. I smiled. Every drop of that was going to help Alice die, and me live. After all, you have to have blood, for a rebirth. Saint Blannad understood that better than anyone.

Chapter Forty

There was a corpse on the bed.

Paula froze in the doorway of Martha Garrett's room. There was no sign of Anderson in the house, so the team had fanned out across the land, searching for him. She had climbed the stairs in the farmhouse, where a chill crept over her skin despite the heat of the day outside. Through the open door, she could see the woman lying on the bed, still as a statue and just as pale, unmoving. Paula began to move towards it, heart in her mouth.

Then the corpse breathed. The woman was old, near the end maybe, but hanging on to life. She turned her head slowly, and Paula could see that her mind was as sharp as ever, ticking like a clock inside that husk. The voice came from somewhere far away. Her legs and arms hung, useless. 'You're back.'

'Yes – we've come for your son. I'm sorry.'

She turned her face, slowly, to the light from the window. Paula moved closer. The room was full of the smell of old age, and the death of hope. 'We think he lied. About Yvonne. And you knew too, didn't you? What you said about him being in work – it wasn't true. You got Andrew Philips to lie for you.'

No movement. A faint twitch in the corner of her mouth.

'Mrs Garrett – there's two young people missing over at

Oakdale College. It's too late for Yvonne, if she's dead, which I think she is. But they have their lives ahead of them, if we can bring them back safe to their families. This has gone on long enough. So please tell us what you know. I understand why you lied for him, back then. He's your son. But it's so long ago now. Please help us find Alice. And Yvonne too, if you know where she is.'

Still nothing. Paula decided to play her last card. 'We're here to arrest your son. We think his alibi was a lie that day. So we'll be taking him in again. We'll be questioning him, in the station, for as long as it takes. We'll charge him with killing Alice too, if we get enough evidence. And Mrs Garrett – you know he's not in the best state. It will break him. Just tell me what we need to know, and maybe we can sort this all out quietly.'

There was a rustle. Paula looked and realised the woman was staring right at her. 'You probably weren't even born then,' came the croak.

'I was. Just about.'

'Well, it was a bad time. People dying, people getting shot. And I'd had my accident – they'd told me I would never walk again. I had to do my best to secure our future. The college wanted to buy our land. I knew that would help take care of me, and Anderson too. He'd never have made a real lawyer. He's bright, you know, a very clever boy. But he's . . . sensitive.'

'Yvonne's family wouldn't sell the land. Was that why?'

She sighed. 'A bit of soil was all it was. I'd have given them a good price. But they were stubborn, stubborn and superstitious like all Catholics. Thought the land was special, just because of an old bit of bone. A relic, my foot. Probably belonged to a sheep or something anyway. I never heard the like. I asked Anderson to invite the girl over. She was pleasant enough, for all her idolatry. They both liked to go to the church and help out. I didn't approve of the friendship – Anderson was raised Church of Ireland – but it seemed to give him comfort. He had some silly notion about being a priest for a while. And the girl – he took it badly when she left the convent to get married. I told him to bring her here and give her tea and ask her to reason with her mother.'

Paula held her breath. 'What happened?'

'Oh, I don't know. I was up here, lying in my bed. I heard a scream, and a crash. Next thing I know Anderson is standing by my bed, shaking like a leaf. I've killed her, he says. I've killed her.'

So that was how the truth could come out, after thirty-two years of searching for someone who seemed to have vanished into the air. With three words spoken in a hot, airless bedroom by a near-dead woman. Paula was surprised at how calm she sounded as she asked: 'He killed Yvonne?'

'That's what he said. They'd got into some silly row about the strikes. A lot of Catholics supported it, you know. Political prisoners, indeed. Murderers is what they were.'

Paula wondered if the woman even saw the irony. She went on, 'I never knew whether she fell and hit her head, or she started to scream and he tried to quieten her, or what happened. If he tried to touch her or something. I honestly don't know. But she was dead, in our living room. So I told Anderson he had to hide her.'

'Where did he take her?'

'There's a place. You wouldn't find it unless you knew. So he put her there – he was bawling like a baby – and I said I would sort it. I knew the RUC were too busy to bother with some girl going missing. So I spoke to Andrew Philips and we organised it all. Of course it was a shame. I had nothing against the girl. But it wasn't worth my son rotting in prison for. He didn't belong in there with that terrorist scum. He tortures himself enough anyway, with his silly hair shirts and those spiked belts. Catholic nonsense.'

'And Yvonne's mother? Waiting all this time?'

'If she hadn't been so needlessly stubborn, none of this would ever have happened.' The voice, old as it was, was as cold and sharp as a blade.

'Did you see her? Did you see Yvonne dead?'

A pause. 'She looked peaceful, if that's what you want to know. I don't think she suffered. Why should my son go to jail for an accident?'

'It happened in the living room? I noticed he was looking at something there, when we interviewed him. I couldn't tell what.'

Her voice was steady. Almost tranquil. 'Her finger, most likely. It's in the jar there. Well, the bone of it.'

'You mean . . . he took it? A trophy or something?'

'Don't be silly, dear. I made him put it there. To remind him. Since he was so obsessed with that stupid relic, why not have the girl's as well?'

Paula's head swam. 'Remind him he'd killed her?'

'Remind him what he owed me. I saved that boy. He owes me his life. He'll never leave me now.'

Paula took a deep breath. 'I have one more question, Mrs Garrett – where is she? Where is Yvonne, after all those years? She's close by, I think. It's time her mother knew where she is.'

The woman didn't move for a while, and then there was the sound of rustling. She dragged herself from the bed and into the wheelchair by the side. Paula knew better than to offer help, as the woman moved slowly, slowly, dragging her legs like a dead weight. Then the squeak of the wheelchair turning. Paula watched as the claw-like hands propelled her over the room. On the wall was a framed map of the church. After a minute she realised Mrs Garrett was trying to point to something on it.

She took the stairs two, three at a time. Corry was in the kitchen, searching through cupboards of stale food, gloves on, nose wrinkled. Paula panted it out: 'She's in the church.'

'Alice?'

'Yvonne. They put her in the church.'

It was so close. They were there in minutes, Corry on her phone to gather the remaining officers. Two uniforms with guns opened the door, and there was Anderson Garrett. Crouched like an animal over the stone steps, still marked with Alice's blood. At the sight of them his hands crept up, dazed. 'I'm sorry,' he gasped, and Paula, hovering at the back, saw he'd been crying. 'She . . . she was so pure. She was a nun. Then she stopped – for a man! I had to help her.' He sank down, choking, the words forced out. 'She supported those murderers. The hunger strikers. She brought flowers for them, here! At the shrine! It wasn't right – I had to help her be pure again. I'm sorry. I'm so sorry.' He sagged down, and Paula saw he'd rolled up his sleeve so his pale arm hung, white and limp. Around it, a medieval-looking device, a belt of spikes digging into his doughy flesh.

Corry stepped into the church, lowering her own gun. 'Anderson Garrett,' she said, and her voice was clear in the still air. The stained glass threw colours over her face – purple and red and blue. 'I'm arresting you for the murder of Yvonne O'Neill.'

Later, there were the usual ceremonies. The church sealed off, the white-suited officers examining it yet again. This time finding the small space under the steps, where the gravestone lifted up, and the body inside – just bones now, but enough left to show she had died wearing a yellow dress. And the scrap of newspaper too – the date on it 31st July, 1981 – that Yvonne had wrapped around a spray of white roses, when she left the house, expecting to be back safe in a few hours. Expecting to live out the rest of her life. Fall in love again, maybe. Get married, have children. Live to be thirty, forty, fifty even. She'd have been fifty-eight now, had she not gone to Anderson Garrett's house on that hot day in July 1981. That was how it worked. One moment, one step out of place, and the rest of your life was paused like a film. A bullet shot out of a gun, never hitting home.

There were TV vans, and the rush of a solved crime, especially after so many years. The jar on the mantelpiece was removed, and the living room where Yvonne died sealed too, though there was unlikely to be anything left after thirty-two years. Despite all this, despite the solve, despite finding the bones of a girl everyone had given up on, Paula found she felt nothing. They had thought Yvonne was dead, and she was. They'd thought Garrett killed her, and he had, and thanks to his cunning, cold mother he'd got away with it all this time. He'd been arrested, weeping and shaking, and confessed, though he still denied knowing anything about Alice, and Paula thought this was probably true.

Later still, they were carrying Martha Garrett down the steps of her house in her wheelchair, taking her in to make a statement about her false alibi for her son.

'God forgive you!' They all turned at the shout. Dolores

O'Neill was approaching, on shaky old legs. She still wore her slippers. 'They found her, Martha. They found my Yvonne. And you knew where she was all this time! How could you? How can you live with yourself?'

Martha turned her head away. As officers helped Yvonne's mother, and her legs went under her, weeping that her daughter had slept all these years, just on the other side of a hedge, the older woman closed her eyes. 'Take me away.'

'You shouldn't have spoken to her by yourself,' said Willis Campbell. Paula turned to see him on the church steps, suit pressed, hair neat, an irritated expression on his face now the cameras were gone. 'It isn't part of your role, Dr Maguire. It won't be admissible.'

'But she talked to me. And we've found Yvonne because of it.'

'Yes. All the same I can't have you behaving this way. We need to have a conversation about your behaviour, once this has all died down.'

Paula opened her mouth, her tolerance for him at an end. 'Listen—'

'Sir?'

He turned, annoyed, as Corry approached, peeling off her protective gloves. 'What is it, DS Corry?'

'I'm concerned about Constable Wright,' Corry said. 'She hasn't checked in for the last two hours. There's a party tonight, and her last message was a bit worrying. Maybe we should pull her out.' Corry looked uneasily at the sky, turning all the colours of a ripe bruise as the evening lengthened. Red fire in the west. Night soon.

Campbell sucked in his breath. 'But this is the worst possible time to take her out! If the lad's about to show his hand, we should do our best to see it through.'

'You mean . . . deliberately leave her in a dangerous situation?'

'It isn't dangerous yet, is it? Has something actually happened?'

'Well—'

'I think you're missing the point of undercover work, DS Corry. You shouldn't have sent the girl in if you didn't think she could handle it. Just monitor things and go in only – and I mean *only* – if something happens. This is your last chance not to muck it up.' He buttoned his jacket, smoothed his hair. 'Now if you'll excuse me, I have to do an interview with UTV Live in five minutes.'

'But—'

'What part of no do you not understand, DS Corry? Dr Maguire, we'll continue this another time.'

After he went, Corry turned to Paula. 'Listen to the message that came through. She only turned the mic on for a minute, but she must have known I'd hear it.'

She held up her phone. Through it came not Avril's voice, but Katy's, shouted over the noise of a party. Music, shrieks, laughter. '. . . you OK? You look a bit out of it.'

Avril's voice. 'Don't know. That wine's gone to my head.'

There was a splashing noise, as if they were in a bathroom. 'Come on, do you want some fresh air?'

'Yeah. Good idea.' Avril's words were slightly slurred.

'Let's bring you outside. Down to the lake where it's quiet. I'll get Peter for you.'

Avril made a sort of mumbled noise, and the recording went dead.

Corry switched it off. 'See? Peter's obviously given her something. And you know what happens after that.'

'But Katy's with her. Could she just be drunk?'

'Katy didn't stop something happening to Alice, did she? And you know as well as I do Avril hardly drinks. She wouldn't risk it in this job.'

Paula was moving already. 'We should go to Oakdale then. On our own, if Willis won't give us the back-up.'

'I'm going too.' Gerard had appeared in the porch of the church. He was pulling off a white boiler suit, ripping at it. 'Come on, I'm driving. If we go by the back roads we'll beat the traffic.'

Corry said, 'Monaghan, you shouldn't . . . DCI Campbell has said we're not to go yet. You'd be going against his express orders.'

'I can't leave her there! He's a big lad, this Franks, isn't he?'

'Big enough. All right, you can come. But it's on your own head.' She looked at Paula too. 'That goes for both of you.'

Alice

Please forgive me. Forgive me.

I couldn't believe it when I saw him. When he came in I froze – he's always telling me off for being there late, so I just sat quiet in the dark. He went to the steps, and I saw him kneel down. He was making a strange noise. After a while I realised he was crying. He stayed there for ages, crying and choking over the stones. I crouched there, praying to a God I don't believe in that he would leave. He was wearing something strange – a sort of top made of like rope or something. A hair shirt? Did those actually exist? He spoke out loud. I'm sorry, he said. Please forgive me. Forgive me.

He went, after what seemed like a hundred years. When I heard the church door close, I let out a big, shaky breath. I went to where he'd been, and I realised I could feel a small draught coming up from the steps. I knelt down, feeling around the old, cold stone. It seemed solid, heavy. Then I saw it. Cracks, where the dust hadn't settled. I dragged the stone off – I was seeing stars, but luckily I have a bit more heft these days. Immediately I could smell it – rot. That weird smell that follows me round the church, but stronger. It was only a little space, big enough not to be noticed. But there was something down there. Bones. Bones around a yellow dress. I knew it was her right away. I just looked in, and there she was crammed in, broken and dead. There was still some hair on her skull. Blonde.

I sat there a long time, crying a bit. I had to tell someone. He'd done it. He'd be arrested. Yvonne's mother would finally know what happened to her. Not like my mother – if I disappeared she'd just be glad. She wouldn't spend years looking for me. No more difficult, ugly Alice. She could forget me, lie about her age without me there, living proof she was at least forty-two or had been a teen mum.

I don't know how long I sat there for. I was numb – shock, probably. I couldn't feel my hands or feet. I sat there thinking about Yvonne and Rebecca and bloody Katy and Dermot and Peter. Garrett. Everyone who hurt me, rejected me, didn't want me. And then it came to me. A way I could help people find Yvonne, and still vanish, not have to talk to the police. A way I could punish all of them – the people who'd brought us to this, me and Yvonne. Her broken in bits. Me whole, but only on the outside.

So I did it. I took the photo out of Yvonne's old house. I made my plans. Then I let my blood run onto the altar – onto poor Yvonne. After all, it was the right time of year for it. Lúnasa. Sacrifice and blood running into the ground. An offering. And I knelt down and spoke to her. I'm sorry. I don't mean to leave you. But they'll find you now. I blessed myself, like I'd seen people do in the church. Maybe I was getting quite into this Catholicism thing.

After it was done and it was all too late, I looked back at the relic. It looked lonely to me, suddenly, in its case. Shining away, preserved forever. And I sort of got it, right then. Why people think it can save you. Because it was part of her, something real across the centuries. And I want to believe too. I want to believe things can change and I'll feel different one day. I want to believe there are miracles, because God knows I need one. I want to believe I can do this, and bury Alice, and be able to live. To eat. To feel all right. I looked at her for a while, the gold winking under the tired lights, and I felt myself walking towards her. Come on, I said. Let's get out of here.

After that it was easy. Sometimes it's just as simple as deciding to do something, then doing it. I almost wished I could have told Tony. It's what he always said (when he wasn't knobbing my nannies, of course). Just decide to do something, Alice, and then do it. *Hope you're proud, Daddy.*

Both of them, my loving mummy and daddy, were on the news earlier, pleading with whatever nasty man took me to give me back. I watched it in a pub, where I was charging Katy's phone – I've been keeping it off now I know Dermot's looking for me. I hope it's not too late. It was a close one. They kept showing the footage of when Rebecca stood up and asked me to stop punishing them. No. No, I'm not done yet. There were old men in flat caps at the bar and they muttered to themselves. As well they might. Who wouldn't run away, if they had a mother like that? Poor wee Alice. Poor wee me.

All right? I jumped, spilling a bit of my Coke (full fat, I'll have you know). *The barman – a bit younger, a bit sharper – was clearing glasses.*

Um – fine. *I tried not to sound English. Usually it comes out sort of American.*

Have you ID? *he asked.*

I'm drinking Coke.

Even so. We need ID for you to be in here.

Of course I don't have ID. I'm dead, after all. Dead people do not carry ID.

I left it at home. *Home being my tent in the damp woods. He was still watching me. My damn picture – thin, blonde, sad – was on the screen. I wonder if he'll call someone. Why can't he just be a sozzled mess like the rest of the guys in this fucking country?*

On my way back, through the horrible dripping bracken,

my hood pulled up tight, I think someone is following me again. I hear a small sound. I stand very still. Around me, the rain drums on leaves. Hello? I try, quietly. No answer. Birds call out, enjoying the freshness of the rain. I go back to my damp tent. It smells of mildew and the crisps I ate last night. Alice has been gone for nearly three weeks now. It's real. It's on TV. I can't stay here forever.

At first I was terrified in the woods. I'd never even been camping – it's horrible. Having to wash with wipes and eat stuff out of packets and talk to no one. It wasn't quiet, like I'd expected. There were all kinds of noises, animals and birds and the trees moving.

But after a few days, I started to feel safe there. There weren't any mirrors, so it didn't matter what I looked like. I wasn't Alice any more. Alice was thin, and blonde, and careful. This girl . . . she's got short dark hair, and she's fat, and she smells. But she doesn't care. And she has Saint Blannad, the bones of her, wrapped in a pillow case. That will keep her safe.

That barman has shaken me. My heart is beating hard under my stupid raincoat. I don't want this any more. I don't know why Alice is taking such a fucking long time to die. A crack outside, like someone stepping on twigs. I'm very still. Suddenly I realise I'm not angry any more. What I am is afraid.

I think someone else is here. I think someone is coming for me.

Chapter Forty-One

Night was falling as they reached Oakdale College. In the dark, the lake looked like an open eye, white with moonlight. The boathouse was a smear of black against it. Corry had drawn her gun. 'Should we not ring again for back-up?' whispered Paula.

'Peter can't be that dangerous. He's no access to weapons, and he won't be expecting us.' But still, a pulse of fear beat between them.

Paula hung back. As a civilian, she didn't have the regulation firearm PSNI officers held. 'What's your advice?' asked Corry. In her black clothes, only her fair hair stood out in the dark. Gerard was dressed the same. He moved from foot to foot, and no wonder – his girlfriend was maybe in there with Peter.

'I think he could be dangerous,' said Paula. 'Any of them could, if they're pushed far enough. So – be careful. Try not to make him feel threatened, if he's even here.'

There was no sign of any life round the lake. The boathouse was almost hidden beneath trees. Weeping willows, trailing their hair in the water like mourning women. Corry put a finger to her lips, indicated Gerard should approach the door while she took back-up. Paula, watching from further up the lakeside, saw them move through the trees, shadows in their dark clothes, until they were on the path with a very slight crunch underfoot, and almost at the door and . . .

'Jesus!' She jumped suddenly, stifling a scream as a hand clasped her arm. 'You scared me!'

Guy was also zipped up in a black raincoat. 'I thought I'd better come. The TSG are at the gates.'

'But Willis—'

'Screw him. I wasn't going to let you go in here without back-up just because Willis can't see what's obvious. Any sign of Franks or Avril?'

Paula shook her head. 'Not yet. He hopefully hasn't hurt her.' She didn't want to say it, but the word *yet* was in her mind.

He stood back, and she felt the radiated warmth of his body. Wanted to tuck her head under his chin, where she knew it fitted exactly, and have him tell her it was all going to be all right, Avril would be fine and Alice would turn up safe and the inconvenient fact that Paula's fiancé was in prison could all be sorted out. She stayed where she was.

He nodded towards the lake. 'They're going in.'

In a swift motion, Gerard had kicked the door open, followed by Corry with her gun aloft. Paula tensed, and felt Guy do the same. It was just Peter, she told herself. Dangerous against helpless, drugged women, but not with guns pointed at him. Sure enough, there was a sound of raised voices, and Gerard came out soon after, Avril scooped in his arms. She was limp, head lolling. From the lake shore, Gerard shouted something: '. . . ambulance!'

Guy got out his phone and spoke rapidly into it. 'We've located Constable Wright. She appears unhurt but unconscious – they're on their way? Good.' He put a hand on

Paula's arm. 'Don't worry. She'll be fine.'

'Where's Peter?' said Paula.

Because it wasn't him who Corry was leading out of the boathouse in handcuffs, swearing and fighting. It was Katy.

'I don't understand,' said Guy.

But Paula did. Too late, she saw it. 'Katy. It was Katy gave Avril the drugs. She was never with Peter at all.'

'But that doesn't—'

Then, suddenly, Corry cried out, and stumbled. Gerard froze. There was a clatter as her gun fell to the ground and Gerard was shouting, Avril still in his arms, fumbling for his own firearm: 'It's Healy! It's Healy!'

Dermot was on the path. The moonlight gleamed off his glasses. Somehow, he had Corry's gun and was holding her by the arm. She gave a smothered yell – was he stronger than he looked? He cleared his throat. 'I know you're up there. Come down. I've got her gun.'

It was pointing now at Corry's head. She had gone very still. Katy was straining on her cuffs. 'What the hell, Derm—'

'Shut up,' said Dermot. 'I'm done listening to you and your dumbass ideas. You and fucking Peter – you ruined the whole thing. You couldn't just act normal.'

'I just . . . I . . .'

'Of course the police were on to us. You and your stupid lies. Of course they wouldn't believe Peter was your boyfriend.'

Katy spat at him. 'You were the ones who raped her! Why do you think she ran away? And now we're all in trouble. I'm just trying to do something about it.'

Dermot waved the gun at Avril, who seemed to be slipping in and out of consciousness. 'She's a fucking cop, your mate there. And I bet you told her all about how Alice wouldn't talk to you any more, how she was so upset by what the bad boys did. Poor little Katy. Because it's all about you, isn't it?'

'Shut up! What do you mean, she's a cop?'

Paula and Guy were still frozen on the path. He'd put up a hand to stop her moving when Dermot appeared. She waited. Corry tried to twist herself from Dermot. 'Look, there's an operation in progress here. Don't do anything stupid. Dermot – Katy – it doesn't have to happen like this. Just put the gun down, Dermot.'

For a moment it looked as if he might. He began to lower it slightly, move it away from Corry, and the tension calmed just for a second – until they heard footsteps on the gravel path.

Dermot put the gun up again. 'Who's that? Fucking answer!'

'Dermot?' said Peter, who was coming along the path. He held a paper cup in one hand, and looked totally nonplussed. 'Dude. What's going on?'

'You tell me.' Dermot's voice shook. 'Why the fuck are the police here? Did you tell them anything?'

'Mate, I don't know what's going on. Katy told me to come here.'

'Fucking Katy. Not surprising, is it?'

Peter still looked confused. 'I don't get it. What's going on?'

Dermot gave a trembling sigh. 'Think about it. Katy's given the cop girl something. So if anyone comes they'll find you here, and her out of it – how do you think that looks? I think Katy's trying to drop us both in it. *Mate*.'

'Dermot!' said Katy. 'I wasn't, I swear! I was trying to

help! I even gave him an alibi – and all you do is shut me out, both of you. You wouldn't tell me anything!'

'Just shut up, will you? Just shut the fuck up.'

Guy signalled to Paula to hide by the trees – it was possible Dermot hadn't seen how many of them were there, in the dark. He called, 'Now Dermot, let's keep calm—'

'You shut up. Come down here.' He looked up. 'Both of you. I know that woman's there as well.'

Guy grasped Paula's hand; she let him. His skin felt warm, the pulse beating under the skin. She thought of Maggie, safely at home with PJ and Pat. She'd been in worse scrapes than this, she told herself. Dermot was no killer, just an angry boy. As they went down the grassy slope towards him, she could see his eyes were huge, shiny in the dark. OK, so he was an angry boy who'd taken something. Corry met Paula's gaze, shook her head slightly. Annoyed with herself, maybe, for being caught off guard.

Gerard had half-put Avril down, holding his own gun. Avril's eyes rolled, and she muttered to herself. 'Come on, son,' said Gerard, his voice reasonable. 'Do you even know how to use that thing?'

'I know enough.' Dermot's hands shook. He was holding the gun in both of them now, like a gangster.

'What do you want, Dermot?' asked Corry, also reasonable. 'We came here to stop your friend assaulting a woman—'

'He's not my friend,' snapped Dermot. 'And you were right. He's done it before. He rapes people.'

'Well, yes, we know that.'

'But *I* didn't. I didn't rape Alice.'

'Course you fucking did,' said Peter. 'You were there. You had a go.'

Dermot had started to cry. 'I thought she liked me. I thought she wanted to. Then she said it was rape. She went to the principal!'

'Well, Alice is fucked in the head, she'd say anything. She probably killed herself. She probably just went off somewhere and—'

Dermot laughed. A short, bitter sound, cracking on the edges. 'Mate, you've no idea. She didn't kill herself. Those messages, all the WhatsApping – with Katy? Wasn't Katy. She doesn't even have WhatsApp. Alice had her phone. Remember she lost it way back? It took me ages to figure it out. Stupid. I could have just looked at Find my Friends. Katy never turned it off. Would have led us straight to Alice. It was her the whole time.'

'Fuck, no way. I don't believe it.'

Katy was crying. 'It wasn't me! I don't know anything, I don't understand what's going on.'

'It's true. Alice hated us. She – she did all this to try and fuck with us.' Dermot's voice broke. 'But I'm not a rapist. I'm not like you. And I'm not a killer – I saw what they said about me on the news. I never hurt Alice and I can prove it. Once I figured out about the stupid phone, it was easy.' He took a step back, looking up at the thicket of trees. 'Come out. Show them.' Nothing. His voice cracked. 'You *promised*!'

The bushes moved aside, and into a patch of moonlight stepped a girl. Jeans, an Oakdale hoody. Dark hair, cut short. Paula held her breath. She had seen this girl before.

The girl did an ironic smile. 'Surprise!'

'Alice?' said Corry uncertainly. 'Is it . . . Alice Morgan?'

'Yep. I hear you've been looking for me. Fuck's sake, Dermot. A gun? What's with the dramatics?'

'Shut up! This is all your fault. All this – setting us up. Making it look like we – hurt you.'

'You did hurt me,' she said calmly, stuffing her hands in the pocket of her hoody. 'You and Peter and Katy too. You raped me.'

Katy howled. 'Alice! I never did anything! How could I?'

Alice shot Katy a look of pure hatred. 'You were there, weren't you? Don't think I don't remember what you did. All of you.'

Dermot was crying. 'I didn't! I'm not a rapist . . . I thought you wanted—'

'You can't want it when you're off your face.' She glanced at Avril. Gerard was still trying to support her, while keeping his gun on Dermot. 'You should know that. It's pretty fucking obvious. If you're not awake you can't consent.'

'I never . . . You said it was OK! When I fixed your phone, you said we were cool!'

'Well, we weren't. You hurt me.' Her voice rang out. Paula could hardly believe it was Alice, after all this time looking for her. Not so ethereal, not so tiny, but pretty all the same, her skin luminous under the scrappy dyed hair. Her face animated, alive, when they'd been imagining it dead, buried somewhere in a wood, soil kicked over it. Alive, but twisted in one emotion – pure rage. Then she realised – it was the girl from the search. In Donegal. She'd spoken to Alice, seen her alive, and not even known it.

'I was a virgin,' Alice said casually.

'Fuck!' swore Peter. 'As if you were. Don't lie. How could you be?'

'Well, it's hard to lose it when you spend your teens in psych wards.' She threw him a contemptuous look. 'If you'd just listened, I'd have told you. If you'd ever for one second give – not just take take take. All three of you. You think you can take whatever you want. Just – use me up. Own me. So yeah, you raped me. Blood all down my thighs. I couldn't pee without crying for a week. You did that, all of you. So maybe you didn't kill me but you may as well have done. You killed something. You killed Alice.'

Paula found her voice, deep in her throat. 'Alice. Why did you do it?'

Alice looked her way, her chin moving in a clear slice. 'Because. If you hurt someone, you should be punished for it. This was the best way. I would have come back.' She twisted her mouth in the ghost of a smile. 'Also – I guess people just pay you more attention when you're dead.'

'FUCK!' screamed Dermot. 'It was your own bloody fault! All that oh Dermot, you're like my gay best friend, oh Dermot, you're like my brother – I'm not fucking gay! How do you think I felt? You and fucking Katy. You made me do it. I had to *show* you. *I'm not gay.*'

Paula felt Guy move behind her, and did some very quick calculations. He didn't have a gun, surely, as he'd been in London until recently – and Gerard didn't have a clear sight line – and Corry had a gun to her head – but then Guy was drawing one anyway, and quite calmly shooting Dermot in the arm. Paula felt her bones jump at the noise. The boy howled, dropped the gun he was holding. Corry sprang away, picked it up. Avril cried out, deep in her throat. Gerard laid her down on the grass, head between her knees, and lunged for Dermot, who was writhing in pain. 'Jesus Christ!' shouted Peter. Katy was on her knees, sobbing, still handcuffed.

'Right,' said Guy, moving forward. He motioned to Peter. 'You. Keep your hands where I can see them. Dermot Healy,

I am arresting you for rape, kidnap, assaulting a police officer—'

'He's got a knife,' said Alice, matter-of-factly. Her hands were still in her hoody pocket. 'How do you think he got me back here? I didn't exactly *offer*.'

Gerard and Corry stopped, backed away from Dermot, who had rolled onto his front, moaning. 'It hurts! It hurts!'

Corry was back in control now, blowing her hair out of her face. 'Turn around, Mr Healy.' Both guns were trained on him. 'Put your hands where we can see them.'

He turned, slowly, as if in great pain. In one hand he had a small knife, like a Stanley, with a dully gleaming blade.

'Put the knife down,' said Corry, almost irritated. 'It's over now. We're going to take you to the station, call your parents, and then—'

Dermot was turning. There was gravel stuck to his face, his glasses askew. He had the knife in the hand that wasn't cradled to his chest. 'I'm not a rapist,' he breathed. 'I'm not – going to jail . . . I can't . . . *I'm not gay.*'

'Shit.' Corry ran forward to grab his arm, but he had already drawn the knife against his throat, and a shower of red arterial blood hit her and Katy in the face, and Gerard too, and even Peter nearby. 'Jesus fucking Christ, he's killed himself!' said Peter, stupidly. Katy let out a long howl, like a dog in pain. Her face was splashed with the blood, running over her eyes and down her cheeks.

Corry was scrabbling in Dermot's throat, trying to close the wound, his blood bubbling up under her hands. Beside her, Paula heard Guy speak into his radio. So calm, she remembered afterwards. He didn't even break a sweat. 'We need that ambulance. Now, please.'

Alice

But wait, you say. What actually happened to the relic, Alice? Well, of course they asked. It's supposed to be priceless. Worth way more than I am, anyway. I said I'd lost it in the woods. I said I was so upset and traumatised I'd blacked it all out, and by the time Dermot turned up to find me I'd lost her. What a shame. That should keep them busy for a while, searching in the trees.

But that's not the real story, of course. I can't let them have all my secrets. So where is Saint Blannad? You know, I think we understood each other, by the end. I think she was sick of people staring at her, stripped down to her bones as she was. I think she wanted to hide herself. And so they won't find her, not where I put her. And I know that someday I will come back to the lake shore, where she lies under the water, in the middle of all the mud and weeds and rubbish. I'll come back and I'll thank her. For helping me kill Alice, so that I could live.

She knew about the hunger. I know she'd recognise it, what you find on the other side of the pains. Those are just your body crying, like a baby, for what it's used to. On the other side you see things. Your eyes blur and dance. Your breath is slow, gentle. Your heart slows way down and you feel light as air, the blood moving under your skin. You understand the hunger is only there to distract you from what's really going on. When you get down to the bone, that's when you've really won, really beaten the hunger, the flesh, the pain.

I looked up the meaning of 'relic' once, back when I still cared about books and grades and study. For an essay. The tutor loved that, you could tell. He congratulated me on my 'etymological curiosity'. Anyway, I looked it up and it's from Latin. It means 'what is left behind'. These days, I find myself thinking about that. A lot.

Chapter Forty-Two

'Any news?' The day after was Paula's favourite part of any case. When the loose ends were tied off, and the blood cleaned up, and everything put back in its proper place. Alice Morgan had been treated for shock and minor injuries, then released to her parents, who were insisting the press not hear any of the details of how their daughter had planned her own disappearance. When she recovered, she would be in for a lengthy questioning session as to how she'd managed to evade the police for three weeks. Peter and Katy were in custody. Dermot Healy's parents were at his hospital bed, as he recovered from emergency surgery to repair his carotid artery. Paula herself was filing a report when Corry came to find her at her desk.

'Well, Healy will be fine, though he might have quite a scar to show off in prison where, fingers crossed, he'll be ending up before too long. Avril's grand too. I'm going to recommend she be fast-tracked to CID – that was some good, brave work she did.' Corry brightened. 'Oh, and poor Willis is having a bad time of it – seeing as he refused to pull an officer out of danger.'

'Will he get in trouble?'

'We can but hope. Off the record, I heard that the ACC is planning to sound me out about going back up a level.'

'That's great!'

'Well, we'll see. And who knows what'll happen after that. Willis isn't really suited to Ballyterrin, I don't think. He doesn't quite grasp the . . . what's the word?'

'The subtleties?' Paula suggested.

'Exactly. The subtleties.' Corry smiled. 'Good work, Maguire. One body, long dead, and two solves, with no fatalities. That's not a bad ratio. There's even going to be an investigation into what they get up to at that anorexia clinic.'

Paula was glad something had come of her trip. There had to be a better way to save people, rather than holding them back from the grave with tubes and cuffs and never a second of privacy. 'Maybe we're getting the hang of this after all.'

'Let's not go too far. We both still need to explain to the powers-that-be why we ended up with someone pointing a gun at us, yet again.'

'I guess it's just a Northern Ireland thing.'

'Still. You need to be more careful. You've that wee girl to think of now.'

And once again, she was Maggie's only parent. Paula looked down at her desk, nodded. 'I know. In fact I was thinking of going early, picking her up from my dad's.' Pat had started chemo now, and they'd have to rethink the childcare situation. They'd have to rethink a lot of things.

'I'm sure I can turn a blind eye. Oh, and—' Corry turned back, and the look on her face was a study in discretion, and exasperation, and understanding. 'Brooking wants to see you, before he goes. He's in the wee interview room.'

'There's something I need to say to you.' Guy was waiting for her in there, in his grey suit, working on a stack of reports. Paula hovered, not sitting down.

Me too. Me too. But she still couldn't. 'Oh?'

He ran his hands through his hair. He'd a fine head of it for a man of forty-two. She always wanted to push it back into place, run her hands through it, fair and springy. As she had on that one occasion – just one – when they'd been able to touch. How ridiculous it seemed. She'd had his child, carried her for nine months, fed her, nursed her. Yet only ever spent a few hours with him alone. How was she ever going to tell him?

'Um.' Guy sighed. 'Well, you probably know I'm going back to London. The case is done now and I only came over to consult. My job's there.'

She was nodding. Of course he was going back. 'What are you . . . ?'

'I just need to say this before I go. I wouldn't have come back if I'd thought it would hurt you in any way, or make things hard for you, or disrupt your life. I hope you believe that. And I am so, so sorry for what's happened. I thought if I went away – if I gave you space, you and Aidan could sort things out. You were always meant to be together. Weren't you?'

Her voice was dry. 'I don't know. I don't know anything any more.'

'Well, I just wanted to say that. I never meant for any of this to happen. And – I don't know if this is helpful now, or unhelpful – but there'll always be a job for you on my team. Once things are sorted out here. If they can be sorted out. You'll always have a place to go.'

'I . . .' Paula seemed unable to finish her sentences.

'I know Aidan's here. But Paula, he's maybe going to be in there a long time. You know that. You and Maggie could have a new life.'

With him? Was that what he was offering? *Just tell him, for fuck's sake. Just say, guess what, Aidan isn't her dad after all, so you know what that means, surprise . . .*

And then what? He'd know she'd let him think Aidan was Maggie's dad, all this time, even though she hadn't been sure? She realised she couldn't bear to lose him again, not with Aidan gone too. She couldn't tell him. She had to. But she couldn't.

A nasty idea was forming in Paula's mind. A hard, cold little voice that said Aidan was in prison and he might not be around until Maggie was grown, maybe even at secondary school. And if she and Maggie were both in London – safe, anonymous London, big enough to drown any secret, where none of the crimes touched them personally – then who knew what might happen? God. Could she do that? Was she really so calculating?

'Say something.' Guy gave a nervous smile. 'I'm sorry if that was inappropriate. I just wanted you to know – there are options.'

'I mean – it's a lot to think about. And there's Dad, and Pat and everything—'

'There are flights too. Back and forth.'

'I know. I'd like to think about it, if that's OK.'

'So . . . maybe yes?'

'Not definitely no. That's the best I can do right now.' The look of joy on his face was real, unfaked, and she felt as if her chest were splitting and breaking with it, a kind of fierce, hurtful hope. Could she do this? Work with Guy, and not tell him the truth? Could she burn her life to the ground and start again, as Alice Morgan had? She pushed it to the back of her mind. Classic Irish coping mechanism. She'd think about it soon. Not right now, but soon.

Guy stood up. 'I better go; my flight's tonight and I haven't packed. But maybe I'll see you soon?'

'Soon.' She nodded. Her phone beeped and, distracted, she picked it up. In PJ's usual clipped style it said: *builders done out of house said they found load of rubbish down behind cupboards could you take a look mags fine see you later dad.*

They were finished. Her mind began to race ahead. Maybe this didn't have to be it, stuck in this sad town, with all its memories, all its pain. She could sell the house, if the work was finished. She could do what she'd done at eighteen and refuse to be dragged down by it, by Ballyterrin, the weight of it sinking her like a stone into dark water. Refuse to let Maggie be dragged down either. She would go home now, and look around, and later she'd pick up Maggie and talk to her dad about what they might do next.

Guy turned back in the doorway. 'I'm so pleased, Paula.' His face open, happy.

'Me too,' she said. And meant it, for the first time in ages.

It was hard to believe, after the months of waiting, of coughing on dust and rinsing dishes in the bath, that it was finished. The builders, with their radio and crude jokes told not-quite-quietly enough and always calling her 'love', were finally out. The new cupboards were in, sticky with labels that would need to be cleaned off. The floor was gritty with sawdust, and the new hob still wrapped in plastic, but it was all there, clean and new. Paula ran her hands over it, smelled the fresh pine. For a moment she allowed herself to believe change could happen. This old kitchen, where she had said goodbye to her mother for what she didn't know would be the last time, was transformed. Maybe someone would actually buy it, some young, sensible family who didn't mind that a woman had gone missing from there back in the dark old days of the nineties, didn't know or care so long as it was a good investment.

She found she was holding her breath as she looked round the kitchen, motes of dust turned to glitter by the afternoon sun. If she could leave this place, maybe she wouldn't long for Aidan around the corner every time she came home, drinking his beer outside, watching *Peppa Pig* on the sofa with Maggie, or stuck in the paper and reading out bits of stories she didn't understand. Maybe she wouldn't be punched in the guts by loss every time she put her key in the lock. Not just for her mother now, but for something else too – the life she'd almost had. She tried hard to put those memories away, fold them inside her. That time was over, and the future had to be faced, whatever it brought. She knew that now.

On the counter was a small pile of things – this must be the rubbish her dad had alluded to, which the builders had found behind the old washing machine. She glanced at it – wooden clothes pegs, furred with dust; the instruction manual for a toaster that had been thrown out in 1997; a fridge magnet in the shape of a tomato. And what looked like a folded piece of paper. She moved it out of the dirt, half-glancing at it as she started tidying, shutting the cupboard doors, scraping at one of the sticky labels with her thumb nail. She opened it.

Paula . . .

And then her legs had gone from under her, getting the news much faster than the rest of her. She grasped the counter to keep herself upright. It was her mother's handwriting. Not seen for almost twenty years, but she'd have known it anywhere. The rest of the note swam in front of her. How . . . ? She sat down heavily on the floor, smelling the fresh paint and sawdust-newness of it all. A note. But that didn't have to mean anything. It could have been a shopping list. A reminder to turn the oven on. Anything.

But she found that, as the quickening in her heart grew instead of dying away, a memory was returning. That day in 1993. Late October, winter seeping into town, the light already fading as she got home. And her, aged thirteen, rushing in, tired and starving after school. Cold from the walk up the hill. And what did she do every day when she came in, though her mother told her not to? She threw her schoolbag up on the counter while she opened the fridge to rifle through it. Usually Margaret would be there to tell her off. *Get that bag down off there don't spoil your dinner now.* But that last day. The silence of the house, the uncurtained windows, the feeling of unease that hadn't quite reached Paula's brain yet but was creeping up the backs of her legs and hands. Had there been a movement? Had something skittered away as she threw her bag up there, so careless? Had she knocked something down the back, unseen, unnoticed?

Had this note lain down there for nearly twenty years?

Her hands shook. The paper was so thin, the ink faded. And before she could bear to see what it said, Paula lay down with her head on the new kitchen floor. Begging for the strength to read it, and face what it held, however much it felt like it might kill her.

Dear Paula. When you get this you'll realise I'm not here . . .

Alice

The teacher says, 'Can anyone tell me what is meaning millefeuille?'

There's a hesitation from the rest of the class, a buzz of sudden back-in-school fear. I put my hand up. I can do this, because the person I'm being right now – Ali – would. She's a bit of a swot, Ali. And why not? After all, she doesn't have to pretend not to know things, or not to care.

'Oui, Ali?' The teacher likes me, despite her stern French manner. She's right to be stern anyway. Baking requires discipline. Numbers, maths. It has right and wrong answers. Not like life.

'It means a thousand leaves,' I say, imagining the forest, where it was peaceful. Where I buried Alice, with blood and bone.

'Exactement.' She nods, and begins to tell us the recipe – the butter, the flour, the sugar. So many calories. The ingredients are on my cool marble block in front of me. Good for making pastry, firm and cold. The afternoon sun slants in the window and my fellow students shade their eyes. They're an OK bunch. Mostly angsty mums or nervy young men who think they're Gordon Ramsay. All here because they want to be someone else. They don't want to be Patricia or Odette or Tim any more, housewife or accountant or working in a Little Chef. They want to change.

Not me, though. I already changed who I am. And I would tell them, if they asked, that rebirth is not without pain. You have to bleed, and cry, and be alone and be broken, and after it, when the truth is out, your friends and family won't want to see you any more. The police will want *to charge you, but they won't know what with – seeing as you were the victim, of rape, of kidnap. Your parents, who if we're honest haven't ever known what to do with you, will pay you off with enough cash to keep you away. They'll come back to you one day, probably, when they're old and sick, because blood is thicker than water. But my blood is thicker still, red and dark and clotting. I know. I've seen it. So here I am.*

I reach for the butter in its gold packet, the beads of moisture dripping on its side. Not melting but malleable, just right. When the teacher is helping Monique read the recipe, dumb, sweet Monique, I slip a bit into my mouth with my finger, and it's cool and soft and salty. It tastes like good times, and comfort, and joy. It tastes like being happy. And as it slips down, oily and fatty, ready to be churned through my body and settle on my hips, I know one thing for sure – I won't ever feel the hunger again. Finally, I am full.

A remote island. A missing couple.
A community with deadly secrets.

BLOOD
TIDE

Read on for an exclusive extract from the next novel
in the gripping Paula Maguire series.

'Thoroughly satisfying and intelligent' Elly Griffiths

Out Spring 2017

HEADLINE

Prologue

Margaret
Ballyterrin, Northern Ireland, 1993

Dear Paula. By the time you read this, you'll see that I am, *gone . . .*

No. It was all wrong.

She threw down the pen, angry, and it rolled away over the sheet of paper and clattered onto the kitchen floor. It was no good. How could she explain? She couldn't. Was she really going to do this? It didn't seem real.

She glanced uneasily at the clock: 3.17 p.m., getting dark already. He should have rung by now. He'd promised to ring, tell her what to do, say when he was coming to take her somewhere safe. Because mad as it seemed, her kitchen, with its old seventies units and tiled floor, was not safe any more.

3.18 p.m. Her hands clenched, thinking of Paula, of PJ. At least they'd be safe, if she was gone. She could come back, surely, once it all died down. It was nearly over again, they all said it, the peace process creeping ahead, back one step, forward two, back again. She just had to finish this letter, try to explain it, why she had to run now, today. Explain she might still look exactly like Margaret Maguire, mother of Paula, daughter of Kathleen, wife of PJ, but she wasn't. She was someone else now. The things she had done. The lies she had told. But no, she couldn't explain any of that. Not if she had a week to write the letter.

3.19 p.m. Outside, the cough of a car engine in the street. The gun-crack snap of a door. Her hands began to shake. Not Edward, surely – he never parked near, in case they traced the car. Not PJ, he'd been called out on some case before dawn, something so bad he hadn't even told her what it was. Voices outside. Men. Two or three. Her heart rose up in her throat, and she scrabbled on the floor for the pen, scratching down the last few lines in the seconds she had left. Trying to find the words to explain what could not be explained. Failing.

3.20 p.m. Footsteps, coming to her door. They were here. It was too late.

Chapter One

Ballyterrin, Northern Ireland,
February 2014

'Mummy. *Mummy!* A bad man's at the window!'

Danger. Up. Run. Paula was on her feet before she knew it, heart hammering as she surfaced from sleep and realised where she was. In the doorway stood a small figure in My Little Pony pyjamas. Paula's heart slowed. 'There's no bad man, pet. It's just the big wind outside. It makes the trees scratch at the window, see.'

'Don't *like* it.' Maggie, almost three now, had started sucking her thumb again, something Paula herself didn't much like. The child's breath was hitching in her chest; her top rucked up to show her little rounded tummy.

Paula patted the side of her bed – cold and empty for nearly eight months now. 'It's just the wind. Come on, get in with Mummy here.'

Maggie climbed up, so light the bed might as well have been empty still. Paula pushed the damp red curls off the child's face, as her tears subsided into hiccups. 'There now. You're OK. There's no bad man. Just the wind.'

'Daddy'll get the bad men,' Maggie mumbled, from the edge of sleep. Paula said nothing, as she felt the child uncurl and sag beside her, and outside the wind howled and worried at the house like a boat tossed on the ocean. How could she explain to Maggie that it wasn't true – that she'd lied to her? Of course there were bad men, lots of them, and Aidan – 'Daddy', as she called him – wasn't around to get them because he was one himself.

The child was asleep now, her chest rising and falling. Paula got carefully out of bed and went into Maggie's room, which had been her own for eighteen years, and then again for a year when she'd moved back in with her dad in her home town of Ballyterrin. Twelve years in London, only to find herself here, back to the beginning as if in some crazy real-life version of Snakes and Ladders. Her old desk was stacked with Maggie's soft toys, and the glassy eyes watched Paula as she knelt down and opened the bottom drawer. No need to hide it really. Maggie couldn't read and Aidan was gone, and PJ and Pat were unlikely to go snooping. But just in case, she'd filled the drawer with some little vests of Maggie's. It felt wrong, somehow, those innocent clowns and ducks so near to the horrors at the bottom of it.

Paula reached under the vests and took out the folder. Plain manila, a little worn. On the front, a name – *Margaret Maguire*. The same name as her child. She and Aidan had talked about what to call her, whether to add O'Hara or not, but then the wedding had never taken place and it seemed now Maggie's name would not change. Sometimes, on nights like this, she'd lie awake and wonder if it was for the best. It would have been a lie, after all.

Paula knew the contents by heart. The handwritten reports, the interviews, the picture of her mother on a beach.

She'd taken that herself, playing at photographer. Margaret's red hair whipping in the wind, laughing against the gale and rain that constituted an Irish summer day. The August bank holiday, 1993. Two months after that picture was taken, in October, Paula had come home from school to find her mother gone, the house cold and dark. And there had been no sign, no trace of her for a further twenty years. No body. No answers.

Until the previous summer, tidying up after builders had finally redone her kitchen, Paula had found her mother's note. An innocuous scrap of lined A4 – torn, she was fairly sure, from her own school notebook – but it had changed everything. And now, six months later, she had still told no one. How could she? Her father PJ had remarried, finally declared her mother dead. And she might be, Paula had to remind herself. Even if her mother had gone of her own accord, as the note suggested, she'd gone for a reason, and it didn't mean whoever was hunting her hadn't found her soon after. Either way, Pat was PJ's wife now. And Aidan was Pat's son, and anyway Paula couldn't talk to him at all at the moment, because he was gone. Saoirse, Paula's best friend, was busy trying and failing to get pregnant, and she and Pat saw each other all the time. It was too much of a burden to place on anyone. There was only one other person who knew the whole story, knew the weight of it. And he was gone too. She touched the note lightly, mouthing its short lines by heart.

Dear Paula

By the time you read this you'll see that I am gone. You won't understand why, pet, and I can't explain, but I have to go now. There are bad people after me

*and I need to keep you safe. I'm so sorry, pet. If you
hear things about me, please try to understand I was
doing it for you. Someone had to try and stop the
killing.*

*I love you. If I had any other choice I would take
it, but I just can't stand it any more.*

Look after your daddy, pet, and be good.

Mummy

Look after your daddy, and be good. Well, she hadn't
done either of those things. She'd run away to London as
soon as she could, and now here she was, a single mother
with a fatherless toddler. Who of course had a father – but
one she couldn't know about. Who thought her father was a
different man, currently sitting in a jail cell several miles
down the road.

Paula stood and looked out the window over town, the
lights winking against the dark of the surrounding mountains.
Some nights she convinced herself she could see the beam
from the prison, a bald white laser over a hulk of concrete,
but she wasn't sure it was even true. He was there –
somewhere out there, anyway – and it was eight months
since he'd let her visit, or anyone bring Maggie to see him,
and Paula was alone, swimming hard against a current that
kept dragging her back, back into the dark.

She pushed the folder angrily away, and rubbed at her
tired eyes. What a mess. What a bloody mess she'd made of
everything.

Fiona

Looking back, it all began to go wrong on the day Jimmy Reilly cut Manus Grady's throat. Or maybe it was sooner, maybe it had been growing and metastasising long before that, the way a wave will rise to the shore in a gentle green curve before suddenly cresting, battering you down, raking you over the stony bottom. But even if it had, I only realised how wrong things were going, how badly something on the island was awry, when Jimmy walked into Dunorlan's pub with that old knife in his hand. It was one you'd use to gut fish, the Guards said later. Rusty, bent, but still sharp enough to kill a man.

Manus and Jimmy had bad blood, of course, everyone knew that. Most people on the island had bad blood with someone or other. In Jimmy and Manus's case it was that Manus had sold some land Jimmy thought rightly belonged to him. It had been sold, like most of the spare land on the island, for what I hear was more than enough to keep even Manus in whiskey. This was several years ago, when the company first came over. It was old news. Not something that should have ended with Manus on the spit-and-sawdust floor of that beer-soaked pub, gasping and spasming like a slashed fish on the deck of a boat. But it did.

It was a clear day in January, rinsed out and shining from the usual rain squalls. Before I came to the island, I didn't realise there were as many types of rain as there are days in the year. Patchy rain. Drizzle. Thick showers. Freezing rain that soaks through any layers of clothes you care to put on. Jimmy had encountered Manus in the village Spar around eleven. (I heard all this from Bridget who works at the post office counter and was in to see me about a persistent cough. Never underestimate what you can find out when you have a government post and a letter steamer.) Jimmy asked Manus had he filled in some forms from Jimmy's solicitor. Looking for compensation or some such. Manus said something along the lines of, don't be bothering my head with that old shite now, I am off for a pint. And words were exchanged about the moral character of their respective mothers, before they were kicked out by Oona who owns the shop, much to Bridget's chagrin.

Then Manus set off across the harbour to Dunorlan's, skidding on wet seaweed thrown up by the overnight storm. Shaking, no doubt, from his morning whiskey. He'd been in to see me already about early-stage liver fat, and I'd told him he had to stop or he'd die, but there is no reasoning with an Irish alcoholic – and Jimmy walked the twenty minutes back to his farm, and found the knife in a drawer in the kitchen (or so Bridget said). Even though most people on the island buy their fish ready-gutted in the Spar these days, they also never throw anything away. Jimmy took time to sharpen the knife, then walked back to the pub. Several people claimed to have seen him with the knife in his hand, but thought nothing of it. He might have been going to mend a fence, or cut wood. He entered the pub and approached Manus, who was on his usual barstool, watching a hurling match on the TV. Meath versus Tipperary, I believe. Jimmy said something like, are you going to fill in those fecking forms or not. Manus repeated his earlier comment, with some added swearing. At that, Jimmy lifted the knife and caught at Manus's head like he was shearing a sheep, and drew the blade along the man's neck. The bar and the TV and the packets of Scampi Fries and the barman, young Colm

Meehan – nice lad, brought his mammy in to me last week – were instantly sprayed with Manus's blood. Although at that point it was probably mostly whiskey.

People said afterwards, enjoying the drama of it all – oh, if only you'd been there, doctor, you could have done something for him. And maybe I could, if I'd pressed my fingers right to where the blood gulps out, quick and hot, if I'd stopped him up like an old leaking boat, but as it was, everyone stood gawping and Manus was quickly dead. Colm, who is that rare thing, a fast-thinking islander, took Jimmy and locked him in the bottle store, where he sat quite docile among the crates of Harp and boxes of Tayto crisps until Rory came to fetch him to the mainland. And that was it.

In statistics, two points are just two points. They signify nothing. But three points, that's a line. That's a pattern. And after the incident with Manus and Jimmy, I began to think about the thing at the primary school, and that awful business with the Sharkey baby, and I started to draw some lines. I wonder now, after the blood in the sea and the boat and the box full of dead things, whether I could have stopped it all that day. Pressed my fingers to it like I might have pressed them into Manus's gaping neck. Or whether things were already too far gone by then. I don't know, but I've written it all down anyway, at the very least so I can try to understand it myself. To see what exactly it was I did wrong. For what it's worth, I, Dr Fiona Watts, date the happenings on Bone Island from the date of Manus Grady's death – 5th January 2014 – but if you look back, no doubt you will find that this was only the moment when the building wave began to crest.

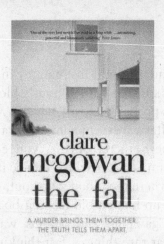

claire
mcgowan
the fall

A MURDER BRINGS THEM TOGETHER.
THE TRUTH TELLS THEM APART.

What would you do if the man you love was accused of murder?

Bad things never happen to Charlotte. She's living the life she's always wanted and about to marry wealthy banker, Dan. But Dan's been hiding a secret, and the pressure is pushing him over the edge. After he's arrested for the vicious killing of a nightclub owner, Charlotte's future is shattered.

Then she opens her door to Keisha, an angry and frustrated stranger with a story to tell. Convinced of Dan's innocence, Charlotte must fight for him – even if it means destroying her perfect life. But what Keisha knows threatens everyone she loves, and puts her own life in danger.

DC Matthew Hegarty is riding high on the success of Dan's arrest. But he's finding it difficult to ignore his growing doubts as well as the beautiful and vulnerable Charlotte. Can he really risk it all for what's right?

Three stories. One truth. They all need to brace themselves for the fall.

978 0 7553 8636 9

HEADLINE

Not everyone who's missing is lost

When two teenage girls go missing along the Irish border, forensic psychologist Paula Maguire has to return to the hometown she left years before. Swirling with rumour and secrets, the town is gripped by fear of a serial killer. But the truth could be even darker.

Not everyone who's lost wants to be found

Surrounded by people and places she tried to forget, Paula digs into the cases as the truth twists further away. What's the link with two other disappearances from 1985? And why does everything lead back to the town's dark past – including the reasons her own mother went missing years before?

Nothing is what it seems

As the shocking truth is revealed, Paula learns that sometimes, it's better not to find what you've lost.

978 0 7553 8640 6

HEADLINE

Stolen. Missing. Dead . . .

Forensic psychologist Paula Maguire, already wrestling
with the hardest decision of her life, is forced to put her
own problems on hold when she's asked to help find a baby
taken from a local hospital.

Then the brutal, ritualistic murder of a woman found lying
on a remote stone circle indicates a connection to the
kidnapping and Paula knows that they will have to move
fast if they are to find the person responsible.

When another child is taken and a pregnant woman goes
missing, Paula finds herself caught up in a deadly hunt
for a killer determined to leave no trace, and discovers every
decision she makes really is a matter of life and death . . .

978 1 4722 0439 4

HEADLINE

Victim: Male. Mid-thirties. 5'7".
Cause of death: Hanging. Initial impression – murder.
ID: Mickey Doyle. Suspected terrorist and member
of the Mayday Five.

The officers at the crime scene know exactly who the victim is.
Doyle was one of five suspected bombers who caused
the deaths of sixteen people.

The remaining four are also missing and when a second body is
found, decapitated, it's clear they are being killed by the same
methods their victims suffered.

Forensic psychologist Paula Maguire is assigned the case
but she is up against the clock – both personally and
professionally.

With moral boundaries blurred between victim and
perpetrator, will Paula be able to find those responsible?
After all, even killers deserve justice, don't they?

978 1 4722 0442 4

HEADLINE

THRILLINGLY GOOD BOOKS
FROM CRIMINALLY
GOOD WRITERS

CRIME FILES BRINGS YOU THE LATEST RELEASES FROM TOP CRIME AND THRILLER AUTHORS.

SIGN UP ONLINE FOR OUR MONTHLY NEWSLETTER AND BE THE FIRST TO KNOW ABOUT OUR COMPETITIONS, NEW BOOKS AND MORE.